PRAISE FOR ABIGAIL DRAKE

First Abigail Drake grabs you with her fresh writing, then she keeps you in the throes of her story with an incredible voice and a gifted talent for spinning tales that will amaze and delight. I am stunned. Tiger Lily will consume you, and before you know it you are fighting for air yet begging for more. You've been warned!

This is one of those hidden gems that you long to come across. It has a little bit of everything in it; romance, paranormal, mystery and lots of action. There are so many twists and turns. A book that packs a punch you'll never see coming.

Absolute perfection!

D0808118

LOVE, CHOCOLATE, AND A DOG NAMED AL CAPONE

ABIGAIL DRAKE

Cover Art by Najla Qamber

Edited by Ramona DeFelice Long, Lara Parker, and Marylu Zuk.

To Capone's loving and devoted followers. You help me start each day out right, by laughing at life, and at myself.

ONE

A list of things not to do on a horse farm:

1. Irritate the horses.
2. Mess with the cows.
3. Make an enemy of the barn cat.

First of all, stampedes happen. It's a fact of life. But how could I have known horses spooked so easily? And cows—don't get me started on cows. It took nothing but a whinny or two from some neurotic horses, followed by a few random stomps of their hooves, for the cows to get themselves worked into a tizzy.

Cows. Such idiots.

Mr. Collins, the barn cat, never saw it coming. He was too busy lecturing me at the time.

"What are you doing?" he asked, jumping down from his perch on the fence post to march after me with a swish of his fluffy orange tail. "You aren't supposed to be here. You know the rules. No puppies in the pasture. Go back to the house, where you belong."

I ignored him, even though I knew he was right. This was against the rules, and rules existed for a reason. I'd learned this the hard way.

One time my caretaker, Mistress Sue, warned me to stay away from bumblebees. She told me it was a rule. I should have listened to her, but the creature looked so fuzzy and yellow and delicious. Sadly, it did not taste as nice as it looked.

Note to self: Never eat something with a knife growing out of its butt.

But no bumblebees buzzed around the pasture on this bright autumn day. And even though Mistress Sue told me never to bother the horses, surely sneaking under the fence to nibble on a teeny-weeny bit of horse poo did not constitute a crime.

We all had our weaknesses. Mine happened to come from the back side of an equine. I'd never met a pile of poo I didn't like.

"Capone, you're disgusting," said Mr. Collins, watching me eat the horse droppings with revulsion. "And you're going to get in trouble again because of this. Why can't you make good decisions? You're the worst dog I've ever met."

Since Mistress Sue bred Labradors, Mr. Collins had encountered a lot of dogs. If I was the worst he'd ever met, I must be pretty bad.

"I don't know what you're talking about. It's like you have a personal vendetta against me, but I've never done anything to deserve it," I said, pausing between mouthfuls. "Well, other than the time I bit your tail by accident. And the time I ran too fast and knocked you over. And the time I ate your food. And the time—"

"Enough. We both know the truth. You're a menace, and no one wants you. That's why you're still here. Your brothers and sisters were adopted ages ago." He narrowed his eyes, spitting out words that felt like daggers to my heart. "You are a bad dog."

He'd gone too far. Feeling defensive, I barked at him. A lot. And I may have chased him around too, but I didn't expect the cows to go crazy. I certainly didn't want Mr. Collins to get hurt.

When the cows charged, rushing toward us, I ducked under the fence and ran away as fast as my puppy legs could carry me. Mr. Collins wasn't so lucky. With one well-placed kick by a cow to his backside, Mr. Collins went flying into the air, over the fence, and onto the green, green grass of the meadow.

He didn't die. In fact, other than having a limp for a few days, and a severely bruised ego, he recovered rather quickly. But now he had a new goal in life; to make me as miserable as possible.

Goals, like rules, are important. And Mr. Collins took his seriously.

He insulted me and called me names every chance he got. The horses joined in, like they always did when Mr. Collins bullied me. He told me over and over again I was a bad dog, but I refused to believe it. I knew I had the potential somewhere deep down inside to be something great. Something interesting. Something...more.

Needing love and reassurance after an especially intense round of bullying and verbal abuse by Mr. Collins, I went back to the farmhouse and snuggled up on the couch next to Mistress Sue to watch PBS. It always soothed me. Everything I knew about humans came from Mistress Sue and the Public Broadcasting Service. Well, that and books. With little to do on the farm at night, and because we lacked cable television, we had limited options for entertainment. Mistress Sue either read me a book or turned on PBS. On this particular evening, as the sun set in the sky, we watched a program that changed my life.

The Rules of Being a Regency Gentlemen.

At last. I now had rules to follow which actually made sense.

I watched, spellbound, and learned about tying cravats and waltzing and helping ladies alight from carriages. The more I watched, the more a plan formed in my little Labradorean brain. I'd prove Mr. Collins and those nasty horses wrong by becoming the one thing a lab had never been before.

A proper gentleman.

There was only one problem. I had few opportunities to learn how to become a gentleman while living on a horse farm. Although a lovely place, it was basically only a stretch of grass, a few glorious piles of horse poo, a mean cat, and some exceedingly unfriendly horses. Not a single person to practice the waltz with, and definitely no one to teach me more about becoming a true gentleman. It was hopeless and I sank into a deep pit of despair.

The next morning, I woke up, wishing I had a cravat to tie, and a valet to tie it, when I heard a knock at the door. We never had guests this early, which meant perhaps someone had finally arrived in response to Mistress Sue's advertisement in the local paper.

Full bred Labrador retriever puppy for sale. Black. Male. Energetic and extremely friendly. Three months old. Last of the litter. Will consider all offers. Must have previous puppy experience.

Not exactly a ringing endorsement of my many virtues, but Mistress Sue knew what she was doing. I hoped for the best, but what greeted me at the door was even better than

I'd ever imagined; an elegant, red-headed vision in a mossy green skirt.

She was a lady. She had to be.

Mistress Sue grabbed me by the collar to keep me from jumping all over our guest. I wiggled to escape, but to no avail. Mistress Sue had a grip of iron.

The stranger smiled at me. "I'm Anne Weston. I'm looking for a puppy for my friend, and I hear you have one available for adoption."

Mistress Sue stared at Ms. Anne with a critical eye, taking in her fancy clothing and high heels. "Who is your friend?"

"Her name is Josephine St. Clair. She's the owner of Bartleby's Books of Beaver. I want this to be a surprise gift for her."

"Are you sure your friend even wants a puppy?"

In spite of the wording in her advertisement, Mistress Sue did not give her puppies to just anyone, but this might be my only chance. I squirmed and wiggled until Mistress Sue released me, then I ran over to Ms. Anne. I licked her high heels and slim ankles, and she bent down to give me a pat and a scratch behind the ears.

"She doesn't just want a puppy, she *needs* a puppy, and this one is so sweet. What's his name?"

"Capone," said Mistress Sue.

Ms. Anne let out a laugh, the most beautiful thing I'd ever heard. It sounded like bells tinkling, or the wind chimes Mistress Sue had out back.

"How perfect. A tough guy wrapped in an adorable, furry package. Josie will love him."

"I'm not sure this is such a good idea. Capone requires a great deal of supervision," said Mistress Sue. "He's very...curious."

Ms. Anne seemed unfazed. "Not a problem. He can stay with Josie all day while she works, so he'll be well supervised. He'll love it at Bartleby's. It's a beautiful bookstore."

Mistress Sue eyed me carefully as I pranced around in a circle, nearly exploding with excitement. I loved books, and Mistress Sue knew it. I'd already heard wonderful stories about barn spiders spinning miraculous webs, rabbits in velveteen jackets, and faithful dogs doing heroic things. To live in a bookstore would be a dream come true.

Mistress Sue offered Ms. Anne a spot on the couch. "Capone's a strange little dog, and he likes books, oddly enough. There isn't much to do in the evening here, so I read to him almost every night. Even so, I'm not sure he'd be the right fit for your friend."

Ms. Anne leaned down to pat my head again, and I stared up at her with adoration. I liked the way she smelled, like flowery perfume and scrambled eggs made with butter and cheese, which was probably what she had for breakfast that morning. I crawled onto her lap and licked her fingertips, which still carried a trace of butter, and Ms. Anne smiled.

"Josie will love him," she said, and I thought I heard a hint of sadness in her voice. "She lost her parents a few years ago, and she's all alone. She needs him for companionship, and also for protection."

Mistress Sue's eyebrows lifted in surprise. "Don't let the name deceive you. Capone's not guard dog material. He's a licker, not a fighter, and he has the attention span of a gnat."

I wanted to protest but got distracted by a bit of dust on the floor. I wiggled my bum, eyeing it the way a lion stalks a gazelle on the Savannah, and pounced on it. Several times. Then I hopped up and down on it to make sure it was dead and barked at it, too. When I finished, I looked up to find both Mistress Sue and Ms. Anne staring at me.

Curse my overactive imagination.

"He'll grow out of it," said Ms. Anne after a long moment. "I always trust my instincts, and right now they're telling me Josie and Capone belong together."

I sat up straighter, hard to do when my rolly polly puppy belly kept getting in the way. This might be the answer to all my problems. I could live at the bookstore with Miss Josie, become a faithful and attentive companion, and learn how to waltz and play Whist. I could also protect her from rogues and miscreants. Gentlemen always provided this service to ladies. They were extremely clear about that on the special on PBS.

I stared at Mistress Sue, hoping she'd see the longing in my eyes. To my great surprise, it seemed to work. "Fine," she said. "I'll let you take Capone, but only on a trial basis. I'll come check on him in two months. If he's not adjusting well, I reserve the right to bring him back to the farm. Are we clear on this?"

"Definitely." Ms. Anne stood, a smile lighting up her face. "Josie will be so happy. She loves surprises, and Capone will be the best surprise of all."

TWO

Ways not to greet a lady:

1. Lunge at her.
2. Stick your nose up her skirt.
3. Lick the back of her thighs.
4. Get a tiny bit of lint from her stockings caught on your tongue.
5. Make gagging noises as you attempt to dislodge it.
6. Urinate on her favorite potted plant.

Bartleby's Books had a bright blue façade and gold lettering above the door, but I barely noticed its splendor. Instead, I panted nervously as a cloud of white dandruff erupted from my skin, making it look like I'd wandered through a snowstorm.

Curse my high-strung nature.

I forced myself to calm down through sheer power of will. I had to make an excellent first impression on Miss Josephine St. Clair, but how?

Although butt sniffing was a time-honored tradition among members of the canine persuasion, and animals in general, I doubted it would work when meeting a lady. I never saw any gentlemen sniffing butts on the PBS special, not even once. I suspected it might not translate well between species, so I chose not to smell Ms. Josie's bottom.

Well, not on our first encounter at least.

As I wracked my brain, trying to decide what to do, I came up with a great idea. Hand kissing. The perfect solution. On the PBS special, it worked like a charm. Women generally responded to hand kissing by fluttering their fans and blushing adorably. If I kissed her hand, Miss Josie would be so amazed by my manners and comportment; she'd want me to stay with her forever.

I walked into the shop with Ms. Anne, desperate to do well. It intensified when I saw Miss Josie.

She was lovely. The prettiest human I'd ever seen. She stood at the cash register, engrossed in a book, as the sun streamed through the windows, bathing her in its light. Her hair shone in a curly halo around her head, the color of spun gold. She'd stuck a pencil in her bun and had black-framed glasses perched on her tiny nose. Her eyes, the dark grey of a summer storm, focused on her book, and a little wrinkle of a frown formed between her brows.

She looked worried, and I wanted to make all her worries go away. I knew the moment I saw her she was my human, my destiny, and I loved her with an intensity that surprised me. I wanted her to love me back so badly it was nearly agonizing.

I went over my plan again in my head. Kiss the hand. Flutter of the fan. Coquettish smile. Success. But there was one problem.

Miss Josie did not have a fan.

How could she flutter a fan as she stared at me adoringly if she didn't have one? Also, I faced a logistical problem as well. I could not reach her hand to kiss it.

Curse my short puppy legs and my lack of a decent vertical leap.

I had no choice. Desperate times called for drastic doggie measures, so I found another solution. I stuck my nose under the woolen folds of her grey, pleated skirt and licked the back of her thighs.

I'll be frank here. This technique was never mentioned on the PBS special, but it felt right. Judging by Miss Josie's reaction, however, I'd committed a terrible faux pas.

She jumped, making an odd squeaking noise, her expression akin to blind panic as she looked down at me. "What is that?" she asked.

"Your new alarm system," said Ms. Anne. She extended her arm, showing me off as if I were a prize on a television game show. "A purebred Labrador retriever. Isn't he gorgeous? You should pet him. He's as soft as black velvet. His name is Capone."

Miss Josie stared at me, her grey eyes huge behind those black-framed glasses and wisps of her blond hair falling in a tumble around her face. I didn't know a lot about human behavior, but I knew enough to gather Miss Josie had been rendered momentarily speechless.

To make matters worse, the lint from Miss Josie's stockings stuck to my tongue and made me gag. They didn't cover this particular problem, gagging on fluff from a lady's stockings, in the rules on being a gentleman either. I had no idea how to proceed.

Ms. Anne came to my rescue, fishing the offending bits out of my mouth. I licked her hand to express my gratitude and rolled over to show off my irresistibly soft and slightly chubby tummy. It worked like a charm. Even Miss Josie was not immune. She came out of her stupor, reached down (probably against her better judgment), and gave me a scratch.

"He's cute," she said. "But I don't understand why you brought him here. A bookshop is no place for a puppy."

"You need a better alarm system, and you also need a companion. Capone is both. Surprise."

Miss Josie, it seemed, did not like surprises as much as I'd hoped. She studied me dubiously as I rose clumsily to my feet and sniffed around. "He's not going to pee on my books, is he?"

In truth, I hadn't considered relieving myself on her books until she brought it up. Funny how it happens. Now it was the only thing I could think about.

Ms. Anne, with her ninja-like reflexes, scooped me up and rushed me outside. We made it just in time. I lifted my leg near a large, potted plant as Miss Josie cringed.

"I bought those mums this morning," she said.

Note to self: Never pee on pretty potted plants.

As a small river of urine trickled its way down the side of the plant and onto the sidewalk, I tried to hop away but hadn't entirely stopped peeing yet. A strange splatter pattern appeared on the ground, as even more pee ran down my legs in a humiliating stream. Oh, calamity. I was not making a good first impression on Miss Josie at all.

Curse my overactive bladder.

Ms. Anne pulled me away from the mum with a gentle tug of my leash and cleaned my pee-splattered legs with a wet wipe from her purse. "Behave, Capone," she said softly. "You have to keep out of mischief, or you'll end up back on the farm, and she needs you, remember?"

I ducked my head, ashamed. She was right, but who

knew there would be so many new rules? I mean I loved rules, but the PBS special didn't cover any of this.

Miss Josie stared at me, probably wondering what I might pee on or lick next. "What on earth were you thinking, Anne?"

"He needs a home, Josie. And a family."

"A family?" she asked. "But why me?"

Ms. Anne gave Miss Josie a sad, gentle smile. "Because you need a family, too," she said. "I know it was hard after you lost your mom and dad, then Mr. Bartleby, but you barely even leave the bookstore these days."

"I have a business to run. If I fail, I'll have to sell the shop and find a new job. Bartleby's is all I've ever known." Miss Josie folded her arms across her chest, her eyes sad. "I'm on my own here. It isn't easy."

"Which is why you need Capone. Trust me. The last time you had a break-in they did a lot of damage. Even with your new security system, each layer of protection you add will help. Think of him as an additional layer."

"But a dog, Anne? Really?"

"Do it on a trial basis. His breeder will come to check on him in two months. If it's not working out for you, she'll take him back. No harm, no foul."

Ms. Josie tapped her foot nervously on the sidewalk. Her shoes were grey, like her tights, and tied with old-fashioned looking rose-colored ribbons. I'd never seen anything more beautiful or tempting in my life. I leaped at the ribbon, taking it into my mouth and yanking on it. She moved me away with a none too gentle push of her leg and shot Ms. Anne a dirty look as she knelt to retie her shoe.

"You're employing emotional blackmail."

"I'm doing it because I love you and have your best

interests at heart. I've been worried about you, and it's gotten so much worse ever since you broke things off with Cedric—" Miss Josie held out one hand to silence her, making a hissing noise, and Ms. Anne rolled her eyes. "Sorry. Since you broke up with he-who-shall-not-be-named, your life has been a train wreck."

"I'm a mess, but it has nothing to do with him. It has to do with this." She pointed at the shop next door, First Impressions Café. A "Grand Opening" banner waved across the front, and crowds of people streamed in and out, sipping large cups of hot coffee and fancy drinks like espresso, lattes, and cappuccino. It smelled delightful. I lifted my nose for a better whiff. Mmmmm. Could it be pumpkin spice?

"The coffee shop?"

"From the moment they moved in, it's been nothing but trouble."

As she spoke, a woman in a large SUV attempted to back out of her parking space while juggling what looked like a large iced coffee in one hand and her cell phone in the other. She nearly hit a passing car. The man in the car honked at her, making a rude gesture out the window.

Ms. Anne didn't blink an eye. "But books and coffee go together, right? Those might be your future customers."

Miss Josie shook her head as two teenaged girls posed for selfies. They made duck faces and held up their coffee cups in a mock salute.

"They are not my customers," she said. "They wouldn't know a rare book if it knocked them on the head. And don't even get me started on the manager. He's a nightmare. Oh, great. Here he comes now."

A tall man with curly brown hair wearing a First

Impressions Café T-shirt walked out of the shop, a big smile on his face as he greeted customers. His smile disappeared as soon as he saw Miss Josie. He stomped over to where we were standing.

"Josephine St. Clair," he said, a muscle working in his jaw. "Did you seriously call the police yesterday because one of my customers dared to park in front of your store?"

"Nate Murray." She spat out the words, as if she found each syllable of his name offensive. She squared her shoulders, cheeks flushed and eyes bright with anger. "I called a tow truck, not the police. As you can see, these spots are marked, 'Parking for customers of Bartleby's Books only. All others will be towed.' Is that not clear enough for you?"

I watched their interaction closely. When faced with an awkward social situation, a gentleman must always do his best to smooth the waters. I wagged my tail and gave Mr. Nate my paw. His face immediately softened, and he leaned down to scratch me behind the ears. Crisis averted, and the scratching felt wonderful.

Note to self: A little cuteness goes a long way.

Ms. Anne gave him a friendly smile. "Hello, Nate Murray. I'm Anne. Nice to meet you."

"It's nice to meet you, too," he said, straightening and shaking her hand. I realized he looked quite handsome when he wasn't scowling. A fat pug waddled up to Mr. Nate and plopped down on the sidewalk. "And this is my dog, Jackson."

When Jackson breathed, he inhaled with a snort, and exhaled with a sort of wet, slobbery pant. It was disturbing, like listening to an obscene phone call.

"Oh, I know Jackson. He keeps pooping in front of my store," said Miss Josie as she glared down at the portly pug, but, to my surprise, Jackson was not offended in the least.

"Guilty as charged, cutie pie." He laughed, the sound a rough chortle, and scratched his sizable belly.

Mr. Nate did not laugh. He frowned again.

Oh calamity.

"It happened one time, and I apologized," he said, his face darkening. "I cleaned it up right away and sent you coffee as a peace offering. What more do you want from me?"

"I want you to keep your animal on your property, and don't bother with the peace offerings. I don't drink coffee."

He rolled his eyes. "Of course, you don't. I bet you drink kombucha and herbal tea."

She glowered at him, which meant he was probably right. It made me wonder, though...what the heck was kombucha?

As the animosity between them intensified, I let out a bark as a way to change the subject. It worked. Mr. Nate dug in his pocket and pulled out a treat.

"Where did this puppy come from? He can't possibly be yours," he said.

"Why?"

"Because you're a cat person if I ever saw one."

"You don't know anything about me," Miss Josie huffed.

"I know enough. Crazy cat ladies always drink herbal tea. It's a dead giveaway."

I suspected he might be teasing, mostly because of the glimmer of humor I saw in his eyes, but Miss Josie did not seem to notice. She took the leash from Ms. Anne with a scowl.

"Well, Mr. Know-It-All-Nate, Capone happens to be mine. And I'm not crazy, nor am I a cat lady. For your information, my cat doesn't even like me."

I cringed, knowing she probably wished she hadn't said

the last part, but she recovered quickly, lifting her chin and looking down her nose at Mr. Nate. He didn't seem fazed.

"Capone? Cool name."

"I can't stand it. I plan to change it as soon as possible. Good day, Mr. Murray."

"Good day, Miss St. Clair," he said. "And good luck, Capone. You're going to need it."

He gave me a final pat and returned to the café. Miss Josie and Ms. Anne went back into the bookstore, and Miss Josie let out a groan, covering her face with her hands.

"What was I thinking? Why did I tell him Capone is my dog?"

"Because Capone *is* your dog, Josie, but I'm confused about the parking thing. You're not the kind of person who has someone's car towed away for no good reason."

Miss Josie's shoulders slumped. "I know, and I hated to do it, but I'm in a bind here. I need all the customers I can get. If there aren't spaces in front of my shop, they might drive right past. Most of the people who shop here are older. They don't want to walk for blocks and blocks to get here. Thank goodness I have a steady online business to keep me afloat. Otherwise, I would have already closed."

Ms. Anne put a comforting hand on Miss Josie's shoulder. "I had no idea it was this bad."

"When Mr. Bartleby left me this shop in his will, it was the kindest thing anyone had ever done for me. I love this place, but it's a money pit. First, I had to get a new vault because Mr. Bartleby's wasn't moisture controlled. Then I had to update the entire computer system and create a website. And then there was the accounting. Do you know Mr. Bartleby did all of his record keeping by hand?"

"He did?"

"Yes, which is part of the problem. He recorded everything in old-fashioned ledgers, and the most recent one has gone missing. I've been searching for it everywhere, and I've been looking for a bunch of valuable books that disappeared from the inventory as well. I don't know if they were lost or stolen, but I can't make any insurance claims until I have some documentation that they were purchased in the first place."

"I'm guessing the documentation would be in the missing ledger?"

"It should be," she said, with a despondent note in her voice. "And I had to pay for a pricy new security system as well. It's one expense after another."

"The security system is a good thing. The idea of someone breaking in when you live upstairs is scary. Have any of the other shops on the block been broken into?"

Miss Josie laughed, but it had a brittle edge to it. "No, because Beaver is the safest place in the universe. Except for Bartleby's. We're a hotbed of criminal activity. And guess what? Now we even have Capone himself living here. It seems oddly appropriate." She blew out a sigh, and stared down at me with a woebegone expression. "This is the last thing I needed Anne. Dogs are expensive, and I'm barely getting by as it is."

"You won't have to pay for a thing. Capone is a gift, and so are the costs associated with him." When Miss Josie tried to protest, Ms. Anne shushed her. "I've arranged a vet and obedience training. I've even opened an account for you at Percy's Pet Palace. Percy owes me one. I do a lot of shopping there, and he gave me a huge discount."

"But it's too much—"

Ms. Anne stopped her. "You're like a little sister to me, and I've wanted to get you a puppy for ages, but it was never the right time. This is the right time. I'm sure of it.

And don't worry about the money. I'm loaded. I made out well in my last divorce."

Miss Josie's lips quirked. "You made out well in your first two divorces, too."

"I did," she said with a wink. "The point is I have money to spare, and I'm worried about you. I think this will help you get out of the slump you've been in. I'm older and wiser than you, so you should trust me on this."

Miss Josie snorted. "Only ten years older, and not so wise."

Ms. Anne ignored her. "I have to tell you your hot neighbor is right. If you aren't careful, soon you'll be a strange old lady who lives alone and eats cold soup out of a can."

"I will not, and I don't live alone. I have Rocco."

"Rocco hates you."

Miss Josie frowned at first, like she might argue the point, but ended up agreeing with Ms. Anne's statement. "Okay, fine, but Rocco hates everyone. He's that kind of cat. I don't take it personally. And it's not like I chose him. I inherited him from Mr. Bartleby."

"Didn't you inherit Mrs. Steele in the same way?"

"Yes, but she actually helps out around the shop," said Miss Josie, and Ms. Anne raised her eyebrows. "Well, at least she *tries* to help. Rocco...not so much."

"Mrs. Steele is nice, but we both know she's a hot mess. You're a softie, Josie. You can never say no to a stray or to someone who needs you. Which is why you'll give Capone a chance."

Miss Josie grimaced. "It has nothing to do with me being a softie. I've backed myself into a corner this time. If I give Capone back, Nate Murray will be a total jerk about it, and my desire to prove him wrong supersedes my desire to maintain my sanity."

"What are you saying?"

She let out a sigh. "I'm saying, for the time being at least, Capone is my new dog."

THREE

Rules and regulations for the proper behavior of puppies in the bookstore:

1. No books shall be eaten.
2. No books shall be licked.
3. No books shall be chewed on.
4. No books shall be touched.
5. No books shall be (ahem) peed on.
6. Stay away from Miss Josie's shoes.

"That's all I can think of for now," she said, after going over her monotonous list of rules. "But I would like to change your name eventually. I don't think it suits you."

Change my name? What an excellent idea. I hoped she'd choose something remarkable. Something manly. Something memorable.

"How about Shadow?"

What? The generic name for every pet ever born with black fur in the history of recorded time? I even knew a black horse named Shadow back on the farm. No, thank you. And no thanks to Midnight, either. Ugh.

"Or maybe Darcy?"

I stared at her in disbelief. Wasn't Darcy a girl's name?

She frowned, thinking hard. "Fitzwilliam? Wentworth? Bingley? Knightly?"

I tilted my head to one side. Were those all characters from books?

Miss Josie sighed. "We'll work on it later. The rules are the most important thing, and, remember, rule number one is to stay away from my books." She led me to a pile of books on the floor. When I sniffed them, she yanked on my leash and said, quite firmly, "No."

She did this over and over again. I wanted to tell her I got it the first time, but she didn't understand Dog, so I had no way to communicate with her. Instead, I tried to speak with her telepathically.

I understand. You don't have to repeat yourself. I am not a complete fool, and I love books as much as you do.

It did not work. I sadly lacked telepathic ability. Miss Josie continued her diatribe as I struggled to maintain my composure.

"No books," repeated Miss Josie. "No. No. No."

I rolled my eyes, hoping she'd get the hint. She glanced at her watch.

"I'll close the shop, and we'll head upstairs," she said. "Then we can go over the ground rules for the apartment."

How wonderful. More rules. Yippee. Even for a dog who loved rules, this seemed excessive.

As we walked into the apartment, I heard a strange growling sound. Two glowing eyes stared down at me from high on a bookshelf. I whimpered and hid behind Miss Josie's leg.

"That's Rocco. My cat. Don't worry about him. He's crabby."

What kind of weird cat lurked on a bookshelf and growled at people? Rocco definitely had issues, but I ignored him and looked around. The upstairs apartment, nice and cozy, looked in no way similar to Mistress Sue's Spartan white clapboard farmhouse. It was like entering a different world entirely. Decorated in jewel tones and plush fabrics, with antiques and curiosities sprinkled throughout, it was the perfect abode for a gentleman.

Although I loved it immediately, I saw hidden dangers lurking in each room. Things to tempt me, chewable objects, fragile items I could bump into and knock onto the floor, a plethora of potential problems. The blue velvet couch near the window seemed safe enough, but when I tried to climb on it, Miss Josie stopped me.

"No," she said, using her favorite word once again. "No sitting on the couch."

How unfortunate. I stared at it longingly, but Miss Josie ignored my pleading eyes.

"We'll go to the pet shop first thing tomorrow morning to get you a nice bed and whatever else you need. Anne gave me this." Miss Josie held up Orange Snuggle Bunny. "I hear it's your favorite."

I hopped up and down because I loved Orange Snuggle Bunny. I'd slept with it every day of my life, and I was so glad to have it here. When Miss Josie gave it to me, I pranced around the room with it in my mouth. Lovely and squishy, it reminded me of home.

"And she also brought over some dog food. Would you like to eat?"

I dropped Orange Snuggle Bunny and gave Miss Josie

my biggest, happiest smile. I loved to eat even more than anything, even more than Orange Snuggle Bunny.

She put my food in a bowl and filled another with water. I ate my kibble, lickety-split, and slurped up all the water, too. I turned to thank my kind hostess for the meal, as is my custom, but ended up dripping water all over the beautiful, shiny hardwood floor.

Miss Josie grabbed a paper towel and cleaned it up. "We're going to have to work on your manners, mister."

Too tired to worry about it, I curled up in a ball, resting my head on Josie's feet as she sat on the blue couch, and fell promptly asleep. When I woke, the only light in the room came from the television and a small stained-glass lamp on an end table. Miss Josie perched on the couch, a tissue in her hands. I sat up, wondering what had her so enthralled. It was a program I'd never seen before.

Pride and Prejudice.

Mesmerized, I watched the entire movie, and realized I had a new goal. I wanted to be like Mr. Fitzwilliam Darcy.

Note to self: Practice brooding more.

Nothing would be better than to live at Pemberley, wear a suit with a snowy white cravat, and view the world with mild disdain. I wished I had not scoffed at Miss Josie when she suggested his name for me. Now I wanted it. Badly. Darcy or Fitzwilliam. Either way, it didn't matter, and I wanted something else as well, something that had nothing at all to do with the works of Jane Austen.

I wanted to go to the bathroom. I had no idea how to communicate this to my new owner, however, so I was in quite the pickle.

Curse my inability to speak Human.

Miss Josie sat on the couch, crying over *Pride and Preju-dice,* or maybe crying over the fact Mr. Darcy did not exist in real life. Either way, it was touching, and I didn't want to disturb her, but if I didn't get outside soon, I might have an accident. I whined, not knowing what else to do.

"What is it, boy?" she asked, so I padded over to the door and whined some more. "Do you need to go out?"

I wagged my tail and barked encouragingly. Miss Josie slipped on a pair of shoes, grabbed my leash, and led me swiftly down the stairs and out to the fresh green grass of the back garden.

Not huge by any means, and nowhere near as large as the horse farm, it provided an area entirely sufficient for my needs. I squatted, looking around as I...uh...performed the task at hand. Three ivy-covered brick walls enclosed the garden. A narrow wooden door provided an exit to the alley Miss Josie shared with Mr. Nate's café. The soft strains of live music came from his establishment. Miss Josie frowned in annoyance when she heard it, but after a few minutes, she hummed along to the tune. I wondered if she even realized she was doing it.

She did not like Mr. Nate. Not one bit. Odd because I liked him very much.

After I relieved myself, I inspected the area in greater detail, pleased to see she took her security seriously. She'd shut the outside door to the garden tight, and a large, sturdy-looking padlock hung on the handle. A good idea, considering the recent break-ins Ms. Anne had mentioned, but something puzzled me. I loved books, but were Miss Josie's books actually so valuable, or had the robbers been after something else?

Not that it mattered. Miss Josie had me now, Capone the Super Protector, as her guardian. I'd keep her safe, and I'd keep the shop safe, too.

I could be both an upstanding gentleman and a capable

guard dog. Mr. Darcy would never have let any harm come to his Lizzie. If he could guard his love and still look great doing it, surely I could do the same.

When we got back inside, I couldn't stop thinking about *Pride and Prejudice*. "Why, oh, why could I not have been named after Mr. Darcy?" I asked aloud to no one in particular. "There is simply no justice in the world."

Well, there was some justice. Mr. Collins, the barn cat, had likely been named after the annoying Mr. Collins from *Pride and Prejudice*, a fact which made me happy indeed. I bet he had no idea, and I wanted to go back to the farm to tell him, but my little revenge fantasy was interrupted by something unexpected.

"You know," said a voice coming from high above me, "you're called Capone for a good reason."

At first, I thought God spoke to me directly, but then I realized it was a large, fluffy, gray cat with a smushed up face perched on the kitchen table. I sat up straighter. "Rocco?"

"Who else would it be, dimwit?"

"No one, I guess. But what do mean about my name?"

"You're named after Al Capone."

"Who was Al Capone?"

He paused in licking his paw, and stared at me, an evil smile forming on his flat, furry face. "Oh, my. You have no idea. Is it a secret? I do love a good secret."

"I don't have secrets. A true gentleman does not need them."

"Whatever. Ignorance, I suppose, is bliss." When Miss Josie came back into the room, Rocco yawned, turned, and pretended to be asleep.

"Time for you to go to bed, too, Capone," she said,

tossing a blanket on the floor and pointing at it. "Here you go. Sit. Lie down. Sleep. Stay. Goodnight."

Did she just throw four commands at me and leave? She had to be kidding.

When she walked down the hall, heading to a door in the back of the apartment, I followed her. She looked at me in surprise. "No, Capone. Your bed is out there. Not here."

I tilted my head to one side. No way would I be able to sleep out there with the mean kitty Rocco and all those strange sounds and noises. Had she lost her mind?

She stepped into her room and tried to block me from entering, but I stuck my nose in and pushed my way through. I trotted inside and took a look around. Fluffy white comforter. Lace pillows. Pretty lamps. The place of a lady.

I loved it.

I spied a soft armchair in the corner, hopped onto it, and curled up in a little ball, thoroughly satisfied. Miss Josie did not approve of my choice of seating arrangements.

"No, Capone. Get down."

Grudgingly, I lowered myself to the floor, giving her my best sad puppy dog look. It didn't work. Miss Josie pointed down the hall to the blanket, and said, "Go. Now." And she did the unthinkable. She shut the door in my face.

Did she not realize I was a puppy? Temptation overwhelmed me. I could not do as she commanded. I stayed right outside her closed bedroom door and sang the sad song of my people in the loudest possible voice. I barked. I whined. I howled in misery.

Miss Josie opened the door minutes later, but it felt like hours. "What is your problem?" she asked.

I tried to appear as pathetic as possible. Not a difficult task.

Why did she ask me these things? Wasn't it obvious? Even for a person who could not speak a word of Dog, didn't she realize I was sad, lonely, scared, and needed the comfort of her presence?

She did not. She called Ms. Anne and asked for advice, putting her on speakerphone as she marched around the room. "He won't go to sleep," she said. "What do I do?"

"He's a puppy, Josie. And he's in a new place. He's sad, lonely, and scared."

Ms. Anne understood the inner workings of my soul. Miss Josie did not.

"But I gave him a blanket."

"He doesn't want a blanket. He wants you."

Miss Josie hung up the phone and put her hands on her hips. "Fine. You can stay in my room, but only for tonight. And no sleeping on my chair or in my bed. It's the floor or nothing."

She got my blanket from the front room and put it next to her bed. I circled once, and then twice, before curling up on it. I kept my eyes on Josie, though. I'd been brought here to guard her, after all.

She put on a white nightgown resembling something Elizabeth Bennet herself would have worn and turned off the small lamp on her bedside table. "Goodnight, Capone," she said. "Be good."

Goodnight, Miss Josie. Sleep well.

FOUR

A list of things I should not have done as Miss Josie slept:

1. Eaten the rose-colored ribbons from her spiffy pumps.
2. Chewed on the shoes, removing one of the heels and making a hole in the toe.
3. Shredded her grey tights. I couldn't stop myself. They were delightfully boingy.
4. Destroyed her decorative, goose down pillow.

Although I passed an enjoyable evening, I regretted my actions when Miss Josie awoke to the feather-coated destruction of her bedroom. She yawned, stretched, got out of bed, and tripped on the remnants of her shoes. Staring around in horror, she took in the entire scene. It probably looked like a blur since she didn't have her glasses on. I'd knocked them off her bedside table sometime during my attack on the pillow.

It amazed me she hadn't heard any of my shenanigans, but Miss Josie slept like a rock. She didn't even wake up when I licked her toes in the middle of the night, but she was fully awake now, and not happy.

I tried to blend in, hoping she wouldn't notice me and realize I created this mess, but a black lab covered in white feathers tends to stand out.

"Capone. What have you done?"

Note to self: Some questions are better left unanswered.

I tried to appear as guileless as possible. I wagged my tail (just a little, too much would have been overkill), and stared around the room as if to say, "What on earth happened in here? Wow. It must have been Rocco the cat."

She didn't buy it. Miss Josie is so stinking smart. The words she said next nearly broke my heart. "Capone, you are a bad dog."

My wagging tail stilled as I contemplated the possible repercussions of my actions, but now I faced an additional problem. If I didn't get outside soon, I would add something both significant and stinky to this whole mess.

I ran to the door, wagging my tail hopefully to convince Miss Josie to let me out. Sadly, she could not focus, both because of the destruction of her room, and because she couldn't locate her glasses.

Poor Miss Josie. She also searched in vain for the ribbons that once adorned her pretty pumps. If I could have spoken, I would have told her I highly doubted she'd ever use them again. Those ribbons now lay buried somewhere deep inside my intestines.

I whined, then barked, as my need to get outside increased with each passing second. I even scratched on the closed bedroom door but to no avail. Finally, with all hope gone, I circled and squatted.

"No," she screamed, understanding at last and flying toward me. "Nooooooo."

She flung open the door, and we raced through the apartment and down the steps. Miss Josie still wore her sheer white nightie, her hair a tangled mess. She didn't bother with a leash. She also didn't bother with slippers or a robe. Time was of the essence, and she knew it. We did not have a second to spare.

We made it in the nick of time. If we'd waited a moment longer, I would have messed on the floor of the shop, and I'm sure it would have made Miss Josie even more displeased.

Squatting on the edge of the grassy part of the back garden, relief flooded my body as I finally did my business. My relief proved to be rather short-lived, however, since something had gone terribly wrong. Something was...stuck. I turned, trying to locate the source of my discomfort, and saw it. Rose-colored ribbons dangled out of my behind.

I squatted, walking around the yard, hoping to dislodge the offending items, but couldn't. Two little ribbons hung out of my backside, fluttering in the breeze like streamers on the handlebars of a bicycle.

Miss Josie didn't notice at first. She was too busy trying to keep warm. The chill of early fall permeated the bright October morning, making her shiver. She had no shoes on either and hopped back and forth trying to keep her feet from freezing.

When she finally perceived my predicament, I turned away, mortified. What an impression I must be making on her. Not once in the entire two hours of *Rules of Being a Regency Gentleman* did it address what to do if one had brightly colored ribbons dangling from one's rectum.

"Oh, no." Judging by the look of pure horror on her face, she had no idea what to do next either. "I can't."

I didn't know if she referred to the current ribbon situation, or to dealing with me in general. Due to the glazed and shocked look in her eyes, I had a sinking suspicion it might be both.

As I continued to squat walk around the small confines of her garden, she leaped into action. Grabbing her gardening gloves from the potting bench, she approached me with a determined gleam in her eye.

"Come here, doggie."

I tried to squat walk away from her as fast as possible but didn't make it far. She got a good grip on my collar and held fast. I looked up at her, miserable, begging her to put an end to my humiliation.

Miss Josie pinched the ends of the ribbons with her gloved fingers and pulled them slowly and carefully out of my anus. I stood utterly still, not moving a muscle, both terrified at what might happen next and elated because it would soon be over.

"Almost got it," she said softly, concentrating on the task at hand. Within seconds, the ribbons were out. I turned and licked Miss Josie's face, thanking her in the best way I knew how for relieving my agony. "You're welcome," she said, making a gagging noise when she looked at the ribbons. She walked over to the garbage bin, threw them in, and tossed her gloves in as well.

"Come on, Capone," she said. "Let's go inside."

Grabbing the handle of the door, she tried to open it, but nothing happened. I stood next to her, tail wagging, hopeful I'd get breakfast soon but concerned about the expression on her face. The door refused to budge.

"We're locked out," she said.

She ran to the wooden door in the middle of the brick wall, the exit to the alley. Rubbing her arms frantically with her hands, she lifted the giant padlock with a groan. "The key is inside the shop. This can't be happening."

She played with one of the back windows, testing it, and pushed against the door, hoping it might be stuck and not locked. Nothing. Nada. No dice. She eyed a large rock, and as I wondered if she might toss it through a window and climb in, I heard a noise from next door. Someone was whistling. Miss Josie and I looked at each other for a split second and then charged toward the wall.

"Help," said Miss Josie. "Please."

The whistling continued. Whoever stood there didn't seem to hear us. I barked as loudly as I could. Miss Josie grabbed a ladder tucked into a corner near the opposite side of the garden. She ran back with it, slipping in a pile of fresh poo. She nearly fell, ladder and all, but managed to right herself.

"For Pete's sake," she muttered. I understood her distress. I hated stepping in my poo, too, but nothing could be done about it now. Time was, once again, of the essence.

The ladder, tall enough to reach the top of the wall, caused another dilemma since jumping down would be a problem. Miss Josie couldn't lift the ladder from such an odd angle and swing it over. It was too heavy and awkward. And if she jumped, in her poor, bare, poop-covered feet, she might break an ankle. She did the only thing possible. She stood on top of the brick wall in her nightgown, waved her arms in the air, and screamed at the top of her lungs. I assisted her by barking my head off and running around in circles. Eventually, I heard the voice of our savior, Mr. Nate, from the other side of the wall. Through a small crack in the wooden door, I saw his face as he took out his earbuds and gave Miss Josie a look of pure disbelief.

"Are you okay?"

His eyes scanned her. I gazed up at her, too. She was sort of mesmerizing. Her blond hair hung loose down her back in a riot of curls. Standing on the wall in her old-fashioned white nightgown, she looked like an angel, albeit one with filthy feet.

Well, maybe she looked more like a fallen angel. The nightie, although buttoned up to her neck, became positively scandalous in the bright morning sun. The view left nothing about Miss Josie's generous curves or long, shapely legs to the imagination, and, for a moment, Mr. Nate did nothing but gaze at her.

She placed tightly clenched fists on her hips, and somehow managed to look haughty. "Obviously, I am not okay. I got locked out, and I'm freezing to death. Can you please help?"

"Of course," said Mr. Nate, biting his lip in what I had to assume was an attempt not to laugh. "I'd never leave a damsel in distress."

As soon as he said those words, I froze. Miss Josie was a damsel in distress? If true, rescuing her was a sure-fire way to prove my gentlemanly qualities. Chances to rescue damsels in distress didn't happen every day.

"I'm not a damsel in distress," she said, but a woman in her nightie on a wall with poopy feet seemed pretty distressed to me, and she must have realized it, too. Her voice took on a grudgingly conciliatory quality when she spoke again. "But I do need assistance."

"And I'll help you...on one condition."

She gasped. "Are you kidding me?"

As I peeked through the crack in the door, I saw his lips quirk into a smile. "I want to make a deal. I hate this animosity between us. We're neighbors, and we ought to get along."

"I agree."

"I've come to the conclusion you don't like me because you don't know me. I suspect the same is true regarding your obviously misguided dislike for coffee, and I plan to prove it to you."

"How?"

"I'll bring you a different kind of coffee daily, and you'll agree to keep trying it until we find one you like, or I give up and admit defeat. If that happens, you can go back to drinking your kombucha in peace and I won't bother you again."

She scoffed at his words. "I've already told you. I don't drink coffee."

He stared up at her, squinting in the sunlight. "What's the harm in trying, Josephine? Are you afraid you might end up enjoying it?"

"No chance," she said, her words clipped.

"Then you'll agree to my terms?"

"Fine, since it's the only way I can get off this wall, but I have terms of my own."

He raised one dark eyebrow. He looked dashing when he did it, and I wished I could raise one eyebrow. Sadly, I couldn't, mostly because I didn't have eyebrows.

"You're giving me a condition in order to rescue you?" he asked.

"Yes. First of all, let's be clear. This isn't a rescue. You're simply offering assistance to someone in a difficult predicament."

He snorted. "Okay. So, what's your condition?"

"You sell coffee, I sell books. If I drink your coffee, you'll agree to read a book of my choice," she said, a challenge in her voice.

He considered it. "A book for a cup of coffee? You're being completely unreasonable."

"How about a chapter per cup. Fair enough?"

"I guess so. Shall we shake on it?"

She stomped her foot, which seemed like a dangerous move for a person standing on top of a wall. "I obviously can't shake on it when I'm standing up here. Now hurry before I freeze to death."

He brought a ladder from his side of the wall and held it steady for her as she descended. When she got closer to the ground, he took her elbow and led her down the final few steps. It was an outstanding rescue. I couldn't wait until I got my turn to do the same.

"A cup of coffee per day?" he asked, extending his hand.

She shook it, although she didn't seem thrilled about the deal they'd made. "And you'll read one chapter a day from a book of my choosing?"

He gave her a little bow. "It's a deal. I'll go make your coffee."

He went back to his café, and I heard Miss Josie muttering as she punched in the code for the keyless entry on the front door of the shop. Within minutes, she marched through the shop and opened the back door to let me in. I was so grateful, I found one spot on her foot not covered in poo and gave her an appreciative lick.

"You're not out of the woods yet, buster," she said.

Uh-oh. I didn't want to be in the woods. That sounded scary.

I accompanied her to the bathroom and waited as she took a hot shower, warming up her body and washing her poor poopy feet. I discovered it's hard to wait patiently. Waiting is boring. And soap tastes so good.

She stuck her head out from behind the shower curtain

to chastise me. Thank goodness she didn't notice I'd already eaten the spare bar of soap she kept next to the tub, paper and all. "It's between my toes, Capone. You're disgusting."

I gulped, trying not to burp out soap bubbles. Oh calamity. She sounded like my old arch-nemesis Mr. Collins, but how could Miss Josie blame me for what happened this morning? I didn't lock myself out. She locked both of us out. I only did as nature intended.

Well, except for the ribbons. Nature never intended for me to eat Miss Josie's ribbons. Or her soap. Or feathers from her pillow.

Note to self: Sometimes I defy the laws of nature.

After she washed, she stepped out of the shower and wrapped herself in a towel, her skin warm and damp. I padded over to her and licked the droplets of water on her legs. Yummy.

She grimaced. "Stop it. You're gross."

She went to her bedroom to dress, sighing as she took in the carnage. It's incredible how many feathers can come out of one small pillow. When I'd clutched it in my teeth and swung my head back and forth, the feathers resembled snowflakes falling from the sky. I saw snow on a PBS special once. I wish Miss Josie could have witnessed it, but she may not have appreciated the ethereal beauty of the experience.

She put on a black skirt, thick black stockings, and a white blouse with a narrow black grosgrain ribbon tied at the neck. She looked bookish and yet stylish, especially with her blond hair in a messy bun and her funky, hipster glasses perched on her nose.

She'd found her glasses behind the nightstand, and, thankfully, they were still intact. I didn't want to be in trouble for destroying those, too. Grabbing a cardigan from a shelf in her closet, she put on a pair of pumps, and headed down the steps as a knock sounded at the front door.

I immediately went into frenzied puppy mode. Was it a stranger? If so, how exciting, and yet potentially dangerous. This could be my chance to show Miss Josie my incredible guard dog skills. She'd be so impressed.

I pushed past her on the steps, clipping her with the strength of a small freight train. Barking for all I was worth, I charged toward the door. Miss Josie let out a squeal and grabbed onto the stair railing to keep from falling.

Oopsie. My bad.

I should have been more careful, but I couldn't control myself. The mysterious and unexpected knocking at the door unleashed something wild and primitive inside me. I was a puppy on a mission, ready to attack, or maybe just lick someone. Probably the latter.

When I saw Mr. Nate stood outside holding a cardboard tray with two cups on it, I hopped up and down until Miss Josie opened the door. Mr. Nate had come to visit. What could top this?

Jackson stood next to him, looking bored. "Yo, pupster. How's it hanging?"

I stared at him in confusion, not sure how to respond. "Excuse me?"

He laughed, a rough sound, his little pug face squinching up. "You're a riot. I forgot you still have your cojones. How cute."

I checked out the place between my legs. Of course, I still had them. What a strange comment.

Mr. Nate handed one of the drinks to Miss Josie and knelt to pet me. "Hey, big guy. Did you get into trouble today?"

His friendly brown eyes crinkled at the corners as he

played with me, rubbing my head and tickling my belly to help me get my wiggles out. An expert dog whisperer, he unfortunately seemed to lack any such skills with the ladies.

Miss Josie, acting even more annoyed than usual, frowned as Jackson sniffed around the shop. She probably wondered if he planned to lift a leg and pee on something. I wondered the same thing myself. Jackson was an unpredictable kind of guy.

"I can't believe you're making me drink this," she said, staring at the contents of her cup.

"Well, I can't believe you managed to lock yourself outside nearly naked, so I guess we're even."

She gasped. "I was not naked."

He winked at her. "I said 'nearly,' and you were pretty close. You should thank Capone for barking his head off. I may not have heard you otherwise."

Jackson took a break from licking his butt to laugh. "Nearly naked. I wish I'd seen it."

"She was completely clothed at all times. The important thing is I helped her get rescued." I sat up taller, now the hero in this saga. What wonderful news.

Miss Josie shot me a look like we were at a formal dinner and I'd picked up the wrong fork. It crushed my pride.

"It's his fault we got locked outside in the first place."

"Wait, you're blaming the dog?"

"Yes." She told him all about what had happened this morning in detail. The feathers. The ribbons. The willful destruction of property. It embarrassed me, and yet Mr. Nate didn't seem fazed by it.

"Sorry, but you're the one who's to blame for what happened this morning," he said, and lectured Miss Josie about puppy proofing, having a schedule for meals, and how often I needed to go outside. Mr. Nate knew a lot about dogs. He may have known almost as much as Mistress Sue, but he didn't know when to stop. Miss Josie's eyes glazed over.

"Well, it doesn't matter," she said. "After this morning, I'm not sure if this is going to work out."

My heart thumped to a stop in my chest, and I shot Jackson a worried look. He couldn't quite meet my eyes, and I swallowed hard. Sent home already? This was a disaster.

Mr. Nate sided with me. "He's a good dog, and he deserves an owner who loves and appreciates him. If you can't do that, he'd be better off with someone else."

She blinked, her cheeks reddening. "It's not that I don't want him. I'm just not sure we're the right fit for each other."

I flopped down on the floor, disheartened. Jackson came over and licked my head sympathetically, a rather kind thing to do. Maybe I'd read Jackson all wrong. Perhaps he wasn't wholly uncouth.

"Cheer up, buttercup," he said, then turned around and farted in my face.

Or maybe I'd read him correctly in the first place.

"A gentleman always trusts his instincts," I muttered under my breath, glaring at Jackson, the scoundrel. I'd been right about him.

I'd been right about Mr. Nate, too. He was honestly upset for me. "He's going to be a great dog someday, and he's smart, too."

Taking my side again. Mr. Nate was a peach.

"Let's agree to disagree on the last part, but there's something you don't quite understand. Anne brought him to me because she thinks I need companionship or protection or something. But she didn't take into account that I know nothing about dogs. I don't even know where to start. And you standing there, trying to make me feel guilty about this, is not helpful at all."

Her voice shook, and Mr. Nate winced. "I'm sorry. I was out of line. I thought you got him on impulse and regretted your decision once you realized how hard it was. I didn't know Anne got him for you. It's kind of a weird gift."

Composing herself, she gave him a rueful smile. "Anne is kind of a weird friend."

Mr. Nate shoved his hands into the pockets of his jeans. "I'm about to head out to the pet store right now. Would you like to come with us? I could help you pick things out. I'm afraid of what you might get on your own. The last thing Capone needs is a princess bed, or a rhinestone covered collar."

He must have been teasing. A princess bed? Surely not.

"I wouldn't buy him anything so silly." She narrowed her eyes at Mr. Nate, but it seemed necessity, in this case, overruled pride. "Are you sure you don't mind?"

"As Capone's neighbor and friend, it's my duty. But, first things first, we had an agreement." He nodded toward the cup of coffee she'd set on the counter.

She glanced around the shop, and as soon as her gaze alit on a book sitting on the table next to her, she smiled. "And here's your book." She handed him a copy of *Pride and Prejudice.* My favorite. I wagged my tail in delight.

Mr. Nate did not seem quite as thrilled. "Jane Austen? Please tell me you're kidding."

"Stop whining. It's a classic." She took a whiff of her coffee and wrinkled her nose. "Do I seriously have to drink this?"

"It's a mocha. It's basically flavored hot chocolate. Even children drink it."

She didn't seem convinced. "I'd rather just have hot chocolate."

"You're impossible."

"I'm being realistic." She took a sip of the mocha and grimaced. "What if you can't find the right coffee for me? Will this go on and on forever?"

He gave her a crooked smile. "Nope. I'm good at what I do, and I'm good with people, too. Eventually, somehow, I'll figure it, and you, out."

FIVE

Items required for the care and maintenance of one energetic Labrador retriever:

1. A large crate with a comfy cushion inside.
2. Soft treats for training and manipulation
   purposes.
3. Hard treats to get rid of the urge to chew on
   shoes (but not so hard to hurt sensitive puppy
   teeth).
4. Poop bags. No other explanation necessary.
5. A cozy dog bed.
6. A sturdy water bowl and a food bowl.
7. Doggie shampoo.
8. A brush.
9. A pooper scooper.
10. A toy reminding me of Mr. Darcy.

Perhaps the Mr. Darcy toy, a little stuffed man in a black
top hat and tails, was unnecessary, but I saw it and had to have

it. Jackson called me a rude name when I chose it, but Miss Josie seemed charmed as well. She didn't even argue when I pulled it off the shelf and trotted around the store with it in my mouth.

Mr. Nate insisted she get more dog food, a wise idea, and he carried our purchases back in his First Impressions Café truck. A man with a truck is a handy thing, and I certainly enjoyed riding in it. I sat on the seat between them, grinning ear to ear. Jackson flopped down next to me, and I felt a certain amount of camaraderie between us, in spite of the events of this morning,

"What did you think of the mocha?" asked Mr. Nate.

"Almost as good as hot chocolate."

He tapped his fingers on the steering wheel as we waited at a red light. "Hmmm. Not a mocha girl. We'll have to try something else tomorrow."

"I'm a tea person, Nate," she said. "I'm not going to change."

"We'll see," he said, and it suddenly occurred to me this might be a ploy for Mr. Nate to spend more time with Miss Josie. If so, his genius extended far beyond the magic of hot beverage preparation. I gave him a steady look, trying to assess if his intentions were honorable or not. He caught me staring at him and patted my head. "So, what made you name this little gangster Capone?"

"I didn't," she said. "He came with the name, but it doesn't suit him."

"Are you going to change it?"

"Oh, definitely."

I held up my Mr. Darcy toy hopefully. This could be my big chance. "Please call me Mr. Darcy. Please call me Mr. Darcy."

Jackson looked at me out of the corner of his eye. Or at

least I thought it was the corner. It's kind of hard to tell with a pug. "Are you kidding me?"

"No," I said, although it came out muffled with Mr. Darcy in my mouth. "He's the epitome of a multi-dimensional literary character and a fine example of a gentleman. Why wouldn't I want to be named after him?"

Jackson laughed, and the sound hovered somewhere between a chuckle and a raspy guffaw. "He, he, he, he," he said. "Because a dog named 'Mr. Darcy' would get beat up by the other dogs. It's a name chicks give to dogs, but no self-respecting pooch would want it. Asking for a name like Mr. Darcy is like asking to be humped, frankly speaking."

"Humped?" I asked, confused.

Jackson rolled his googly eyes at me. "I'll explain later, when you're older. The point is don't ask for a stupid name. Stick with what you have. Your name is awesome. It demands respect."

"What do you mean?" I asked. "Who was Capone anyway?"

Jackson blinked his buggy puggy eyes in surprise. "You don't know?"

I shook my head. "No. Was he someone important?"

"Well, in certain circles, I guess," said Jackson. "He led an interesting life, and even though he died from the pox, he was tough and tough guys are cool."

"What's the pox?" I asked, confused by so much of what Jackson said.

"Uh, we'll discuss that later. When you're older. But trust me, kid. You have an impressive name. Much better than Darcy."

Mr. Nate spoke, interrupting our conversation. "He looks like a Capone to me."

Jackson gave me a knowing nod. "See what I mean? Real men like the name. Trust me."

I didn't trust him. I knew Mr. Darcy would be a much better fit for me.

"What names are you thinking about?" asked Mr. Nate. "For Capone."

"Well, probably something literary," she said. I nudged her with my Darcy toy, but she ignored me. "If he'd been a girl, it would have been easy. I would have named him Jane."

"For Jane Austen?"

"Of course. But a boy dog is trickier. Naming him Austen doesn't feel quite right. Nor does Brontë. I thought about doing something substantial and classical, like Shake- speare or Chaucer, but neither of those fit." I climbed on her lap and tried to stick the Darcy doll in her face, pleading with her. She shoved it away. "Stop it."

Mr. Nate considered the options. "I don't know. Capone seems perfect."

Miss Josie rolled her eyes. "I cannot have a dog named Capone."

"When the name is right, you'll know it, but you'd better decide soon. You don't want to confuse him."

"Thanks," she said. "Your advice is so appreciated." Even though she sounded a little snooty, he winked at her, a smile tugging at his lips.

"It is a truth, universally acknowledged, that a dog in possession of a name like Capone, must be in want of a new one."

Her eyes widened in surprise. "You're already reading *Pride and Prejudice*?"

"I read the first two chapters before I brought your

coffee over this morning, so I'm ahead of the game. You're going to have to drink more to catch up."

She snorted, not a ladylike sound, but still somehow adorable. "Not going to happen."

He ignored her attitude and kept talking. "So how did you become the owner of Bartleby's?"

"I worked for the old owner, Benjamin Bartleby, since high school. When he passed away, I'd just finished my master's degree in library science, and he left the shop to me. It was a huge shock, and upset some of the other employees, but I think he understood how I felt about old books, and knew I'd carry on the tradition."

"How do you feel about old books?"

She gazed out the window at the passing scenery, a faraway look in her eyes. "Old books aren't like new books. They have more character. From the bindings to the detailed artwork inside, each one is a mystery and a delight. It might look worn and misused on the outside, but then you open it, and you realize it's magic. When I'm in a place full of books, especially old books, it's like I'm less...alone. Like I'm with old friends, people I know and love, and it's the best feeling in the world."

Mr. Nate seemed fascinated by every word coming out of her mouth. I understood why. I felt the same way. "Are there any books you dream of acquiring?"

"I'd love to have an original, first edition, signed copy of the book I gave you this morning, *Pride and Prejudice*. It's a pipe dream, though."

"Why?"

"Jane Austen barely signed any books," she said. "Before Mr. Bartleby sold the shop to me, he had a lead on one. Unfortunately, it fell apart. According to his records, he purchased the book, but he never listed it in his inventory. It's like it disappeared."

"Books can't disappear, but inventory certainly can. I once thought I'd lost an entire shipment of Brazilian coffee only to find someone had mislabeled it. Maybe something similar happened to you," he said as we pulled into the alley on the side of the shop.

She gave him a sad little smile. "I'm not so lucky."

"Well, perhaps your luck is about to change," he said, and when I barked in agreement, he laughed. "See? Even Capone thinks I'm right."

We got out of the truck, and Mr. Nate helped carry Miss Josie's purchases inside. "I'll bring your coffee over first thing in the morning. Do you need any help with Capone?"

"No. I can manage."

He raised an eyebrow at her words. "When dogs misbehave, it's the owner who's to blame."

"Is that so?" she asked.

Mr. Nate, oblivious to the brewing storm, plowed ahead. "Yes. A puppy needs a safe environment, and this place is a dog disaster zone. There is far too much temptation. Do you want him to eat your books?"

"Of course not."

"Then be proactive. Study things from Capone's perspective. See the world the way he sees it. Get down on your hands and knees if you have to."

Jackson fell over on the floor laughing. "Get down on your hands and knees. Hilarious."

I decided Jackson was a complex and confusing creature. Better to ignore him.

Miss Josie opened her mouth, likely to respond to Mr. Nate's unsolicited advice, but she got distracted by something, and her gaze went to the front window of the shop.

She let out a frustrated huff and marched outside, cell phone in hand. Cars occupied two of the spots directly in front of the bookstore. Miss Josie muttered to herself as she took note of the license plate numbers on each of the cars.

"What are you doing?" asked Mr. Nate, watching Miss Josie punch in numbers on her cell phone.

"Calling a tow truck," she said, enunciating each word. "This parking is for my customers only."

He frowned at her. "But your shop isn't even open yet. What's the harm?"

She glanced at her watch. "It opens in twenty minutes, but that's beside the point. These are my spots for my customers. Your customers can park anywhere else on the block but not right here."

"I get it, but do you have to have them towed? I'll run over to First Impressions and let them know..."

She shook her head, holding up one finger to silence him. "Hello, is this Gilarno's Towing? I'm Josephine St. Clair of Bartleby's Books, and I have two cars parked in front of my shop illegally. Will you please come and remove them? Thank you."

She shut off her phone. Mr. Nate made a noise of disgust. "You are a real piece of work. I can't believe you called a tow truck."

"And I can't believe you don't provide adequate parking for your customers."

He didn't answer. He gave Miss Josie another dark look and stomped away. Jackson waddled off behind him. We went back into the shop, and a few minutes later, a rather harried-looking woman with a toddler in tow rushed toward one of the parked cars. She shot Miss Josie a dirty look before climbing into her minivan. Following her was a middle-aged, balding man who hobbled over with a brace on his foot and jumped into his car. He shot Miss Josie a dirty look, too.

Miss Josie went inside and inhaled a deep, shaky breath as she slumped against the door, her shoulders drooping. "I'm right, you know," she said.

I'm not an expert on women or humans in general, but I think we both knew one thing. A person could be right and wrong at the same time.

SIX

A list of things required before a puppy can start obedience training:

1. A visit to the vet for shots.
2. A new dog registration form.
3. A terms of agreement form.
4. A dog behavior form.
5. A recent photo.
6. A pre-training mandatory orientation session.
7. A bait bag and a special Easy Leader collar.

On Monday morning, Ms. Anne arrived early, accompanied by her miniature sheltie, Gracie, and gave Miss Josie the list of items we would need for the training sessions at Misty Mountain Dog Kennel and Spa. Miss Josie frowned as she read over it.

"What the heck is a bait bag? It sounds like something you'd take fishing."

"A bait bag is a pouch you wear around your waist so

you can dole out treats as you train him. Labs are food motivated."

Gracie was not food motivated. Gracie did not seem motivated by much of anything.

"How long do we have to stay in this dreary place?" asked Gracie. "I'm bored. And a weird pug is staring at me through the window."

I glanced up. "His name is Jackson. He's harmless."

Jackson winked at Gracie and licked the window provocatively. He turned around and wiggled his little pug bottom at her. Gracie shuddered. "He's disgusting."

I couldn't argue with her. "Jackson is an acquired taste."

Gracie was a lady, and I treated her accordingly, giving her the best spot to sit and letting her have the first treat. She seemed to appreciate it. I even allowed her to curl up on my new bed.

"It's nice to meet a pup who knows his manners," said Gracie. "You should see the riff-raff I encounter at Misty Mountain."

"Miss Josie is signing me up today. Is it bad?"

She yawned, patting her mouth delicately with one tiny paw. "Let me say; you have to be careful whose butt you sniff there. You could bring home something nasty if you aren't careful."

I pondered this as Gracie snoozed. I had no idea what she might be talking about, and both Ms. Anne and Miss Josie seemed unaware of the potential dangers lurking at Misty Mountain. With regard to my upcoming obedience classes, their concern centered on something entirely different.

"Make sure you ask for the younger trainer," said Ms. Anne. "He's gorgeous. I call him Sexy Trainer Dude."

Miss Josie snorted. "You do realize that's STD for short, right?"

"No, I did not," said Ms. Anne with a laugh. "But, trust me, this guy is hot. He's all muscular, and stern, and oh, so strict. If he told me to sit or lie down, I'd listen." She fanned herself.

Miss Josie groaned. "You've got to be kidding. You want me to go to dog obedience training to meet men?"

"The trainer could be what you need right now. A distraction. Anything to help you get over Cedric the loser."

Miss Josie made a sour face. "You said his name. Again."

Ms. Anne held up her hands in defeat. "Sorry. I know he hurt you, but he is so not worth it."

"I realize you're right, but I need to go through a proper mourning period first."

"And how long does this mourning period last, exactly? It's been...what? Six months? You broke up with him not long after you inherited the shop. And you were not at fault. He was the one who conveniently forgot he already had a wife, the jerk."

Miss Josie didn't say anything, but she looked away quickly as if to hide the hurt in her eyes. I saw it and put my head against her leg to comfort her. She smiled down at me, patting me on the head. "Thanks, buddy."

She called me "buddy." Definitely the best thing ever. I wagged my tail happily. Nothing would bring me down now.

"I managed to snag an appointment for Capone at the vet," said Ms. Anne, checking her watch. "It's in half an hour. If he gets his shots today, you can go to the orientation for dog training on Wednesday. They only have the orientation once a month, so you lucked out. And I signed you up for Puppy Preschool tomorrow. You can attend as a warm-up of sorts."

It was the best of times, and now the worst of times. Shots? Training? Orientation? Puppy Preschool? A gentleman had no time for such things.

Apparently, neither did Miss Josie. "I can't, Anne. I have a business to run."

"Gracie and I will take care of the shop. You need to get him trained. You have a narrow window of opportunity here. The more time you spend on him now, the less you'll have to do in the future." She handed Miss Josie my leash and pushed us out the door. "And you'll like the vet. He's cute. I call him Doc McHottie. He's a dreamboat."

Miss Josie narrowed her eyes at Ms. Anne as I tugged on the leash. "First Sexy Trainer Dude, then Doc McHottie. Are you using Capone as a way to fix me up with strange men?"

Ms. Anne shrugged. "Yes, and also to force you out of this bookstore once in a while. Now go. Doc McHottie is waiting."

As we walked the short distance to the vet, Miss Josie muttered to herself under her breath, but her demeanor changed as soon as she met Doc McHottie. Slim and tall, he had dark hair, green eyes, and he carried the faint aroma of dog treats on his clothing, probably from the residual crumbs in his pockets. He might have been the perfect man.

He shook her hand. "So, this is the new puppy," he said, leaning down to pet me. "He's a real beauty. I'm not supposed to be partial, but I'm a lab guy myself. I have one like this at home. His name is Wrigley. We should get them together to play sometime."

Wait a second. We'd been at the vet all of two minutes, and we'd already been set up on some human/canine double date? Strange, but intriguing. I wanted to hear more about Wrigley, but Miss Josie seemed more interested in Doc McHottie.

"That would be nice." She flushed. Miss Josie was definitely out of practice with this whole flirting thing. She sat up a little straighter and pushed a lock of hair behind her ear. "What made you decide to become a vet?" she asked as he examined me. He had strong, capable hands, but a gentle touch and his eyes were kind. In all honesty, Miss Josie could do a lot worse. If they dated, he might even give her a discount on my veterinary care.

"I grew up on a ranch out west, surrounded by animals. I learned how to ride a horse before I could walk."

"So, you're a cowboy?" she asked, her voice sounding oddly husky. Either she was coming down with a cold, or my bookworm of an owner had a thing for cowboys.

"Yes, ma'am," he said.

Miss Josie let out a tiny gasp. A cowboy and a gentleman. What more could she want? The only thing better would be if Colonel Brandon and Captain Wentworth walked through the door together and took turns making passionate love to her. Who could turn down Brandon and Wentworth?

"I know nothing about dogs," Miss Josie admitted. "I'm learning as I go. I found some books on basic care and training, but do you have any recommendations?"

"Sure," he said. He went to a cupboard and pulled out a few paperback books on obedience training and how to care for a puppy—basic stuff, but precisely what Miss Josie needed. "And I meant what I said about getting together for a playdate with Wrigley. Dogs need to be socialized, the sooner, the better. Wrigley is a calm boy. He might be a good influence."

They watched as I inspected each nook and cranny in the examination room, tail wagging, and my body so full of wiggles I thought I might burst. Miss Josie looked concerned.

"Is it normal for him to be this energetic?" she asked as I ran into the door and fell over. In my defense, it was a reflective door, shiny and metallic. I thought I saw another dog.

"Capone is definitely on the active side."

He scooped me up in his sinewy arms and lifted me onto the exam table. Shiny and metallic, like the door, it gave me the heebie-jeebies. My feet kept slipping, and I felt miles above the ground.

As I experienced a wave of vertigo, I crouched down and clung to the table for dear life. Then Doc McHottie did the unthinkable. Without any warning at all, he stuck a thermometer in my...well...it wasn't my mouth. Yowza. What a shock. But he pretended there was nothing at all out of the ordinary about it. Like people go around on a daily basis shoving things in the nether regions of innocent bystanders. He gave me a little scratch under my chin, not an easy thing to do while muscling a thirty-pound puppy to hold still on a shiny metal table and keeping a rectal thermometer in place.

"Good boy. We're almost done." He shot Miss Josie a glance. She averted her eyes as he took my temperature. I appreciated it more than she'd ever know. "Let's get the dogs together soon. Maybe we could even turn it into a picnic or something."

Getting asked out on a date with a man and his dog was probably a first for Miss Josie, as was getting asked out by someone taking a temperature reading from a dog's anus, but she handled it smashingly. Doc McHottie was a professional. He knew what he was doing. And this was the moment of truth. Would Miss Josie put herself out there and start dating again, or would she go back to the bookstore alone, shut the door, and watch reruns of *Downton Abbey*?

"Sure. It sounds like fun."

"Super." He smiled and removed the thermometer from my bum. "His temperature is normal, and he looks great. My assistant will be in to give him his shots. By the way, his anal glands need to be expressed. We can do it for you here unless you'd rather do it at home."

I'd never seen a human's eyes grow as wide as Miss Josie's. "Anal glands?"

Doc McHottie gave her a detailed explanation about the glands located near what we can politely refer to as the exit door for the intestinal tract. Aka, the place where Doc McHottie shoved his chilly thermometer. Although I didn't realize I had anal glands either, it could explain the odd sensation pulsating from my backside ever since the rose-colored ribbon debacle. I wasn't a doctor, but even I knew a throbbing itch and funny aroma coming from the rear area was never a good sign.

"You see," he said, pulling up a large photo of engorged anal glands from a file on his computer. "Normally fluid is expressed with each bowel moment. In the case of Capone here, they're backed up. What we'll do is milk the glands to clear them out."

"You *milk* them?" asked Miss Josie, her face pale. I honestly thought she might yak. She did not, but for a minute or two, it was close. "Take care of it, please. Do it right now."

"Okay." He flashed her his megawatt smile. "We'll be back in a minute."

I won't go into detail to describe what happened when Doc McHottie took me into the back room for my anal gland expression, but I will admit to feeling relief and intense gratitude after we finished. Doc McHottie knew his stuff.

He gave me my shots and brought me back to Miss Josie. "How about getting the dogs together on Saturday for a picnic in the park?"

I was only a puppy, but even I understood Doc McHottie wanted a human playdate with Miss Josie as much as he wanted a canine playdate for me and Wrigley, but I don't think Miss Josie minded.

"Okay," she said. "What can I bring?"

"Nothing," said Doc McHottie. "I love to cook. Do you mind if it's vegetarian?"

"No," said Miss Josie, smiling. "I'm a vegetarian, too."

"Awesome." He beamed at her. "I'm looking forward to it."

As we walked back to the shop, I noticed a bounce in her step and a smile on her lips. Miss Josie looked happy. And I wanted nothing more than to make sure she stayed that way.

SEVEN

Things I do not like about sleeping in my crate:

1. I'm alone.
2. I'm not with Miss Josie.
3. I'm alone.

I didn't suspect a thing when Miss Josie put together a giant cage on Monday evening. In all honesty, I had no idea she intended it for me. I even helped her assemble the metal monstrosity, mostly by standing on it and wagging my tail. I'm such a good assistant.

"Okay, Capone," she said after she finished. "Time to lock you up in Alcatraz."

Lock me up? I didn't want to be locked up, but I am so easily fooled. As soon as she tossed a treat into the crate, I hopped right in.

Curse my naiveté.

I couldn't possibly protect Miss Josie while locked up in a prison. I freaked out when she closed the door, trapping me inside.

"Settle down, Capone. This is for your own good, and I'm right down the hall."

Her room felt miles away. Did she not realize how dangerous this was? How easy it would be for rogues and cads to take advantage of her if I weren't able to stop them? Also, I was lonely. I needed her.

Sighing, I pulled Orange Snuggle Bunny close. This was the worst night of my life. To make matters even more unbearable, Rocco tortured me as soon as Miss Josie went to bed.

"Locked up, I see. It shouldn't come as a surprise to you."

I growled at him. He curled up on top of my crate and stared down at me, his green eyes glowing in the darkness, his grey, fluffy fur appearing almost black.

"What are you talking about, Rocco? Spit it out."

He laughed, stretching and licking one paw. "The blondie called your crate Alcatraz. What a funny little joke."

I couldn't stop myself from taking the bait. "What do you mean? What's Alcatraz?"

Rocco snorted. "I'll let you figure it out. At least Josie knows you belong in a cage."

I barked, startling him. He hissed at me, jumping off my crate and moving to the blue couch. Miss Josie shouted from her bedroom for me to be quiet.

"We're not allowed to sit on the couch," I said, keeping my voice low.

He smiled at me, an evil, feline sort of smile. "*Dogs* aren't allowed on the couch. Cats can do whatever they like."

"I hate you," I said as I curled up in a ball and tried to go to sleep.

"Trust me. The feeling is entirely mutual."

I slept fitfully, cold and alone in my cage. Well, not cold. Miss Josie had provided me with a blankie for warmth. And not precisely alone, either. I had Orange Snuggle Bunny, my old friend, to comfort me, but I hated this crate. It felt like a punishment, and it made me so confused. I knew if I wanted to be a good dog, I should accept it and go to sleep, but to protect Josie, I needed to be free. It created quite a moral dilemma for me.

I woke as the first golden fingers of dawn fell upon my humble jail. I sat up, wondering what decorum demanded I do at this point. At no time, in the entire program about being a gentleman, did it talk about what to do if one found oneself locked up in puppy prison.

As much as I would have liked to let Miss Josie sleep, I had a more pressing issue. My bladder. I whimpered and whined, and a few minutes later, Miss Josie emerged from her room, bleary-eyed. "Good morning, Capone. Do you need to go outside?"

We went out together. Miss Josie had on her robe this time, and her slippers and glasses. Fully prepared, she made sure the door did not shut behind her. She'd also taken the precaution yesterday of hiding the key to the padlocked garden door under a potted plant on the back patio. It seemed like a safe idea. We didn't want to get trapped in the back garden again.

As I frolicked in the dew-covered grass, Miss Josie grabbed a cup of hot tea and sat on one of the wrought iron chairs next to a café style table in the back. Her garden was small, but pleasant, with beds of flowers against the walls and rose bushes throughout. Vines crept over the brick, covering it and the back side of the shop as well.

"The rose bushes are from Mr. Bartleby," she told me as she sipped her tea. "After his wife died, he planted one each year in her memory. Sweet, huh?"

I looked around. There were quite a few rose bushes, which meant Mr. Bartleby had spent many years here without his wife. Sad, and yet beautiful. The whole garden was, in fact, lovely.

There was something so comforting about ivy on brick, although some of the leaves were turning brown due to the crisp fall weather. And even if most of the flowers in her garden had peaked, I could see it would be delightful in the spring and summer months.

Miss Josie patted my head and smiled at me. "We have Puppy Preschool today at Misty Mountain. Anne arranged it, and Mrs. Steele will be here to mind the shop for us, which is always interesting. She tries her best, but she seems to have the same capacity for organization as Mr. Bartleby."

Mrs. Steele, a large woman with greying hair and a kind face, arrived at the shop as Miss Josie and I came downstairs after breakfast. When she saw me, she clapped her hands together, a huge smile on her face.

"What a nice puppy," she said, bending down so she could pet me as I wiggled around her legs. She laughed at my antics, even when I accidentally stuck my nose up her floral dress. "Oops. You are a cheeky one. I brought some treats for you today. Would you like one?"

Mrs. Steele gave me a homemade dog biscuit shaped like a bone. As soon as the delicious, peanut buttery taste hit my tongue, I decided Mrs. Steele was my new best friend.

"Thank you," said Josie, putting on my leash as I munched on the biscuit. "You're so thoughtful, Mrs. Steele."

"You're welcome. Is there anything in particular you want me to do while you're gone? I thought I'd get to work on rearranging the historical fiction area for you today."

I saw a hint of panic in Miss Josie's eyes. "No," she said, and then cleared her throat. "I mean, I already took care of it."

Mrs. Steele frowned. "I see. Should I work on something else? Maybe biographies?"

Miss Josie shook her head. "Just mind the front desk for me. I won't be gone long. I'm expecting a few deliveries, but not until later."

"Good luck, Josie," she said and leaned down to cup my face in her soft hands. "And good luck to you, too, Capone."

We got into the car, and I hopped around, exploring every fascinating part of the vehicle until Miss Josie locked me in a travel crate. Such a buzzkill. Luckily, I could still stare out the window.

The winding road to the dog center snaked up a mountain and was lined with giant evergreen trees. The Ohio River flowed past far below, covered in a blanket of dense fog. The name Misty Mountain probably came from that fog, and because of its location high on top of a mountain. I'm a genius at putting these things together.

The facility itself looked like a hunting lodge. In this setting, I'd never felt so much like a true gentleman. I imagined the interior of the building would be dimly lit and decorated with lots of plaid. It was the sort of place where men gathered around a fireplace to smoke cigars and drink port wine, with faithful dogs by their side. Most likely those dogs would be Labradors. We're extremely faithful, and partial to plaid.

Sadly, the interior didn't live up to my expectations. No

plaid, no port, and no men with cigars. Clean, plain, and a little dull, it looked like any other building, except for one factor.

It contained puppies. Lots and lots of puppies.

As soon as I saw them, I let out a bark of pure joy and jumped into the fray. We played and frolicked and sniffed and wiggled as Miss Josie signed me in.

She handed the receptionist my vaccination record and the forms she'd filled out the night before in painstaking detail (three sheets, single-spaced, with over fifty questions). She'd told Ms. Anne it felt vaguely like a psychiatric evaluation from the National Security Agency, and in it, Miss Josie had to explain her goals for me.

I didn't believe Miss Josie had very lofty aspirations as far as I was concerned. I think she wanted me to stop eating her shoes, destroying her pillows, and pooping out ribbons.

Note to self: I needed new hobbies.

As we stood in line, waiting with all the other happy puppies, the receptionist perused my paperwork with a frown. "Are you here for obedience class?"

"Puppy Preschool. We have our interview and orientation for obedience class tomorrow."

"Oh. You're in the wrong place. You'll be over there," she said, pointing to a door on the opposite side of the room. "And it looks like the other dog you'll be with today is also a black lab. Isn't that nice?"

As the herd of puppies pranced down the hall to obedience class, we waited inside the Puppy Preschool room. It was dark and quiet and kind of dingy. Moments later, an older couple with a tiny black lab joined us.

The man smiled and fussed over me, but his wife didn't seem as entranced. Her thin, penciled-in eyebrows rose to her hairline as soon as she saw me. "He's huge. What's his name?"

"Capone."

The nearly non-existent eyebrows rose even higher. "What an odd name. Our puppy is called Luke. After the apostle. We named all our dogs after apostles. Matthew, Mark, John, and now Luke. It's from the Bible."

"How nice," said Miss Josie.

Even though the woman's eyebrows made her look perpetually surprised, her expression changed when her husband put Luke down on the floor next me. She turned serious very quickly.

"I don't know if this is a good idea, Daddy," she said.

"Let 'em play," he responded. He had an impressively big and bushy mustache. Maybe he overcompensated for his wife's lack of eyebrows by producing excessive facial hair. I had no idea, but he liked me, which meant I also liked him. I couldn't say the same about No Brows. She emitted a sort of anti-Capone vibe.

At first, Luke and I got on rather well. We approached each other tentatively and sniffed with wagging tails. He smelled so good a dam burst somewhere inside me and I had a sudden love eruption. I sniffed Luke so aggressively I knocked him over. Total accident.

Note to self: Watch out for love eruptions.

"Oh, my," said No Brows to her husband. "Daddy. Pick Luke back up."

Her husband guffawed. "They're playing—"

No Brows refused to listen. "Pick him up. Now. Get him away from that mean dog."

Mean dog? Me?

"Sorry, Luke," I said. "I didn't mean to knock you over. My bad."

"No problem," he said. "You outweigh me by like twenty pounds. It's not your fault. Ignore Mumsy. She's annoying. Daddy is cool, though, and he likes you. I like you, too. Maybe we can hang later."

"Sounds like a plan."

The whole time we chatted, which I guess sounded like barking aggressively at each other; No Brows and Miss Josie grew increasingly nervous. By the time the instructor arrived, poor Miss Josie had started to sweat.

Unfortunately, we did not get Sexy Trainer Dude, the one Ms. Anne had mentioned. He was teaching the puppy obedience class today. I know this because all the ladies, including the canine ones, sighed when he walked by. Instead, we got Mr. Grumpy Trainer, the one no one wanted. He arrived late and made it clear he didn't want to be there. He mumbled a greeting and asked if we had any initial questions. No Brows placed a dainty finger on her chin.

"Luke likes to bite my calves. I tell him no. Is that okay?"

Miss Josie looked down at me. We hadn't done an official count, but I believe she'd told me no about ten million times already today.

Even the instructor seemed perplexed. "That's fine, but you don't want the dog to think you're playing. You have to be firm."

Miss Josie nodded. At least she'd been doing something right. She sounded firm when she disciplined me. And loud. And scary.

She raised her hand to ask a question. "How do I know what's appropriate when he's playing with other dogs?"

The instructor ran a hand over his head. "Think back to when you were growing up. If you and your siblings got into a fight, you'd stop before anyone got a bloody nose, right?"

Miss Josie's jaw dropped. What kind of family did this man have?

"I was an only child..." she said.

He let out a sigh. "Let both of them go, and we'll see how they interact."

She had my leash wrapped around her hands and leaned back as far as she could to keep me from climbing all over Luke and squashing him like a bug. "Are you sure?"

He nodded. "Let go of the leash, both of you."

No Brows didn't look convinced either, but she let go at the same time as Miss Josie, and, let me just say, it did not end well. Mr. Grumpy Trainer should have known better. Within seconds, I hopped on top of Luke, and he yelped and curled into a submissive ball of black fur.

"Capone. No," said Miss Josie, mortified.

She definitely meant it. She spoke so firmly she frightened me. I took one look at her angry face and darted out to the reception area, nearly knocking over a cute little girl in a sequined skirt.

"Puppy!" the little girl squealed.

"I'm so sorry," Miss Josie said to the girl's dad as she rushed past him, in hot pursuit. She had seconds to grab me before I caused a fiasco in the reception area. It would not be good if we got kicked out of Misty Mountain on our first day.

The little girl's father laughed. "We have a big dog, too. It's okay."

Miss Josie managed to wrangle me into submission by the front desk and brought me back to the Puppy Preschool area. Luke and Daddy seemed sympathetic to our plight, but No Brows and Mr. Grumpy Trainer met us with accusing glares. It got worse from there. I'd reached a frenzied state of puppy overload. I hovered low to the ground, mad with excitement, sniffing and pulling Miss Josie back and forth as she struggled to control me.

"Look at him," said No Brows. "He's crazy. And Luke is so good. We named him after one of the apostles." She nodded at the instructor, and he nodded back at her.

"Dogs eventually live up to their names," said Mr. Grumpy Trainer sagely.

Oh, calamity.

"I didn't choose his name," said Miss Josie. "And I'm going to change it."

Mr. Grumpy Trainer shrugged. "Do what you want, but once the name sticks, it'll be his for good. I don't know about you, but I wouldn't want to go through life with a name like Capone. It's dog abuse."

Miss Josie made a strangled squeaky noise, something I noticed she did when she got unusually upset. Her sounds were a clear indicator of her current emotional state.

Mr. Grumpy Trainer asked Miss Josie to lift me onto the shiny silver table. I heard Miss Josie sniff and looked up at her in surprise. Was she about to cry?

Mr. Grumpy Trainer, not realizing her fragile emotional state, kept talking. "Your dog is, what we like to call here, a dog bully. He belongs out there. In doggie daycare. They'll whip him into shape," he said, looking over his shoulder at the large, glass window which served as a viewing area for the doggie daycare room. Inside, a crazy-eyed spaniel jumped on a poodle and proceeded to bounce up and down on it. Aggressively. We all watched in stunned fascination. This must be the humping thing Jackson had mentioned. Not at all what I'd pictured.

To my horror, Miss Josie's lip wobbled. "You're wrong

about him. He's not a dog bully, and he's not a bad dog," Miss Josie said, her voice shaking.

Mr. Grumpy Trainer stuttered in shock. "I didn't mean to infer he was bad. He needs to spend more time with dogs his age. He needs to be corrected so he can learn the right way to behave."

He did have a point. I'd never spent much time around my fellow canines.

Mr. Grumpy Trainer lifted me off the table, perhaps as a sort of apology for upsetting poor Miss Josie. He led us over to the scale, and it took Luke several tries to understand he had to sit on it. Even then he didn't fully cooperate. It took three people feeding him treats for him to stay on.

I hopped up and sat down right away, no treats required. I wanted to make up for my previous bad behavior and attempt to be good for once. My efforts impressed all the humans in the room—even No Brows.

"If he weren't so crazy all the time, he'd probably be easy to train," she said.

I mentally stuck my tongue out at her. I couldn't help it. I think Miss Josie mentally stuck her tongue out at No Brows, too.

At agility training, I kicked Luke's hairy little butt again. I walked up and down ramps and steps and different surfaces with ease. I had the makings of an agility rock star.

I couldn't resist smirking at No Brows. Luke kept forgetting what to do. He didn't make it through a single obstacle. Daddy cheered him on, but No Brows turned livid.

"The breeder stuck me with the runt of the litter. She gave me the wrong puppy."

I felt bad for poor Luke, but he shrugged it off. "And my owner has no eyebrows. You win some; you lose some, I guess."

Miss Josie pulled me close and gave me an extra treat. "Well, I got the right puppy," she said softly. "The best puppy." She winked at me, and I just about burst with happiness. Miss Josie was mine now, whether she knew it or not.

EIGHT

A list of things I'm currently good at:

1. Eating.
2. Pooping.
3. Begging for treats.
4. Looking adorable.
5. Being naughty.

I was especially good at the last one. If being naughty qualified as an Olympic sport, I'd have earned a gold medal by now.

After our early morning adventure at Puppy Preschool, Miss Josie and I returned home exhausted. Ms. Anne and Gracie waited inside for us. Mrs. Steele worked in the back, cataloging books, but she stuck her head out the door and greeted us.

"How did it go?" she asked.

"It could have been worse," said Miss Josie, breezing in and taking off her coat. "No one died, and we aren't banned from the dog center. Yet."

Ms. Anne winced. "Was it so bad?"

"Oh, yes," she said, wiping the sweat from her brow. "Although Capone did rock agility training."

"Well, that's something, right?"

"I guess so. Thanks for helping this morning. I appreciate it."

"Gracie and I like hanging out here, and it's my fault you had to go to Misty Mountain in the first place."

"True," said Miss Josie, giving her a dirty look.

"Did you get to meet Sexy Trainer Dude?"

"No, but I saw him at a distance."

"Oh, dear. You probably had the grumpy guy."

"Yep," said Miss Josie sadly. "And he told me dogs live up to their names. I have to think of a new one for Capone."

I ran to get my Darcy toy and bumped her in the knee with it. Repeatedly. She took it from my mouth and tossed it, completely not understanding my message.

"You can't be serious, Josie," said Ms. Anne. "Do you think by naming him Capone he's going to form an organized crime ring and start bootlegging?"

Miss Josie looked at me. "No, but he deserves a better name."

Ms. Anne gave her a knowing smile. "You like him."

"Of course, I like him," said Miss Josie with a frown. "Which is why I want to come up with a different name. He is not a Capone."

I brought her the Darcy toy again, brimming with hope. She dashed it immediately. "How about Lancelot?"

"Not Lancelot. It's pretentious."

She sighed. "Quixote?"

"Even worse."

She took the Mr. Darcy toy from my mouth and barely

even glanced at it before tossing it across the room. "Fetch, boy."

I didn't want to play fetch. I hated playing fetch. I wanted a new name.

Oh, calamity.

Note to self: Miss Josie is not as smart as I thought.

Ms. Anne handed her a cup with the First Impressions logo on the side. "Here. A little caffeine will help. It'll wake up your brain."

Miss Josie wrinkled her nose. "I don't drink coffee," she said but took a sip anyway. "Mmmm. Is this caramel?"

"I'm not sure. Nate brought it over this morning."

Miss Josie put the cup down. "I thought it was from you."

"No, but he's a nice guy, Josie. Don't get bent out of shape."

She chewed on her lower lip. "I know. You're right, but he brings out the worst in me. I'm so crabby and mean around him. I'm sure he hates me."

Ms. Anne raised one eyebrow. "A man doesn't make coffee for a woman he hates."

"He wants to prove he can turn me into a coffee drinker like he has some magical power. But I have news for him. It's not going to happen."

"Good to know. By the way, this was attached to your cup." Ms. Anne handed Miss Josie a folded piece of white paper. Miss Josie opened it with a confused frown on her face.

"Unbelievable," she said, laughing. "He's actually reading *Pride and Prejudice*."

She showed Ms. Anne the note, and Ms. Anne read it out loud. "*So far, Mr. Darcy is kind of a jerk. I'm on chapter four. Drink your coffee.*"

"He's so bossy," said Miss Josie, but she took the note from Ms. Anne and read it again, a smile on her face, before folding it carefully and putting it into her pocket.

Ms. Anne studied her closely. "I think you and Nate got off on the wrong foot."

"I think you're right," said Miss Josie grudgingly. She picked up the coffee and took another sip. When she caught Ms. Anne watching her, she put it back on the counter again. "But I'm still not going to start liking this stuff."

"Whatever you say, cupcake. What's on the schedule for today?"

Miss Josie pursed her lips. "Inventory. It's taking forever. Mr. Bartleby left a mess behind, but it wasn't his fault. His memory was going, and he misplaced several of the ledgers. I found two on a shelf in the garden shed."

"Why would he put them in the shed?"

"Who knows? The most recent ledger is still missing. I'll probably find it ten years from now, in an old cookie tin or something."

"Hidden treasure," said Ms. Anne. "Maybe he also left behind a pot of gold. He did resemble a leprechaun."

She pointed to the photo on the wall above the cash register of a little bald man with sparkling eyes and an infectious grin. I didn't know anything about leprechauns, but Mr. Bartleby seemed like the sort of man who would slip me treats under the dinner table. In other words, my kind of guy.

Miss Josie pulled out her laptop. "Back to work," she said. "Mrs. Steele, shall we try this one more time?"

"Certainly," said Mrs. Steele, bustling over to her. "I finished packing up all the online orders for the day, and I don't have to send out the books for the university library until tomorrow. I have nothing else to do at the moment. Many hands make light work."

Miss Josie smiled at her. "I appreciate your help."

"I love this shop, Josie. It's provided a great deal for me over the years..." Mrs. Steele got so teary her glasses fogged up, and she had to wipe them with a hankie she pulled out of her pocket. She cleared her throat. "I'm honored to help in any way I can."

"Thank you," said Miss Josie. "Although you might regret your offer once you see what we have to do."

Mrs. Steele patted her arm. "We'll get through it, dearie. Don't you worry. I know this shop like the back of my hand, and Benjamin always said I had a good nose for sniffing out a valuable manuscript. We'll find what's missing. I promise."

I discovered I thoroughly enjoyed doing inventory, especially when Miss Josie leaned down to look at the books on the bottom shelves. It gave me a chance to lick her face, paw at her glasses, and nibble on her hair.

"Capone. Please," she said, as I stole her pen for the one-hundredth time and ran around the shop with it. I wanted to play chase. She wanted to get work done—a problem since we had different goals.

As she attempted to wrestle the pen from me, the bell above the door tinkled. I let go of it so suddenly Miss Josie fell onto her bottom, but I didn't help her to her feet. I rushed toward the door, barking and hopping at the same time, the Labradorean equivalent of a hyperactive kangaroo.

A man stood in the doorway. He towered above me and shot me a decidedly dirty look over the rim of his wire-rimmed glasses before letting out a loud sneeze.

"A dog, Josie? Are you kidding?" he asked, pulling a tissue from the pocket of his tweed coat to wipe his nose.

Miss Josie, still on the floor, gaped at him. "What are you doing here, Cedric?"

"Yes, Cedric," said Ms. Anne with a snarl. "Shouldn't you be at home with your wife?"

Mrs. Steele popped in from the rear of the shop. As soon as she heard Ms. Anne's words, she turned on her heel and went straight back from whence she came. Miss Josie didn't appear to notice. She kept her gaze on the man in front of her.

Cedric the Betrayer.

I hated him instantly. I placed my body between Cedric and Miss Josie and let out a soft growl. I'm an inexperienced growler, so the effect was not as terrifying as I'd hoped.

Miss Josie patted me on my head, and said, "Good boy," under her breath as she got to her feet.

"I came to collect some items from the shop belonging to me," said Cedric, sneezing again.

"I've never seen anything of yours here," said Miss Josie, her brow wrinkling in confusion.

"Mr. Bartleby promised me several books from his private collection."

Ms. Anne snorted. "He did not. You're such a liar, Cedric."

I sidled closer to Miss Josie, and she stood a little taller, holding her ground even though it must have been hard for her. "I'm not obligated to give you anything," she said. "Unless you have some kind of written proof."

I wanted to stand up and cheer. Gosh, I hated Cedric the Betrayer. I wished I could pee on his shoes or something, but that might upset Miss Josie further, so I refrained from following through on my urge. I still wanted to, though. Badly.

Cedric did not give up as quickly as I'd hoped. He took

off his glasses and wiped his eyes, which seemed to be watering.

"Cedric, are you crying?" asked Josie.

"No, I'm allergic to dogs. Obviously." He let out a long sigh and appeared to count to ten. "Look, Josephine, those books would be of little or no value to you, but they hold a great deal of sentimental importance to me. I worked for Mr. Bartleby long before you came here. I traveled the world and procured many of his finest pieces for him. By all rights, this shop should be mine."

I felt a subtle shift in the air and knew if Miss Josie had hackles, they would have been rising right now. "Mr. Bartleby left me the shop because he trusted me to carry on his legacy. He didn't feel the same way about you."

"His legacy?" he asked with a snort. "You must be kidding. You'll be lucky if you can stay open another year. Two at tops. You have no idea what you're doing, and one word from me could destroy you. Like that." He snapped his fingers for emphasis.

Miss Josie folded her arms across her chest and lifted her chin into the air. "You don't scare me, Cedric. After you tried to pass off a fake *Doria Atlas* as the real thing, you've lost all credibility."

His cheeks reddened. "I don't have to defend myself. Just give me my books, or I promise you'll regret it."

"Stop right there," said Ms. Anne. "No one threatens Josie. It's time for you to go, mister."

Miss Josie agreed. "Anne's right," she said, a weary sadness in her eyes. "Leave now, or I'll call the police."

He blinked at her in surprise, straightening his jacket. "This isn't the last you'll hear from me."

"Oh, goody. I'm looking forward to it." Miss Josie sounded so brave, but I heard a deep sadness in her voice.

Cedric must have heard it, too. He changed tactics, lowering his voice and adopting a gentler tone. "I know how badly I hurt you, and I'm sorry. Truly, I am."

"You're only sorry she found out the truth," said Ms. Anne.

Cedric snarled at her. "This doesn't concern you."

"It most certainly does—"

"Anne. Please." Miss Josie shot her a pleading look. Ms. Anne lifted her hands in surrender and went to the back of the shop. Still within listening distance, but far enough away to provide them with a modicum of privacy.

Cedric's gaze returned to Miss Josie's face. "I understand why you hate me, and I don't blame you, but I miss you, Josie. You were my best friend, my partner, my equal. We made a great team, personally as well as professionally. You know it's true. Together we could have done something spectacular."

She stared up at him, her eyes all misty and melancholy and sad. She wasn't thinking straight, so when he reached for her, I reacted. I had to protect her.

Although tall, Cedric had a thin frame and the reflexes of an elderly sloth. One push from me sent him falling into a display of books about the joys of autumn in Western Pennsylvania. I narrowly avoided getting concussed by a sizable volume on fall foliage, but Cedric wasn't as lucky. As he slipped to the ground, a book about avian migration hit him in the face, causing his glasses to fall off his nose. When I picked them up with my mouth, this led to another fun game of chase. Cedric followed me through the shop as I ducked and weaved, avoiding him with ease. Cedric seemed to have little or no experience with those of the canine persuasion.

"Give me my glasses now," he said, growling with frustration.

Miss Josie let the game continue for a few minutes before she said, ever so casually, "Drop it, Capone."

For the first time ever, I listened to her, dropping the glasses into a mangled heap on the floor. Cedric picked them up gingerly. He tried to wipe off the drool with a tissue, but it got soaked in minutes, and the glasses were a twisted mess. He placed them on his nose, where they hung awkwardly, damaged beyond repair. He sneezed again, and, when he spoke, he sounded stuffy.

"You haven't heard the last from me. I will get back what is rightfully mine, and I expect to be compensated for these glasses, too."

"Don't waste your time," said Miss Josie, giving him a smug little finger wave. "It's not going to happen."

After he left, Ms. Anne clapped. "Way to go, girlie. I'm proud of you."

"Thanks," said Miss Josie, but her bravado slipped away as soon as Cedric walked out the door.

"What did you ever see in him?"

She leaned against the high table near the vault. "He used to be so nice. So kind. We understood each other. He was smart and funny and knew more about books than anyone, even Mr. Bartleby. I never had to explain things to him. We clicked. He was the first man I ever loved." She stared out the window, a faraway look in her eyes. "The only man I ever loved."

Oh, calamity. Could Miss Josie still be a little in love with Cedric? Didn't she pay any attention at all when we watched the BBC version of *Pride and Prejudice*? He was Mr. Wickham and not Mr. Darcy. How could she have missed it?

"I'm sorry, kiddo, but he's not worth it. I never liked him, and the best thing you can do now is get over him as quickly as possible."

"Is that why you've been trying to set me up with all the men in Beaver?" Miss Josie asked wryly.

"Well, yes," said Ms. Anne. "This place is like a smorgasbord, and you've been on a starvation diet. You need to get out, get back into the game, and get over that loser. Also, you should spend more time with people your age. I know a lot of your friends moved away after graduation, but I'm sure some of them are still here. It's better than hanging out with us. Mrs. Steele and I are both too old for you."

"You are not," said Miss Josie with a sigh. "Of course, I'd love to spend time with my friends, but I doubt they'd want to see me."

"What do you mean?"

"While I dated Cedric, I spent all my free time with him. It was so wrong of me. For a while, my friends tried to make plans with me, but eventually they gave up and drifted away. I don't blame them, but I couldn't exactly call them after we broke up. First of all, I didn't want to explain what had happened. It was too embarrassing. Secondly, I didn't deserve their friendship anymore. I messed up. I'm not sure how they'd forgive me."

Ms. Anne squeezed her arm. "Don't be so hard on yourself. I'm sure your friends would love to see you. And the best way to get over Cedric is to move on."

Miss Josie raised an eyebrow at her. "I can tell you aren't going to drop this, but I have horrible luck with men. That should be obvious by now. I'm not exactly a social butterfly, you know. I'm not even sure what kind of man I want, or what kind of man would want me."

I knew exactly what kind of man she needed. Why

couldn't she see it? I grabbed my Darcy toy and bumped her with it, trying again to get my message across. Miss Josie took the toy from me and stared at the little top-hatted version of Mr. Darcy in her hands. For a second, I thought maybe she understood, but then she tossed it across the room.

"Fetch," she said.

Hopeless. I needed to find another way to communicate with her.

Miss Josie stared at me. "Why doesn't he fetch?" she asked. "Aren't Labradors retrievers? Shouldn't they retrieve? He doesn't seem to understand. This is so frustrating."

Welcome to my world, Miss Josie. And "frustrating" doesn't even begin to cover it.

NINE

How to terrify Miss Josie a few weeks before Halloween:

1. Find an old bat decoration in the garden storage shed.
2. Sneak outside (with the music from *Mission Impossible* playing in my head).
3. While Miss Josie isn't looking, hide the bat under a bush.
4. Bark at it. Several times.
5. Grab it and make her scream.
6. Run around the yard with it in my mouth.
7. Try not to laugh as she chases me with a broom.

Ah, such good times we had that afternoon. Who knew there were so many wondrous things in the small shed in the back garden? The bat was the main prize, but I found lots of other delightful and exciting objects as well. Dangerous chemicals. Sharp gardening tools. Fertilizer with the words "Hazardous if swallowed" written on the box. I consider these sorts of things a personal challenge. Hazardous if swallowed? Well, let's see.

Miss Josie stopped me from trying it out, though. She immediately assessed the potential risk of the items in the shed and closed the door in my face. The only thing I managed to sink my teeth into was the bat, and acquiring it took a great deal of stealth and sneakiness.

It had been a long day. We'd gone outside right after Ms. Anne and Mrs. Steele left. The conversation with Cedric the Betrayer clearly disturbed her. She kept staring off into space with a hurt look in her eyes. Poor, sweet Miss Josie.

I honestly thought the bat trick might cheer her up and make her laugh. It did not. After we finished our merry chase through the garden, we headed straight to the basement of the shop and she picked out a bottle of red wine from a storage rack.

I had no idea there was a basement in the shop. It fascinated me. First, I'd discovered the shed (a Cave of Wonders), and now I got to see the basement (the Deep, Dark, Dungeon of Mystery). If I included the time spent at Misty Mountain and the not-so-delightful visit from Cedric, I had to admit today had positively teemed with adventure.

Miss Josie fed me dinner, grabbed a copy of *The Complete Works of Jane Austen,* and carried her bottle of wine outside. She poured a glass, and sat quietly for a long time, sipping on it. She'd changed into a comfy pair of yoga pants, and had on a thick, woolen cardigan to keep her warm. Although it was a mild evening for early October, a slight chill pierced the air. She was reading *Pride and Prejudice*, probably to make sure Mr. Nate didn't lie about his progress. Fortunately, she read it aloud so I could enjoy it, too.

I snuggled close to her, hanging on every word. When she noticed my attentiveness, she gave me a warm smile. "A fellow Janeite, I see," she said. "Do you know why I like Jane Austen, Capone?"

She wanted to discuss Jane Austen with me? This might be the best day of my life so far. I wagged my tail, hoping she'd continue. She did, patting my head as she spoke.

"In Jane Austen's time there were rules. I like rules."

Her words made me wag my tail even harder. I liked rules, too. We were obviously soulmates.

"Men were honorable. They followed a strict code of ethics." She wrinkled up her nose. "Well, not Wickham, of course. He was pond scum."

After her second glass of merlot, she spoke in a much louder voice, waving her arms around and sloshing drops of wine on my back, but I didn't complain. Miss Josie could slosh me anytime.

"You know, Capone, I'm not the kind of girl who dates a married man," she said. "I'm not the kind of girl who dates anyone at all."

Acting on instinct, I placed my head on her lap and stared up at her with my big, puppy eyes. I wanted to psychically convey my sympathy to her, and it seemed to work. She lost the haunted look on her face and gifted me with another smile.

"I've never had a dog before, but I wish more people were like dogs. Dogs are simple. People are so much more complicated."

I heard a noise on the other side of the wall near the wooden door. I sat up and sniffed. Recognizing the familiar scent of Mr. Nate, I wagged my tail, wondering why he didn't say something. He could most certainly hear every word Miss Josie said, and it seemed weird.

Well, I guess the fact she held a private conversation with her dog while drinking an entire bottle of wine alone in her backyard might be the weird part. Mr. Nate listening in? Pretty minor in comparison.

"Take Nate over there at First Impressions Café." She waved her wine glass in the general direction of the coffee shop. "He thinks I'm a real..."

She lowered her voice and said a word that rhymed with "witch." I won't repeat it. A gentleman does not curse.

Miss Josie took a deep breath and stared into the contents of her glass. "And he's right. I haven't been nice to him at all." I licked her ankles, hoping to make her feel better. Oddly enough, it worked. "Thank you, boy. That feels kind of nice."

Note to self: Miss Josie has a kinky side.

As I continued licking her ankles, she continued talking. It felt quite companionable, and I rather enjoyed it.

"I'm such an idiot. Cedric seemed perfect, but who falls for a man named Cedric? Not exactly the kind of name you want to scream out in a moment of passion." She made her voice high pitched and nasal. "*Oh, Cedric. Yes, Cedric.*" She looked at me. "See what I mean? It's awful. Yuck."

I heard Mr. Nate stifle a chuckle on the other side of the door. I wanted to warn Miss Josie about our intrepid eaves-dropper but couldn't figure out how to do it. "Capone, what am I going to do? I miss Cedric. I know I shouldn't, but I do. He understood me, and he understood books, and, other than the fact he was a lying jerk face and a married man, he treated me well. I realize it sounds pathetic, but how many men do you know who can quote Jane Austen and keep all the Brontë sisters straight?"

She slurred the last few words, and it came out kind of like, "slisters slaight," which made no sense at all. Wow. She was toasted. And she continued to pour more wine.

"I thought he might be my Mr. Darcy, but he was not Darcy at all. He was..."

Mr. Wickham. He was your Mr. Wickham.

Curse my inability to speak even a single word of Human.

"You're right," she said, and I looked at her in surprise, since I hadn't said anything. "I need to stop whining about my problems. Yes, I lost my parents, and it was hard, but it shouldn't define me. They wouldn't want me to live like this, all sad and alone. I have to force myself to get out more. Do you know sometimes it's almost hard for me to leave the shop? I get stressed out even thinking about it, and I'm tired of feeling like this. I want to reconnect with my old friends. I also need to make new friends. And I think I should force myself to date as well. I haven't been able to date since Cedric, but it might be the only way to fix this. I need to get over him and be the person I used to be before he broke my heart into a million tiny pieces."

A little dramatic, but she wasn't done yet. She was only warming up. She rose to her feet and stumbled around the yard, wine glass in hand, as she went through all the things she planned to change about her life.

"The next time Cedric comes here, insinuating I've stolen something from him, I'm going to say, 'Get out of my shop now. You are a stinking...'" She paused, brows furrowed, as she tried to think of a good insult. Unable to come up with something powerful enough, she waved the hand not holding the wine. "I'll think of something. It'll be good, too. You'll see. I'll show him."

She took another gulp of wine. Her sipping had turned

to chugging at this point. I wondered if perhaps I should bring her a straw so she could drink it straight from the bottle.

"And I'm going to be nicer to Nate over there." She pointed to the fence. "Yes, his customers are annoying, and yes, his fat pug pooped in front of my shop, but he seems like a nice guy. Cute, too. He might even be the most attractive man I've ever met. And he's reading *Pride and Prejudice*, which does not seem like it's in his wheelhouse at all, but he's making an actual effort and it's sweet. If only he would stop it with the coffee. It's like coffee, coffee, coffee. All the time, coffee. Geesh. Enough already."

Mr. Nate laughed, a muffled sound, but it made Miss Josie stiffen. "Did you hear a noise? Is someone there?'

She grabbed the key to the padlock, but couldn't move fast in her inebriated state, so her run ended up being more of a drunken stumble. I ran beside her, barking the whole way. By the time she staggered to the door and unlocked it, Mr. Nate had already gone.

"Huh," she said. "I could have sworn I heard something, but I think your barking scared them away. Maybe Anne was right. You are a good guard dog."

After patting me on the head, she closed the door, locked the padlock, grabbed the now empty bottle, and headed back into the shop. "Come on, Capone. Time for night-night."

I trotted along beside her, and she did something unexpected when we reached the back door. She crouched down, leaning against me, and hugged me tightly around my neck. A little awkward, and suffocating, but beautiful.

"Thank you, Capone. You were the friend I needed tonight."

I didn't even mind it when she locked me in my crate. I fell asleep, a smile on my face, a song in my heart, and Orange Snuggle Bunny tucked under my chin. For the first time since I joined Miss Josie, I felt like I'd genuinely come home.

TEN

Why Miss Josie should not drink an entire bottle of wine by herself:

1. Waking up on time the next morning is a challenge.
2. Being hungover makes her extremely grumpy.
3. She will sleep in her clothes and probably won't have time to change.
4. She'll forget to do important personal hygiene things, like washing her face.
5. Sticking her hair in a ponytail and shoving on sunglasses will not disguise anything.

"Come on, Capone," she said, pulling me out of the shop the morning after her drinking session in the back garden. "We're going to be late, and this interview is important. We want to make a good impression."

I looked up at her. Did she seriously just say that? She slapped herself on the forehead.

"I hate my life."

As we walked to her car, Mr. Nate called out to us, a cup in his hand. "Wait," he said. "I have something for you."

She turned around in surprise, nearly falling over. "Whoa." She grabbed the car door for support. As soon as she regained her balance, she glared at Mr. Nate. Even though she had on dark sunglasses, I could tell she glared, mostly because of the angry set of her mouth and the way her eyebrows drew together in a frown. She was a regular ball of sunshine this morning. "What do you want? Please don't make me drink coffee today. I mean it. I can't."

She winced, her face pale, as if the thought of coffee made her want to hurl. I leaned against her, hoping she wouldn't throw up in front of Mr. Nate. How embarrassing.

"Not coffee. It's my hangover smoothie. Chamomile tea, lemon, ginger, slippery elm bark, and lavender flowers. I put in a little apple and banana, too, for sweetness. Try it. It's yummy. I promise."

She lifted her glasses to the top of her head, and glared at him again, but took a sip. Her bleary eyes widened in surprise. "Wow. It's good."

He shoved his hands into his pockets. "Glad you like it. I always drink it the morning after I overindulge."

She took a few more sips, the color coming back into her face, and frowned. "Wait. How did you know about my hangover?"

Mr. Nate didn't answer. Miss Josie seemed as prickly as a cactus this morning, and twice as mean. He was wise to be cautious.

Her eyes narrowed, comprehension dawning on her face. "You eavesdropped on me, didn't you? I thought I heard someone by the door. You dirty, sneaky snooper you."

"Eavesdropping?" he asked. "On the conversation you

had with your dog? No insult intended, Capone. I'm sure you are a great listener."

He patted my head. Did I mention how much I adore Mr. Nate? He's a peach.

Miss Josie did not feel the love. She stamped her foot, poking her finger at him. "It's a violation of my privacy."

"I didn't violate anything. I took out the garbage and happened to overhear you blathering on and on about your ex. Cedric, right? He sounds fantastic."

Miss Josie stared at him mouth agape. "I can't believe you stood there and listened to me. You're so weird."

He shoved his hands into his pockets. "I only listened because I thought you might have locked yourself out of your shop again, but I kept listening for entertainment purposes. You're pretty funny when you drink. Funnier than when you're sober, at least."

I blanched. Oh, no, you didn't, Mr. Nate. Nothing good ever came from poking a bear, and nothing good would come from poking a hungover Miss Josie either.

"You...you...you...terrible person."

What a comeback. For someone so well-read, Miss Josie had a limited arsenal of insults. She needed to work on her smack talk. Maybe she should try Shakespeare instead of Austen. He had a lot of good comebacks.

Note to self: Her wit's as thick as Tewkesbury mustard.

"I'm wounded to the quick," said Mr. Nate.

Ah, both impressive and Shakespearean. Sadly, Miss Josie didn't seem to notice.

"I would go on," she said, spluttering. "But I have an important appointment this morning. Capone has an interview for obedience training, and I'm already running late." Miss Josie winced, probably realizing how downright ludicrous she sounded. "And, anyway, I've got to go. Bye."

She climbed into her car and turned on the ignition. Mr. Nate tapped on her window.

"What?" she asked. "Haven't you humiliated me enough? I realize I seem like a total idiot, and my life is a big joke for you, but I'm a woman on the edge here. Please don't push me any further."

"First of all, I meant the smoothie as a peace offering, but it backfired. I wasn't trying to make fun of you. Honestly."

"Thanks," she said. "But I have to go."

"Did you forget something?" he asked. He pointed to me, still sitting patiently next to him on the sidewalk. He opened the back door to Miss Josie's car so I could jump in. I did so, wagging my tail happily. A car ride? Yippee. I loved riding in the car.

Miss Josie groaned. "Thanks. Again. Bye."

She put her glasses back down and drove off. A quick escape was sometimes the only way to avoid future embarrassment.

We got to Misty Mountain five minutes late. Unfortunately, as soon as we arrived, I realized I had to poo, which delayed us an additional five minutes.

Curse my poor time management skills.

"Crap," said Miss Josie, looking at her watch, and probably not intending to make a pun. "Please don't let it be the grumpy guy. I can't handle him this morning."

When we entered, the reception area was quiet and empty except for a rather stern-looking blond man with a clipboard in his hands. He glanced at Miss Josie, and then at his watch before shooting her a disappointed look.

"Josephine St. Clair? You're late."

Sexy Trainer Dude in the flesh. And we had not made

an excellent first impression. "Sorry," she said, pointing at me. "He had to poop."

Way to throw me under the bus, Miss Josie.

He breathed out a long sigh, clenching his chiseled jaw and writing something on his clipboard. "A good dog owner can anticipate these things ahead of time and incorporate them into the schedule. You will learn," he said.

"I will learn," Miss Josie repeated, like a good little robot.

Sexy Trainer Dude led her to a small table and waved a hand to indicate she should sit. He spoke, in a monotone voice, staring vacantly out the window, but we hung on each word. Judging by the bored expression on his hand- some face, he'd gone over the rules for obedience school a million times already, but it was all new for Miss Josie. She listened attentively to him, taking notes on a piece of scratch paper she'd found wadded up in her purse. She'd forgotten to bring a notebook. Heck, she'd even forgotten to shower.

Sexy Trainer Dude paused in his speech, his glorious blue eyes lingering for a moment on Miss Josie's raptly attentive face, his golden brows furrowed in a frown. "Excuse me," he said. "I think you have something stuck to your cheek."

"I...what...?" She reached up and felt her cheek, pulling off a piece of dog kibble from my breakfast this morning that had somehow gotten stuck there. She stared at it a moment, then, without losing a beat, handed it to me. Bonus treats. Yum. "I like to carry around spare dog food on my face. It's my way of anticipating his needs and being prepared. Like a good pet owner should."

He stared at her a long moment before his lips twitched. "Funny. Yes, it's good to have a sense of humor, especially when dealing with a lab. Capone can start training on Monday. We have an eight am class. Sound good?"

"Yes," she said.

I got a little antsy and sniffed around, pulling on my leash. Sexy Trainer Dude looked me right in the eye. "Sit, Capone."

He didn't speak loudly, but his voice pierced my soul. I sat, unable to stop myself.

"How did you do that?" asked Miss Josie. "He never listens."

He shrugged, his face softening as he looked at me. "He's a good dog, and smart, too. Given enough time, I could train him to do anything."

"Do you think so?" asked Miss Josie, and I practically saw the wheels turning in her head. The idea that someone might be able to control me appealed to her at the moment.

"Yes." He stood up and shook her hand. "For now, I'd suggest frequent walks to help him get rid of some of his excess energy, but he'll learn what he needs to know once he starts his classes. I'm looking forward to training you, Miss St. Clair."

She faltered. "You mean you look forward to training Capone."

He shook his head. "Nope. The dogs are fine. It's the people we train here."

"Oh," said Miss Josie, getting pink in the face. I had to wonder what went through her mind. I had a feeling it had to do more with the obvious appeal of the ruggedly handsome Sexy Trainer Dude and less to do with getting me to follow her commands. "Um, bye."

He nodded. "See you on Monday. Don't be late, or I'll dock you for time. Training the dog starts and ends with training the owner. If you can't be on time, you aren't committed, and I'll have to punish you." His eyes grazed over Miss Josie. In spite of the messy hair and the bit of dog food she'd had stuck to her face, she was quite lovely. Suddenly, his words seemed to have a sexual undertone. He cleared his throat uncomfortably and got as pink in the face as Miss Josie. "As much as I'd, um, hate to do such a thing."

Miss Josie gave him a mock salute. "We'll be on time. I promise."

"Okay then. I think we're done here. See you on Monday, Josephine St. Clair."

After he left, she turned to me. "Wow. If he were any hotter, I might self-combust," she said softly. "I'm actually looking forward to obedience training. Thanks, puppy. It's kind of a good thing you're so bad."

Hmmm. Not exactly a compliment, but if she liked Sexy Trainer Dude, I would do my best to help her. In fact, I'd be the best worst dog they'd ever seen.

ELEVEN

Things I am not allowed to do while Miss Josie works in the garden:

1. Steal and unroll a ball of twine.
2. Run around the yard with scissors in my mouth.
3. Bump into Miss Josie and push her into one of the rose bushes.
4. Eat clippings from the rose bushes.
5. Eat cuttings from the peony bushes.
6. Eat clippings from any of the bushes.
7. Knock over the trash can full of clippings.
8. Relieve myself on the trash can full of clippings.
9. Lick Miss Josie's face while she's weeding.
10. Chew a hole in Miss Josie's favorite gardening glove.

"Maybe we need to take a walk," she said. "You're driving me crazy."

We set off walking through the town of Beaver, and I licked everyone I met. In my opinion, there were no strangers, only friends I hadn't licked yet. And all the people out walking on the main street were fair game.

I licked people having savory pastries outside Café Kolache. They tasted like sausage and happiness. I licked people at Two Rivers Olive Oil. They smelled like garlic. Yummy.

I licked the window at Zugliani's Hair Design. Ms. Nicole, the nice lady who worked there, came out and slipped me a doggie biscuit.

"Hi, Capone," she said. "Are you being a good boy today?"

Good was a relative term, and open to interpretation. Miss Josie summed it up nicely.

"He's being...Capone-ish," she said.

Ms. Nicole laughed. She had beautiful hair the color of lavender. I licked her hand, which tasted like shampoo, and we continued down the street.

Nearly everyone we passed knew Miss Josie and said "Hello." Each time it happened, her smile got a little wider. Miss Josie needed this.

When we reached the middle of the block, I jumped up and tried to lick the plate of a person eating a salad at Sproutz, but they had lightning quick reflexes, and I didn't even get a taste. But I felt better when a kind girl named Mackenzie, who worked at the donut shop, told me I was cute. Then Kristin from Don's Deli came outside and gave me a slice of capicola. If heaven and happiness had a meaty Italian love child, it would be capicola.

I pulled Miss Josie toward Kretchmar's Bakery, wanting to see the sweet delights displayed in the front window. I got up on my hind legs and pressed my nose to the glass, but she refused to let me go inside. What a party pooper.

When I tried to steal a ball from a child in front of

Castle Toys, Miss Josie decided she'd had enough walking for the day and led me back to the shop. She locked me in my crate and went back outside to finish her yard work.

I flopped down in annoyance. What an infuriatingly short walk. To make matters worse, Rocco decided to perch on top of my crate and bother me.

"Locked up again, I see," he said, with a laugh. "That's rich for a dog named Capone."

I glared up at him, wanting to bite his fat, fluffy tail. "What are you trying to tell me, Rocco? You've been hinting around at it since I came here."

"I'll tell you, but only because it's hilarious," He stretched out on top of my crate, his green eyes glowing with malicious pleasure. "You don't seem to know anything at all about the person you're named after. Al Capone was one of the worst criminals in American history; a gangster and a murderer and a thief. Who would give a marshmallow like you a name like that?"

Things clicked in my mind like spent shells from a tommy gun. "Hold on a second. Was John Dillinger also a criminal?"

"Yep."

"And Lucky Luciano?"

"Definitely."

"And Ma Barker and Opal Mack Truck Long?"

"Yes, and maybe. I've never heard of Opal Mack Truck Long. Why are you asking?"

"Those were the names of the other puppies in my litter," I said, my voice soft. "My brothers and sisters."

Note to self: Mistress Sue has an odd sense of humor.

Rocco laughed. "Entertaining, especially because Al Capone was the worst of them all." He narrowed his eyes.

"You're named after him for a reason. Your breeder saw it, and I saw it, too, the minute I met you."

"What did you see?"

"You're a bad dog." He leaned closer, his eyes locked on mine. "It's your destiny, and there is nothing you can do to change it."

I bristled, shocked by how much he sounded like Mr. Collins. Cats were awful creatures, but I was stronger now, and more confident. I refused to let Rocco's words bother me.

"No. It can't be true. I mean, I've made some mistakes, but I'm learning."

"With a name like Capone, your path is set." He stretched, seemingly oblivious to my distress. "Look, my hairy little friend. I know you imagine yourself as a gentleman, as a modern-day Mr. Darcy. You're actually the furthest thing from it, and there isn't a single thing you can do about it."

I sat up straighter. "I don't care what name Mistress Sue gave me. I know she loved me. She cried when I left the farm. I also know I'm not destined to be anything. I choose to be a gentleman, and therefore I shall become one."

"How?"

"I'll start by convincing Miss Josie to change my name."

"What makes you think you can get Josephine to change your name when you can't even get her to let you sleep on the couch?"

The couch remained a sore spot for me, and he knew it. "The epitome of gentlemanly behavior is saving a damsel in distress. I'll save Miss Josie."

"From what?" He snorted. "She's perfectly capable of taking care of herself. Why would she need help from a furry idiot like you?"

Hmmm. Rocco had a point. But I remembered her drunken rant in the garden; her sad, lonely, soliloquy, and I knew exactly what I had to do.

"I'm going to help Miss Josie find her one true love, her own Mr. Darcy. When I do, she'll change my name to something more appropriate."

"Like what? Doofus?" He laughed, and it was a horrible sound. "Good luck. Men like Mr. Darcy don't exist. They never have."

"Yes, they do, and I will find one. Now leave me alone. I have a lot to think about, and this will be complicated."

"For you, finding your tail is complicated."

"Shut up, Rocco," I said as he slunk away. "And thank you."

He turned and looked at me over his shoulder, his smushed up face confused. "For what?"

"For spurring me to action. You're a good..." I paused, thinking about it, not sure what to call him exactly. "Associate."

Rocco snorted and mumbled something derogatory under his breath, but I ignored him. As I curled up in my crate and formulated a plan, I realized things were not as bad as they first seemed. Yes, Mistress Sue named me after Al Capone, the furthest thing possible from a true gentleman, but I had the opportunity to change it, and improve myself. All hope was not lost. The power to fix the terrible blow karma had dealt me now rested in my paws. I had a chance to prove to myself and everyone else I had the makings of a true gentleman, and I was not about to waste it.

TWELVE

A partial list of things a puppy should not eat:

1. Piles of grass.
2. Parts of a peony bush.
3. Miss Josie's slippers.
4. The cap from a Sharpie marker.
5. Rabbit poo.
6. Mulch.
7. A rock.
8. An empty plastic container of mango juice.

Not long after I learned the truth about my name, something terrible happened. What began as a rumbly feeling in my tummy quickly turned into explosive diarrhea, and it lasted all night long.

Poor Miss Josie. She had to take me outside over and over again. On one of those trips, Mr. Nate called out to us over the garden wall. "Are you okay?"

Miss Josie, in her robe and pajamas, opened the gate. Mr. Nate stood there with Jackson by his side. Without saying a word, she pointed to me as I squat walked around the yard, making offensive noises with my derriere as I tried to rid myself of whatever ailed me. Jackson laughed so hard he fell over. Mr. Nate didn't seem to find it as funny.

"Uh-oh," said Mr. Nate. "What did he eat?"

When Miss Josie told him the list of things I'd eaten recently, even Jackson was shocked. Or he may have been impressed. I couldn't tell. "Dude," he said as he followed me around the yard. "Why didn't you eat the kitchen sink while you were at it?"

"Shut up. I'm in agony. It's not funny."

My brain felt foggy, probably due to dehydration. When would I learn to make better choices?

Note to self: Explosive diarrhea is as bad as it sounds.

Although Miss Josie praised me for not going in the house, she reminded me this would not have happened if I had a more discriminating palate. I wanted to tell her I was a gourmand. I lived to discover new tastes and textures. But she may have had a point.

"Why isn't he more careful about what he eats?" asked Miss Josie. She had yet to discover what had happened to her slippers, but I felt too sick at the moment to care.

Mr. Nate shrugged. "He's a puppy. Puppies try to eat things they shouldn't. It's probably the peony bush making him sick. Those are mildly toxic for dogs."

Her face filled with worry. "Toxic? Will he be okay?"

"Yes, but you should take him to the vet first thing in the morning. If it is the peony bush, he'll need medicine. At least that's what always happened to Jackson."

I looked at Jackson. "You did stuff like this, too?"

"All the time," he said. "I once ate an entire tube of antibacterial cream. The plastic cap hurt like a mother as it came out."

Another spasm hit me, and a spray of diarrhea shot from my bottom like water from a fire hose. Jackson jumped out of the way.

"Whoa. Watch your aim," he said. "You're dangerous."

"I'm ill. Be kind. And be careful where you step. It's everywhere."

"Don't worry, my friend. This, too, shall pass," he said with a gravelly chuckle.

Mr. Nate offered to take a shift and stay up with me so Miss Josie could get a little sleep. "I'm not tired," he said, giving her a sheepish grin. "I had way too much coffee today."

"A man who works at a coffee shop drank too much coffee? How strange," said Miss Josie with a giggle.

"Hazard of the job, I guess."

The friendship between them, something new and sweet and fragile, made me happy—a bright spot on a dark day.

"Speaking of your coffee addiction, I've heard First Impressions is the hot new thing," said Miss Josie. "Do you enjoy working there?"

"Uh, yeah. Sure. I do."

"Are you the store manager or something?"

He shoved his hands into his pockets. "We're not really into titles. I'm here to help this new shop get on its feet."

Miss Josie tilted her head to one side, looking almost as adorable as I did when I made the same motion. "So, I guess you won't be staying in Beaver then?" she asked, and I heard an odd catch in her voice.

He gazed down at her, his expression unreadable. "I'll be here a while. You never know how long it'll take. Each store is a little different."

"I guess." She nibbled on her lower lip. "Thanks for the

smoothie this morning. It helped. And I'm sorry I was mean to you again."

"I'm sorry I eavesdropped on your discussion with our man Capone here." He nodded toward me. I remained in a hunched position, trying to expel the toxic peony pieces from my digestive tract. How humiliating. And having Jackson there to witness it didn't make it any better.

Note to self: Make better choices.

When it finally ended, Miss Josie cleaned me off and lifted me into her arms. "Poor baby."

I *was* a poor baby, and Miss Josie looked no better. She nearly drooped with exhaustion.

"Let me carry him," said Mr. Nate.

She handed me over, and he followed her up the stairs to the apartment. Rocco hissed at the sight of Jackson.

"Shut up, furball," said Jackson. Rocco skittered away and ran down to the shop to hide.

"Rocco is my cat," said Miss Josie with a rueful smile. "Sort of. He came with the shop, and I'm pretty sure he hates me."

"Nice," said Mr. Nate.

"Rocco hates me, too," I said to Jackson, as Mr. Nate lowered me carefully onto the floor. "Do you know what he said last night? He told me I'd never become a true gentleman."

"He's an idiot," said Jackson, without any hesitation at all.

In spite of feeling ill, I almost glowed with pride. "You think I have a chance to make myself into a proper gentleman?"

"Heck, no," said Jackson, immediately deflating my hope. "I just think the cat is an idiot."

My shoulders slumped. "It's not only Rocco. The cat

back home on the horse farm, Mr. Collins, said almost the same thing. He got mad at me for causing one tiny stampede, then he called me disgusting because I liked nibbling on horse poo."

"Horse poo is delicious," said Jackson. "So grassy and oaty."

"I know, right?" I let out a sigh. "But maybe they're correct. Maybe I am disgusting."

Jackson rolled his puggy eyes at me. "Why would you listen to cats? That's the stupidest thing I've ever heard. No good ever came from it. You might be disgusting, but you're a good kind of disgusting. Trust me on this one."

"Thanks for being such a great friend, Jackson." I gave him a half-hearted lick. I didn't have the energy to do much else.

"You're welcome, pup," he said. "Now get some rest. You're going to feel like crap in the morning. No pun intended."

Miss Josie gave Mr. Nate a blanket and showed him to the blue couch. She nearly swayed on her feet from exhaustion.

"Go to bed, Josie. I'll take care of him," said Mr. Nate.

"If I could get a few hours of sleep, it would help," she said. "I'll set my alarm, so I won't sleep too long, but thanks again for doing this. I appreciate it."

She went to bed, and Mr. Nate turned on the television, keeping the volume low. When Jackson jumped on the couch, too, I stared at him in shock, but Mr. Nate didn't seem to care. He patted the spot next to him. "Come here, Capone."

Now I faced a moral dilemma. I knew the rules, and the right thing to do would be to decline his kind offer and go to my crate. Alone. But I heard the voice inside my head, the one always telling me to do naughty things. It said, "Get up on the couch, stupid. How many chances will you have to sleep on a soft, blue velvety slice of heaven? Stop worrying and carpe the heck out of this diem."

Alas, the voice proved to be too compelling to ignore. I felt powerless to stop it. I hopped onto the couch and curled up next to Mr. Nate, putting my head on his lap. I sighed contentedly, experiencing a moment of absolute bliss.

"Would you like to watch some football?" asked Mr. Nate. Then he realized Miss Josie didn't have cable. "Or we could watch PBS."

I wagged my tail happily because, of course, PBS was my favorite. Mr. Nate smiled at me. "PBS it is."

We watched a program about the Brontë sisters as Jackson snored on his corner of the couch. PBS had an almost narcoleptic effect on him but not on me. I found it riveting and nearly as good as reading books.

When Mr. Nate led me outside again, barely anything came out, and I took it as a good sign. Hopefully, this whole horrible episode would be over soon.

When I finished, I heard a noise from the garden door. It sounded like someone playing with the latch. Unfortunately, Miss Josie had taken off the padlock when she let Mr. Nate inside.

Mr. Nate whistled softly for me. "Come here, Capone."

I padded over to his side and stood there, shaking from fear and from being ill. I needed to find a way to protect Mr. Nate and Miss Josie, but I was sick and weak. What could I do?

Mr. Nate located the switch for the outdoor light, and turned it on, bathing the entire area in a bright glow. "Who's there?" he asked, grabbing a broom. This show of bravado made me nervous. Who knew what kind of foul villain lurked behind the door?

In spite of my doubts, Mr. Nate's plan worked. When he opened the door, broom in hand, whoever had been fumbling with the latch was now gone.

"Good dog," he said. "If not for your nocturnal diarrhea, they might have broken into the shop as Josie slept. I've heard from some of my customers that she's already had a few break-ins. We'll have to call the police first thing in the morning. But who wants to rob a bookstore? It doesn't make sense."

I had to agree. Although Miss Josie's books were valuable, she kept the most expensive ones locked in a temperature-controlled vault, and she barely had any cash in her store. What might they want?

After putting the padlock back on the garden door and making sure all the doors and windows remained securely locked, Mr. Nate snuck into Miss Josie's bedroom. I watched from the hallway as he shut off her alarm clock, and then stared at her a minute as she slept. Her face looked relaxed and quite pretty in the moonlight, and she didn't seem at all worried or ticked off, the two expressions typically on her face when around Mr. Nate. I wondered if he'd ever seen her not looking angry. Right now, she appeared sweet and kind of vulnerable.

What if Mr. Nate had not been the one to come outside with me? What if Miss Josie had been out in the garden all alone in the dead of night? Things could have ended quite differently. The thought made me feel even worse than the toxic peony bushes.

By the time I settled onto the couch, sore, miserable, and exhausted, I could barely keep my eyes open. Mr. Nate made me drink some water and lifted me so I could sleep on top of him. It felt cozy, for me at least. The couch was too small to accommodate Mr. Nate, and his long legs hung off the side.

Jackson took up an entire cushion. He sprawled out as he slept and snored like the devil. I couldn't imagine anyone sleeping through such noise, but I snoozed as soon as my head went down on Mr. Nate's chest. In spite of the fear over the potential robber and feeling sicker than I ever had in my life, somehow, I was oddly content. I'd found a good friend in Mr. Nate, and Jackson, too.

Almost in response to my thoughts, Jackson rolled over and farted in his sleep. It was even louder than his snoring, but I was far too tired to care. I snuggled up to Mr. Nate, gave him one last sleepy lick of gratitude on his cheek, and fell asleep.

THIRTEEN

Reasons why Mr. Nate would be the perfect man for Miss Josie:

1. He likes me.
2. He lets me sleep on the couch.
3. He feeds me treats.
4. He understands dogs.
5. He scared away the bad guy who tried to break into the garden.
6. He's kind to Miss Josie, even when she's prickly and thorny.
7. He's reading *Pride and Prejudice*.
8. When Miss Josie isn't looking, he stares at her like she might be the prettiest thing he's ever seen.

Reasons why Mr. Nate would not be the perfect man for Miss Josie:

1. He's leaving.

I stretched and yawned, still on top of Mr. Nate, as Miss Josie emerged from her room. I lifted my head and gave her a half-hearted wag of my tail, too sick to get up and greet her properly. I hoped I wouldn't be in trouble for breaking the Sacred Rule of the Couch, but she didn't seem mad. In fact, I saw something soften in her eyes as she looked at us.

Jackson let out a snore. It nearly made the windows shake. A giant pool of drool marked his spot on the couch. But, to my surprise, Miss Josie didn't get angry.

"Do you want to eat, Capone?" she asked, her voice soft. I lowered my head back to Mr. Nate's chest. I did not want to eat. I never wanted to eat again.

Her face filled with concern. "Poor puppy," she said, and then her eyes rested on Mr. Nate, who was twisted in an uncomfortable position on the small couch. "Poor man."

She touched his shoulder, and his eyes opened. "Good morning," he said, his voice scratchy and rough. He sat up carefully, keeping me on his lap. "How's the patient this morning?"

"He doesn't want to eat. I already called the vet. I'll take him there in an hour." She paused. "Thanks for staying last night. I set my alarm, but I must have shut it off in my sleep."

"No. I turned it off. The last time I took him out, I had a feeling he was done. He slept the rest of the night." He tilted his head back and forth, stretching out his neck. "By the way, it's a good thing Capone had his little problem last night. We interrupted someone trying to come in through the side door."

Miss Josie put a hand over her mouth. "Are you serious?"

"Unfortunately, yes, but I scared them by turning on the lights and making threatening noises. I also grabbed your broom, which was extremely intimidating," Mr. Nate said with a little laugh.

"It's scary," she said. "I don't understand why this keeps happening."

"You've already had a few break-ins, right?"

"Yes, which is why Anne got Capone for me in the first place. I have a new alarm system, too, but she thought a dog might help. I guess she was right," said Miss Josie. "Although she thought his barking would keep intruders away, not his intestinal distress."

"Diarrhea is an unusual theft deterrent, but it worked," said Mr. Nate, petting my head. "It worries me, though. What could they be after?"

"I have no idea. The first time I had a break-in, they left before doing any significant damage, but the second time they tried to get into the vault. That's the place where I keep the most valuable inventory." Miss Josie looked down at me, her eyes kind. "Anyway, I'm glad Capone didn't have to do anything heroic. He's a licker, not a fighter."

I gave her another half-hearted wag of my tail. *Thump, thump, thump.*

"I put the padlock back on the door," said Mr. Nate, "but you should still call the police."

"I will as soon as we get back from Capone's appointment."

Jackson woke up, bleary-eyed, and got awkwardly to his feet. "Where the heck am I?"

Mr. Nate cringed when he saw the puddle of drool Jackson left on Miss Josie's pretty couch. "Sorry. I'll clean it. Where are your paper towels?"

She touched his arm. "It's fine. Jackson is welcome to drool on my couch anytime. I owe you that much, at least."

His gaze locked on hers. "You don't owe me. It was the neighborly thing to do."

"Neighborly," said Miss Josie with a tiny frown. If I didn't know better, I would have almost said she seemed disappointed, but I didn't understand why. Women were such confusing creatures.

He glanced at his watch. "I'd better go. We'll see both of you later."

Mr. Nate and Jackson left, and by the time Miss Josie dressed, I had gone from feeling poorly to trembling in absolute agony. I grew so weak I could barely stand. She ended up carrying me to the car, not an easy task. A First Impressions coffee cup sat on the roof near the driver's side. She put me down, then read the words written on the side of the cup in black marker.

"Chapter Four: He should have danced with Lizzie at Meryton. Big mistake. Almost as bad as Capone eating the peony bushes." She rolled her eyes, a smile tugging at her lips. "He does not give up."

She put me on the passenger seat and stuck the coffee in the cup holder in between us. It smelled good, like whipped cream and happiness, but I was too sick to appreciate it. I flopped down on my belly and moaned. Being on death's door was awful.

Miss Josie sipped on her coffee as she drove the short distance to the vet, shooting me worried glances the whole time. My stomach made funny, gurgling sounds, but nothing else shot out. Although happy about no longer erupting like Old Faithful, I was definitely dying. How could a dog feel this bad and survive? I wish I'd written out a will. I would have left my Orange Snuggle Bunny to Jackson and my special chew rope to Gracie. Miss Josie could have the rest, but I didn't want to leave Rocco anything. My only regret was I didn't poop on his bed last night. I thought about it, and the naughty voice inside my head told me to do it, but I resisted.

Note to self: Next time, poop on Rocco's bed.

As we waited in the exam room for Doc McHottie, Miss Josie continued to sip her coffee as she gently stroked my head. She'd pulled me up onto the chair next to her, and I sprawled across her lap.

"Poor puppy," she said. "You'll be better soon. I promise."

I gave her hand a small, sad lick. I didn't have the heart to tell her she was wrong. She'd be so sorry when she realized I wouldn't make it. I'd be sad too. What I wouldn't give for one more day, and another chance to help Miss Josie find her Mr. Darcy.

Doc McHottie came in, all raven black hair and kind green eyes, and made a tsking sound when he saw me. "Capone. What happened to you, buddy?" he asked as he washed his hands. "I didn't expect to see you until Saturday."

"Saturday?" asked Miss Josie, frowning in confusion.

He raised one dark eyebrow at her. "The picnic with Capone and Wrigley. Did you forget?"

Her cheeks turned bright pink. "Of course, I didn't forget." He gave her a steady look, and she winced. "Yes, I forgot. I'm sorry."

"Don't worry about it. You've had a lot on your mind. Let's have a look at poor Capone."

He let me stay on Miss Josie's lap rather than taking me to the shiny metal exam table. I was grateful for his thoughtfulness. Since I would die soon, I wanted it to be in the arms of the woman I loved.

Doc McHottie put on his stethoscope and listened to

my tummy. "Has he eaten anything unusual?"

I looked up at Miss Josie as she looked down at me. "Define unusual," she said.

He sighed. "Why don't you tell me what he ate in the last twenty-four hours or so?"

"Well, let me think. Rabbit poo. Rocks. Shoes. A leaf. Part of a pen. A ponytail holder. There could be more. I can't find my tights, and I pulled ribbons out of his bottom the other day. He also ate part of my peony bush. My neighbor said those are mildly toxic for dogs."

Doc McHottie stared at her in shock. "We're going to have to do an x-ray. Many of those things could get lodged in his digestive tract and cause a serious obstruction. He should be better supervised, Josie. If something is stuck, he'll need surgery."

"I'm sorry," she said, and I heard a catch in her voice. "I do watch him, I swear, but he's sneaky. He has a gift."

Note to self: I'm gifted. Who knew?

"Let me get the x-ray. I'll bring Capone back in a few minutes."

As he carried me out of the room, I stared over his shoulder at Miss Josie and whimpered, knowing this could be the last time I saw her. It was tragic. She finally liked me, and now she was about to lose me forever.

I wondered what might show up in the x-ray. Miss Josie had no idea about the other things I'd ingested when she hadn't been looking, like the slippers, an entire stick of butter (wrapper and all) and some of Miss Josie's dental floss. I'd also done some counter surfing while Miss Josie took a shower yesterday. The floss had been a bonus find, but I'd chewed on her toothbrush, too. She had no idea. I'd left it on the counter, and she used it as soon as she got out of the shower. She didn't seem to notice it was covered in dog drool and had tooth marks on the side. I blame the steam-filled bathroom and the lack of glasses on Miss Josie's part.

When Doc McHottie brought me back to the exam room, Miss Josie clutched a tissue in her hands and dabbed her eyes. "What did you find?" she asked.

He smiled at her reassuringly. "Nothing at all. Whatever he ate, he seems to have gotten it all out. Your dog's intestines are empty, except for a great deal of gas."

Almost on cue, a loud fart erupted from my nether regions. I ducked my head sheepishly as Miss Josie waved a hand in front of her nose. "What made him so sick?"

"Your neighbor's hunch about the peony bushes might be correct. I'm going to give him anti-nausea meds, antibiotics, and special food. It's bland, and it'll help him recover. He should be as right as rain in time for our picnic on Saturday. If you still want to go."

"I do," she said, giving him a grateful smile. "Are you sure he's going to be okay?"

"Yes," he said. "I'll send what he needs to the front desk. Keep a better eye on him and call me if he has any problems. Otherwise, I'll meet up with you at noon on Saturday. Sound like a plan?"

"It does," said Miss Josie. "And thank you."

"All in a day's work, ma'am," he said, and he swooshed out of the room, his white coat fluttering like a cape.

A superhero, a gentleman, a cowboy, and a vet. Also, he wasn't leaving any time soon. I may have found the perfect man for Miss Josie. What more could she possibly want? And she'd met him all because of me.

At the rate I was going, I'd have this wrapped up in no time. I'd found a Mr. Darcy for Miss Josie on my first try. This good deed stuff? Not as tricky as I'd thought.

FOURTEEN

An itemized list of charges incurred during my visit to the vet:

1. Antibiotics.
2. Anti-nausea medication.
3. Probiotics.
4. Special dog food.
5. Pill pockets to help me take the medicines.
6. Fee for the exam.
7. Fee for the x-ray.
8. Powdered clay to firm up my...problem.
9. A doggie electrolyte solution for my dehydration.
10. A bottle of wine.

Miss Josie didn't get the last one from Doc McHottie. She bought it on her way home and planned to consume it later, because the vet bill ended up being approximately the same amount as a car payment.

The receptionist patted her hand. "But we can't put a price on our dog's health, now can we?"

Miss Josie may have disagreed with that assessment, but she took pity on me. "It's not your fault, boy. Apparently, I'm a horrible dog parent and didn't take proper care of you."

I wanted to tell her it was, most definitely, my fault, but now Miss Josie felt terrible. I felt awful, too. The only person who didn't feel bad? Rocco. After Miss Josie gave me my medicine and got me set up in my crate, Rocco came over to torture me.

"You didn't die? How unfortunate. I thought surely you would."

"Shut up, Rocco." I tried to sound harsh but still felt too sick. It came out as pathetic.

He laughed at me. "All bark and no bite. What kind of gangster are you, Al Capone?"

"I'm not a gangster. I'm a gentleman."

"You know the truth as well as I do," he said, his eyes narrowing. "You have a heart of pure darkness. Evil lurks within you."

"That's not true," I said, even though a part of me feared he might be right. "I've made some mistakes, but I'm not a bad dog, and I'm certainly not evil. Don't be ridiculous."

"You're the one who's ridiculous. Aspiring to be like Mr. Darcy, when he was nothing but an arrogant snob."

I wanted to cover my ears. "No. Mr. Darcy may have seemed arrogant, but he was kind and loyal and good. He loved his family and his friends. He just wasn't comfortable with strangers."

Rocco rolled his eyes. "Have you read the book, or were you too blinded by Mr. Darcy's handsome face on the BBC program to see the truth? Mr. Darcy was kind of a twit."

"No," I said, wishing Rocco would stop talking. "You're lying."

"Whatever. Believe what you will, but I know the truth." He leaned close. "You'll never be a gentleman. Badness is in your blood, little dog. You can't fight it."

I sat up taller. "So, I should stop trying?" I asked. "Is that what you're saying?"

He shrugged. "If the shoe fits...oh, wait. There is no shoe. You ate it, didn't you? The first night you arrived. And you ripped apart my favorite pillow, too. It's more evidence that you'll never be a gentleman, no matter how hard you try."

It was the final straw. "I'm going to prove you wrong, Rocco. If it's the last thing I do."

He walked away, chuckling in his evil feline voice. "We'll see, pup. We'll see."

Note to self: Rocco is a jerk face.

I spent the next few hours resting in my crate, torturing myself with what Rocco had said. Miss Josie came to check on me several times, making sure I drank enough water. When I went outside to pee, we celebrated. It felt good not to be sick and dehydrated anymore. And although Miss Josie might disagree, I thought the anti-nausea medicine was worth every penny.

Miss Josie let me spend the rest of the afternoon in her shop, curled up on a blanket by her feet as she went over Mr. Bartleby's ledgers. Ms. Anne peeked over her shoulder.

"The man wrote in code."

"It's convoluted," said Miss Josie. "And I still can't find the last ledger. I have no idea where it might be."

"He was nearly ninety when he passed away. I think the bookstore was the only reason he lived so long."

"I agree, and he never got over Mrs. Bartleby's death. Not a day went by that he didn't talk about her."

"It's so romantic," said Ms. Anne. "I'm sure all three of my ex-husbands talk about me, too, but mostly to curse and call me vile names."

Miss Josie laughed. "Not quite as nice, or as romantic. But it hurt watching Mr. Bartleby deteriorate. Part of my job entailed finding what he lost."

"Like ledgers?" asked Ms. Anne. "Isn't it odd he didn't have a safe or something?"

"He told me once he kept a safety deposit box hidden in the shop, but I've never saw one."

"Could he have meant the vault?"

"Anything's possible, I guess."

The vault, which sat in the back of the shop, resembled a large walk-in closet. A complicated locking mechanism secured the door. Temperature controlled and carefully sealed, it contained the most valuable pieces in the shop's inventory, precious old books with crumbling leather covers and delicate gold lettering. Of course, I'd never gotten close to the vault, or those special books. Miss Josie kept me far away, but I'd caught a glimpse of what was hidden inside.

She wore white gloves whenever she handled her treasures, and she made others use them, too. Her customers were typically professors, intellectuals, and other people wearing tweed and wool. Most of them made appointments to see books they wanted to buy.

A high, narrow table sat in the middle of the vault, enabling potential buyers to examine the merchandise without leaving the room. Even something as innocuous as exposure to oil from someone's hands could be all it took to ruin one of those treasures forever.

The books had a distinctive smell, something which

tickled my nose with a mixture of vanilla and lavender. I'd overheard Miss Josie tell a customer old books smelled this way due to the breakdown in their chemical composition as they aged. New books smelled harsher and more artificial. Because of scent alone, I understood why Miss Josie preferred old books. The aroma of ancient tomes delighted my entire olfactory system.

"It's a mystery," said Ms. Anne. "Maybe there's a box somewhere in the shop you know nothing about."

After Ms. Anne left, Miss Josie took another look around, and I followed, tail wagging. It felt like a game. As she worked her way through a large display case at the front of the shop, the bell over the door tinkled and Mr. Nate came in. He smiled when he saw me.

"Well, hello," he said, patting me. "You're looking better."

I snuggled against him happily. We'd bonded yesterday when I nearly died, and spending the entire night sleeping on Mr. Nate's chest made us special friends.

Jackson came in, looking bored. "Hey, poopy pants."

"I don't wear pants." Much of what Jackson said confused me. I didn't understand his humor at all.

"Maybe you should," he said. "Or maybe you need one of those doggie diapers. I've never seen anything quite like what you did last night. It was like an explosion of poo. It positively spewed out of you. It was impressive."

"Are you here to torture me?" I asked.

"Nah. We're here because my man Nate has the hots for the blondie. He digs the whole sexy librarian thing she has going."

I glanced at Miss Josie. In a grey cashmere sweater that matched her eyes and emphasized her curves, she did give off that sort of vibe. The hipster glasses and the pen currently stuck in her messy bun added to the effect.

"Thanks for your help last night," said Miss Josie. "I appreciate it."

"Don't mention it. I had fun," said Mr. Nate, shoving his hands into the pockets of his jeans.

"Oh, yes. Fun," Miss Josie said, rolling her eyes. "First you took care of my sick dog, then you slept on my couch. Lucky you."

"I enjoyed it. Honestly." Their eyes locked for a long moment before Mr. Nate's cheeks reddened. "Capone feels better; I take it."

"Yes, and the vet thinks you were right about the peony bush. Good call."

"Jackson was like a walking textbook on all the bad things a dog could do," he said. "I learned a lot from him."

Jackson scratched his fat belly, looking rather pleased with himself. "We had some good times, Nate and I," he said. "And I regret nothing. Well, maybe a few things. Like the time I ate an entire box of chocolate. Never do that, Capone. Trust me. You'll end up at the vet so fast you won't know what hit you."

Note to self: Life is not a box of chocolates.

Mr. Nate shot a glance at the ledgers. "Wow. Old-style record keeping."

"Courtesy of the former owner," said Miss Josie. "Benjamin Bartleby. He knew more about books than anyone I'd ever met but nothing about bookkeeping. He never felt comfortable with technology. This was his system," she said, pointing to the messy ledgers. "The good news is I've finally finished inputting most of this onto my computer. The bad news is I'm still missing one of his ledgers, and it's an important one. It has all of the most recent inventory posted in it."

"Where could it be?"

"He told me once that he had a safety deposit box in the shop. I doubt it even existed, but I thought I might as well make sure there isn't a box here somewhere."

Mr. Nate glanced around the shop. "It wouldn't have to be huge, right? Just large enough to hold a few books or a ledger."

"I guess so," she said. "But if a mysterious box had been lying around, I'd have noticed it by now."

"Can you do a physical inventory, and then compare it to what's in the ledger when you find it?"

"That's what I've been doing. I finished up today." She stretched. "Finally."

"You should reward yourself for all your hard work. I heard there's a special exhibit Saturday on the history of fashion, including ball gowns, at the Beaver Museum. Want to go?"

Jackson and I shared a look. Ball gowns? How strange. Mr. Nate did not seem like a ball gown kind of guy, but Miss Josie didn't notice.

"I wish I could, but Capone and I sort of have a date on Saturday."

"A date?" he asked.

"Yes. With the vet. He thought it would be good to socialize Capone with his dog."

Jackson grunted. "You've got to be kidding. Socialize her pet? It's the oldest scam in the book. That's code for fornication. Trust me. The vet must have a thing for hot librarian types, too."

I found this disturbing but decided Jackson was wrong. Doc McHottie comported himself like a total gentleman, and I felt certain his intentions regarding Miss Josie were honorable.

"But I'm free tonight," said Miss Josie. "I'd love it if you and Jackson could come over for dinner. It wouldn't be fancy, only pizza or something."

Mr. Nate lifted an eyebrow. "Are you talking about a vegetarian pizza with soy cheese and kale? Because I know bookshop owning cat-lady types are into kale."

A smile tugged at the corners of her lips. "No kale, and I'll get the pizza from Vic's Oven. Yours will be meaty and magnificent. Have you tried their kielbasa and pierogi pizza? I've heard it's awesome. For carnivores."

"Intriguing," he said. "I'll bring the wine. After all, we both know how much you like wine." He gave her a wink, making her blush.

"Come over around seven?" she asked.

"We will. Thank you, Josie."

Jackson laughed, in his throaty and slightly perverted way. "He, he, he," he said. "And you know what pizza and wine are code words for, right?"

"Fornication?" I asked.

He looked shocked. "No. Dinner. And Mr. Nate always lets me have the crust. You have a sick mind. See you later. This pug is planning a pizza pig out tonight. It's going to get ugly."

Although impressed with his use of alliteration, I had a feeling my interpretation of this event actually might be closer to the truth. This seemed like a date, and if Mr. Nate still planned on moving away once the coffee shop got up and running, dating him could be a potential disaster for poor Miss Josie and her sweet, fragile heart.

And I had absolutely no idea what to do about it.

FIFTEEN

Ways to stop humans mid-coitus:

1. Bark.
2. Hop on the couch next to them.
3. Act like you need to go outside.
4. Stare at them awkwardly.
5. Lick any exposed skin.

Mr. Nate and Jackson arrived promptly at seven. They'd both bathed, and Mr. Nate had shaved and put on a clean T-shirt, one without any holes in it. I had to assume my first analysis of the situation had been correct. This was a date.

I sniffed at Jackson. "Why do you smell like vanilla?"

Jackson flopped down on the floor. "He made me do it. I rolled in something nasty I found behind the shop, and the boss wanted me to smell nice for tonight. Where's the pizza?"

The doorbell rang, and I ran to it with joyful anticipation. Miss Josie had ordered two pizzas. One smelled like spinach and cheese, and the other smelled like a dream.

"What is that glorious aroma?" I asked.

Jackson took a deep whiff. "It's kielbasa, my friend. A fantastically fatty delight."

"I think I've died and gone to heaven," I said, as we went upstairs to Miss Josie's apartment.

Jackson laughed. "You won't get any kielbasa tonight. Your intestines are still in recovery mode. You're probably on the special diet from the vet. It comes in a can. It doesn't taste anywhere near as good as kielbasa."

He was right. As Mr. Nate and Miss Josie sat on the couch, nibbling pizza, and sipping red wine, I ate a meal of canned meat and rice. Yes, it felt good on my sore tummy, but I still wanted to try kielbasa. Sadly, Mr. Nate refused to give me any.

"Sorry, Capone," he said when I put my paw on his knee and looked up at him longingly. "No people food for you tonight."

Realizing I would get nowhere with him, I flopped down on his feet in despair. Not even getting a bite of pizza filled me with regret for my earlier indiscretions.

"I called the police after I got home from the vet," said Miss Josie. "Officer Stahl came over to check on us."

"I'm glad. Even our shop in New York hasn't had as many break-in attempts as yours, and this is the safest town I've ever visited. It doesn't make sense."

"Officer Stahl told me the same thing. He's happy about the new alarm system, the padlock on the garden door, and about Capone. He said a barking dog is an excellent deterrent."

"He's right," said Mr. Nate. "So, I guess you've finally realized Capone is perfect?"

"Not by a long shot. But he's mine. Speaking of which, I need to change his name. He deserves something better. What do you think of Darcy?"

I jumped to my feet, hoping this might be my big moment, but Mr. Nate ruined it. "I think Capone suits him, but I'm biased. I grew up in Chicago."

"Well, I guess that explains your fondness for my dog's awful name."

He laughed. "I wouldn't call it a fondness. It's more like a healthy level of respect. How about you? Are you from Beaver?"

"Born and raised," she said.

"And your parents live in Beaver, too?"

She shook her head and took a sip of wine. "They died. It happened a few years ago."

"I'm so sorry. I didn't know."

"It's okay," she said softly.

"Do you have other family here?"

"No." She gave him a sad little smile. "I was an only child, and my father traveled a great deal for business. My mother homeschooled me so we could travel with him, but this was always our home base. We had a house on River Road, and Anne lived next door. She's ten years older, but we've been friends forever." She dusted some crumbs off her skirt. "When I had the offer to work for Mr. Bartleby, it seemed like the perfect fit. Beaver has always felt like home to me."

"I get it," he said. "Travelling isn't always easy. It must be nice to stay in one place."

"I think so. Do you travel a lot?"

"I do."

"How long have you been working at the coffee shop?" she asked.

He reached for the wine and poured her more. "For a few years now."

"I've heard it's a great company."

"It is," he said. "I know you aren't particularly fond of coffee..." She made a face, and he laughed. "But First Impressions is innovative, both because of the coffee and how it's acquired."

"Do you mean the whole free trade thing? I read about it online."

He wiped his mouth with a napkin. "You've been investigating us?"

She blushed. "No, but I'm curious."

"I'm teasing you. I'm proud of what we do. We offer a great product, and we're helping coffee farmers all over the world have easier lives. What could be better?"

"How did you get into this?"

"Well," he said, leaning back on the couch, "It's kind of a long story. I joined the Peace Corps after college and lived in Guatemala. I saw the struggles of farmers first hand, and I wanted to do something to help. I went back home, got my MBA, and then started working."

"What did you study undergrad?"

"I had a dual major. Math and anthropology."

She twirled a lock of hair with her finger. "An interesting combination."

"I also have a minor in gender and women's studies, but I got it by accident."

"How?" she asked with a giggle.

"It overlapped with anthropology, but I thought it would be useful, both personally and professionally. I grew up in a house full of brothers."

"How many?" she asked, tucking her legs beneath her on the blue velvet couch.

"Five," he said, and laughed at her startled reaction. "Jimmy, Ricky, Tommy, Billy, Mickey, and me."

"You're fortunate. I always wished I'd had brothers and sisters," she said, with a slightly loopy smile. They'd nearly polished off the entire bottle of wine, and Miss Josie, from what I could tell, was a lightweight. "It was always just me and my parents."

"You have no other family at all?

My heart squeezed in my chest at the expression on her face. "I have Anne, who's like family, but a brother or a sister would have made it less lonely. Are you close to your brothers?"

"I am."

She grinned. "Did they call you Baby Nate? I bet they did."

"Stop," he said, covering his face with his hands. "You're bringing back so many painful memories of wedgies and noogies and being dared to do things that always got me in trouble."

She giggled, pulling his hands away from his face. "Poor you," she said. "Poor Baby Nate."

"You'll pay," he said. I'm not sure what he intended to do, but somehow Miss Josie ended up on his lap and he was kissing her. Enthusiastically. And she kissed him right back. It made me wonder what this man learned in his women's studies classes.

"Grab some popcorn," said Jackson, his jaw dropping. "I think we're about to get quite the show."

"Whatever do you mean?" I asked.

"Blondie and the boss man are about to get it on." He punctuated the last few words with pelvic thrusts, the effect both disturbing and mesmerizing.

"They're going to consummate their relationship?" I

asked, horrified, but one glance at Miss Josie and Mr. Nate told me it could be a real possibility. Miss Josie had gone from sitting daintily on his lap to straddling him, and Mr. Nate now had his hands in places his hands had never been before.

"I prefer to call it something else, but no matter how you say it, the results are the same. They are about to do the deed. This is awesome."

This was not awesome; it was a disaster. Who knew how long Mr. Nate would stay here before he left to open another coffee shop? It probably wouldn't be long. Falling in love with him had to be the worst idea ever. I needed to save her from herself.

If I could have spoken, I would have said, "Stop! Stop this madness before you both make a mistake you'll live to regret." Instead, I jumped on the couch and barked in their faces.

Mr. Nate continued to kiss his way down Miss Josie's neck, but Miss Josie came out of whatever trance he had her under and looked at me in surprise. "What is it, boy? Do you need to go outside?"

I ran to the door, tail wagging. If that was what it took to get Miss Josie off Mr. Nate's lap and away from his lips, I certainly did need to go outside. Now. Immediately. Pronto.

Miss Josie pulled away from Mr. Nate gently, giving him a shy smile. "I'd better let him out."

"I'll go with you," said Mr. Nate, getting to his feet and entwining her fingers with his. "Jackson and I could both use some air."

"Don't bring me into this, Mr. Casanova," said Jackson. "I wasn't the one locking lips with the librarian on the couch a few minutes ago."

I shuddered at his imagery. "Please don't. I saved them from making a huge mistake."

"The night is still young, pup. Maybe they intend to do it al fresco."

"Al fresco?"

"A fancy way to say outside," he said with a lustful gleam in his eye. "Which was how I always did it before I lost my you-know-whats. There was a poodle back in Chicago I got to know well, if you understand my meaning. Those were the days. Poodles are crazy but so worth it. Take my advice on this."

"Uh, okay."

Note to self: Don't take Jackson's advice on anything.

I honestly had no idea what Jackson was talking about, but I had other concerns. I needed to fake pee on several bushes so Miss Josie wouldn't get suspicious. Fake peeing is hard, especially since I had to keep my eye on Miss Josie and Mr. Nate to make sure they didn't start on the path to perdition once again.

Fortunately, it seemed the night air had cooled their ardors and brought them back to their senses. Mr. Nate took both of her hands in his and stared down at her. The stars sparkled above them like diamonds, and the moon shone full and bright. If there hadn't been so much at stake, I would have thought it was the perfect night for a romantic rendezvous. As things stood, however, I exhaled in relief when Mr. Nate announced the time had come for him and Jackson to return home.

"Thank you for a wonderful, amazing, perfect evening."

He punctuated the last few words with soft, sweet kisses. Had I actually thought Mr. Nate was shy? I'd been wrong about him. He seemed un-shy at the moment. Mr. Kissy McKissypants.

Miss Josie let out a breathless sigh and leaned against him, her body molding to his like it was meant to be there. Like they somehow fit. As their kiss deepened, I had no option but to start barking again. And hopping. And body slamming both of them until they broke apart.

"What the heck, Capone?" asked Miss Josie, her eyes still dazed from the kisses.

Mr. Nate grinned. "He's jealous. Capone doesn't like it when I kiss you." To prove his point, he kissed her again. I couldn't let them continue, so I had to start barking again, which made both of them think Mr. Nate had been right.

"How funny," said Miss Josie with a laugh. "Capone is jealous of Baby Nate. Who'd have thought?"

Mr. Nate rolled his eyes, pulling her close for one last kiss. "On that note, I think Jackson and I should say goodnight. Lock up after I leave, okay?"

"I will."

It may have been my imagination, but both of them seemed rather disinclined to part ways. I barked again to speed up the process, and they laughed.

"Goodnight, Nate."

"Goodnight, Josie. And Capone."

As the door to the garden closed behind them, Miss Josie firmly locked it and leaned against it, a happy smile on her pretty face and her eyes sparkling nearly as much as the stars above us. I didn't have any experience at all in matters of the heart, but if Miss Josie fell for the wrong guy, she'd never find her Mr. Darcy.

Oh, calamity. This was very bad indeed.

SIXTEEN

Things I should not do when meeting a septuagenarian:

1. Jump on them.
2. Lick their sweet, wrinkly, old face.
3. Knock off their hat.
4. Attempt to eat their hat.
5. Succeed in eating part of their hat.

"Capone, leave Mrs. Norris alone." Miss Josie grabbed my collar and pulled me away from the elderly woman who'd entered the shop. "Sit."

I jumped at the harsh tone of her voice. I hadn't meant any harm. I wanted to greet my new friend, but I'd never seen anyone quite so wrinkled before, or so small.

"It's quite all right, dearie," said our visitor. "I like dogs. But when I heard you had a puppy, I didn't expect such a large one. Is he dangerous? He won't bite, will he?"

"No. Capone will lick you though, and sometimes he destroys private property." Miss Josie picked up the rather large hat I'd knocked off Mrs. Norris's tiny head. "I'm so sorry about your hat, Mrs. Norris."

Curse my insatiable curiosity.

I'd crushed the brim of the hat and dented it on one side. I also stepped on it, sat on it, and ate one of the beautiful feathers decorating the top. I already regretted that particular decision. It hadn't been as tasty as it looked.

Mrs. Steele came rushing from the back. "Are you all right, Henrietta?"

Mrs. Norris smiled at her. "I'm fine, Lucy. He didn't mean any harm. What's the sense of owning a haberdashery if you can't fix your own hat?"

"Speaking of which," said Miss Josie, wincing at the damage to the hat, "how are things going at your shop?"

"It's been challenging lately. I love the new coffee shop, but..." She paused, as if not sure what to say. "Well, parking has always been a headache, but now it's nearly impossible. I'm managing, though."

Poor Mrs. Norris. I felt sorry for her. I also felt kind of queasy.

Note to self: Do not eat feathers from old ladies' hats.

"You and Mr. Bartleby were good friends, weren't you?"

"Yes." Mrs. Norris put a hand on the frothy bit of lace near the collar of her blouse. "Dear, sweet Benjamin. I miss him so."

"Me, too," said Miss Josie. "Did he ever mention anything to you about having a safety deposit box inside the shop?"

"Isn't a safety deposit box usually found in a bank?" she asked, her voice tight. Something in her demeanor had changed. Maybe she was annoyed at Miss Josie for asking so many questions, or maybe she was annoyed at me for eating part of her hat. It was probably the latter.

"He specifically said he had one in the shop. If it exists, I'm hoping it might contain his most recent accounting ledger."

"Oh, that man," said Mrs. Norris, rolling her eyes. "Organization was never his strong suit, and it only got worse as he got older. Such a brilliant person, and yet fighting a battle against the one enemy we all face."

"Which enemy?"

"Time," she said with a little smile. "The problem is you always think you have enough of it." She sounded so melancholy, I gave her a lick on the hand. She tasted strange, like talcum powder and menthol joint cream. She patted my head. "You're a rather nice puppy when you're not trying to eat my hat."

"I apologize," said Miss Josie. "Again."

Mrs. Norris waved her words aside. "No worries, dear. But I got so distracted, I didn't tell you my news." She took a long, deep breath. "I'm closing the haberdashery."

Miss Josie's eyes widened in surprise. "What? Why?"

"Well, because I'm nearly eighty. I love my shop, but I want to enjoy what time I have left. The offer from First Impressions came at the right moment."

Miss Josie, who'd been sorting piles of books, froze. "What offer from First Impressions?"

Mrs. Norris scratched me behind the ear, my favorite spot. "This branch is going to be their flagship. They talked about it at the last city council meeting a few months ago."

"I missed it," said Miss Josie. "I had the flu. What did they say?"

A customer entered the shop and browsed through a display on local history. When Mrs. Norris spoke, she kept her voice low. "It wasn't so much what they said. It had more to do with what I saw. They brought their expansion plans with them. Eventually, they'll need a bigger place, you see, and city ordinances don't allow buildings over three stories tall on the main street. They don't have a choice."

Miss Josie's eyebrows furrowed into a worried frown. "Their expansion plans included tearing down your lovely shop?"

Mrs. Norris reached out and placed a wrinkled hand over Miss Josie's smooth one. "Not only my shop, pumpkin —your shop, too."

SEVENTEEN

Ways to know Mr. Nate is in the doghouse:

1. Miss Josie looks like she sucked on a lemon.
2. She slams things.
3. She mutters to herself.
4. She swears she'll never trust him again.

As soon as Mrs. Norris left, Miss Josie put me on my leash, and we marched over to the café. People looked at her in surprise as she went straight up to the counter, but she ignored them.

"I need to speak with Nate," she said. "It's important."

The barista had purple hair, a nose ring, and a slightly bored expression on her face. "You mean Mr. Murray?"

"Yes," said Miss Josie. She sat at a corner table, crossed her legs, and tapped her foot impatiently. She had on a black and grey checked skirt with a grey cardigan twinset. Her legs were bare, probably because I'd destroyed most of her tights, and her shoes were charcoal grey with pointy toes.

I loved the pointy toes. I hopped on them, batting at them as Miss Josie tapped her foot. Such a fun game, but Miss Josie ignored me, even when I drooled on her. She seemed both preoccupied and pissed off. This analysis was confirmed as soon as Mr. Nate appeared, wearing a navy sweater with a cable knit pattern and a pair of faded jeans. He had his copy of *Pride and Prejudice* in his hands. His face lit up when he saw us, but his joy quickly diminished when he noticed the expression on Miss Josie's face.

"What happened?" he asked. "Did Capone eat something else? Is he okay?"

"He's fine," she said, her voice icy. "But I'm not."

He frowned. "What's wrong?"

She straightened her shoulders. "Do you like putting little old ladies out of business?"

He looked confused. I was confused as well. Mrs. Norris said she planned to close her shop, but she'd never said Mr. Nate forced her to do it.

Mr. Nate pointed over his shoulder to the coffee bar. "Let me grab you a coffee, and we'll chat."

"I don't drink coffee," she said through tightly clenched teeth.

"Fine. Tea. I'll get you some tea."

She stood up and stamped her foot, which I had to admit looked kind of funny, especially with those pointy-toed shoes. "I don't want beverages. I want to know the truth. Are you buying Mrs. Norris's store?"

He swallowed hard and nodded. "Yes, but—" Miss Josie cut him off.

"And did the plans you showed to the city council a few months ago include Bartleby's as well?"

He ran a hand through his curly brown hair. "It's not like that, Josie. I swear."

Her jaw tightened. "You haven't answered my question. Yes, or no? It's pretty simple. Did your plans include tearing down both Bartleby's and the haberdashery to expand your coffee shop?" He gave her one curt nod, and her shoulders slumped. "Then, I don't need to know anything else."

"Let me explain..."

"No, Nate. There is nothing left to say."

She walked out the door, her expression grim. "Never again," she said, looking down at me. "I trusted Nate, but he's a man, and they're all the same. They aren't like men in books, men in real life are..." She paused, trying to come up with the right word and couldn't. "Well, they're not like Mr. Darcy. Not even a little."

Her words made me so upset for her. I licked her bare ankles as a way of showing I cared. She got the message.

"Thanks, buddy," she said, patting me on the head. "Let's go home."

Note to self: A little ankle licking goes a long way.

Mr. Nate might want to give the whole ankle licking thing a try. After all, he couldn't be in more trouble than he was right now.

I let out a frustrated groan. With dogs, it was simple. We sniffed each other's butts and could tell right away if we liked each other or not. Humans were so much more complicated. They puzzled me. Yesterday Miss Josie and Mr. Nate had kissed each other quite affectionately on the couch, but today he made her furious. The PBS special didn't cover this kind of stuff. The back and forth nature of their relationship gave me a bad case of whiplash.

I needed to solve this and soon, before Miss Josie headed down a dark, lonely road. A bitter person could not fall in love or find happiness. I had to help her fix this before it was too late.

EIGHTEEN

Things I should not do during a picnic:

1. Eat all the food.
2. Sit on the picnic basket.
3. Steal the blanket and roll around in the dirt with it.
4. Chase a jogger.

Saturday, the day of our picnic with Doc McHottie and Wrigley, had the makings of an utterly glorious fall day. The sun shone in the sky, and the leaves had begun to change, turning the small park near the municipal building bright with autumn colors.

Ms. Anne had agreed to watch the shop, and Miss Josie promised to be back right after lunch. Doc McHottie packed a large picnic, and Wrigley and I hit it off right away. An older, calmer lab, he provided the yin to my yang, and I felt confident he'd be not only a great friend but also a good influence on me. In my quest for perfect gentleman status, I needed all the good influences I could get.

As soon as we found our picnic spot, Doc McHottie let Wrigley go off leash. Miss Josie hesitated only a second, and then followed suit, eying me warily. I eyed her right back, not sure what to do next. I'd never been unleashed in a public place before, and it felt simultaneously exhilarating and terrifying.

"You're vegetarian, not vegan, right?" asked Doc McHottie as he spread out a red and white checkered cloth on the grass along with some comfy pillows. He'd thought of everything. He even had a bottle of white wine chilling in a tub.

"I'm more of a pescatarian," said Miss Josie.

A big smile spread across Doc McHottie's face. "Me, too. We have so much in common."

"We do," said Miss Josie, her cheeks getting pink as she played with a button on her wool cardigan and smoothed the skirt of her dress. She didn't seem entirely comfortable with this whole dating thing, but how could she not feel great around Doc McHottie? The man was perfect.

As if on cue, he took a dish out with a flourish. "I hope you like quiche."

A veterinarian, a vegetarian, a cowboy, and a homemade quiche maker? If Miss Josie did not fall immediately in love with this man, I decided I might have to snatch him up myself.

As Doc McHottie set up lunch, Wrigley graced me with his wisdom. "The best place to find bunny poo is over here," he said, showing me to an area of grass that seemed greener than the rest. "Free-range bunnies produce the tastiest poo, don't you think?"

I nodded, although I didn't have an opinion on this matter. All bunny poo tasted like good bunny poo to me.

"Are you always off leash like this?" I asked.

"Yes," he said. "But it's important you prove yourself trustworthy. Ignore your instincts and don't get distracted."

Ignore my instincts? I guess I could. I wasn't sure I even had instincts. "It doesn't sound too hard."

He laughed. "You'd be surprised. Of course, I'm older than you. I mastered it a long time ago. Do you know what the most important thing is?"

"What?"

"When your owner uses the command, 'come,' always listen. Run to her as fast as you can, and she'll give you a treat. It never fails. It's like clockwork."

I nodded, absorbing his words. "Run as fast as I can. Got it."

As Doc McHottie pulled one delicious thing after another out of the wicker picnic basket, I tried to investigate all the lovely smells, but he shooed us away. "This is people food, not dog food. And we don't want you to end up with a tummy ache again, do we, Capone?"

Most definitely we did not. I backed away from the quiche, even though it smelled of cheese and I loved cheese.

Doc McHottie lectured Miss Josie about dogs as he poured her a glass of wine. "It's all about your energy. If you're stressed, the dog will be stressed, and it'll make him misbehave."

Miss Josie took a sip. "What if the dog is the cause of my stress?"

I hoped she was joking, but Doc McHottie took her question seriously. "As long as you have rules in place, and follow them, you should have no stress from Capone. He's a great dog. What could go wrong?"

Thank goodness I'd nipped Miss Josie's relationship with Mr. Nate in the bud. Destiny had led her to the handsome cowboy-veterinarian-vegetarian sitting on the blanket next to her. He probably even drank herbal tea. Miss Josie had found a keeper.

"Cheers," he said, raising his glass to her. "May this be the first of many picnics."

"Cheers," she said, and, as they took their first sip of wine, it happened. I heard something, a sound that caused my ears to tingle in anticipation. Was someone running toward us?

Doc McHottie and Miss Josie, with their weak human hearing, were oblivious, but Wrigley heard it too. I saw it on his face. He rose to his feet, ignoring the pile of bunny poo he'd been munching on, and sniffed the air.

"Uh-oh," he said, as the sound of pounding footsteps grew closer. "Don't do it, Capone. We shouldn't..."

His words got cut off by the appearance of a jogger on the path at the far side of the clearing. He hadn't seen us yet, but we'd most certainly seen him.

I did what I had to do. I guess I have instincts after all. I ran straight toward the jogger, and Wrigley followed right behind me.

"Capone, no," screamed Miss Josie. I looked over my shoulder to see her jump to her feet so fast she spilled her chardonnay. "Stop."

I did not stop. Wrigley did not stop either. We ran like the wind.

What was our goal? To catch up with the jogger. What would we do when we reached him? I had absolutely no idea, and I suspected Wrigley didn't either.

The jogger had headphones on, so he didn't hear our approach, nor did he hear Doc McHottie and Miss Josie screaming for us to stop. When we were only a few feet away from him, he turned, incredulous, and what happened next was a total accident. Neither of us intended for the poor man to fall. We wanted to run with him—that was all—to join him as he jogged on the path circling the park. Sadly, we misjudged his speed, and we misjudged our speed, too. When Wrigley and I jumped onto the path in front of him, we blocked his way, and, he lost his balance. He ended up falling, almost as if in slow motion, in a tangle of long legs, tight running shorts, and two slobbery black labs.

Once he landed on the ground, the fun did not end. Oh, no. Wrigley and I positioned ourselves on top of him, paws on his chest, and proceeded to lick his face and the other bits of exposed skin. He had on shorts and a tank shirt, and he was a tall, lanky man. We had a great deal of exposed skin to lick.

The jogger seemed stunned and maybe a little shell-shocked. I licked him some more, thinking it would help. It didn't, especially when my tongue accidentally slipped into his mouth as he called for help.

"Come. Now," said Doc McHottie. Wrigley shot up and ran, quick as a wink, back to Doc McHottie's side.

"Capone. Come here right now. I mean it," said Miss Josie.

When I actually listened to her, I think it surprised us both. I got up and ran as fast as my puppy legs would carry me. I ran past Doc McHottie, who scolded Wrigley (now on leash), and past Miss Josie, who held a dog biscuit in one hand, and my leash in the other. I shot past both of them and headed straight to the place with the highest volume of delectable treats. The picnic area.

Let me say, although I do have some regrets, they are mostly about the jogger. A nice guy, he probably wouldn't file charges against Doc McHottie and Miss Josie for allowing their dogs off leash in a park marked with signs saying clearly, "All dogs must be kept on a leash." He insisted we hadn't hurt him, although he had a skinned knee and probably a bruised ego as well.

What don't I regret? Running straight back to the picnic lunch and scarfing up as much food as possible. Let me tell you, quiche tastes as delicious as it smells, but sandwiches made out of tofu instead of chicken salad? Uh, no, thanks. Tofu was not something I ever cared to taste again.

Miss Josie caught up with me as I polished off the last of the quiche. I didn't even see her coming since I was so completely engrossed in eating. Before I noticed, she had me hooked to the leash again. She shot Doc McHottie a dirty look.

"It was not a good idea to let the dogs off leash."

Doc McHottie frowned. "I didn't realize Capone couldn't follow simple commands."

Ms. Josie's dirty look got dirtier. "Wrigley didn't listen to you either."

He held up his hands. "Point taken, but I still think—"

She cut him off, looking at her watch. "I'd better get back to work," she said and began picking up the remains of the picnic scattered all over the grass in front of her.

"Stop, Josie. You don't need to help. I'll clean it up. It's the least I can do."

"Well, fine. It's been...interesting. See you later."

As we left, Doc McHottie gave Miss Josie a sad little wave. I felt bad for him.

Note to self: Doc McHottie is a Bingley, not a Mr. Darcy.

Being Charles Bingley didn't signify he was a bad guy. I mean, Jane Bennet liked him well enough. But Miss Josie needed to understand she could never be like Jane Bennet, which meant she could never fall for Charles Bingley.

"You were a bad dog today," said Miss Josie as we

stomped back to her car. "I'm glad I signed you up for training. Monday can't come soon enough."

Was she angry at me, or at Doc McHottie? I had no idea. Human behavior remained a mystery. Unfortunately, dog behavior was a mystery as well. Monday was going to be interesting.

NINETEEN

Ways to rock an obedience class:

1. Listen to the instructor.
2. Listen to Miss Josie.
3. Stand next to the worst dog in the room.
4. Make the other dog owners green with envy.
5. Try to come home without any infectious diseases.

Monday morning, we arrived at obedience training early. Miss Josie did not want to suffer the wrath of Sexy Trainer Dude if she came in late. He'd already chastised her once. She preferred not to repeat the experience.

"You're going to behave," she said, as we pulled into Misty Mountain. "You'll listen to the trainer and me, and you won't be so...." She looked at me, trying to come up with the right word. "Capone-ish."

Oh, calamity. I was Capone-ish. I mean, I didn't murder anyone, and I hadn't transported illegal contraband, but I lacked the same thing Al Capone had.

Impulse control.

If I'd learned anything from watching the PBS special on Regency gentlemen or *Pride and Prejudice*, it was that being a gentleman required many things, but impulse control topped the list. If a gentleman couldn't contain his baser instincts, he wouldn't be a gentleman at all.

Note to self: Stop being so Capone-ish.

As we lined up for obedience class, my thoughts churned. How could I manage to control these urges? I decided this might be my chance to learn and prove to Miss Josie I could be taught. She had her doubts, although I didn't blame her.

Before class, Sexy Trainer Dude gave Miss Josie a nod. "I see you made it on time, Miss St. Clair. I'm glad I won't have to punish you today."

"Me, too," Miss Josie said with a snort. "Although there's always next time…"

As her voice faded, I shook my head in embarrassment. Could she be more awkward? She'd attempted to sound witty, I guess, but instead, she came off as kinky.

Sexy Trainer Dude cleared his throat. "Well, let's get started."

We gathered in a large, open training room with easy to clean mats on the floor. I understood why those mats were necessary when the schnauzer next to me squatted and peed. The little dog's owner looked mortified.

"We've only been here two minutes, for heaven's sake," she said, and quickly ran to grab paper towels and a bottle of spray cleaner. When another dog peed, Sexy Trainer Dude rolled his crystal blue eyes.

"First rule of puppy class. Your dogs should relieve themselves before they come inside. If they didn't, please go outside and take care of it now."

About half the class shuffled out guiltily. Miss Josie did not. She'd taken me out to pee twice already, which probably made her feel rather smug.

Luke the Lab had come with his owner, No Brows. They stood across the room from us. Luke gave me a friendly wag of his tail. No Brows scowled at me. She scowled at Miss Josie, too. She was a scowly kind of person.

Sexy Trainer Dude stood in the center of the circle, his expression bored and yet resigned. "Welcome to puppy training. By the time you finish this class, your dog will know how to sit, stay, lie down, and come when you call. We'll also work on loose leash walking and how to behave around other dogs."

Most of the puppies either vibrated with excitement or barked at each other. I sniffed the poodle next to me, remembering Jackson's words about poodles being a good kind of crazy, but otherwise remained calm. The effort required was extraordinary. I wanted to bark and wiggle and prance, but I kept saying to myself, "Be Mr. Darcy. Be Mr. Darcy," and somehow it worked.

Would Mr. Darcy pee on the floor? No. Would Mr. Darcy bark at other puppies? No. Would Mr. Darcy lick his cojones? Definitely not.

By channeling Mr. Darcy, I turned my first obedience class into a rousing success. And when Sexy Trainer Dude taught a new skill, he used me four times to demonstrate how it should be done.

I'd turned into an obedience training rock star. It was awesome.

"Capone is doing great," said Sexy Trainer Dude as the other dog owners milled around, working on loose leash walking. "Hiking is a good way to release some of his energy. Do you like to hike?"

Miss Josie nodded. "Sure. Of course."

I had to laugh at the outright lie. I'm sure Miss Josie enjoyed reading about hiking, but I doubted she'd ever spent any real time in an actual forest. Her idea of being outdoorsy meant sitting on the back patio as she sipped wine.

"Maybe we could hike together sometime. I could bring my dog, Hans. He's a German shepherd. He'll teach Capone the ropes."

Dear Lord. Didn't any of the males in this town have girlfriends? Or wives? They all seemed to be on the prowl, and they were all abnormally interested in Miss Josie.

Maybe she emitted a smell I hadn't picked up on yet. Although I knew little about mating in general, and even less about mating in humans, I knew dogs sent out specific signals while in heat. Was Miss Josie in heat? It certainly seemed that way.

Miss Josie gave him a coquettish look. I'm sure part of his allure was the fact Sexy Trainer Dude could teach her how to control me, so she agreed to meet him for a hike in Brady's Run Park.

As we resumed class, she and Sexy Trainer Dude kept sharing flirty smiles. I liked it when Miss Josie smiled. When he called me over to demonstrate the final skill for the class, I thought No Brows' head might explode. Luke was an obedience class failure today, and No Brows had a bad case of dog envy.

Luke and I discussed it when we went to the dog park after class so all the puppies could play together. "She's intense," he said. "But she makes homemade dog biscuits. Cool, right?"

"Does she let you sleep in her bed?"

"Of course," he said.

I shook my head. "You're so lucky, dude."

"I am," he said. "By the way, I pretend not to understand this obedience stuff to mess with her. When I screw up in class, she lets me stay extra-long at the dog park, and forces Daddy to work with me at home. I love Daddy. He's not a lunatic like Mumsy."

"You call them 'Daddy' and 'Mumsy'?"

He laughed. "I know. Weird, right? Hey, whatever makes them happy."

Maybe Luke wasn't as dumb as I thought. No Brows had turned into putty in his paws, and he took Machiavellian glee in tormenting her.

Brilliant, and with an evil streak. Who would have thought?

Note to self: Scary things often come in small packages.

No Brows approached and grabbed my little buddy by the collar. "Get away from him, Luke. There's something wrong with his eye."

"What do you mean?" asked Miss Josie.

No Brows pointed at me. "Your dog's eye. Look at it. It's goopy."

Miss Josie frowned. "It is not."

"Yes, it is," said No Brows with a laugh. "Don't say I didn't warn you."

It turned out No Brows was right. I ended up coming home with more than just happy memories of my time at the puppy park.

"What is wrong with your eye?" asked Miss Josie as she opened my crate the next morning.

I smiled up at her, as pleasant as could be, although it was a little hard to see her through the thick mucus covering my eye. I wiggled over to her and wiped my goopy eye on her robe. I couldn't help it. It itched, and she provided a handy scratching post of sorts. She grimaced in disgust.

"This means I have to take you to the vet. Again."

I perked up. Another trip to the vet? Cool. Maybe Miss Josie would forgive Doc McHottie for the picnic debacle and agree to go out with him again, although I wasn't sure how it worked since she'd already decided to go out with Sexy Trainer Dude. Miss Josie's dating life resembled a revolving door at this point. I'd only seen revolving doors in movies, but they seemed terrifying.

Miss Josie called the vet and managed to snag an appointment. Ms. Anne agreed to come to hang out in the shop until Mrs. Steele arrived so Miss Josie could take me. She didn't bring Gracie, probably because she didn't want her dog to get "The Crud," and she waved away Miss Josie's apology about the added expense of yet another vet visit.

"This is how things go with puppies," she said, clucking her tongue sympathetically. "Think before you lick, Capone. That's what I always say."

Wait. Licking caused this? Curse my wandering tongue.

Miss Josie shot her a dirty look. "This is all your fault, you know," she said, but Ms. Anne didn't seem upset.

"You love Capone, admit it, and he's been great for your social life. You haven't had this many dates in, well, ever."

"I don't need a puppy to meet men," she muttered, but then she frowned, as the wheels turned in her head. "Oh, gosh. Maybe I do."

"Speaking of men, how's your friend from next door?"

She seemed surprised by Ms. Anne's question. "Nate? He's not my friend. Do you know what he did to poor Mrs. Norris?"

"The hat lady?"

"He's putting her out of business."

She proceeded to tell Ms. Anne the whole sordid tale. Oddly, Ms. Anne didn't seem as upset by it as Miss Josie. "So basically, she's retiring?"

"Because he's forcing her to do it," said Miss Josie, still full of righteous indignation. "He's throwing a sweet, old woman out on the street. It's awful. And he had plans to put me out of business, too. He admitted as much himself."

Ms. Anne frowned. "It doesn't sound like that, Josie..."

A knock at the door interrupted their discussion. Mr. Nate stood on the doorstep with two coffees in his hands.

"Speak of the devil," said Ms. Anne with a cheery smile as she opened the door. "Hello, Nate."

Miss Josie turned away from him and began shelving books in the back of the room. Her shoulders were tense, and she didn't so much as glance his way, but Mr. Nate couldn't seem to keep his eyes off of her.

"I think I'm still in the doghouse," he said.

"Not in my book, Mr. Murray, especially if one of those coffees is for me."

He took a cup out of the carrier and handed it to her. "Two creams and one sugar," he said. "The way you like it. The other is for Josie."

"What did you make for her this time?" she asked.

"Café Bombón," he said. "A Spanish coffee. My usual tricks weren't working on her, so I decided to pull something crazy out of the bag."

"Crazy is probably a good idea," said Ms. Anne, her voice soft. "She's mad at you, you know, but you bring it out in her for some reason. I've never seen her get this mad at anyone else."

I listened, intrigued. What was Ms. Anne trying to say exactly?

"Any idea why?" asked Mr. Nate.

She pursed her lips. "I have a theory, but I think you need to figure it out on your own."

His gaze went back to Miss Josie. "On my own? That's doubtful."

"It's worth the effort. Trust me."

Were they speaking in code? I was so confused.

Mr. Nate pulled a letter out of his pocket and handed it to Ms. Anne. "What's this?" she asked.

"Josie didn't want to hear my side of the story," he said. "But I thought maybe if I put it in writing..."

"You wrote her a letter?" asked Ms. Anne, her eyes twinkling as she put a hand over her heart.

He stuttered. "To explain what happened. Josie misunderstood. She's quick to jump to conclusions, you know."

"I do know," said Ms. Anne with a wink. "And she's pretty quick to forgive and forget as well. I'll make sure she gets it."

"Thanks, Anne," he said, his brown eyes filled with sincerity. "I mean it."

"I'm not doing this for you, silly man, although I do like you, and your coffee. I'm doing it for Josie. I think you're good for each other."

He leaned closer. "I'll bring you coffee all the time, if that's what it takes."

She grinned at him. "Deal."

TWENTY

Things you can acquire at a dog park:

1. New friends.
2. Great memories.
3. Social skills.
4. Conjunctivitis.
5. Herpes.

Doc McHottie looked down at me, his face sympathetic and kind. Or, at least I thought his expression conveyed those emotions. It was hard to tell for sure due to all the mucus covering my eyes.

"Conjunctivitis. It's common when dogs hang out around other dogs," he said, wiping away the slime.

"Pink eye?"

He nodded. "The canine form, but he has something else as well."

"What?"

He touched my lip with his rubber glove. "Doggie herpes. Or, rather, canine oral papilloma."

All the color drained from Miss Josie's face and she sank into a chair. When her eyes met mine, I recalled all the lovely doggie kisses I'd given her recently. Lots and lots of doggie kisses. Sweet, slobbery, enthusiastic doggie kisses. All over her face.

Note to self: At least it wasn't syphilis.

"Is it contagious?" asked Miss Josie, a hand on her throat.

"Yes," he said, and when she let out a gasp, he waved his hand and clarified. "Not to humans, of course. He probably picked it up at Misty Mountain, along with the conjunctivitis."

"He got the conjunctivitis yesterday?"

He wiped some of the goo from my eyes. "No. It takes a few days for it to set in."

"Luke," she muttered under her breath. She might be right. No Brows seemed to notice my symptoms, and my goopy eye, pretty quickly.

Doc McHottie prescribed some cream for my eye. "He doesn't need anything for the bump on his lip unless it starts to bother him. It should resolve on its own."

"Good," said Miss Josie, still pale from the shock of my herpes diagnosis. I had a feeling I would not be kissing her on the lips any time soon. I also had the feeling she planned to take a hot shower the moment we got home.

As Miss Josie turned to leave, Doc McHottie stopped her. "Josephine, I'm sorry about what happened at the picnic. It wasn't how I intended things to go."

"Me neither," she said.

"And I should have been more cautious about letting the dogs off leash."

"It's okay," she said. "How could you have known Capone is a nut job?"

Hey, wait a minute. Did Miss Josie call me a nut job? I tried to get a good look at her face, but couldn't, due to the thick layer of ointment Doc McHottie had slathered all over my eyes. I blinked, tilting my head to one side. A strange sensation, and it made me think of how poor Mr. Rochester must have felt in the PBS version of *Jane Eyre* we'd seen the other night.

Hmmm. Mr. Rochester could be the right name for me. In my currently visually impaired state, it fit. I nudged Miss Josie, trying to do a good Mr. Rochester imitation. She didn't get it.

"Would you care to try again?" he asked, taking off his gloves and handing her the tube of ointment. "Maybe this Saturday?"

She already had a date on Saturday. How awkward. "I'm, uh, busy that day. Would Sunday work for you?"

"Sure," he said. "Even better."

I looked up at Miss Josie and winked, although, in all honesty, the wink may have been a side effect of conjunctivitis and all the cream on my eyes. Miss Josie, thinking we'd shared a sign of solidarity, gave me a pat on the head.

As we walked back to the bookstore, I realized Miss Josie had come a long way in her quest not to shut herself off from the world. She'd met up a few times with her old college roommate for dinner and drinks. They hadn't seen each other in years. And she'd gotten in touch with some of her other friends as well. No one seemed to hold the whole Cedric thing against her, or resent her in any way, so she'd been worried about nothing.

Also, two handsome men had invited her on dates in two days. At this rate, she'd find her Mr. Darcy in no time flat.

But, when we passed the coffee shop, Miss Josie paused,

her eyes sad. She hadn't read Mr. Nate's letter yet. I wondered if she ever would.

Jackson glanced at me through the window of the café, giving me a forlorn little wag of his tail. I missed my friend Jackson. I missed Mr. Nate, too.

That night Miss Josie made me a special dinner and, after carefully cleaning my eyes, allowed me up on the couch with her to watch *Persuasion*. It gave me a new hero to admire, Captain Wentworth, and it also made me realize the importance of letter writing.

Although I knew I might be making a terrible mistake, I thought Miss Josie should at least take a look at Mr. Nate's letter. I picked it up off the coffee table and brought it over to her.

"You're right, puppy. I should read it."

I wagged my tail encouragingly. She took it out of its envelope and read each word, her face solemn. After she finished, she folded it carefully and put it back. I watched her, trying to figure out what might be going on in her head, but I didn't have a clue. As well as I thought I knew Miss Josie, a lot about her still remained a mystery.

TWENTY-ONE

Reasons why Miss Josie should not hike in the woods:

1. She doesn't like hiking.
2. Her scent is like a siren's call to insects.
3. She lacks the proper equipment.
4. Sweating is not her favorite pastime.
5. Bears.

Sexy Trainer Dude waited for us at the entrance to the trail, a backpack on one strong shoulder and a large German shepherd by his side. He had on khaki shorts, a khaki shirt, and even khaki socks peeking up above his khaki hiking boots. Khaki must be his color.

I greeted the German shepherd with my tail wagging. He sat completely still; his gaze focused intently on a point above my head. He looked more like a statue of a dog than an actual dog. I'd never sat still more than ten consecutive seconds in my whole life.

Miss Josie tried to hold me back, but I was over forty pounds of wiggly, wagging happiness. I wanted to sniff my new friend and give him licks and love, but Sexy Trainer Dude stopped me with one glance of his ice-blue eyes.

"Capone. Sit."

As if on its own volition, my bottom planted itself firmly on the ground. It was the weirdest thing, like my butt had a brain, and Sexy Trainer Dude spoke directly to it.

It didn't put an end to my wiggling, though. And, even though I sat nicely, I couldn't stop wagging my tail.

"This is Hans," said Sexy Trainer Dude, nodding to the German shepherd. Hans still didn't move. I practically vibrated with excitement, but Hans showed absolutely no emotion at all.

Even Miss Josie seemed confused. "Is he okay?"

"Of course," said Sexy Trainer Dude. "And, with enough training, your dog can be like this too."

Miss Josie watched Hans with a confused frown on her face. "How do you get him to move?"

"Easy." Sexy Trainer Dude turned to Hans. "Take a break."

Hans relaxed and gave me a sniff. "Greetings. I am Hans. Who are you?"

"Uh...Capone."

He wrinkled his German shepherd eyebrows at me. "Uh, Capone?"

Wow. This guy took literal to a whole new level. "Capone. Just Capone."

"I am Hans."

"Yeah, you told me." Hans narrowed his eyes at me, and I took a step backward. "But it doesn't matter, of course. It's good to be clear on these things."

He nodded once, and I have to admit I felt relieved. "Walk time. Move it," he said.

Note to self: Hans has issues.

Sexy Trainer Dude took us high into the mountains, up narrow, muddy paths and next to steep, dangerous looking cliffs. I'd assumed this would be a casual trek, but it felt like an endurance test. Not for me, of course. I bounced along happily but I worried about Miss Josie. Power hiking wasn't her thing.

Thankfully, she'd skipped her usual skirt and tights combo today. Instead, she wore yoga pants, a light jacket, and a pair of Toms—perfectly acceptable garb for a walk on a paved path, but not as useful for mountain climbing. After an hour of strenuous hiking, her hair frizzed and fell out of her ponytail, and she looked sweaty and tired.

Sexy Trainer Dude plodded ahead, focused on his steady climb and seemingly unaware of her current distress. To make matters worse, something about the way she smelled, like gardenias and honeysuckle, attracted all the stinging gnats and bugs in the forest. She had so many bites on her face; it looked like a bad case of chicken pox, and a swarm of gnats surrounded her in a buzzing cloud as she climbed.

Misery, thy name is Josephine.

"Didn't you use bug spray?" asked Sexy Trainer Dude as Miss Josie attempted to wave away the bugs hovering around her head.

"I did not," she said. "I thought we were going for a walk."

He stared at her, his expression blank and emotionless. "I specifically said 'hike.'"

"Maybe we have different definitions about what the word means."

When we finally reached the top of the mountain, Miss Josie sank onto a rock in relief and exhaled slowly, looking around. The view was beautiful, the hills around us alight with brilliant fall colors. She still smelled like honeysuckle and gardenia, but now she carried a whiff of sweat and annoyance as well. Hans kept staring at her, and I could tell it creeped her out, mostly because she said as much to Sexy Trainer Dude.

"Why does he keep looking at me?" she asked. "It creeps me out."

Hans sat a few feet away from her, staring directly into her eyes. Definitely the weirdest dog I'd ever met.

Sexy Trainer Dude, who'd been in the process of spreading out a large, blue blanket on the ground, turned and looked at him. "He's guarding you."

"From what?" she asked, frowning and looking over her shoulder. We were alone on top of the mountain. It seemed pretty safe.

"From anything that might want to harm you." Sexy Trainer Dude opened the large backpack he carried and handed Miss Josie an apple. "As would I."

She took the apple, staring up at him with an awed expression. I could understand why. With his broad shoulders, chiseled chin, blond hair, and piercing blue eyes, he looked like a statue of Adonis standing on top of a mountain. Or maybe Bear Grylls. He was neat, organized, punctual, and ruggedly attractive. He appeared capable of protecting not only Miss Josie, but the entire population of Beaver, and he could do it without even breaking a sweat. He was probably a hardcore survivalist as well. He had a certain look about him, like he'd eaten bugs and enjoyed it. Of course, I'd eaten bugs and enjoyed it, too, but I was a dog, not a human.

He sat down next to Miss Josie on the rock. "The first time I saw you, I knew you were special."

Miss Josie nearly choked on the bite of apple she'd

taken. "Because I showed up late and had dog food stuck to my face?"

He brushed a lock of hair behind her ear. "I could tell. I have good instincts."

"Like Hans?"

"Even better than Hans," he said, seriously.

He leaned forward and pressed his lips against hers. A bold move, and I got the distinct impression Miss Josie wasn't into it. Maybe because she absentmindedly scratched at a bug bite on her wrist as he kissed her, or perhaps it had to do with the way she never once climbed on top of him, as she had with Mr. Nate, or ran her fingers through his hair. She just, well, sat there. Until it was over and Sexy Trainer Dude backed away, a satisfied smile on his perfect lips.

"Well worth scaling a mountain for, wasn't it?"

She blinked at him in surprise. "Excuse me?"

He held out a hand, indicating the vista of rolling hills and forest in front of them. "The view. It's spectacular. I bet you regret all of your complaining now."

"I wasn't complaining—" she said, but he interrupted her.

"Yes, you were."

Bored with their conversation, I turned to Hans, who was curled up on a large boulder, relaxing. At least, I assumed he was relaxing. He still looked pretty tense to me.

"What do you do for fun, Hans?" I asked.

His eyebrows drew together in a frown. "Fun? I don't have time for fun. I'm a lethal weapon in fur. I know fifty ways to kill a man and leave no evidence."

I did not want to know what he meant about killing people and not leaving evidence. It sounded like he might eat his victims, which made my tummy feel worse than eating those mildly toxic peony bushes.

"Is that even possible?" I hadn't meant to ask the question out loud, but, when I did, Hans bristled.

"Are you calling me a liar?" His words came out as a growl, which made Sexy Trainer Dude elicit a short, soft whistle. Hans immediately went back into his ramrod straight, seated, robotic dog position. I couldn't decide which was worse, Hans bragging about killing people or Hans acting liked a stuffed replica of a German shepherd.

"Why did he growl at Capone?" asked Miss Josie.

Sexy Trainer Dude shrugged. "It's hard for him to deal with a dog like yours."

"Like mine?"

"Undisciplined. Untrained. Unmanaged," he said, handing her a plastic container. "Jerky?"

"Excuse me?"

He nodded toward the container. "Homemade deer jerky. Have some. It's a great source of protein. I killed this particular deer myself."

She wrinkled her nose. "No, thanks. I'm a vegetarian."

He seemed confused. "Why?"

"Why didn't I tell you...?"

"No. Why are you a vegetarian? Humans are carnivores. You can't go against your nature. You need to accept it and embrace it. Fighting against it is...pointless. And stupid."

"Are you calling me stupid?"

Sexy Trainer Dude, as clueless as he was, realized he'd gone too far this time. "I didn't mean *you* were stupid. I meant being a *vegetarian* is stupid."

"Wow. Okay. This hike has been great fun, but I think I'm ready to go back down now."

He blinked in surprise. "But we just got here. We haven't eaten lunch yet, and I brought a blanket. We could enjoy a romantic interlude under the splendor of the fall leaves."

Miss Josie grimaced, like she'd may have thrown up in her mouth, and shook her head. "Uh-no. It's not going to happen. I'm leaving now."

"You can't go on your own. You'll get lost."

When she turned to leave, he reached for her arm, and I didn't like it—not one bit. I jumped between them, hackles raised and growled at him. He immediately raised his hands in the air.

"He's exhibiting protective behavior. Excellent. A good sign." He grinned at her, for the first time showing real emotion. Smiling made him seem almost normal. "I have great hopes for this pup. Yes, he is rough around the edges, but he's a smart one. With proper training, he could do anything. He could be a service dog, a K-9 search and rescue, or maybe even compete in conformation."

"Confirmation?" asked Miss Josie, looking confused. I was confused, too. Sexy Trainer Dude, it turned out, actually liked me. Who knew?

"Not confirmation, conformation. Capone could be a show dog. He has all the quintessential lab characteristics, and he's a beauty. He could be a winner if only he could learn to control his energy levels. He's still pretty much off the charts." He glanced back at the blanket he'd tossed onto the ground, the one he'd brought for their romantic interlude. "So, what do you say, Josephine? I brought mixed nuts. These are vegetarian, right?" He pulled a giant bag of nuts from his backpack, and the aroma of peanuts filled the air. "Do you want to hang out, nibble on some nuts, and chat before we head back?"

Oddly enough, the phrase "nibble on some nuts" sounded utterly normal. It was the way he said the word "chat," however, that made me think he didn't mean he wanted to engage in a deep and meaningful conversational exchange with Miss Josie. It sounded more like he wanted to exchange something else with her...probably bodily fluids of some kind.

If he kissed her again, I might seriously gag. It would be like kissing Hans.

Note to self: I never want to kiss Hans.

Fortunately, Miss Josie didn't fall for his attempt to play nice. "No. I'm good. See you later." She picked up her backpack and started walking toward the trail but froze when a noise came from the bushes. It sounded like something big, and it smelled awful.

Hans's ears pricked up and he grew even more alert. Sexy Trainer Dude bent his knees slightly, crouching down into what seemed like a martial arts pose, which looked extremely funny since he still held the bag of nuts in one hand.

"Did you hear something?" asked Miss Josie, her voice soft and her eyes focused on the movement in the bushes near the path.

Hans sniffed the air with a whine. "Oh, no, oh, no, oh, no," he said. "I don't like this. Scary, scary, scary."

"You're freaking me out, Hans," I said. "What is it?"

He didn't even look at me. "Scary, scary, big and scary," he said, trembling with fear. The humans, nervous enough already, noticed Hans's reaction and their anxiety levels went up about ten notches.

Sexy Trainer Dude, still in his pseudo-Karate Kid position, sniffed the air as well, getting pale. "It smells like a bear, and something is attracting it to us. Are you wearing perfume?"

Miss Josie's eyes widened. "A little. Honeysuckle and gardenia. Why?"

His jaw tightened. "Who wears perfume on a hike? Are you completely clueless? Honeysuckle and gardenia. Why don't you wear a shirt saying, 'Bear Bait' on it or something?"

"Bears can't read, so it makes no sense at all. You need to calm down," she said, shooting him a dirty look. "And tell me what we have to do."

He edged toward her, still in his crouched position and still holding his nuts. "Hans will take care of it. He's a trained attack dog. He'll get rid of the bear. Watch him."

Hans's eyebrows shot up. "He wants me to take on a bear?"

"You're a lethal weapon. You said it. Go take care of the bear, Hans," I said. "By the way, what's a bear?"

I got my answer when a large black bear lumbered out from the undergrowth and headed straight toward us. Although the bear meandered and didn't charge, he was still huge and pretty scary.

"Go get him, Hans," said Sexy Trainer Dude. "Attack."

Hans turned to me and said, "Run. Run for your life," and took off down the path. I will say one thing for Hans, he might not be courageous, but he was fast.

Sexy Trainer Dude's face flushed with fury. A lethal weapon in fur? More like a super wimp with a hairy coat. Not what I expected from my pal, Hans. What kind of gentleman deserted a lady in need? Hans, I suspected, might be an insult to his breed.

"I don't think Hans is going to help us," said Miss Josie,

her voice surprisingly steady for someone about to get eaten by a bear. "What's Plan B?"

"Plan B?" asked Sexy Trainer Dude.

Uh-oh. He didn't have a Plan B.

The bear came closer, and I did what I had to do. Something primal and instinctual took over, and I jumped in front of Miss Josie, barking and snarling and growling at the bear like a thing possessed, a demon dog of unbridled power and fury. It wasn't a conscious decision. My internal drive to protect Miss Josie at all costs outweighed my fear.

The bear paused, unsure how to deal with me. I may have only been forty pounds, but I was forty pounds of unpredictable craziness as far as the bear knew. I thought I caught a glimpse of indecision in his big, brown eyes. He wondered if dealing with me would be worth the trouble.

Sexy Trainer Dude dropped his nuts and mumbled softly as he backed down the path. "Don't turn, don't run. You are mightier than the bear; you are stronger than the bear; you are smarter than the bear."

Miss Josie blew out a slow breath, heavy with exasperation, and backed down the path next to him, taking slow, measured steps. Sexy Trainer Dude continued repeating his mantra, moving at a steady pace. He'd made it a good ten feet further down the path than Miss Josie, which I thought seemed as ungentlemanly as Hans's sprint down the hill.

I realized something. Sexy Trainer Dude, for all his discipline and dedication, was like Hans. Nothing but a big chicken. I smelled his fear, which probably meant the bear could, too.

Miss Josie, oddly enough, did not smell like fear. She smelled like courage, with a hint of resolve. It surprised me, because this was obviously out of the realm of Miss Josie's experience, but she was resourceful. She reached, ever so calmly, into the side pocket of her backpack and pulled out a pink polka-dot umbrella.

Clever Miss Josie. An umbrella might not do any good against a bear, but she wisely utilized the weapons at her disposal and showed far more composure than Hans and Sexy Trainer Dude combined.

Miss Josie didn't require a gentleman at the moment. She needed something else entirely. To protect her from a wild animal, I had to release my inner wildness. I needed to be both brave and a little psycho.

I needed to be Capone-ish.

I stopped trying to channel Mr. Darcy and let out the beast inside me. My hackles rose. I barred my puppy teeth. I displayed confidence I didn't feel as I continued to growl and bark at the bear, easing my way slowly down the path with Miss Josie.

I stayed right in front of her the whole time. She'd dropped my leash when the bear first made its appearance, but it didn't matter. She didn't need the leash to keep me close. We worked as a unit, without words, toward a common goal—getting out of this forest and back to Miss Josie's shop.

The bear stood up on its hind legs, massive and terrifying, and Sexy Trainer Dude did something surprising. He let out a startled gasp and promptly wet his pants. The muscular man with a khaki obsession and the profile of a warrior god peed in his shorts at the sight of a bear. I smelled it as soon as it happened. Miss Josie didn't have my olfactory abilities, but she heard the soft sounds of his tinkling and turned in time to see the wetness spreading across the front of his shorts. She rolled her eyes in disgust.

"You've got to be kidding me," she said, keeping her voice soft. We now stood nearly twenty feet away from the bear, but, quite literally, we weren't out of the woods yet. Not by a long shot.

I wondered what to do. If I got the bear's attention, it might give Miss Josie and Sexy Trainer Dude (whose name should have been Mr. Potty Pants at this point), the chance to run away, but I didn't want to leave Miss Josie's side. As I pondered this, something interesting happened. The bear went back down on all fours, grabbed Sexy Trainer Dude's bag of nuts, and took off in the opposite direction. In seconds, he left, vanishing quickly into the forest.

Exhaling in relief, Miss Josie pulled me into a hug. She trembled as all the fear she'd suppressed while facing the bear came to the surface in a rush, but she was okay. I licked her face, wagging my tail, and she let me, in spite of the recent herpes scare.

I'd done it. I'd helped protect Miss Josie from the wild creatures of the forest. I was so proud I thought I might burst, and she seemed rather pleased with me as well.

She kissed the top of my head. "You are the best, bravest, most wonderful dog ever."

I had to agree with her. I was rather outstanding. To my great surprise, however, I'd earned this praise not by acting like a gentleman, but by doing quite the opposite.

Miss Josie picked up my leash, and we headed home, not saying a word to Sexy Trainer Dude. He followed us, shoulders slumped, shorts still damp with urine. I imagined it must be uncomfortable, and would probably chafe his inner thighs, but his internal chafing had to be even worse.

Note to self: Sexy Trainer Dude was no Darcy.

He'd revealed his true identity at last. He reminded me of the wimpy John Thorpe, from *Northanger Abbey*, and his dog was even worse. I, on the other hand, had comported myself like an absolute hero. Who would have thought?

When we got to our vehicles, we discovered Hans crouched under his owner's jeep, trembling in terror. When Sexy Trainer Dude opened the door, he hopped inside, tail between his legs.

Sexy Trainer Dude climbed into the driver's seat of his jeep and took off, without a word or a glance at Miss Josie. Oh, well. What could he say?

Sorry I brought a bag of nuts so large they attracted a pre-hibernating bear on a feeding frenzy. Sorry I blamed it on your perfume. Sorry my dog is a coward who ran away when we needed him most. Sorry I wet my pants when the bear got up on his hind legs. Sorry I invited you on this hike in the first place.

Yeah. Not going to happen. Better for Sexy Trainer Dude to drive off and end this painful episode without further ado.

I sat in the passenger seat next to Miss Josie, smiling from ear to ear. I couldn't help it. I'd taken on a bear for her. If my actions didn't prove my love and devotion, what would?

"You deserve a special treat," she said. "How about ice cream? I know just the place."

We drove back to Beaver and had ice cream at a shop called Witch Flavor. They gave me a special dog cone, and it tasted amazing. Even more amazing? The way Miss Josie bragged about me as we stood in line.

"This puppy saved me from a bear. Isn't he incredible?"

They all agreed. One person even called me a superhero.

Capone the Wonder Dog.

It had a certain ring to it. Not as nice as Mr. Darcy, or even Fitzwilliam, but it wasn't half bad.

TWENTY-TWO

How a gentleman shows romantic interest in a lady:

1. He compliments her frequently.
2. He woos her with undivided attention.
3. He bestows flowers upon her.
4. He visits her and strolls with her in the park if properly chaperoned.
5. He writes her letters as a way to show affection.
6. He asks her to dance.
7. He brings treats for her dog.

Okay, I made up the last one. The others hailed from Regency times. I preferred the old ways, but they probably wouldn't have worked out well for Miss Josie. She broke all the Regency rules.

Here we were in the park once again, drinking wine, eating cheese, and flirting with the virile vet. But he worked hard not to mess things up this time. He kept Wrigley on a leash, fed Miss Josie lots of yummy food, plied her with alcohol, and wooed her with his undivided attention.

"Capone fought off a bear?" He leaned back on one elbow on the blanket, grinning up at Miss Josie, his green eyes sparkling. "Did he think the bear was made of cheese or something?"

I looked at him in surprise, long strings of drool hanging out both sides of my mouth. The drool was not my fault. I blamed the brie. It smelled incredible.

Miss Josie, wearing a dark blue dress with tiny falling leaves all over it and a matching blue cardigan, tights, and shoes, looked perfectly dressed for a fall picnic in the park. Doc McHottie had on jeans, a flannel shirt, and (gasp) real leather cowboy boots. I think Miss Josie was kind of into his boots. She kept glancing at them and turning pink in the face.

Miss Josie definitely had a fetish for all things cowboy. It made me wonder what else might lurk under her genteel, bookish exterior.

They had a lovely lunch, and they let me sample the brie—what a delight. I played in the leaves with Wrigley and didn't try to eat a jogger. It was a perfect day, and as Doc McHottie walked Miss Josie back to Bartleby's, he held her hand.

"They like each other," said Wrigley.

"How can you tell?" I asked.

"It's the way she looks at him and the way he's always trying to touch her. It's in the nice things he does for her, such as packing the food and wine he knows she likes for lunch. But, do you know what the real indicator is?"

"No. What?"

"The kiss. It's always the kiss. Either the magic is there, or it isn't."

When we reached the door of Bartleby's, Wrigley and I waited expectantly for Doc McHottie to make his move.

"Here it comes," said Wrigley. "The kiss. You can tell by the way they're looking at each other. It's about to happen."

Sadly, Wrigley was mistaken. Rather than gathering Miss Josie into his arms for a romantic embrace, Doc McHottie gave her a rather tepid, and somewhat brotherly, kiss on the cheek.

I shot Wrigley a look of surprise. "Was that it?"

He frowned. "I'm not sure. I think it has to be on the mouth, but these things take time. You have to be patient."

Note to self: I hate being patient.

"Do you want to go to Beaver Tales together Friday night?" asked Doc McHottie. "It's the storytelling event at the gazebo in Irvine Park. The dogs could come, too."

"Sure," said Miss Josie. "This time I'll bring the food."

"Wonderful. See you then."

As he and Wrigley walked away, he whistled a happy tune. Miss Josie did not whistle, but she seemed pleased. Although a rather anticlimactic end to their date, at least they had another one planned for Friday. And Doc McHottie might be a Charles Bingley and not a Mr. Darcy, but perhaps it wasn't the end of the world. Bingley had his good points. He just wasn't, well, Darcy.

Ugh. I wanted Miss Josie to have a Mr. Darcy.

The bookstore remained closed the rest of the afternoon, but Ms. Anne and Gracie came over to help Miss Josie. Gracie wore a fancy pink collar dotted with rhinestones.

"Love the new collar, Gracie," I said. "It looks fantastic on you."

"Thanks," she said. "You're dapper today yourself."

I did not have rhinestones, but I wore a special bow tie collar. It felt almost like wearing a cravat and made me extraordinarily delighted. "Why thank you," I said. "I appreciate the compliment."

We sat on a dog bed Miss Josie had purchased for me to use in the shop. Although too big for me at the moment, the person at the pet supply store had assured her I would grow into it quickly. But, for now, it was the perfect size for both of us, and an ideal location for us to listen to Miss Josie and Ms. Anne gossip.

"Start at the beginning. Sexy Trainer Dude took you on a hike, and Capone had to save you from a bear?" asked Ms. Anne.

Gracie stared at me, admiration sparkling in her bright eyes. Or maybe it was the reflection of the rhinestones, but it certainly seemed like admiration. "Impressive, Capone. Where was Hans when this happened?"

"Running down the path as quickly as he could and leaving us to deal with the bear on our own."

She laughed. "Typical."

"How do you know Hans?"

"Doggie daycare," she said. "Hans is a dog bully. I had to put him in his place several times. He doesn't mess with me anymore."

I frowned, remembering how I'd been called a dog bully the first time I met Luke. "I think I'm supposed to go to doggie daycare on Monday after my obedience training. Should I be worried?"

She shrugged. "I imagine Hans is pretty upset with you if you made him look bad in front of his owner, but you're too young to run with the big dogs. They'll put you in the puppy group."

"What a relief."

I heard a tap at the door and saw Mrs. Norris outside wearing a large green hat decorated with pumpkins, a scarecrow, and tiny, white ghosts. It should have been tacky, but on her, it looked whimsical.

Miss Josie unlocked the door and let her in. Gracie and I greeted her in our usual way, by barking, licking, and hopping up and down, but Mrs. Norris was ready for us this time. She had dog treats tucked away in her handbag, and she doled them out to us.

"Two puppies. Aren't I the lucky one today?" She handed me an extra treat, earning a dirty look from Gracie, but Mrs. Norris didn't seem to notice. "How's my big boy Capone doing? Aren't you the prettiest dog in the whole wide world?"

"Excuse me, old lady," Gracie said with a huff. "I'm the pretty one here."

I swallowed a chuckle at the look of indignation on Gracie's face, and rushed to appease her. "Mrs. Norris's sight is obviously impaired. You're the prettiest dog I've ever seen."

Mollified, she sank back down on the dog bed. "You're right. I don't like Mrs. Norris anymore. She has poor taste, and she smells funny."

She did smell a little funny, but I had to assume it was a combination of mothballs from storing all her woolen things and the minty hand cream for her arthritis. I only knew about the cream because I'd tried to lick her hands. It had left a bitter flavor on my tongue.

Note to self: Do not lick old people.

"I'm here to ask you a favor, my dear," she said, pulling some papers out of her bag and handing them to Miss Josie. "Could you hang these up for me? I'm advertising for my closing sale. I'm liquidating my inventory."

Miss Josie took them with a sigh. "I'm sorry you're leaving. I loved having you in the neighborhood."

"You, too, Josephine, but to all things, there is a season, right? It's now my time for a little adventure before it's too late if you know what I mean." Her last words came out like a whisper, as if her age was some huge secret. She brightened, giving Miss Josie a big smile. "Have you made any progress in finding out about Benjamin's safety deposit box?"

Miss Josie shook her head. "Which is why we're doing an additional inventory today. It's not only a missing ledger we're looking for at this point. Several valuable books are unaccounted for as well. It's a disaster, to be honest."

"Shouldn't you ask that nice Cedric about it? He worked here quite a long time."

Miss Josie managed to respond in a professional manner. "Cedric was a buyer, and most of his job involved traveling. He never spent much time in the shop and had nothing to do with the day-to-day business. I doubt he'd know anything about accounting ledgers or inventory."

"Oh, too bad," she said. "I wish I could stay and help, but I must be on my way. Happy hunting, ladies."

Mrs. Norris breezed out the door, and Miss Josie gazed around the room at the many books tidily arranged on shelves and showcased on various tables. "They have to be here somewhere."

Ms. Anne frowned. "Unless someone took them."

"Like who?" Miss Josie stared at her a long moment, and they both said the same name at the same time.

"Cedric."

I'd been licking, my, uh, undercarriage, but the sound of his name made me sit up and take notice. Cedric the Betrayer. Had he stolen from Miss Josie? Oh, calamity.

Miss Josie let out a sigh, shaking her head. "I can't see it. Cedric may be a lot of things—"

Ms. Anne cut in, ticking each word off on her fingers. "An adulterer, a scumbag, a liar."

"Yes, all of the above, but he isn't a thief. And what would he do with the books anyway? We move in the same circles. Anyone he tried to sell them to would know him and know me. He wouldn't be able to cover his tracks."

I watched their interaction, wanting to help. Something smelled wrong to me here, but it wasn't the sort of problem a gentleman could solve. To figure this out, I had to do something I rebelled against with every fiber of my being. I needed to think like a criminal. Once again, I had to be Capone-ish.

Who kept trying to break into the shop, and why? Miss Josie and Ms. Anne didn't seem to be connecting the dots. The missing books and the attempted robberies had to be related. Maybe it would take a criminal mastermind, or someone named after a criminal mastermind, to figure it out.

Dang it. I had to put on my gangster hat again. They wore fedoras, not top hats. I'd look terrible in a fedora.

Ms. Anne's lips tightened. "I'm not convinced. If we can't find those books, he's first on my list. He's not happy working for Smythe's Books. He's the lowest rung on the ladder there, which is a huge blow to his ego. Don't you think he should at least be a suspect?"

Miss Josie shook her head. "No. He would never have done that to Mr. Bartleby. He thought of him as a father figure. He was loyal."

"Did he have the same loyalty toward you?"

"Not at all. To Cedric, I was nothing more than..." She frowned, trying to come up with the right word. "A convenience, I guess."

"It must be hard for her to admit," said Gracie, with a

little shake of her head. "To have loved someone so deeply, then to be betrayed by them is bad enough. But if Cedric stole her books, it's so much worse."

"What do you mean?"

"Losing one book would be a hardship for her. Losing several would be a disaster."

A disaster for Miss Josie would be a disaster for me as well. I cocked one ear and listened.

"Which books are missing, exactly?" asked Ms. Anne.

Miss Josie straightened her glasses and studied the list in front of her. "Seven, including the first edition autographed copy of *Pride and Prejudice*."

"The one Mr. Bartleby paid for, but never listed in the inventory?"

"Yes. One and the same." Her eyes misted up behind her glasses. "I'll never find all seven books. I'm doomed."

"We'll find them. We have to."

She put her face in her hands. "Even if we do, they'll probably be ruined by now. What am I going to do?"

Ms. Anne gave her a stern look. "Well, we aren't going to stand here and cry about it. You're a good business-woman, and you know more about books than anyone I've ever met. The books you have in your vault are more than enough to keep this business afloat. If we find those missing titles, it's the icing on the cake, right?"

Miss Josie straightened her shoulders. "You're right. Of course. It's been a stressful week. With Capone nearly eating the jogger, then the encounter with the bear, and my big argument with Nate...." She paused and cleared her throat. "Well, it's been a little rough, but I'm fine. I need to stay focused and get through this."

"And I'll help you," said Ms. Anne, hugging her. "What was in his letter by the way?"

Miss Josie nibbled on her lip. "He made some good points, and it was well written."

Ms. Anne rolled her eyes. "I'm not asking for a literary critique. I want to know what he said. Did he explain why his plans for First Impressions included both the haberdashery and Bartleby's?"

She nodded. "Those were the original plans, created more than a year ago. Once Nate arrived in Beaver, and assessed the situation, he realized the appeal of the location was due, in large part, to the shops surrounding the coffee shop, including Bartleby's. He insists he never asked Mrs. Norris to sell, but when she offered her property, he took it —at an extremely generous price. He said they already have room for their corporate offices upstairs and permits to incorporate Mrs. Norris's property as well. By doing this, they'll have more than enough space and won't need to expand any further."

"Good news, right? Did you make up with him?"

She shook her head. "No. I haven't spoken with him since I barged into his shop and yelled at him. I'm not sure what to say."

Ms. Anne studied Miss Josie's expression carefully, kind of the way I stare at people when I'm trying to figure out what their words mean. "Maybe you should apologize to him," she said.

Miss Josie sighed. "What's the point? He's leaving soon anyway. He said he's only here to get the new location up and running. I'm sure the last thing he's worried about is getting an apology from me. He probably couldn't care less."

"If he didn't care, he wouldn't have written the letter. It's like Captain Wentworth in *Persuasion*. Or Mr. Darcy when he wrote a letter to Lizzie in *Pride and Prejudice*." Ms. Anne fanned her face with her hand. "There is nothing better than a letter written by a hot guy, except maybe when a hot guy sends you diamonds. Diamonds are a good option, too."

Later, after Ms. Anne and Gracie left, I joined Miss Josie outside. It was cold enough now she needed a blanket, and she sat for a long time, staring up at the sparkling stars in the sky.

"They look like diamonds, don't they, Capone?" she asked, as she stroked my head. "But I wouldn't trade you for all the diamonds in the world."

I licked her hand. I thought my heart might explode with utter happiness.

"Come on, puppy," she said, leading me back into the shop. "Tomorrow is a new day. Maybe we'll get lucky and find those missing books."

It sounded like a quest, and gentlemen lived for quests. Or maybe knights did. I wasn't sure. But having a quest certainly wouldn't be a bad thing. I already had a damsel in distress (Miss Josie), and a villain (Cedric). I had a comrade in arms (Jackson, sort of), and a beautiful lady cheering me on (Gracie). I also had the Capone-ish side of my nature, which could be an asset in this situation. A quest could be the thing to push me into the realm of true gentleman status. The only question was where to begin?

TWENTY-THREE

Books currently missing from Miss Josie's inventory:

1. *The Wonderful Wizard of Oz* by Frank Baum, a first edition.
2. *Dracula* by Bram Stoker, a signed first edition.
3. *The Velveteen Rabbit* by Margery Williams, a first edition.
4. *The Hobbit* by J.R.R. Tolkien, a first edition.
5. *Little Women* by Louisa May Alcott, a first edition.
6. *Jane Eyre* by Charlotte Brontë, a first edition.
7. *Pride and Prejudice*, by Jane Austen, a rare signed first edition.

"Holy moly," said Ms. Anne early Monday morning when Miss Josie showed her the list. She'd come in to open the bookstore for us while we went to obedience training. "That's quite the list."

"It is," said Miss Josie, chewing on her lower lip. "But

it's not about the money. Each of these books is a treasure. Something precious. Losing them would be tragic."

Today Miss Josie had on flat shoes and a short dress in a pretty shade of blue. She'd pulled her curly blond hair into a low ponytail, but wisps had already escaped and curled around her face. For such a strait-laced person, Miss Josie had remarkably rebellious hair.

Ms. Anne looked at her watch. "Do you know what else would be tragic? Arriving late for your obedience lessons. Sexy Trainer Dude is probably already upset with you for emasculating him during the bear incident."

"I did not emasculate him," said Miss Josie. "He wet his pants. It had nothing to do with me. But you're right. I don't want to be late, especially because today is Capone's first doggie daycare session. It'll give us a chance to get the inventory done and look for the missing books. Capone can be distracting."

Ms. Anne snorted. "A good word for it." She bent down to pat me. "Be a good boy, Capone. Gracie will be waiting for you at doggie daycare. She has a grooming appointment this afternoon, so I dropped her off on my way over. The two of you will have fun together."

It gave me something to look forward to, time with my pal Gracie. When we arrived at Misty Mountain, however, I was surprised to see the Grumpy Trainer waiting to teach our class. I'd been worried about dealing with Sexy Trainer Dude, and, of course, Hans, but this might be even worse.

Miss Josie seemed nervous, too. Things escalated when I got in a little tussle with a coonhound. We were messing around, but Grumpy Trainer scowled at us.

"Control your dog, please," he said directly to Miss Josie. The coonhound's owner gave her an apologetic look.

Both of us had been equally guilty, but Miss Josie got blamed for it.

It ended up being a terrible class. I didn't get called on to demonstrate, not even once. To make things worse, halfway through the course, Miss Josie realized she'd worn two different shoes today, one black and one blue. She was so embarrassed, but not as embarrassed as she became a few minutes later when I heaved and threw up all over the floor. As if vomiting weren't bad enough, the contents of my stomach revealed something else.

"Is that a thong?" asked a woman with hair the same shade of red as the Irish setter puppy next to her. Did she choose her hair color based on her dog or her dog based on her hair color? I had no idea, but she reacted to the contents of my vomit with a combination of disgust and amazement. "Your dog threw up a pink thong."

Miss Josie stared at the pile of vomit, which did indeed include a hot pink thong. In all honesty, I'd completely forgotten I'd eaten it. It had gone down so quickly. I pulled it out of her lingerie drawer as she showered this morning, and ate it, lickety-split, in one enormous gulp. It came out the way it went in, all in one piece, so no harm, no foul, right? I mean, technically, she could take the thong home, wash it, and wear it again. Other than eating it, and puking it up, I hadn't harmed it at all.

Miss Josie, however, seemed disinclined to bring home a thong which had recently explored part of my digestive tract. Mortified, she grabbed a giant wad of paper towels and picked it up off the floor. She tossed everything into the garbage can, and as soon as the class ended, she took me straight up to doggie daycare to sign in.

"Hi, I'm Jenny," said the girl at the desk. "And I'll be

taking care of Capone today. Don't worry. He's in good hands."

"Thanks," said Miss Josie, not looking worried at all as she handed over my leash to Jenny. I guess after the vomit and the thong she kind of needed time away from me.

As I nervously entered the doggie daycare room, the big dogs, including Hans, mocked me. They played in a separate area but jumped up to catch a glimpse of me through the plexiglass and barked at me from the door.

"Look at the puppy. Isn't he cute? Guess what? I eat puppies for breakfast. I hate puppies."

I highly doubted they actually ate puppies, but one could never be sure when dealing with Neanderthals. I refused to let them bait me into reacting. I marched past them, head held high.

Jenny slammed her fist on the door. "Shut up, you guys. Stop being jerks."

Note to self: I love Jenny.

She brought me to a smaller area containing smaller dogs. Well, most were smaller. Only one dog was bigger than me, a giant, floppy, goldendoodle puppy named Townsend.

"Hi," he said. "I'm Townsend. Do you want to be my friend? I want to be your friend. Let's play. Playing is fun."

"Please play with him," moaned Gracie from her perch in the corner. She sat on top of a carpeted box. It looked almost like a throne, which suited Gracie well. "He's driving us nuts."

I played with Townsend for hours. We jumped and frolicked and tackled each other and licked parts that shouldn't be licked by others. Even though Townsend tended to be a humper, it wasn't a problem. We were young, wild, and free, and by the time Townsend's owner came to pick him up, I knew I'd made a new friend.

I smelled Miss Josie's arrival before I saw her. Her scent washed over me, a perfect mix of old books, and the honey-suckle and gardenia perfume she liked to wear. As I bounded out to meet her, led by the lovely Jenny, a growl coming from the big dog pen startled me.

"Watch your back, Capone." I could barely see Hans through the crack in the door but knew it was him. I smelled his hot breath and caught a glimpse of the tip of his snout. "I'm going to get you. They'll move you to the big dog room soon enough. When they do, I'll get my revenge—I promise you. You humiliated my master and me, and now you're going to pay."

A shiver went over my body. Hans meant it, and he was psycho. Not majorly psycho, but psycho enough to be scary.

I cowered behind Jenny. As much as I'd enjoyed my time at doggie daycare today, and meeting my new buddy Townsend, I wasn't sure if I ever wanted to come back. I also didn't know if I'd have a choice in the matter.

TWENTY-FOUR

Reasons why K-9 search and rescue dogs are fantastic:

1. They help find lost people.
2. They can locate dead bodies.
3. They have cool accessories.
4. They're professionals.
5. They are exceptionally well trained.
6. Their noses are the best in the business.

Once I got out into the sunshine and went back home with Miss Josie, I felt much better. She fed me and gave me a special treat. Then she told me about a surprise.

"I know you're tired," she said, "but my friend Patti is going to stop by with her dogs Clancy and Elliot. They are K-9 search and rescue dogs. Maybe you can learn something from them."

The idea of their visit made me nervous. Clancy and Elliot were heroes. Miss Josie explained it to me as she cleaned up my poop in the backyard.

"They find lost people in the woods. Many of the

people they track have had a medical emergency, or they are older people with memory issues who've wandered off. Clancy and Elliot take a whiff of an article of clothing belonging to the missing person, and they can find them— even if they're miles away. They're amazingly well-trained dogs."

Crap. I was not an amazingly well-trained dog.

Curse my lack of discipline.

What could I do to impress dogs like Clancy and Elliot? I had no skills and no unique ability, but I did have one thing to set me apart from the average canine.

A cravat.

I grabbed my special occasion bow tie collar from the basket where Miss Josie stored it and carried it over to her. She smiled when she saw it. "You want to dress up for your new friends?" she asked, as she put it around my neck. "How cute."

It was more than cute. As soon as I had the bow tie around my neck, I felt much better. I grabbed my Mr. Darcy toy and ran to the front of the bookshop to wait for the arrival of our guests. Miss Josie puttered about, chatting as she tidied up the shop.

"You know, it's because of Patti you're here in the first place. She recommended your breeder to Anne. Clancy is your uncle."

I dropped the Mr. Darcy toy and stared at her. My long-lost uncle Clancy? The uncle I never knew existed? In spite of the obedience class debacle, and vomiting up lingerie, this was quickly turning into the best day of my entire life.

And although I wasn't related to Elliot, I assumed he must be well-educated, well-read, and well-traveled. He probably knew how to waltz and enjoyed playing an occasional game of cards. I could tell by his name. Elliot was the name of a gentleman. What else could he possibly be?

It made me even more nervous, so nervous, in fact, I feared I might piddle on the floor. What a debacle. What if Elliot didn't like me? What if Uncle Clancy thought of me as the black sheep (rather than the black lab) of the family?

I thought about retiring to my bed and hiding under a blanket, but Miss Josie grinned as she glanced out the window. "Look, Capone. There's your uncle Clancy." She pointed to a chocolate lab, with well-defined muscles and a powerful physique. "And the other dog is Elliot."

Elliot was a yellow lab but mixed with something else, maybe a golden retriever. He was sleek and blond and beautiful. Together they were inspiring. How could I possibly live up to two such legends?

When Mistress Patti saw me sitting forlornly by the window, her face lit up. "Here he is," she said, as she entered the bookstore and knelt beside me. "You're gorgeous. What a great puppy. What a fantastic dog."

My tail began to wag. Mistress Patti thought I was gorgeous, great, and fantastic? I felt the same way about her. I gave her a lick on the cheek and put my paws on her knee so I could reach more of her face. I even chewed on her auburn hair. I'd never been so happy. I thought I might cry.

"Hello, pup," said Uncle Clancy, his eyes kind. He had grey around his snout, and I thought it made him look even more distinguished.

No one would ever describe Elliot as distinguished. "Hey, you," he said, bumping me so hard he nearly knocked me over. "Let's play chase. I'll chase you, and you chase me. It's fun. Go."

After a rousing game of chase in the back garden, and a great deal of ritualistic butt sniffing, we took a break on the patio. Miss Josie and Mistress Patti sat by the wrought iron table and shared a bottle of wine.

The night was chilly but comfortable, and a giant harvest moon hung in the sky. As the ladies chatted, Uncle Clancy entertained us with stories about the good old days, and both he and Elliot talked about their work as rescue dogs.

"The key is to know what you're looking for," said Uncle Clancy. "All dogs have a good sniffer, but many don't know how to use it properly. Our noses are ten thousand times more accurate than a human nose. It's a fact, my boy."

Note to self: I may have an actual skill.

I sat up a little straighter, thinking about Miss Josie and her missing books. "Can you use your nose to find other lost things as well, not only people?"

Uncle Clancy nodded. "Of course. But, it's like I said, you have to know what you're looking for, and you have to be able to recognize the scent when you finally come across it. That's the hard part. Do you know what else is tough?"

"What?"

"Ignoring all the other smells getting in the way. You need a special kind of focus."

Elliot jumped up and started chasing his tail. It made me wonder something. "Does, uh, Elliot have the kind of focus you mentioned?"

"He's getting there," said Uncle Clancy. "Life is a journey, Capone. Each step you take, each lesson you learn, leads you further down the path you're supposed to be on. Elliot's path is a little different."

Elliot tripped but managed to catch his tail at last. He shot us a triumphant grin, losing his hold on his tail in the process. "Rats," he said, and commenced chasing it again.

Uncle Clancy sighed. "He's a goofball. It's in his nature,

and there is no fighting it. We are what we are, and we need to accept it, embrace it, and be the best we possibly can."

My shoulders slumped. "But I'll never be a rescue dog like you and Elliot. I'll never be anything important. I'm a stupid little worthless puppy."

I scratched at my bow tie. It chafed my neck, which seemed oddly symbolic to me, almost a metaphor for my life.

Uncle Clancy watched me closely. "Did you know Elliot was supposed to be a service dog, the kind that would help someone with disabilities? Guess what? He failed out. He didn't have the right personality for it. He does have the right personality for search and rescue, though, which is how he ended up where he is today. You must have faith in yourself. You're going to be a great dog someday."

I put my head down on my paws. "How do you know, Uncle Clancy?"

"I'm old. I've seen a thing or two in my day, and I can always spot a good dog when I meet one. You are a good dog, Capone. You have excellent genes and an incredible nose. You could be anything, find anything, do anything. The choice is simply up to you."

I tilted my head and looked at him. He seemed sincere, and it made my heart swell with pride. "Tell me more about finding things, Uncle Clancy. How do I start?"

He winked at me. "The same place you always do—at the beginning. If something is missing, you have to go where it was last located. It's not rocket science. It's olfactory science, and you have all the tools you need. Trust your nose. It won't steer you wrong."

Trust my nose. I closed my eyes and took a whiff of the night air, inhaling deeply. I smelled Miss Josie's perfume, the treats in Mistress Patti's pocket. I also caught the scent of Mr. Nate's shop, the smells of coffee and cream and biscotti.

"Go deeper, Capone. Stretch out your senses," said Uncle Clancy, his voice soft.

I inhaled again, smelling the wool from Mrs. Norris's haberdashery, the pizzas baking in the oven at Mario's down the street, and even the leaves in the park by the gazebo in the town square.

Opening my eyes, I stared at my uncle in surprise. "I smelled things I've never smelled before."

"Good work, pup," he said, letting out a yawn. "With practice, you'll get better and better. In no time, your nose will be your greatest tool, and you'll find what you seek. I promise."

Elliot, who'd left us briefly to take a dump near the rose bushes, trotted back over to us. "Hey, have you guys seen my tail? I left it right here a minute ago, but now it's disappeared."

"Your tail," said Uncle Clancy. "Where could it be? Have you seen Elliot's tail, Capone?"

I pretended to consider his question. "I think I saw it over by the back wall."

"Me, too," said Uncle Clancy, giving me a wink.

"Thanks, guys," said Elliot, as he scampered off.

Uncle Clancy sighed. "Not the sharpest tool in the shed, but he's a good dog. Now, tell me more about what you're looking for, Capone, so I can help you sort out a way to find it."

TWENTY-FIVE

A list of things cats are good at:

1. Being jerks.
2. Knocking things off tables.
3. Coughing up furballs.
4. Torturing puppies.
5. Making fun of puppies.
6. Being mean to puppies.
7. Upsetting puppies.
8. Helping puppies find things.

As I nestled in my crate with Orange Snuggle Bunny by my side, I thought about what Uncle Clancy had taught me. I took a deep breath of the night air and tried to smell the whole neighborhood like I did before, but I couldn't. First of all, Miss Josie closed all the windows, so it hampered my ability. Secondly, Rocco sat directly on top of my crate. All I could smell was fat, hairy cat.

"Do you have to sleep there?" I asked.

He yawned and stretched, staring down at me with his

creepy, glowing eyes. "I do. Mostly because I know how much it bothers you."

Parts of Rocco's belly hung down between the metal bars of my crate. It was kind of gross, and it didn't look comfortable at all. Maybe he'd give up soon and sleep somewhere else.

"Goodnight, Rocco," I said, closing my eyes.

"Wait, Capone. I want to tell you something."

I opened one eye so I could glare up at him. "What?"

He let out a long sigh and stared at the window. "I heard you talking to the other dog, the one who finds lost things. Were you thinking about trying to find the missing books? The ones Josephine has been searching for?"

"Yes. Do you know anything about it?"

He hesitated, seeming almost unsure, a new trick for Rocco. "It may be nothing, but I like to wiggle into small places, and when I was under the stairs the other day, I found something. It might be the last accounting ledger. It's about the same size and shape as the others, and it smelled like Mr. Bartleby."

I raised one eyebrow at him. "You have a good sniffer, too?"

"Of course, I do," he huffed. "Not like a dog's nose, mind you. A cat's nose is more...discerning. Mr. Bartleby always smelled like oregano and mint. He grew both of those in his herb garden, and it stayed on his skin."

I studied Rocco closely. "You liked Mr. Bartleby, didn't you?"

He rolled his eyes at me. "He fed me, which meant he served a purpose."

I sat up straighter. I was onto something here. "And you like Miss Josie, too."

He turned his back to me and shot an evil look over his

shoulder. "As I said before, provider of food. What's not to like?"

Suddenly, it struck me. Rocco's meanness was all a façade. I decided to take it one step further. "I think you like me, too."

"Don't push it, pup," he hissed, swiping a paw at me through the bars of my crate. He nearly got me in the nose, but I ducked my head just in time. I couldn't tell if he missed me by accident or on purpose, but, on second thought, maybe his meanness wasn't a façade. Perhaps he was a nasty soul encased in a fluffy, furry package.

At least Rocco wanted to help Miss Josie, which meant we had a mutual goal, but what motivated Rocco's interest in finding the ledger all of a sudden?

"Why are you telling me this, Rocco?"

He hopped over to the arm of the blue couch, the perfect vantage point for shooting me a dirty look. "Because I need your help, dummy. I can push the ledger to the opening at the back of the stairs, but I can't lift it high enough to get it out, which is where you come in. I'm the brains of this operation, and you're the brawn. I'll push the ledger to where you can reach it, and you yank it out. Use your mouth for something other than licking your privates and tearing apart feather pillows."

I scowled at him. "One pillow. And it happened ages ago. Let it go, will you?" He didn't respond, so I took a deep, calming breath. "But this isn't about you or me. It's about Miss Josie, so yes, I'll help you. But I have to go down to the basement to pull out the ledger. How are we going to manage it? Miss Josie will never let me go to the basement myself. She has rules, you know."

He let out a yawn. "Leave it to me, bone breath. I've got it covered. By this time tomorrow, Miss Josie will have the ledger in her hands, and I can stop listening to her whine about it. What a relief."

Jumping up to the top of the bookshelf, he disappeared into the shadows, but I could still see the faint gleam of his eyes in the darkness and hear the cadence of his breathing. He might deny it, but he cared about Miss Josie. Not as much as I did, of course, but in his own snarky, feline way, he had genuine affection for her.

"Goodnight, Rocco. You're not such a bad kitty after all."

"Shut up. I hate you."

Note to self: I may be starting to like Rocco.

TWENTY-SIX

My to do list:

1. Find the lost ledger.
2. Find the missing books.
3. Find Miss Josie's one true love.
4. Save the day.
5. Get a new name.
6. Become a perfect gentleman.
7. Live happily ever after.

Rocco and I spent the morning trying to convince Miss Josie to go down to the basement. I stood next to the door and barked, hoping she'd open it for me. She told me to be quiet and ignored all my attempts to gain her attention.

Because our first plan didn't work, Rocco stood by the door to the basement and made an ungodly sound. She didn't even look at him. He makes those noises frequently. She was going over the inventory one final time, with Ms. Anne's help, and remained focused on the task at hand.

Mrs. Steele fluttered about, reorganizing the shelves.

She'd brought homemade muffins for Miss Josie and Ms. Anne, and homemade treats for Gracie and me. Mrs. Steele was a dog biscuit baking angel. She didn't bring anything for Rocco, and he gave her a dirty look before pulling me aside so we could work on our plan.

"I'll get down to the basement on my own. There is a narrow opening next to the stairs by the back entrance. I can easily squeeze through. The problem is getting you down there, too. We have to think of a way," he said.

Ms. Anne and Gracie had come over first thing in the morning. We'd told Gracie about our plan, but she declared it too early to be disturbed and curled up on my bed. She somehow managed to ignore my barking and Rocco's noises. Gracie needed her beauty sleep.

Miss Josie could probably use some sleep, too. She'd stayed up late chatting with Mistress Patti and now had dark circles under her eyes.

"I've looked for the books and ledger everywhere," she said, and to my horror, her lip quivered. "They're gone. I know it."

Ms. Anne squeezed her shoulder. "Don't lose hope."

Miss Josie put on a brave face, probably for the sake of her friend. "I'm sorry. It's not only about the books. Nate has been avoiding me. Not that I care, but we are neighbors, after all. It shouldn't be tense between us. But he still leaves the coffee by the front door, and he's still reading *Pride and Prejudice*. He's up to chapter eight."

"How do you know he's up to chapter eight?" asked Ms. Anne.

Miss Josie lifted her First Impressions coffee cup and pointed to the words scrawled across the side. "It says, 'Extensive reading? Like what I'm doing every day to make you drink coffee?' He's enjoying this."

"I have no idea what you're talking about."

"He's reached the part of the story when Darcy talks about what it means for a young lady to be accomplished in Regency society. It's actually kind of cute, and funny, too. He's a nice guy." Her face crumpled in despair. "And I've been so mean to him, Anne."

"Did you respond to his letter?"

She shook her head. "I didn't know what to say. He never had any designs on my shop. Those were the initial plans drawn up by the architects who worked for First Impressions and had nothing to do with him."

"It doesn't sound like he's the evil bloodsucking corporate exec you painted him to be."

"He's not, but what can I do? I accused him of putting an old lady out of business. I screamed at him in his shop. I became the crazy parking Nazi of Beaver. I don't know, Anne. He brings out the worst in me. And then I went and kissed him—"

Ms. Anne's eyes widened. "You kissed Nate Murray?"

"Yes, but—"

"Did you enjoy it?" Miss Anne put her elbows on the counter and gave Miss Josie a conspiratorial wink.

"Oddly enough, I did." She got a faraway look in her eyes, and her fingers went to her lips.

"I can tell."

Miss Josie flushed. "I mean I enjoyed it more than kissing the dog trainer."

"Wait. You kissed STD?"

Miss Josie shuddered. "Please stop calling him STD."

Ms. Anne folded her arms across her chest. "You little harlot. Did you kiss Doc McHottie as well?"

Miss Josie's blush answered for her, but she replied to

Ms. Anne anyway. "He gave me a peck on the cheek. Not a kiss, exactly."

"Are you going to see him again?"

She shrugged, letting out a sigh. "I'm sure I will. He works next door after all. He can't avoid me forever, and I hate things being like this between us. I miss him."

Ms. Anne gave her a knowing look. "I was actually talking about Doc McHottie, but now I understand your dilemma."

Miss Josie narrowed her eyes. "Aren't we supposed to be looking for my books? How did we end up talking about my love life?"

"Because it's so fascinating. You never had much going on before, other than Ced—" Miss Josie silenced her with an icy look, and Ms. Anne gave her an apologetic wave. "Other than your evil ex, but now it's like you're making up for lost time. It is an interesting problem."

"What do you mean?"

Pushing her red hair over her shoulder, Ms. Anne leaned closer to Miss Josie. "I've known you since you were in diapers. Heck, I even changed a few of those diapers. You can't hide anything from me. You've kissed three men in a week, a new record, but only one of them got your panties in a knot, and that's Nate Murray." Miss Josie let out a noise of indignation, but Ms. Anne waved it off. "It's all in the kiss, sweet pea. If the kiss doesn't rock your world, the man won't either. Trust me. I'm an expert."

"You've been divorced three times."

"Which is why I'm an expert."

Miss Josie rolled her eyes. "There is nothing between Nate Murray and me. He's not my type, and he's not planning to stay in Beaver. What's the point?"

"I guess you're right."

"I know I'm right." She let out a long breath. "And maybe Doc McHottie's kiss wasn't quite as earth-shattering as Nate's, but he's the better choice for me. He's a good guy, and we have a lot in common. And he's a vet. He can help me take care of Capone. Convenient since Capone makes bad decisions and needs a lot of vet visits. I'm making the right choice here. A logical, well thought out, reasonable kind of choice."

Ms. Anne laughed. "I've never made that kind of choice before. I give you credit."

"I don't want to get hurt again," said Miss Josie softly.

"I understand, sweetness, and I didn't mean to tease you about it." Ms. Anne patted her arm. "Let me go pick up some lunch. Café Kolache. My treat. It'll make you feel better, and it'll give both of us the energy we need to find those books."

Mrs. Steele came out of the back room wearing her cardigan and carrying an envelope. "I have to go to the post office, and I'm meeting a friend for lunch at Waffles Incaffienated. Do the two of you need anything?"

Miss Josie shook her head. "No, Mrs. Steele. Thank you. Enjoy your waffles."

She waved and stepped out the door. Gracie continued to snooze in the corner, but as soon as Ms. Anne left, her eyes flew open. "It's time. Operation Gracie Saves the Day will commence right now."

TWENTY-SEVEN

Operation Gracie Saves the Day

1. Rocco must sneak down to the basement and knock something over.
2. Miss Josie will naturally rush to figure out what happened. I'll follow on her heels.
3. Gracie can begin her extremely high pitched and annoying "intruder alert" bark.
4. Miss Josie will have to come upstairs to investigate.
5. Rocco can climb into the cubbyhole beneath the stairs and push the ledger to the opening.
6. I'll stick my nose into the opening and pull it out.

It didn't take long for Rocco to put the plan into action. As Gracie and I waited anxiously upstairs, he went to work. A loud crash came from the basement, followed by the sound of glass shattering. Miss Josie hopped up so fast, she bumped her head on a bookshelf.

"Ow," she said, rubbing her head as she ran to the basement door. "What's going on? Is someone downstairs?"

Another crash echoed from the basement, then another. Rocco, never known for his subtlety, took his role on this caper seriously, but, even for him, it seemed like overkill.

I followed Miss Josie as she charged down the steps in a fluttery green dress, green tights, and navy-blue suede pumps. Not the best footwear for a jog down a rickety staircase, and she twisted her ankle on the final step. I bumped into her, and nearly knocked her over, but she grabbed the rail and steadied herself.

"Holy—" Whatever she'd meant to say got cut off when she looked around the basement. Several shattered wine bottles lay on the concrete floor, the glass gleaming in the dim light of a single overhead bulb. Miss Josie let out what I can only describe as a howl of pure fury.

Note to self: Never mess with a girl's wine.

Rocco raised his paw, as if to strike down another bottle, just as Gracie started barking. It sounded like someone was murdering her.

Miss Josie let out a curse and ran back up the stairs, limping because of her twisted ankle. I made a move to follow her, but Rocco stopped me.

"Hey, stupid. It's an act. Gracie isn't hurt. Get over here and help me."

Wow. Gracie was a good actress. I'd almost fallen for it.

Rocco squeezed into a space behind the stairs. I couldn't see what he was doing, but I heard him grunting and pushing something.

It was the ledger. It had to be.

I let out a soft yelp of triumph when I saw the edge of it appear in the narrow crack between steps but didn't want to alert Miss Josie. We were so close, and Gracie continued to do an excellent job of barking her head off.

"Almost there," I said, wagging my tail.

"Can you get a grip and pull it out the rest of the way?"

"I'll try."

I saw the edge of the ledger but couldn't grab it. "Can you push it further?"

Rocco grunted. "That's as far as I can get it."

I tried again but to no avail. Then I noticed one part of the step seemed warped and wobbly. By pushing at it, I managed to create a space large enough for my snout. I'd be going in blind, and I'd have to rely on Rocco to guide me, but it might work.

As I stuck my nose into the hole, I heard the sound of the door to the shop opening, and Mr. Nate talking. We didn't have much time.

"A little more, Capone. You're close."

I could smell the ledger, only a hair's breadth away from my nose. I smelled Rocco, too. I squeezed in even more, wriggling my bottom as I pushed. And then it grew silent upstairs.

"Uh-oh," said Rocco, his voice strained. "They must have given Gracie a treat. We're out of time. It's all or nothing."

I gave a final push, getting my entire snout and most of my head into the opening, and grabbed the ledger with my teeth.

"Way to go, Capone. You have it," said Rocco.

We froze when we heard Mr. Nate ask Miss Josie the one question which might ruin our plans. "Where's Capone?'

Miss Josie squawked, probably realizing she'd left me alone in the basement, surrounded by broken glass and toxic household chemicals. We heard footsteps above us as Mr. Nate and Miss Josie rushed to the basement door.

I tried to pull my head out with the ledger still clutched in my teeth, but I had a problem. Getting my head into the hole was one thing. Getting it out was a different matter entirely.

"What are you doing?" asked Rocco, panic in his voice.

"I'm stuck," I said. Rocco pushed against my head, but to no avail. Miss Josie caught one glimpse of me and screamed.

"He's trapped," she said and pulled on my bottom. "Help."

Curse my big fat head.

Miss Josie, in the middle of a total meltdown, sobbed as she tried to free me. Mr. Nate, thankfully, intervened.

"Stop it, Josie. You're going to hurt him. Let me take a look." Mr. Nate felt around my head and reached an obvious conclusion. "Yep. He's stuck. Do you have any tools I could use? I'm going to pry the step apart and get him out."

Mr. Nate found a crowbar somewhere in the basement. Within minutes, he'd taken the step apart and freed me.

Poor Miss Josie wept even harder, pulling me into her arms. Then she noticed the ledger, still clenched in my teeth. I wagged my tail and held it up to her. She took it from me and leafed through it.

"It's Mr. Bartleby's ledger," she said, her voice tinged with awe. "The one I've been searching for. Capone, you're a hero."

Rocco, who'd slipped out from behind the steps, stared at them aghast. "You've got to be kidding. I do all the work, and yet you get all the glory? This is an outrage."

Miss Josie heard him growl and picked him up into her arms as well. "Don't be jealous, Rocco. I still think you're sweet, even if you did destroy three bottles of my favorite wine for no apparent reason at all."

Rocco looked like he might be choking on a fur ball. "Sweet? I'm not sweet. Ew. Yuck. Unhand me, woman." He wriggled out of her grasp and marched up the steps with a swish of his tail. I heard him mutter "humans," under his breath, his voice dripping with disgust, but when he glanced back at Miss Josie, I caught a glimpse of something resembling genuine affection in his eyes.

Mr. Nate hammered the step back in place, and we went upstairs. Ms. Anne arrived moments later, carrying bags of food. She listened to the story about what had happened as she handed out kolache; pastries made out of a sweet dough with savory fillings. Miss Josie gave me one loaded with bacon and cheese as a thank you for finding the ledger. It was the most delicious thing I'd ever eaten in my entire life. The fact it came from Miss Josie, with her most profound appreciation for my help, made it even tastier.

Gracie and Rocco received kolache, too. Although Miss Josie had no idea the roles they'd played in helping find the ledger, it felt like a party, and she seemed to be in a generous mood.

We sat in a circle around a small table in the shop. Mr. Nate insisted Miss Josie put her foot on his knee so he could examine her injury thoroughly, his brown eyes intent, as he made her wiggle her toes and rotate her ankle. She paused in mid-munch of her spinach and feta filled kolache to watch him, her eyes lingering on his dark, curly head. When he looked up and caught her studying him, he gave her a crooked smile.

"I think he likes her," I said.

"And she likes him, too," said Gracie knowingly.

Rocco, who sat perched on a table above us, licking his

paw, spoke in his dry, gravelly voice. "Love is a many splen-dored thing." Gracie and I looked at him in shock, and he scowled at us. "I'm joking. I hate love. Leave me alone, dimwits."

Note to self: Rocco might not be so evil after all.

Mr. Nate had gone back to First Impressions to pick up a bag of ice for Miss Josie's ankle and three cups of hot tea. He insisted on taking care of her injury himself. "This should help keep the swelling down," he said as he held the ice against her foot. "I think it's sprained, but if it gets worse, you should get an x-ray."

"Thanks. I will." Miss Josie's voice was soft.

Awkward silence ensued. Ms. Anne sipped on her tea. "So, what did Capone find in the basement?" she asked.

"The missing ledger," said Miss Josie. "Under one of the steps. How he knew it was there, and why he went after it is a total mystery."

"Maybe Capone is smarter than we realize," said Ms. Anne. They all laughed. Rocco mumbled something derogatory under his breath. "What's in the ledger, Josie? Is there anything about the missing books?"

"Well, according to what I found in the other ledgers, six books are missing. The seventh, a Jane Austen, is listed in Mr. Bartleby's purchase records as something he bought from an estate sale in England, but he never added it to the inventory list. It's kind of fishy. He wrote down everything, but not the location of one of the most valuable books he'd ever purchased."

Mr. Nate frowned. "If it came from England, there would have to be a bill of lading. Can you find something in the ledger about it?" he asked.

Miss Josie shook her head. "Most of what's in here seems to be written in code. Except for this, of course."

She held up the book, showing Ms. Anne and Mr. Nate what appeared to be a landscaping plan of the back garden. Ms. Anne shook her head in disbelief. "Poor Mr. B. He was losing his marbles."

Miss Josie stroked the diagram of the garden. "These are the roses he planted in memory of his wife," she said, her voice tight with emotion. "He chose special varieties, all with a literary connection. Isn't that the sweetest thing you've ever heard?"

The female creatures in the shop all sighed in unison, even Gracie. I may have sighed too because it was pretty freaking romantic. I'm not ashamed to admit it. I'm in touch with my feminine side.

Miss Josie turned the page, her eyes widening in surprise. She sat up straighter in her chair, a hand over her mouth, as all the color drained from her face.

"What is it?" asked Mr. Nate.

She held up a single piece of paper. It looked like a page taken from a book, and it seemed old. "It's a photograph by Edward Sheriff Curtis. He documented the lives of Native Americans in the early twentieth century. This page came from his series entitled *The North American Indian*. He called this one *In a Piegan Lodge*. The Curtis series was one of my first acquisitions for Mr. Bartleby, so I remember it well."

She limped to the vault in her stocking feet and opened it, bringing out a book. As she leafed through it, her face turned even paler.

"What is it?" asked Mr. Nate, looking over her shoulder.

She put a shaking hand to her head. "The photo in the ledger came from this book. There are others missing as well." She turned page after page, counting, then closed the book and sank into a chair. "At least fifteen pages are gone."

"From one book?" he asked.

"Yes. Someone mutilated this book. It's a total loss."

"Oh, Josie," said Ms. Anne. "Why would Mr. Bartleby do something like this?"

Miss Josie looked like she might be in shock. "I don't know, but now I have to go through each of the books in the shop and see if others are damaged. If I sold a book with missing pages to a collector, it would ruin me. This is a nightmare."

I felt the despair and disappointment wafting off Miss Josie's skin, and I knew I was her only hope. I had to use my super sniffer, find the seven missing books, and save the day.

Rocco summed up my thoughts perfectly. "Oh, crap," he said. "We're going to have to help the humans again, aren't we?"

I didn't answer him, and neither did Gracie. We all knew the answer, and we were in this together whether we liked it or not.

TWENTY-EIGHT

Ways to apologize to someone you care about:

1. Say you're sorry.
2. Mean it.
3. Bring them a gift.
4. Forgive and forget.
5. Make them laugh.
6. Don't make the same mistake twice.
7. Fondle their ankle.

As Miss Josie sat, with the copy of *The North American Indian* still on her lap, Ms. Anne glanced at her watch. "I hate to leave you like this, but I've got to run. Are you okay, Josie?"

She nodded, her expression grim. "I'll be fine. I have a collector coming later this afternoon to look at a few of the books in my vault. I'll have to check and make sure someone hasn't ravaged them, too, and I'm going to study this." She pointed to the ledger, which rested on the table next to her.

"Maybe something in here will tell me why Mr. Bartleby tore pages out of this book."

Ms. Anne's gaze went to Mr. Nate, who showed no signs of leaving. At his insistence, Miss Josie had put her foot back on his knee, and he gently pressed the ice pack against it, shifting it slightly when one spot got too cold.

"Okay, then. See you later."

After Ms. Anne and Gracie left, Miss Josie and Mr. Nate spoke at once, their words coming out in a rush. "I'm so sorry."

They laughed, and Miss Josie shook her head. "What do you have to be sorry about?" she asked. "I'm the one who was rude to you. I jumped to conclusions."

"True," he said. "But I was afraid your good opinion, once lost, would be lost forever."

Her expression turned incredulous. "You're already up to chapter ten?"

"Eleven."

"Wow. I'm impressed. I'll have to drink a lot more coffee to catch up."

"We'll consider the tea and the hangover smoothie I made you part of the deal, so you're only a cup behind."

He removed the ice pack, and she put her foot gingerly onto the floor. "It's better," she said. "Thanks."

"My pleasure. Don't overdo it, though. No disco dancing, pole vaulting, or hiking in the mountains. You won't be able to run away from bears on a gimpy ankle."

She put her face in her hands. "You heard about that?"

"I didn't even realize there were bears in Beaver County."

"Uh, neither did I, but I've also never hiked quite so far into the woods."

"You were exceedingly brave," he said. "It must have been terrifying."

"I think I was more irritated than brave. Capone ended up being the one who jumped in and frightened the bear away."

They both looked at me. "I told you Capone was a good dog," said Mr. Nate.

"And you were right. About a lot of things."

They stared deeply into each other's eyes. Even I could tell it was a romantic moment. But then I burped, thanks to wolfing down the kolache, and broke the spell.

Mr. Nate patted my head. "Capone ended up being a hero twice in one week. First, he saved you from a bear, and today, he found the missing ledger."

"So it seems." Miss Josie sat up straighter in her chair, her hands folded neatly on her lap, and her eyes staring directly at Mr. Nate. "And you're a hero, too. You've helped me so many times, including today, and I never thanked you properly."

His gaze went to Miss Josie's sweet, full lips, and for a moment she stared at him as if entranced. They were interrupted when Mrs. Steele returned, calling out a greeting as she headed to the back room to hang up her coat,

Miss Josie cleared her throat. "There is something I need to say. I haven't been kind to you, Nate, and I'm truly sorry. Can we still be friends?" She reached out a hand, and he took it, giving it a formal shake.

"I'm sure I'm making a huge mistake, and you'll probably think I'm a fool for saying this, but I'm tired of pretending." He stumbled over his words, his face growing red. "I want to be more than friends, Josie."

"But you're leaving, Nate," she said softly. "As much as

I care about you, as much as I like spending time with you, we can't...I can't..."

She reached out and put a hand on his cheek. He closed his eyes like her touch was something he'd craved. For a second, I thought she might kiss him right then and there, but she didn't. She sighed and lowered her hand, giving him a melancholy smile.

"Who are we kidding? You'd hate my tea and tofu and my obsession with books. I'd drive you nuts."

"You already do." He returned her smile, but his eyes were sad.

"So, I guess we agree." I thought I heard a question in her voice, but I may have been wrong. He didn't reply. I had to wonder if perhaps they weren't in agreement after all. Miss Josie cleared her throat and turned the conversation to safer territory. "I need to apologize for a few other things as well. Mrs. Norris deciding to sell her shop and retire was not your fault."

He shook his head. "No, it was not."

"And the parking situation. It wasn't your fault, either."

"Let's blame it on the city planners." He folded his arms across his chest, his tone once again playful and bantering. "They did a poor job."

"Well, since they mapped it out in 1802, there isn't much we can do about it, I suppose." She took a deep breath and blew it out slowly. "I'm sorry about a lot of stuff, Nate. Truly, I am. Will you give me another chance?"

He pretended to ponder it. "Will you let me continue to bring you coffee?"

She rolled her eyes. "If you must."

"I must," he said, getting to his feet. "I have to get back to work, but I'll keep reading *Pride and Prejudice*. I'm enjoying it."

She followed him to the door. "I'm glad. And even if I don't like coffee, I think First Impressions is nice. Do you like working there? I read an article about it in the *New York Times* a few months ago. I don't remember the details, but they said the founder is some kind of crazy genius."

Miss Josie was rambling. It almost seemed like she didn't want Mr. Nate to leave.

He leaned against the doorframe, a twinkle in his dark eyes. "He *is* a crazy genius, and I do like working there."

She tugged on a lock of her hair. "And what do you do there exactly?"

He shrugged. "This and that."

"A little vague," she said with a frown.

"Not vague, mysterious." He gave her a smile which brought out dimples in his cheeks. "My job is so boring I'll spare you the details. I'd hate to put you to sleep in the middle of the afternoon. I've seen you sleep. It's not pretty. You drool a lot, and you snore, too."

Her jaw dropped. "Wait, what? Are you serious? I snore?"

He backed out the door of the shop, grinning, but she held the door open and he kept talking to her from the sidewalk. "A gentleman never talks about what goes on in the boudoir. Your secret is safe with me, Josie. I mean, I thought Jackson snored, but after hearing you the other night, well... wow. Just wow."

He winked at the outraged expression on her face. Miss Josie tried to give him a stern look but couldn't quite manage it. Neither of them noticed Cedric the Betrayer standing a few feet away, partially hidden by a tree, listening to them. He had an angry scowl on his face, and I realized something with a start.

He looked the way I did when the horses back on the

farm got irritated and gave me a well-aimed kick in the belly. It took the air right out of my lungs and made me feel like I might throw up. Cedric the Betrayer, at this moment, looked like a big horse had kicked him, and since there were no horses around, I could only conclude one thing.

Cedric, the Betrayer, still loved Miss Josie.

Curse my empathetic nature. It almost made me feel bad for him.

TWENTY-NINE

Words to describe a man who dates a much older woman:

1. Boy toy.
2. Happy Meal.
3. Cub.
4. Gigolo.
5. Player.
6. Gold digger.
7. Arm candy.
8. Studmuffin.
9. Man hunk.
10. Fortunate.

Back in the shop, Miss Josie sipped the last of her tea as she sat on the high stool behind the cash register and read through the ledger. I gazed out the front window of the shop, letting out a low but rather intimidating growl. Miss Josie, who most likely had no idea Cedric the Betrayer lurked somewhere close by, was not impressed.

"Stop growling at the leaves, Capone. They aren't an

invading force. They're going to keep falling until the trees are bare, so get used to it. Please."

Excuse me? She thought I growled at a bunch of leaves? Well, yes, I have growled at leaves in the past, and paint cans, and my own shadow, but this time, I growled at a real threat. Cedric.

Why had he come here? What nefarious deeds lurked in that dark and evil mind of his? When I could no longer smell his unique wool and starch scent, I knew he'd gone, and I could finally relax.

"My, it's getting chilly outside," said Mrs. Steele, rubbing her arms. "Sorry, it took me so long at the post office. What would you like me to do first?"

"I have to tell you something," said Miss Josie. "I finally found Mr. Bartleby's ledger. This was inside."

She handed Mrs. Steele the Curtis photo, and Mrs. Steele narrowed her eyes. "Is this from *The North American Indian*?"

Miss Josie nodded, holding up the book in her hands. "And it came from our copy. Someone removed not only this photo but many others, and I think I know who did it."

Mrs. Steele's eyes widened behind the thick lenses of her glasses. "You do?"

"Yes. It was Mr. Bartleby. It had to be him. Although I have no idea why he'd do such a thing."

Mrs. Steele sank into a chair, and when she spoke her voice trembled. "Poor Benjamin. He wasn't in his right mind. He probably had no idea at all what he'd done."

"I know." Miss Josie rose to her feet and limped over to the vault. "But it doesn't make it any easier. I have to check over the volumes the collector wants to see this afternoon, and we'll need to look through all the books in the vault to make sure no one tampered with any of the others."

"Of course. I'll wash my hands, and then we can get to work."

After Mrs. Steele went to the back room of the shop, the bell above the door jangled. Mrs. Norris strode into the shop, on the arm of a much younger man.

She smiled at Miss Josie, her bright blue eyes twinkling. Today she had on a long blue coat and skirt. The jacket buttoned to her neck, and she'd decorated it with a colorful broach. Her hat, also blue, sat at a jaunty angle on her white head and was covered in daisies.

"Good afternoon, Josephine. This is my beau, Bill Elliot."

"Please call me Billy," he said with a toothy smile.

Big, blond, and paunchy, he looked to be about fifty. Which made him nearly thirty years younger than Mrs. Norris.

"Cute dog," he said, reaching down to pet me. His touch was rough, and I didn't like it. I backed away, hiding behind Miss Josie's legs

"Were you able to find the mysterious safety deposit box, Josie?" asked Mrs. Norris. She reached into her small, embroidered pocketbook and gave me a dog biscuit. I snatched it up. I'm so easily bought.

"No," said Miss Josie. "But we did find the missing ledger."

"How fortunate. Was there anything useful in it?"

Miss Josie shook her head, her expression melancholy. "Not that I could tell."

"There, there, dear. It'll be okay. And if you need any help searching for things, I can loan you Billy. He's good at heavy lifting, and so strong." Mrs. Norris patted Billy's bicep and fluttered her eyelashes at him. "He's been packing up inventory for me, and he's nearly finished. He can come and help you any time."

Miss Josie stood up, detangling me from her legs. "I appreciate the offer, and thanks for stopping by, but I'd better get back to work. I have a customer arriving in a few minutes, and I need to get organized. Do you need anything else?"

Mrs. Norris's face tightened ever so slightly, as if she didn't like being dismissed. Maybe it was an old person thing. "Not at all. We'll be on our way. Remember what I said. You don't have to do this on your own. Your friends are here to help you."

After they left the shop, Mrs. Steele joined Miss Josie by the vault. "Was Henrietta here?" she asked.

Miss Josie bit her lip to keep from smiling. "And her boyfriend, Billy."

"Oh, I've met him," said Mrs. Steele with a soft giggle. "They are quite the interesting couple, aren't they?"

"They certainly are," said Miss Josie. "You know, it's funny. I always suspected she and Mr. Bartleby had a thing going on. Do you think they dated?"

Mrs. Steele shook her head so hard the bun on top of her head wobbled. "Benjamin never got over the death of his wife."

"Wasn't her name Lizzie?"

"Yes," said Mrs. Steele. "I started working here when she was still alive, you know. I've never seen two people more in love. He called her his special rose."

Miss Josie placed a hand over her heart. "And later he planted the roses out back in her memory."

"It was his way of grieving, I think. She died not long before I lost my own husband. Working here was what kept me going. Well, that and my children. They were small when he died, and I raised them on my own."

"It must have been so hard for you."

"It was definitely a struggle. They went to private school, and then to rather elite colleges. It was expensive and difficult at times, but I did what I had to do." Her eyes grew misty. "And Mr. Bartleby helped me more than he'll ever know."

I looked at the photo of Mr. Bartleby on the wall. He helped widowed ladies. He planted rosebushes in memory of his wife. He left Miss Josie the shop in his will. He seemed like a decent and honorable man, and not the kind to destroy valuable books for no apparent reason. The only question was why did he do it?

THIRTY

Why books are sometimes better than people:

1. They are always there when you need them.
2. They smell good.
3. They never judge you.
4. They aren't moody.
5. They won't misunderstand you.
6. They will never intentionally leave you.
7. They don't cheat on their wives.
8. They aren't allergic to dogs.
9. They don't crush your heart, step on it, and leave you broken and sad.
10. They aren't Cedric.

Our scheduled customer arrived promptly at three p.m., but it was not the person Miss Josie expected. "Cedric?"

I looked up in surprise. Cedric the Betrayer was in our shop?

I let out a long, low growl. I'd gotten better at this whole growling business. I hoped it might even sound threatening someday.

Cedric sneezed, pulling a handkerchief from the pocket of his tweed jacket. He had on new glasses, and he watched me warily. "Is the creature going to attack me again?"

Miss Josie rolled her eyes. "Not unless you provoke him. What do you want, Cedric? Mr. Vernon is about to arrive, and I'm busy."

"I'm here for business, not pleasure," he said. "Mr. Vernon's flight was delayed, so he asked me to come in his place. Is that a problem?"

"Of course not," said Miss Josie, her mouth a tight, straight line. "I have the items ready. I'll get them out of the vault for you. Follow me."

He scowled. "I know where the vault is, Josephine, or did you forget?"

"I never forget anything." She pressed her fingertip to the sensor, and the vault opened with a soft swooshing noise and a burst of cool air. Miss Josie donned white cotton gloves and offered a pair to Cedric.

"Please," he said, with a dismissive shake of his head. "I carry my own."

The temperature in the vault needed to stay at 60 to 66 degrees to keep the books safe and the humidity had to remain constant, too. The vault had specially designed lights because direct sunlight could damage the books as well. Although the books were locked up to protect them from possible thieves, they were also locked up to protect them from outside elements. Improper handling by humans often damaged books, but things like mold, rodents, insects, and temperature changes were far more dangerous.

It's incredible how much I learned by living in a bookshop for a few weeks. I could almost teach a class.

Note to self: I am a bookish wonder.

Miss Josie went into the vault. She picked up three books and brought them out, placing them on a high table. The books, wrapped in thin paper, looked quite old.

Cedric, who'd been waiting rather impatiently for her, pulled on his gloves with an irritated tug of his fingers. He studied the books carefully, turning the pages, inspecting the spines, and checking the publication dates.

"These are exactly what Mr. Vernon has been looking for," he said. "I'll take all three."

"All three?"

"Yes. These books are in excellent condition, and Mr. Vernon is discriminating. He's been searching for the right pieces to add to his collection. These will suit him perfectly."

"Well, all right," said Miss Josie. Judging by how flustered she'd become, I had to assume this surprised her.

Cedric touched her gloved hand with his. "I didn't come here to upset you. This visit is purely business. Even if it kills me inside, I can act professionally."

"Why would it kill you?" asked Miss Josie. She didn't look at his face, but she also didn't pull her hand away. Uh-oh. Not a good sign.

Cedric moved closer, his body only a hair's breadth away from hers. "Because I'm still madly, crazily, hopelessly in love with you, Josie. I know it's wrong, but I can't help how I feel."

For a second, it looked like Miss Josie couldn't breathe. She exhaled in a gasp and moved away from Cedric. "But you love your wife, too."

"I do, but it doesn't make me love you less." He gave her a sad half-smile, and, for a moment, I understood why Miss Josie found him attractive. In many ways, they suited each other. But he was an adulterer, and he'd hurt Miss Josie badly. I had significant issues with both of those things.

I'd thought he was a Mr. Wickham, but maybe he was more of a John Willoughby. I'd been putting him in *Pride and Prejudice* when he belonged in *Sense and Sensibility*.

"Why are you telling me this, Cedric?"

He took off his gloves and cupped her face in his hands. "When I saw you with the guy who owns all the coffee shops, it made me insanely jealous. I've never felt anything like it. I'd been upset about Mr. Bartleby leaving you the shop, and about the books he'd promised me, and some other things as well, but I should have known better. You're the only thing that ever mattered, and I lost you to the First Impressions billionaire because of my stupidity."

Miss Josie frowned and pushed Cedric's hands away from her face. "You mean Nate?"

He nodded. "Nate Murray. The founder of First Impressions. The brains behind the whole operation. He's famous, and I handed you to him on a silver platter."

"Wait. Are you saying Nate, my neighbor, the man who doesn't own a single T-shirt without a hole in it, is rich?"

Cedric seemed confused. "I assumed you knew. He's obscenely wealthy. And when I found out you'd slept with him I nearly lost my mind."

She blinked in surprise. "Who said I slept with him?"

Cedric frowned. "I overheard you talking about it this morning."

She stepped away from him. "I have no idea what you mean, but it's none of your concern," she said. "You're married. You seem to keep forgetting that little fact."

"What if I weren't married anymore?"

She froze. "What are you saying?"

He ran a finger along the edge of the table, not making eye contact with her. "It's a hypothetical question."

Miss Josie narrowed her eyes at him. "Those don't require an answer."

"Josie..." he said, his voice raw with emotion.

Thankfully, she didn't fall for it. "I appreciate you acting on Mr. Vernon's behalf. Let me pack these up for you," she said, all business once again.

He followed her to the cash register. "I miss you, Josie. Please think about it."

She carefully placed the books into a bag and rang up his bill. "There is nothing to think about, Cedric, because there is nothing between us."

He handed her a credit card. "You still have feelings for me. I know it."

She gave him a weary look. "You broke my heart, Cedric, and you're a married man. Act like one."

"But I can't live without you."

She slammed the cash register closed and handed him the receipt. "You're going to have to. Thank you. Have a nice day."

THIRTY-ONE

Things that fill me with regret:

1. Nibbling on those peony bushes. I still feel sick whenever I think of them.
2. Not getting even with Mr. Collins, the barn cat, and all of the idiot horses on the farm for being so mean to me.
3. My habit of startling the deaf, elderly beagle living down the street on purpose each time we take a walk.
4. Eating Miss Josie's thong. What was I thinking?
5. Holding my poo when we walk until I find a house with immaculate landscaping, and then letting it go.
6. Pushing Miss Josie into a rose bush while she gardened.
7. Kissing Miss Josie sometimes right after I lick my bottom. She has no idea.
8. Eating an entire bag of chocolate at Beaver Tales.

Miss Josie spent a great deal of time preparing the picnic she planned to share with Doc McHottie at the evening storytelling event at the gazebo. She made spiced pumpkin soup and put it in a thermos. She also prepared panini sandwiches filled with roasted vegetables, cheese, and homemade pesto, and baked special brownies for dessert. The brownies were piled high with a decadent, fudgy frosting. Her apartment smelled delicious, making me drool like a fountain.

"Control yourself, Capone," she said, wiping away the drool with a paper towel. "This food isn't for you."

Note to self: Miss Josie has a mean streak.

Making someone smell those delicious aromas all day long and refusing to share is not nice at all. It's especially bad for someone with advanced olfactory abilities, but I was excited about the picnic, and seeing my friend, Wrigley, and hearing ghost stories in the park. I hopped around, smiling widely, as Miss Josie packed the food up. She secured a bait bag around her waist filled with treats for me as well—oh, happy day—and grabbed my leash. Her cell phone rang, and she put it on speaker so she could wrangle me into my Easy Leader collar as she spoke.

"Hello," she said, sounding slightly out of breath.

"Josie?" asked Doc McHottie. "Are you okay?"

"Yes, I'm getting Capone's collar on. He's not cooperating."

The Easy Leader fit across my nose and was supposed to stop me from pulling Miss Josie while we walked. Instead it turned me into a nut case. It felt like a medieval torture device. I learned all about medieval torture devices on a PBS program once. Instead of being put on the rack, I had a tickle on my nose I could not scratch thanks to the

Easy Leader. As soon as she put it on me, I fell to the ground and tried to get it off by rubbing my face against the floor.

"Capone. Stop it," she said, her voice an angry hiss. She sweetened her tone for Doc McHottie. "I'm leaving. I'll be there shortly."

"I have some bad news. One of my patients, another lab, ate some broken glass. I have to operate immediately. I won't be able to come tonight. I'm so sorry."

Miss Josie's shoulders slumped. "Oh. Okay. I understand."

"Raincheck?"

"Definitely."

Miss Josie hung up the phone and sighed. Between spending the night listening to ghost stories in the park, or spending the night alone with me, Miss Josie went with the first option.

"Let's go, Capone. It'll be fun."

She was right. Once I got to the park and saw all the people, I sniffed around excitedly and almost forgot about the Easy Leader. Someone had decorated the gazebo with ghosts made from tissues and lollipops, and they'd hung swooping bats as well. The lighting provided an eerie purple glow, and nearly the entire town of Beaver had shown up for the event. Miss Josie spread a wool blanket on the grass, pulled out her picnic basket, and instructed me to sit and behave for the rest of the evening. As she poured a cup of soup from the thermos, someone spoke.

"Do you mind if we join you?"

Mr. Nate stood behind us with Jackson. Miss Josie cocked her head to one side. "Of course you can, Nate Murray, who does 'this and that' at First Impressions Café." She shook her head in disbelief and patted the spot next to her on the blanket. "I can't believe you didn't tell me you owned the place. Why did you lie to me?"

He sat down, stretching out his long legs on the blanket. "I didn't lie. Not exactly. You seemed so anti-coffee, and you were definitely anti-First Impressions. I already had two strikes against me. I thought if you knew who I was, it would be the third and final strike."

She studied him. "I appreciate the baseball analogy, but it doesn't apply. We're friends now. Friends get more than three strikes before they're out."

"Good to know." He wore jeans and a jacket with large pockets. The pockets smelled like treats. I pounced on him, trying to get to them. He laughed and gave me one.

Since we weren't walking anymore, Miss Josie took the Easy Leader off my nose and attached the leash to my regular collar instead. Instant relief. Glory be.

Miss Josie wore leather boots and had a scarf wrapped around her shoulders to ward off the cold autumn air. "Would you like some soup?" she asked.

He nodded, glancing at the contents of her picnic basket. "Either you're hungry, or this was a meal meant for two."

She smiled and handed him a cup of the pumpkin soup. "My date couldn't make it at the last minute. I'm glad you showed up. I'm not sure what I would have done with all this food if you hadn't."

I wanted to raise my paw and volunteer as tribute, but she wouldn't have understood. Instead, I sat next to Jackson and watched the proceedings.

"Who was her date?" asked Jackson.

"The vet," I said. "He's a nice guy. I like him."

Jackson snorted. "You'll feel differently about Doc McHottie after he cuts off your cojones."

"Cuts off my...what are you talking about, Jackson?"

He shook his head sadly. "You'll find out soon enough, my friend."

Mr. Nate took a sip of the soup and smiled. "Delicious. Did you make it?"

She nodded. "Vegetarian food isn't quite as bad as you thought, right?"

"Well, it's not steak..." He laughed at the outraged expression on her face. "I'm teasing. I'm not a caveman. I like vegetables. I consider myself an omnivore—like Capone."

She snorted. "Is there a word meaning a dog who will eat anything, even non-food items?"

Mr. Nate considered it. "A Labradoravore?"

She giggled. "Nailed it."

"I'm almost done with *Pride and Prejudice,* by the way."

"What do you think?"

"I liked it, but parts were frustrating. There was one miscommunication after another, and no one could say what they felt."

"So, you found it unrealistic?"

His dark eyes locked on hers. "Quite the opposite. I think it hit a little too close to home."

Miss Josie's mouth opened, her lips forming a round little "o," and I thought she might speak, but then Miss Edith Strosnider, a retired schoolteacher, got up to introduce the first storyteller. She slipped a pair of glasses onto her nose and read from a pile of notecards she'd taken out of her coat pocket.

"Storytelling has long been a popular means of creative expression," she said. "But this rich and valuable art form is dying out. The purpose of Beaver Tales is to share this wonderful form of oral history with our children and inspire generations to come. Without further ado, let me introduce the first of our storytellers."

We listened to story after story, and each one was fascinating, but the last storyteller was my favorite. Tony Lavorgne, a tall man with a deep voice who worked for the busing authority, shared local ghost stories with us.

"If you've ever climbed Misty Mountain," he said. "You know how it got its name. A mysterious mist swirls around it, often coming out of nowhere. And sometimes, if you listen carefully, you can hear the sound of a lost dog barking far off in the distance. But it isn't a dog at all. It's a demon beast hunting for its next victim." He paused, staring out at the crowd. "The Hell Hound of Misty Mountain."

I whimpered, and Jackson's eyes bugged out even more than usual. "I think I wet myself," he said quietly.

He wasn't joking. He now stood in a small puddle of pee. Thank goodness we sat on the grass and not on Miss Josie's blanket.

"I never want to go to Misty Mountain again," I said.

"As long as you don't go there at night, you'll be fine," said Jackson. "Now, be quiet. I want to hear Tony tell us the legend of Charlie No Face."

Charlie No Face was a man who lived near Beaver. Disfigured during a freak electrical accident, his face and most of his features had melted away. People often saw him walking along country roads at night, and some said his skin had an eerie glow, making him seem not quite human. Rumor had it he could come and go at will, disappearing into the night, and reappearing right next to an innocent bystander. It gave me the willies.

Note to self: Never go outside again.

The story of Charlie No Face, although terrifying, didn't scare me half as much as the Hell Hound of Misty

Mountain. I moved closer to Jackson, pressing against him, but he gave me a dirty look.

"Dude. Scary story time is meant for snuggling with the ladies, not with another guy."

"Oops, sorry." I backed away.

"Look at my boy, Nate, and learn," he said. He nodded toward Mr. Nate, who sat next to Miss Josie on the blanket. They'd finished their meal and now sipped wine. "That's the kind of snuggling you want to do while listening to a scary story. Love is in the air, Capone. Take my word for it."

I frowned. Miss Josie had packed a picnic for Doc McHottie, not Mr. Nate. Had she forgotten about Doc McHottie completely? If so, I had to remind her.

An idea came to me out of the blue. The family on the blanket next to ours had an entire bag of chocolate bars sitting unguarded next to their sleeping three-year-old. I knew I might be making a terrible error in judgment, but I had to do something to make Miss Josie remember Doc McHottie. An emergency visit to the vet would do it.

I lunged for the bag of chocolate, yanked my leash out of Miss Josie's hands, and took off across the darkened park full of people packing up their belongings after Beaver Tales. Miss Josie screamed, and both she and Mr. Nate got up to chase me, but I kept running until I reached a quiet area under a tree, out of sight. I then proceeded to eat the entire bag of chocolate, paper wrappings, and all.

Jackson waddled up to me as I finished, a shocked and horrified expression on his face. "Capone. What are you doing? It'll make you sick. You'll have to go straight to the vet."

I nodded, licking chocolate from around my mouth. For something so poisonous, it didn't taste half bad. "That's the goal. I want to go to the vet. Miss Josie packed her picnic for Doc McHottie, not for Mr. Nate."

Jackson paused, a confused frown wrinkling his already wrinkly pug forehead. "You don't like Nate?"

I burped. Maybe the chocolate wasn't quite as tasty as I'd initially thought. I felt a little funny now. "I love Mr. Nate, but if they get involved, it will break Miss Josie's heart when he leaves. I can't let it happen."

Jackson eyed me with newfound respect. "I don't agree with your methods or your conclusions, but I admire your loyalty, pup. You're brave. Stupid but brave."

"Thanks, Jackson."

Mr. Nate and Miss Josie came up to me, identically worried expressions on their faces. "Capone, what have you done?" asked Miss Josie.

My stomach made a noise loud enough everyone around me heard it. "Uh-oh," said Mr. Nate, picking up the now empty bag of chocolate bars. "This is not good. We have to take him to the vet. Now."

"Is he going to be okay?" asked Miss Josie, her face pale with worry. The rumble in my tummy increased before I made an agonized gagging noise and spewed vomit on Miss Josie's pretty leather boots like a volcano. I didn't erupt with lava, however. What came out of my mouth was a dark stream of chocolate, paper, and foil.

Curse my heroic nature.

To Miss Josie's credit, she didn't get mad. "Poor puppy. I need to get him to the vet. Can you clean up the picnic stuff for me?"

"Of course," said Mr. Nate. "I'll bring it to you later."

"Thanks, Nate," she said, looking at him misty eyed before rushing me toward Doc McHottie's office. Fortunately, it was only a block away from the gazebo, so we didn't have far to go.

I glanced over my shoulder at Mr. Nate. He waved goodbye, a worried frown on his face. Jackson looked worried, too. I wondered if I'd done the right thing, and I wasn't so sure. For the first time in my life, I may have literally and figuratively bitten off more than I could chew.

THIRTY-TWO

The scariest stories of all time:

1. The Hell Hound of Misty Mountain
2. The Legend of Charlie No Face
3. *Poltergeist*
4. *The Exorcist*
5. The Day Capone Ate a Bag of Chocolate

Doc McHottie had been about to leave when Miss Josie rushed me into his office. "Help," she said. "He ate chocolate."

He scooped me up and carried me back to one of the examination rooms. My stomach clenched and I heaved and heaved, but nothing happened. I'd probably gotten most of the chocolate and assorted wrappers out when I puked on Miss Josie's boots. Doc McHottie put on his stethoscope and listened to my belly. It gurgled so loudly, I doubted he needed the stethoscope, but who am I to argue with the best vet in Beaver?

"When did he eat it?" he asked, still listening to my stomach.

"A few minutes ago," said Miss Josie, sniffling. Oh, calamity. I'd made Miss Josie cry again. It made me feel worse than the chocolate. "We were at Beaver Tales, and he grabbed a bag of chocolate some people had on their blanket. It was so unexpected. The leash slipped out of my h-h-h-hands."

"And then what happened?"

"Nate Murray was with me, and we chased him. I was so afraid he might run out onto the street or something, but he didn't. He hid behind a tree and ate the entire bag of chocolate bars. By the time we found him, it was too late. They were all gone."

Doc McHottie nodded, his eyes on me. "Did he vomit? I don't hear anything in his stomach or his intestines."

"He did. All over my boots." Miss Josie held up one vomit covered boot to demonstrate. "Right after we found him."

Doc McHottie stood up and washed his hands. "I think he'll be fine. The vomiting, as unpleasant as it might seem, did the trick. Since Capone seems to eat things he shouldn't eat on a fairly regular basis, I'd suggest keeping hydrogen peroxide on hand. It's great to induce vomiting. Getting him to throw up quickly is the key. Keeping a better eye on him would be the first step, but that isn't something I can help you with."

Miss Josie bit her lip. "It happened so quickly, like he planned it or something. He picked the exact moment I wasn't paying attention and taking advantage of it."

Doc McHottie crossed his arms over his chest, his expression somber. "And why weren't you paying attention?"

She blinked in confusion. "Because Tony Lavorgne was telling the story of Charlie No Face and it's freaking scary."

"Well, it looks like you filled my spot on your picnic blanket pretty quickly."

"Excuse me?"

He sighed. "I realize Nate Murray, with all his fame and money, would appeal to any woman, but I thought you were different. I thought you had more substance. I guess I was wrong."

Oh no he didn't....

Miss Josie went from confused to angry even faster than I'd leaped off the picnic blanket and grabbed the chocolate. It was like, I don't know, record time.

Note to self: Don't ever get on Miss Josie's wrong side.

"Nate is a friend. We didn't plan to sit together at Beaver Tales, but I was glad to have the company. I don't appreciate what you're insinuating."

He studied her face. "I'm not the kind of guy who dates more than one woman at a time, Josie. And, if I'm dating someone, I expect the same in return."

"So would I."

He tilted his head to one side. "Oh, really? Because it's not only Nate. Your ex seems to be around a lot, too. And right after our first date, you went on a hike with the trainer from Misty Mountain. Wasn't that a date?"

"Well, kind of..."

"And do you know he approves of using shock collars on dogs?" Doc McHottie shook his head. "Zapping dogs into submission. What kind of person is he?"

Miss Josie gave me a long look. She probably wasn't opposed to the occasional zap if it meant keeping me in line.

"I apologize. I've been thoughtless," she said. "I should be able to control when my ex decides to show up at my place of business. He borderline harasses me, but that's my fault, too. Also, I should refuse to be friends with the nice man who owns the building next door to mine. Why would I want to cultivate a good, civil relationship with my neighbor?"

"Josie, wait—" Doc McHottie tried to stop her, but it was too late. Stopping Miss Josie at this point would have been like halting a train going full speed down a mountain. It was not going to happen.

"And another thing, I should have considered your feelings when deciding who trains my dog. I mean you did recommend obedience classes to me, but I didn't let you choose the time, place, and the person. My bad. And the hike *was* a date. I won't go out with him again, especially since my first date with him was even worse than my first date with you, but it definitely was a date."

"I'm glad you clarified this," he said, and he may have wanted to say more, but Miss Josie hadn't yet finished

"Our first date was a disaster, but I gave you a second chance because I liked you. I don't like ultimatums, however, and I don't like controlling relationships. Been there, done that. I don't need to experience it again." She shifted her purse on her arm. "And another thing, I realize I'm a horrible dog owner, but I'm honestly doing my best. I'll look for a new vet tomorrow."

"Josie, wait," he said. "I'm a jealous idiot but don't let it affect Capone's care. If you ever need me, I'm here for both of you."

"Good to know," said Miss Josie, her voice icy. "How much do I owe you for tonight?"

He shook his head sadly. "Nothing. I only listened to his stomach. Don't worry about it."

"Thank you, and goodbye."

I almost felt bad for poor Doc McHottie. Yes, he acted like a jerk, but Miss Josie's fury was a frightening thing. The entire way home, she muttered to herself about men and how much she hated all of them. I hoped she didn't include me in that group. I was, after all, a male.

She opened the door to the darkened bookstore. As she searched for the light switch, a sound came from the garden.

"Be quiet, Capone," she said.

We tiptoed to the back of the shop in the dark, and then I saw something that would haunt my nightmares. Charlie No Face...in the window...staring back at us.

Miss Josie let out a blood-curdling scream. I yelped in surprise and hopped away, knocking over a large stack of books, and causing them to fall to the floor with a crash. Miss Josie fumbled for the outside light switch as I barked like a maniac, and suddenly the back garden was bathed in light.

Dressed entirely in black with pantyhose covering his face and distorting his features, a man stood right by our back door. He looked around a moment in shock, then ran to the far corner of the garden. He climbed to the roof of the shed like a chubby ninja monkey and vaulted over the back wall.

As soon as he disappeared from view, loud pounding came from the front door of the shop, and Miss Josie screamed again. She fumbled for her cell phone, ready to call 911. We both melted with relief when we saw who stood there.

"Nate," she said as she ran to the door and unlocked it, flying into his arms. He had her picnic basket and blanket but dropped those to the ground next to Jackson so he could hold her.

"What happened?" he asked. "I heard you scream and Capone bark."

"Someone tried to break in through the back door. I thought it was Charlie No Face." Miss Josie's voice sounded muffled because she had her face in Mr. Nate's neck.

Jackson looked at me in shock. "Seriously? Charlie No Face?"

I nodded. "Yes. It was terrifying. My heart is beating so quickly, I'm afraid it might pop out of my chest."

"It's probably because of the chocolate. You should make better choices" Jackson waddled closer and sniffed the picnic basket. "Wait a second, do I smell cheese in here? Come to Papa, baby."

He stuck his head in the basket and pulled out a wedge of cheese. Mr. Nate and Miss Josie didn't notice.

"Charlie No Face?" Mr. Nate asked, a smiled playing on his lips. "No more scary stories for you, Josephine."

But Mr. Nate hadn't seen the face in the window. He didn't understand how terrifying it had been. Miss Josie scowled but remained in his embrace. "I said I *thought* I saw Charlie No Face, but it turned out to be a man with pantyhose over his head."

Nate frowned his dark eyes filled with worry. "Wait, you're serious, aren't you?"

She took out her cell phone and dialed 911. "Yes, and I'm calling the police. This has gone far enough."

THIRTY-THREE

High crimes in Beaver, Pennsylvania:

1. Change stolen from unlocked cars.
2. A multiple muffin theft at the snack bar in the Beaver County Courthouse.
3. Going over the 25-mph speed limit on Gypsy Glen Road.
4. High school students caught sneaking onto a construction site
5. Illegal parking in front of the post office.
6. Not returning library books on time.
7. Lawn care violations.
8. Jackson pooping on the sidewalk.
9. A delinquent shooting a BB gun at stop signs.
10. The mysterious break-ins at Bartleby's Books.

Officer Stahl of the Beaver Borough Police arrived precisely two minutes after Miss Josie's call. He didn't have far to go. Police headquarters was located in the borough building only a few doors down from the bookshop.

"Tell me again what happened," he said, taking notes on a little pad. He had a square jaw, a soft voice, and a calm aura. We needed a calm aura right now. Miss Josie and I were still pretty freaked out.

Mr. Nate sat next to Miss Josie holding her hand. When I looked hopefully at one of the cookies still in the basket, Jackson shook his head. "No way, Capone. You've had enough people food for the day."

"But you ate a giant wedge of cheese."

"Completely different," he said, with a belch. "And non-toxic. I still don't understand why you did that, pupster. Pure craziness."

I sighed. "It was a bad plan. I need to think these things through a little better next time."

Note to self: No more chocolate.

"Do you know what your problem is, pooch? You aren't separating human business from doggie business. Look at it this way—I love Mr. Nate more than anything, but I don't interfere. Boundaries are important." He leaned closer and sniffed my bum. "Your exit area smells a little funny. Are you sure you're okay?"

My stomach gurgled again. "I'm not sure." I gave him a stern look. "Speaking of personal boundaries, why are you sniffing my anus?"

He shrugged. "I referred to dog/human boundaries. They don't apply to this situation."

Miss Josie went over what happened when we returned home this evening. Officer Stahl took notes.

"Two confirmed break-ins and two attempted break-ins since August," said Officer Stahl, rubbing his chiseled chin. "It's strange, but if you add it all together, I can only come up with one conclusion. It has to be someone who knows the shop well, is familiar with your schedule, and understands the value of the books you're selling here. Is there anyone you can think of who fits this description?"

"Cedric Churchill," she said, her voice tight. "He's a disgruntled former employee, and he's also my ex."

"A disgruntled ex?" asked Officer Stahl.

Miss Josie shrugged. "Not exactly. He cared more about the shop than he ever cared about me, and, well, he's married. I didn't know, of course, when we first started dating. If I had, I never would have gone out with him. It's not typically something I do. Heck, I rarely date at all." She smacked a hand over her mouth. "I'm sorry. Am I rambling?"

Nate nodded, trying not to smile. "You're rambling."

Officer Stahl gave her an understanding look. "It's an adrenaline thing. I see it all the time. At least you aren't crying. Lots of people cry. So, your ex is a married man?"

"Yes." She took in a deep breath and let it out slowly. "But I can't imagine it's him." Miss Josie's lip wobbled, and I had a feeling a weep-fest might be coming on. Officer Stahl must have noticed it, too. He cleared his throat.

"Okay. I'll take it from here. Keep your doors locked, your alarm on, and your eyes open. It might be all it takes to stop this from happening again, but I'm not sure."

"What do you mean?" asked Nate.

"The same person does not try to break into a shop repeatedly unless they are after something specific." He closed his notebook and shot Miss Josie a sympathetic look. "And I don't think he's going to stop until he gets it."

After Officer Stahl left, Mr. Nate stared around the shop, at the tall bookshelves reaching nearly to the ceiling, the tables covered in piles of books, and the smaller items for sale on standing displays, mostly bookmarks, and other bookish oddities. "What could it be?" he asked. "What would a thief want so much he'd risk breaking into this place over and over again?"

"I have no idea," said Miss Josie. "I think we're missing something, some key piece of the puzzle."

"Or maybe it's your ex, and he's out for vengeance."

She frowned. "I honestly don't think so."

Mr. Nate gave her a steady look. "It's hard to imagine someone you once cared about would do something so awful, but it is possible."

"Don't misunderstand me. He's a terrible person, but he's also extremely anal. He'd never hurt a book on purpose."

"But he'd hurt you?"

She gave him a wry smile. "I'm not a book."

"What a loser. Did Mr. Bartleby know about you and Cedric?"

She shook her head. "He would not have approved. Cedric encouraged me to keep our relationship a secret, which should have been the first sign. I thought it was because he wanted to be respectful and professional. I had no idea he did it so his wife wouldn't find out."

Mr. Nate crossed his arms over his chest. "How did Cedric become a disgruntled employee?"

"Cedric worked here much longer than me. He was Mr. Bartleby's main buyer and assumed Mr. Bartleby would sell him the place when he retired."

"But he didn't."

"No, he didn't."

"How did you find out about the wife?"

She sighed. "Completely by accident. Cedric normally wasn't in the shop much, but one day, Mrs. Norris stopped by when he and I were both working here alone. Mr. Bartleby hadn't been feeling well and went upstairs to rest.

She'd come to drop off chicken soup for Mr. Bartleby, and asked Cedric how his wife was doing. Apparently, Cedric's wife had caught the same cold as Mr. Bartleby."

"What did you do?"

"I held it together long enough to smile and thank Mrs. Norris for the soup, but as soon as she left, I lost it. I called Cedric every name in the book. I may have even invented a few new ones of my own."

Mr. Nate stuck his hands into the pockets of his jeans. "None of this is your fault."

She shrugged. "I know, but Mr. Bartleby must have heard my little tirade. He fired Cedric the next day and left the shop to me in his will. He was such a remarkable gentleman."

My ears perked up. I glanced at the smiling photo of Mr. Bartleby on the wall, his blue eyes twinkling over his wire-rim glasses. A remarkable gentleman? Interesting.

"And Cedric was a slime ball."

"I understand that now." She glanced at him from under her eyelashes. "Have you never been crossed in love, Mr. Murray?"

He gave her a crooked smile. "Not quite as dramatically as you. I don't date much, to be honest. Work always seems to get in the way."

"Well, I suppose being a corporate genius keeps you busy."

"I guess. Although hearing you call me a genius is a little weird. How I went from being a Neanderthal to a genius in such a short period is beyond me." He glanced around the shop. "What can I do to help?"

"I hate to keep you up past your bedtime."

He laughed. "Which is why coffee is so helpful," he said. "I provide a community service."

"You're a regular Mother Teresa," she said with a smile as she took off her cardigan and rolled up the sleeves of her white blouse. "But, if you're seriously willing to help, I'm happy to accept your offer. I'm certainly not going to be able to sleep tonight."

He rubbed his hands together. "Where do we start?"

She frowned, biting her lower lip. "I'd say we start where the thief did."

"Where?"

She pointed to the steel door with the sophisticated, illuminated keypad next to it. "The vault. The intruder wanted to get in there badly, but why?"

She put her finger on the keypad, and the door opened with a swish. Mr. Nate's eyes widened. "I feel like Aladdin, and you've opened the cave of wonders. I'm strangely excited about this. Is that weird?"

"Nope," she said with a smile of genuine pleasure. "Because I've opened this door hundreds of times, and I feel exactly the same way. It's a treasure trove. These books are fragile. Irreplaceable. It's my job to protect and guard them."

"You sound like one of the Knights Templar guarding the Holy Grail."

"Exactly," she said, quite seriously. "It's a sacred trust. Mr. Bartleby knew I felt this way about books, which is part of the reason he left me the shop. Cedric felt the same way, but with one small difference."

"What do you mean?"

"Cedric valued books for what they're worth, for the money they brought to him. I value them simply for what they are."

"And what are they, Josephine?"

Her smile lit up her whole face as she stared at the

books in the vault with a dreamy expression. "Voices of people long gone. Beautiful bits of history. The whispers of ghosts. Their hearts are on these pages. Their souls. These are precious bits of humanity, and it's up to me to keep them safe."

THIRTY-FOUR

A list of the highest prices paid for books and manuscripts:

1. *Codex Leicester*, $52.1 million.
2. *Book of Mormon*, $35.8 million.
3. *Gospels of Henry the Lion*, $29.4 million.
4. *Magna Carta, Original Exemplar*, $25.7 million.
5. *Rothschild Prayerbook*, $20.2 million.

Miss Josie and Mr. Nate spent an hour looking through the vault. I knew from the disappointed expressions on their faces that they had found nothing. Before closing the door, Miss Josie stared around the narrow interior, at the walls lined with books with older volumes resting in specially designed drawers, a puzzled frown on her face.

"There are rare books in the vault, and valuable books, too," she said, shutting the door. "But I don't understand what someone would want so badly they'd risk jail for it. I mean it's not like we have the *Codex Leicester* or anything."

"How much would it be worth?"

She shrugged. "It depends. Probably about $52 million."

Mr. Nate's jaw dropped. "For a book?"

"For a priceless piece of history," she huffed. "It's a collection of scientific writings by Leonardo da Vinci. You can't express the true value of it in monetary form."

"You just did. It's $52 million. That's expressing quite a lot."

I wagged my tail, happy they were done with the vault. I hated it when Miss Josie went anywhere without me. Jackson seemed less concerned. He snoozed on his back with his legs spread open. He snored so loudly the windows nearly rattled. Rather than being an annoying sound, however, I found it kind of soothing. I'd gotten used to the idiosyncrasies of Jackson the Pug.

Usually, Miss Josie gave me a treat for being obedient when she came out of the vault, but not tonight. When I sat prettily and stared up at the treat jar, all she gave me was a stern look.

"No treats for you, Capone. You need to give your tummy a rest after that chocolate." She shook her head in bewilderment as she stared at me. "What do you think made him do it? Why would he grab an entire bag of candy and eat it? It seemed almost like he had a dastardly plan."

Mr. Nate laughed. "With a name like Capone, he's destined to be a lawbreaker."

I stared at Mr. Nate, horrified, but Miss Josie immediately came to my defense. "It's not his fault his name is Capone." She frowned. "I need to change it, but I can't seem to figure out the right name for him."

"It's a cool name," said Mr. Nate, studying my face. "Why change it? It suits him. He's Capone, to me at least."

Miss Josie cupped my face in her hands. "Not to me,"

she said, staring deeply into my eyes. "I don't know what your name is yet, but I'm going to figure it out."

Thank heavens for small miracles. Maybe I wasn't doomed after all.

Mr. Nate glanced at his watch. "I'd better go. I have an early day tomorrow."

Miss Josie blushed. "Sorry to keep you here so late. I appreciate your help."

"My pleasure," he said. They stared at each other a long moment, the kind of moment when time stands still. Incredibly romantic, but I ruined it by producing the most protracted, loudest fart ever to come out of my body. Why did these things always happen at the worst possible moment?

Curse my irritable bowels.

Miss Josie's eyes widened. "Gracious," she said. "I'd better take him out back."

"I'll walk you out there," said Mr. Nate. He probably suspected Miss Josie might be nervous after the whole Charlie No Face incident. I felt nervous, too.

Although I'd thrown up most of the chocolate I'd eaten, the rest decided to come out a different direction. Not the projectile diarrhea I'd produced when I ate the peony bushes, but still an icky stream of watery, chocolaty poo. Not a good visual, I know, and not a good thing to experience first-hand either.

"So," said Mr. Nate, making conversation as he attempted to avoid looking at what I was currently doing all over Miss Josie's back garden. "Mr. Bartleby was a gardener. Do you like to garden, too?"

"I do. It calms me, but Mr. Bartleby had a green thumb. His roses always bloomed in the most gorgeous colors, and he kept a little vegetable garden as well. I never had to buy a tomato or a zucchini when I worked for him. He always kept me stocked." She smiled wistfully at the memory.

"Don't you think it's interesting he had a diagram of the garden in the last ledger you found?"

She frowned. "It is odd."

"Do you know what else is weird? He mapped out each rose bush and plant, and he included the dimensions of the patio, but he didn't put the old potting shed in his drawing." He nodded toward the corner of the garden. "Why not?"

"Good question," she said and grabbed her flashlight from the hook inside the back door. "Do you want to take a look?"

As they walked to the shed, Jackson sat on the patio and waited. "I'm not tramping through that grass," he said, scratching his round belly. "You had the runs. It's like a minefield. No, thank you."

Mr. Nate and Miss Josie didn't seem to have a problem with it as together they marched through the grass and went straight to the shed. Miss Josie opened the door to take a peek inside. I came with them, sticking my head in, too. It felt like a party. I wagged my tail happily. How fun.

"It's hard to see much of anything right now," said Miss Josie. "I'll have to come back and look again in the morning."

She turned to leave and bumped right into Mr. Nate. He put his hands out to steady her, and they stared at each other a long moment before he leaned his dark head close to hers. "I'd really like to kiss you right now, Josephine."

Her breath came out with a hitch. "I'd like to kiss you, too, but I can't. Not when I know you'll be leaving soon."

He still had his hands on her upper arms, his face

somber and a bit confused as he stared down at her in the darkened shed. "You won't kiss me because I have to go to Seattle next month?"

"It's not the trip to Seattle. You have a business to run, not one little shop." She shook her head. "Getting involved would be a mistake."

"I don't understand—"

She put a finger to his lips. "In the last few years I've lost my parents, my mentor, and also Cedric; the man I thought I loved. Right now, I'm on the verge of losing this shop, too." I heard the pain and emotional exhaustion in her voice, but I heard something else, too. Fear. "It's not only about business. If I lose the shop, I might have to give Capone back, and it would break my heart."

Oh, calamity. It would break my heart, too.

This was tragic and also proof I'd been correct. Mr. Nate might be one of the most excellent men I'd ever met, but he could not be her Mr. Darcy. Mr. Darcy would not leave Lizzie to go open a new coffee shop. True love does not gallivant off to Seattle. True love stays.

I was running out of options. Doc McHottie? No longer a contender. He'd basically called her a skank and dumped her. And Sexy Trainer Dude had failed, too. The man was a terrible kisser, and also, he peed his pants in front of her, which is never a good sign.

The only question was—who remained?

I got my answer the next day after Miss Josie updated Ms. Anne on the events of the night before. She'd left out the part about almost kissing Mr. Nate, oddly enough, but she told her the part about me eating chocolate.

Gracie looked at me in shock. "It's toxic. Why would you eat something toxic?"

"I was trying to help Miss Josie find her true love." I explained my efforts to find a Mr. Darcy for my beloved owner.

Gracie looked misty-eyed. "How adorable. You risked your life to help her."

"But I'm failing. Miserably. And at this rate I'll never get a new name."

"What's wrong with your name?"

I gave her a sidelong glare. "Seriously?"

She shrugged, looking exceptionally fluffy and pretty this morning. She smelled sweet, too, which meant she must have been at the groomer recently.

"Okay. Fine. Capone may not be the perfect name for you, but you're more than your moniker. Your name isn't what's important. It's what's in your heart that matters, and your heart is good. Trust me. I've seen some bad dogs in my day, and you're not one of them. You're a nice puppy."

It was the kindest thing anyone had ever said to me. "Thank you, Gracie."

"Don't mention it, and don't give up. You'll find someone for Miss Josie. Someone perfect. I know you can do it."

The bell on the door tinkled and Cedric burst into the shop. Miss Josie had been putting a dictionary back on the shelf, and she held it in front of her, like a shield.

"What do you want?" she asked.

Ms. Anne, who'd been behind the counter, came to stand next to her. "Good question. Tell us what you're doing here, Cedric, or we'll call the police."

I leaped in front of Miss Josie and Ms. Anne and let out a low growl. If Cedric wanted to get to them, he'd have to go through me. Oddly enough, he didn't seem like a man on the warpath. He looked more like a man on the verge of tears.

I studied him carefully, noticing the dark circles under his eyes and the paleness of his skin. Although he'd been fastidiously dressed the last time he visited, Cedric seemed rumpled this morning, like he'd slept in his clothes.

"Josephine St. Clair. Did you tell the police I broke into your shop?"

Miss Josie's face turned so red it looked like the lobsters I'd seen once in a PBS special. "I didn't think you did it, Cedric. But they asked me for the names of disgruntled former employees who might know about rare books."

He sighed, his shoulders slumping. He reminded me of a deflated balloon, as if all the air had gone out of him as soon as he heard Miss Josie's words. "I guess I would be the first person to pop into your mind. But I didn't do it, Josie. I swear."

She slowly lowered the dictionary she'd been holding and put it down on the table in front of her. "I believe you, Cedric."

At her words, Cedric put his face in his hands and moaned. I'd been right in my earlier assessment. He stood on shaky emotional ground. What was going on here?

Ms. Anne called Cedric a rude name under her breath and went back to the cash register. Miss Josie led Cedric to a chair in the corner of the shop and gave him a cup of tea. She sat in the chair next to him.

"What's going on, Cedric?"

He sniffed, wiping his nose on a napkin. "My wife kicked me out."

Miss Josie sat back in her seat, her expression blank. "Oh."

He nodded. "She suspected I hadn't been faithful to her." He let out a long shaky breath. "The police confirmed those suspicions when they came to our house last night."

"This was not a vengeful act on my part. I never intended to break up your marriage."

"I know," he said, reaching out to hold Miss Josie's hand. She pulled it away from his grasp. Good girl. "And I got what I deserved. Our marriage hasn't been the same since I fell in love with you. I tried to make it work, but my heart wasn't in it. It remained here. At Bartleby's. With you."

Miss Josie's eyes narrowed. "What are you saying, Cedric?"

He fell on his knees in front of her. "I love you, Josie. I always have, and I always will. Please forgive me. Please take me back."

Cedric took Miss Josie's hand and kissed it fervently. I'd licked her entire hand only moments before he'd arrived. In essence, it was almost like Cedric kissed me.

Note to self: Ew.

The bell above the door tinkled, and Doc McHottie walked in, a bouquet in his hands. Mr. Nate came in behind him, carrying two cups of coffee. They both froze when they saw Cedric on his knees in front of Miss Josie.

Ms. Anne ushered them in, trying hard not to smile. "Form a line, gentlemen."

Miss Josie hopped to her feet, and away from Cedric the Betrayer, but Mr. Nate and Doc McHottie didn't stay long. Doc McHottie put his flowers on the counter and left without saying a word. Mr. Nate watched him go, his expression unreadable, before turning back to us.

"Your coffees, ladies," he said. The only indication he gave he might be upset was a slight flush in his cheeks.

Cedric shot him a condescending look. "Josephine doesn't drink coffee."

Miss Josie took the cup from Mr. Nate. "Yes, I do. I love coffee now. Thanks, Nate." She took a sip and smiled. "This is the best one yet. What is it?"

"It's black, actually," he said, biting his lip as if trying not to laugh. "But a nice Sumatran. One of my favorites."

"Mine, too."

"Good choice. I'd better get back—" he said, but Miss Josie interrupted him.

"Did you get any further in the book?"

He stuck his hands into his pockets and leaned against one of the bookshelves, his pose casual. Cedric's was not. He stood ramrod straight and watched the interaction between Miss Josie and Mr. Nate with something icy and calculating in his eyes.

"I finished it, actually," said Mr. Nate.

She blinked at him in surprise. "I can't believe you read it so fast. What did you think?"

"Well, I relate to Mr. Darcy more than I ever thought I would. See you later, Josie."

She waved to him, a bemused expression on her face, and Cedric watched him go. "You never drank coffee before," he said, sounding a bit peevish.

"Things change," said Miss Josie, her eyes still on Mr. Nate's retreating form. "People change."

"I want to change. I want to be better," Cedric said. "For you."

Ms. Anne made a gagging noise. Clearly, she was not Cedric's biggest fan, and judging by the hostility in his eyes when he looked at her, the feeling seemed to be mutual.

"I'm so glad I came this morning," said Gracie, watching

Miss Josie and Cedric. "I was going to stay home and sleep, but this is much more interesting."

Although not certain I agreed with Gracie, I knew one thing for sure. Miss Josie was in a pickle, and not the yummy kind of pickle they gave out with the sandwiches at Don's Deli. She was in a bad kind of pickle, and I didn't know how to help her get out of it.

THIRTY-FIVE

Why Cedric the Betrayer ended up sleeping on Miss Josie's couch:

1. His wife kicked him out.
2. He had nowhere else to go.
3. Miss Josie was the kindest person in the world.
4. Miss Josie harbored residual guilt over things which weren't her fault (aka she'd dated a married man).
5. Cedric was a master manipulator.
6. Whether she liked it or not, Miss Josie still had feelings for the creep.

The last one was the kicker. Unresolved relationships were dangerous quagmires full of heavy emotional baggage.

"Wait, she still cares for him?" asked Rocco. The room was dark, but I saw the shocked expression on his smushed up face. "Is she a total idiot?"

"No. She has a soft heart. And she tends to love the unlovable. She can't help herself. Take you, for example."

I thought for a second I saw something close to admiration flash in Rocco's eyes, but it could have been a trick of the light. "Right back at you, bully stick breath."

A fair shot, since my breath did smell like bully sticks. Miss Josie gave them to me as a way to keep me from chewing on other things, like her shoes. Unfortunately, they were made from the male appendages of bulls, and they reeked.

"Point taken. To answer your question, I think Miss Josie is lonely."

"But she has us," said Rocco. "What more could she possibly want?"

"Um, someone human. Someone to hang out with, and drink wine with, and, well, you know..."

"Of course, *I* know," said Rocco, giving me an odd look. "I'm surprised you do."

"We live in a book store. Duh."

Rocco frowned, wrinkling his furry eyebrows at me. "What exactly are we talking about, pup?"

"The fact that she would like to have someone to discuss books with, of course."

"I see," he said, but he looked like he tried not to laugh. Felines are such a mystery.

"Yes, and she and Cedric the Betrayer had books in common."

"Cedric the Betrayer? I love it. I wish he were allergic to cats. I'd make him suffer."

A plan formed in my mind. "Cedric isn't allergic to cats, but he is allergic to dogs. Hey, Rocco, is there any way you can spring me from Alcatraz tonight?"

He laughed. "I like the way your mind works, pup."

Rocco opened my crate with ease as Miss Josie slept in her room, the door closed and locked. We all heard the click when she went to bed. Cedric the Betrayer snoozed on her blue couch. He'd put his glasses on the end table and curled up in a slightly uncomfortable looking ball.

"What do we do now?" I asked, my voice a whisper.

"Sleep as close to him as possible so he gets the full effect of your allergens."

I hopped onto a soft velvet Ottoman. It matched Miss Josie's blue couch and was the closest I could get to Cedric. It put me only inches away from his face. "Is there anything else?" I asked as Rocco climbed on the bookshelf to sleep.

"Yes," he said. "Control yourself this evening. Don't eat anything toxic or chew on anything that doesn't belong to you. Behave. We don't want a repeat performance of the night you destroyed Miss Josie's room."

"No way," I said, and I meant it, but sometime around midnight, my puppy instincts took over. I couldn't help myself. I got bored, and when I get bored, I become Capone-ish. I needed something to occupy my time. Cedric's wallet seemed like the right choice.

After I pulled out all the credit cards, photos, and ID, and shook it until cash flew around the room like single's night in a strip club, I settled down to enjoy the buttery soft leather. Lovely, and such a pleasant texture, so I chewed and chewed until the leather got even more malleable and fell apart. Then I did what came naturally to me.

I ate Cedric's wallet.

Yum. What a perfect, leathery treat. I belched and looked around the room, bored again. I spied Cedric's expensive Italian loafers on the floor next to the couch, and once again ignored my baser instincts.

Let me tell you, Italian loafers do not taste like Italian food—no sauce, and no meatballs, and yet delicious in their own right. I didn't eat the loafers, of course. I just nibbled on them, and they were sublime.

Note to self: Italian shoes are *perfetto* and *delizioso*.

I finished chewing as the sun came up in the sky and retreated to my post next to Cedric's face. He breathed through his mouth at this point. His nose seemed stuffy, and his eyes looked red and swollen.

Way to go allergens, I thought to myself as I yawned and closed my eyes. My belly was full of Cedric's wallet, and I'd been up most of the night making mischief. Now I felt utterly exhausted.

I awoke a short time later to someone sneezing violently right in my face. I guess I'd scooted to the edge of the Ottoman in my sleep and now had my nose right next to Cedric's. He opened his eyes and pulled away in shock.

"What the—" He fumbled for his glasses, knocking over the lamp on the end table in the process. It caused a big crash and Miss Josie opened the door of her room, rubbing her eyes.

"Cedric. Are you okay?"

He sneezed again. "No. Capone slept next to me, and I'm having an allergic reaction."

Cedric glared at me through puffy, swollen eyes. His nose seemed puffy and swollen, too—not a great look for him—and it dripped like a leaking faucet. He sniffed, grabbing a tissue from the box on Miss Josie's coffee table, and sneezed again.

He was a mess. His hair stood on end. He held his head oddly to one side, wincing as he tried to stretch his neck, perhaps to relieve a crick from sleeping on the small couch.

Miss Josie straightened the lamp and patted me on the head. I wagged my tail and licked her hand. "Why did you let him out of his crate?" she asked. "I pushed it as far away as I could from you, hoping you wouldn't breathe in his dander all night."

Cedric blew his nose. "I didn't let him out. You must have left it open."

"I did not."

For a second, it seemed like he might want to argue with her, but he thought better of it. "It doesn't matter. Thanks for letting me stay. I appreciate it, Josie. I'll be out of your way as soon as possible. Two days tops."

"Two days?" she asked. "I thought you only needed to stay the night."

Cedric's lip trembled, the most pathetic thing I'd ever seen. "I don't want to inconvenience you. I'll find somewhere else to crash... a park bench or something."

Rocco rolled his eyes. "Ridiculous," he muttered. "He's scamming her. He wouldn't last two seconds on a park bench."

Miss Josie, however, fell for it. "You can stay another day or two, I guess," she said rather grudgingly.

Cedric pursed his thin lips. "You don't sound happy about it."

"I'm *not* happy about it, Cedric. Why would you even think I could be?"

"Well, you'll be rid of me soon enough," he said, his voice snippy and cold. "I have a lead on a place. I put the contact info into my wallet. Do you see my wallet anywhere?"

Miss Josie looked around and noticed the money all over the floor. "Uh-oh," she said. When she leaned down to pick up the bills, she saw the credit cards lying beneath the couch. "This is not good."

"What is it?" asked Cedric as he folded the blanket he'd borrowed from Miss Josie, a pale pink afghan.

"Um, Cedric," she said wincing. "Capone may have gotten ahold of your wallet last night."

Cedric froze. "What?" He knelt to gather the cash and credit cards. "Why would he do this? And where is my wallet?"

They both stared at me. Realization dawned on Miss Josie's face. "I think he ate it."

Cedric's eyes widened. "The whole thing?"

"Well, he did remove your cash and credit cards first," she said meekly. "That's something, right?"

"It was an expensive wallet."

"I'm sorry, Cedric, but you shouldn't have let him out of his crate."

Judging by the way his jaw tightened, Cedric wanted to argue the point. Instead, he took a deep, measured breath, and when he blew it out, he gave Miss Josie a tense little smile.

"Enough about my wallet," he said. "Let's go have brunch at Waffles Incaffienated. You love their bananas Foster waffles, and I want to thank you for helping me out last night."

"I don't know... "

"I insist. It's the least I can do."

She couldn't seem to come up with an excuse not to go. "Fine, but I have to feed Capone and let him out first."

"I'll take him out," he said. "And you can get ready. Now, where did I put my shoes?"

I hid under the kitchen table, terrified, as Cedric searched for his Italian loafers. This situation would not end well. Miss Josie took one look at me and immediately knew what had happened.

Curse my guilty conscience.

"Oh, no," she said. "Capone, what did you do to Cedric's shoes?"

Cedric let out what can only be described as a muffled scream of agony when he spotted them. "Not my Italian loafers. I bought these in Rome. I haven't even paid for them yet."

"I'm so sorry," said Miss Josie.

Cedric sat on the couch, staring at the mangled loafers in his hands. "My shoes. My poor, beautiful shoes."

Miss Josie let out something that sounded like a smothered laugh. When Cedric glared at her, she cleared her throat. "I need to take Capone outside. I'll be back in a few minutes. We don't have to go to breakfast. I know you're upset."

He shook his head. "No. I'm taking you to breakfast," he said, slipping the loafers onto his feet. They looked ridiculous, and were still damp from my drool, but at least they seemed wearable. "And I'll take Capone outside. I insist."

We went outside, and Cedric knelt next to me, his face a mask of fury. He grabbed the back of my neck and squeezed, pinching me so hard I yelped in pain. "If you touch any of my things again, you'll regret it. Do you understand me, Capone?"

I stared at him, knowing I had a big problem on my hands. Cedric looked murderous, and it was bad news indeed, especially since I appeared to be his intended victim.

Oh, calamity.

THIRTY-SIX

What I discovered after destroying Cedric's belongings:

1. Cedric the Betrayer was a monster.
2. If Miss Josie took him back, I'd be forced to leave.
3. Leather is yummy.

"We need to get rid of this guy," said Rocco, as he sat perched on top of my crate. "He's a nightmare."

"I know, but how?"

He stretched. Oddly enough, I didn't even mind that he lay sprawled out on top of my crate. Rocco and I had bonded, I guess.

"Let me think about it," he said. "Unlike you, I possess a magnificent brain."

"Think fast," I said. "Miss Josie and Cedric will be back from breakfast soon, and he already threatened me once. I'm scared it could happen again."

"He was mean to me, too," said Rocco. "He pushed me off the couch last night. He has some nerve."

Rocco cleaned himself, because it soothed him, and it seemed much cheaper than therapy. In between licks, he muttered derogatory things about Cedric. I agreed with him. Hearing Rocco complain about Cedric helped. It made me seem less alone.

When Miss Josie and Cedric got back from breakfast, smelling like vanilla-infused syrup and waffles, I realized we stood on dangerous ground. Although Cedric had hurt Miss Josie terribly, the first tentative efforts toward forgiveness had sprouted between them. I needed to trample those sprouts, and Rocco felt the same.

He eyed them as they sat down on the couch to watch PBS together. Miss Josie let me out of my cage, and I tried to get close to them, but Cedric gave me the stink eye and scared me away. I sat all alone, suffering in silence, but Rocco did not suffer in silence. He did so vocally.

"This is not good, pup. Look at how Cedric has his arm on the back of the couch. It's one step away from snuggling, I'm telling you. This whole situation spells trouble, big trouble, for both of us."

I had to admit Rocco might be right. Scary thought.

Miss Josie glanced at Cedric. "What's the plan for tomorrow?"

He touched her cheek with one finger. "I'll do whatever you're doing."

She edged away from him. "Stop it, Cedric. You're making me uncomfortable. I meant I'm taking Capone to obedience training, so you'll have to leave the apartment."

"I see," he said, shifting in his seat. "Well, then I guess I'm taking Capone to obedience training, too."

"I'd prefer to go on my own."

"Please don't be like this, Josie. I want to help, and I think Capone and I got off on the wrong foot."

"Fine," she said, her eyes still wary. "But don't read into this. I'm serious."

We arrived at Misty Mountain the next day at eight a.m. sharp. Cedric had on a wrinkled pair of khakis and his damaged loafers. He held a soggy tissue in his hands and kept wiping his nose with it. Miss Josie didn't look happy herself, and she let out a little groan when she saw Sexy Trainer Dude working behind the desk.

"Ms. St. Clair," said Sexy Trainer Dude, unable to look her in the eye. "Can we talk?"

"Certainly," she said, keeping things formal and polite. She turned to Cedric. "I'll be right back."

Cedric nodded as he studied the display of shock collars with interest. He was a horrible human being.

Sexy Trainer Dude, the man who sold those collars, led us to the corner of the room and spoke in a hushed voice. "Look, Josephine, I want to make sure nothing regarding our hike becomes public knowledge."

"Which part?" asked Miss Josie, her brow wrinkling in mock confusion. "When your dog ran off, or when Capone saved the day, or when you, uh, didn't quite make it to the bathroom in time?"

He leaned closer, twin spots of color appearing on his cheeks. "Capone did not save the day. If he helped, it was a complete and total accident. He doesn't have the level of intelligence required to do something so..."

"Extraordinary?"

"Exactly," he said, running a hand through his golden blond hair. "It's the other stuff I'd rather you didn't mention. It would cause me a great deal of embarrassment and ridicule, especially from Jenny. She's ruthless."

"Yeah, Jenny looks like a monster," said Miss Josie, eyeing Jenny, who had dimples and sported a high ponytail.

"But don't worry about the rest of it. We'll pretend it never happened. I won't tell a soul, and neither will Capone. Are you teaching the class today?"

He nodded. "Another reason I wanted to talk to you beforehand. I didn't want it to be awkward."

"I'm glad you did. You'll have no issues on my end."

"Thank you." He eyed Cedric, who'd moved from shock collars onto choke collars and held a large silver one in his hands. "And is he your...uh..."

She filled it in for him. "My ex. He's staying with me for a few days. He's allergic to dogs."

"Oh, really?" asked Sexy Trainer Dude. "Well, this might be an interesting morning for him, and for Capone, too. He's reached the weight limit for the small dog and puppy area. He'll be with the big dogs now." He looked down at me and gave me a pat on the head. "You get to play with Hans today. Won't it be fun?"

Fun? More like terrifying. I didn't want to play with Hans and his friends. They would eat me alive. I wanted to go home. Now.

I tried to pull Miss Josie away from the training area and out the front door, but she refused to let me have my way. "What's wrong with him?" she asked Cedric as she pulled me toward the training room. "He's acting so weird."

Cedric, who walked next to her, shrugged. He obviously didn't care about me or my problems. He cared only about one thing. Getting into Miss Josie's...well, her good graces.

"You know, they sell special collars near the front desk. One zap, and it'll cure Capone of anything."

Miss Josie came to a dead stop. Even though she'd probably considered the benefits of shocking me once or twice herself, she didn't seem to like hearing it from anyone else. "A shock collar? For a puppy? Are you serious?"

He had the decency to look embarrassed. "As a behavioral tool. Not permanently. Even you have to admit Capone has issues."

As he spoke, I threw myself down onto the floor and tried to remove my Easy Leader nose harness by rubbing my snout against Miss Josie's leg. She had on a short skirt and heels today. Not exactly sensible obedience training gear. Wearing the bait bag around her waist kind of ruined the whole effect, as did the fact I now thrashed around on the floor next to Miss Josie's feet.

"Capone. Stop it," she hissed, trying to adjust the nose harness.

The harness was a big problem. I hated having anything touch my nose. For me, this was torture.

Miss Josie held my face in her hands and looked me right in the eyes. "Stop it. We aren't going to do this today."

I tried to behave. Honestly, I did. But between my anxiety over the imminent threat from Hans and my discomfort from the harness, I was a mess before class even started. To make matters worse, the German shepherds in the class all seemed to be good friends with Hans.

"You wait, Capone," said one of them, a large puppy named Brutus. "Hans has special plans for you today. You're going to regret you ever messed with him."

The other German shepherds; Goliath, Crusher, and Stevie, joined in on the teasing. "Yeah, he's going to teach you who's boss," they said, laughing.

It felt like a flashback to my days on the farm when the horses would tease me mercilessly, and it made me feel all quivery and sad and inadequate inside. Getting harassed by the horses was one thing. The cat, Mr. Collins, coaxed them into it, and they were a different species, after all. For it to come from other dogs, however, seemed so much worse.

Also, who names a dog Crusher? It was even scarier than my name.

Note to self: I do not want to be called Crusher.

"I don't think he likes his collar," said Cedric.

Duh. What was your first clue? Perhaps because I writhed in agony on the floor of the training room trying to get it off? I would have thought I'd made it kind of obvious.

Miss Josie watched me, a perplexed frown on her face. "He'll have to get used to it. This is only the second time he's worn it, but he can't pull me when he's wearing it. He's so big now pulling has become an issue."

Luke wagged his tail when he saw me. He had on an Easy Leader, and it didn't bother him at all. He stood with his owner, No Brows, and her husband. The other labs hung out close to them. No one wanted to be my obedience class buddy today.

"Newsflash. Capone is the worst dog in the class," said Cedric softly.

Miss Josie didn't have to answer. We both knew it was true. It was even more of a nightmare than Puppy Preschool, and even more embarrassing than the time I threw up Miss Josie's pink thong.

"I don't know what happened," said Miss Josie. "He's usually so good."

Sweaty and disheveled, she'd torn her black tights in one spot, and dog drool marked her clothing. Her glasses were askew, and her hair had fallen out of her neat bun and cascaded part way down her shoulders. Sadly, I still flailed about on the floor, trying unsuccessfully to get the Easy Leader off my nose.

Sexy Trainer Dude stepped in to help. "Do you want me to run him up to doggie daycare for you?"

"Thank you," said Miss Josie, practically throwing my leash at him.

As Sexy Trainer Dude led me away, I looked over my shoulder, hoping she'd watch me go. If Hans had his way, this might be the last time we ever saw each other, and the thought made me whimper. She didn't look, but Cedric did, a cruel and ugly smile curving his lips.

This was bad. If she had to choose between Cedric and me, I might be on a one-way trip back to the farm. The thought made me sick with grief. I couldn't let it happen. I just couldn't.

THIRTY-SEVEN

The rules of doggie daycare:

1. Do not talk about doggie daycare.
2. DO NOT talk about doggie daycare!
3. If someone goes limp or taps out, doggie daycare is over.
4. Only ten dogs in the big doggie area at a time.
5. No fancy collars, no doggie sweaters, no chew toys.
6. Doggie daycare will go on as long as it has to.
7. Do not show weakness.
8. Do not be a dog bully.
9. Do not hump without prior consent.
10. If this is your first time in the big dog room, you will get hazed.

As Sexy Trainer Dude led me to doggie daycare, my little Labradorean heart filled with terror. Brutus, Goliath, and Stevie already waited for me in the big dog room, as did

Hans. The only good news was that my buddy Townsend, the giant goldendoodle, romped around the room, too.

"Hey, Capone," he said happily. He didn't seem to notice the four German shepherds, or, if he did, he didn't care.

"Hi, Townsend." I looked nervously over his shoulder, hard to do because Townsend kept bouncing.

"I'm so glad you're here," he said. "This place is great. We can run and play and hang out with our new friends. We're going to have a blast."

"Come play with me, little puppy," said Hans, baring his teeth. I nearly peed myself.

Hans was big, intimidating, mean, and out for revenge. Thankfully, Townsend stood next to me, a big pile of doodle happiness, and a good friend. I didn't know if I could handle this alone.

"Townsend?" Jenny's voice made me jump. "What are you doing in the big dog room?"

One of the other Misty Mountain employees, a slim young man named Kyle with tattoos and purple hair, raised a pierced eyebrow at her. "But Townsend is huge. He's bigger than all the other dogs."

Jenny pursed her lips, digging through Townsend's fur to find his collar and leash him up. "We separate them by weight. Townsend might seem big, but he's all fur. Underneath this," she said, grabbing a handful of his fur. "He's tiny."

As she pulled Townsend out of the room, my hopes for a peaceful resolution to the conflict with Hans went with her. Besides the pack of growling German shepherds, the only other dogs around were an elderly golden retriever snoring in the corner of the room and a stressed-out boxer who did not want to get involved. When I tried to make eye contact with him, and plead for help, he looked away.

I understood it. If I were a random dog, I wouldn't want Hans and his gang to notice me either.

Jenny had barely closed the door behind her when the other dogs moved in, all pointy teeth and open hostility. They were big, hairy, mean, and filled with a thirst for vengeance.

"I'm going to tear you apart limb by limb," said Hans.

"Limb by limb," growled the others in unison.

"I'm going to make you wish you never insulted me."

"Yeah," said the others, getting into it. "No one insults Hans."

"I'm going to tear your little hairy balls off and have them for lunch."

The other dogs looked at each other in surprise. "Uh, you're going to do what, Hans? Tear off his balls? Are you serious?" asked Stevie. It gave me hope that perhaps they weren't all as keen on this idea as Hans.

"It seems harsh," said Brutus. "I mean, sure, rough him up, but castration? You're kidding, right?"

"Dude," said Goliath. "I am not okay with this."

Hans spoke through gritted teeth, his voice soft. "Back me up on this. I'm engaging in hyperbole. I'm not going to... you know..."

"Ohhhhh," they said, nodding in unison. They shot me a wilting glare, enjoying how I trembled from head to toe.

"Stand up for yourself, Capone," said a voice from beyond the partition. It was Gracie. "Don't let those morons intimidate you."

Curse my timid nature.

I couldn't be a gentleman right now. I needed to be, well, Capone-ish. I uncurled from the fetal position and forced myself to stand, even though my legs shook. As I walked toward them, I straightened my spine and lowered my head as my hackles went up.

"Go ahead and bite off my balls," I said. "I dare you."

Okay, maybe not my best idea. I honestly didn't want Hans or his friends anywhere near my balls, but I'd issued an ultimatum. The other German shepherds backed off, but Hans stood his ground.

He growled, and I growled back at him. When he lunged at me, I felt a sharp tug, followed by a stinging sensation coming from my ear.

"What happened?" I asked, turning my head from side to side.

Hans backed off, his expression mortified. He spit something onto the ground, and although I couldn't see it, the other dogs stared in horrified fascination.

Something wet and warm splattered all over the floor. I didn't know what it was, nor did I understand why Hans and his friends suddenly turned and ran away from me. I followed, trotting along behind them.

"What is it? What's going on?" I asked.

What began as a gang of German shepherds trying to intimidate a lone puppy turned into a strange game of chase. When Jenny came in a few minutes later to check on us, she screamed, and called Sexy Trainer Dude over to help.

"He's bleeding," she said. "There's blood all over the place."

Blood? What blood?

When Sexy Trainer Dude rushed in, I realized flecks of blood covered the floor and the cowering pack of German shepherds. There was also blood on the boxer, who looked like he wished he had not come to doggie daycare today, and on the sleeping golden retriever, who still lay snoring in the corner. Most of all, there was blood on me.

"What happened?" I asked, turning my head back and forth as more blood splattered in all directions.

"I'm so sorry," said Hans. "I didn't mean to do it."

"Do what?" I asked, turning my head again—another spray of blood shot around the room.

Hans groaned. "Stop moving your head. It's your ear. I bit off part of your ear. *Mein Gott*. I've never seen so much blood."

The blood did seem to come from my ear, but, oddly enough, my ear didn't even hurt. Sexy Trainer Dude, who was being kind, took me to the back room and carefully bandaged my ear after he managed to stop the bleeding.

"You're a good dog," he said, patting me on the head. I licked his face in gratitude, and he laughed. "And now we have to call your owner. Prepare yourself. I suspect there will be tears, and there is nothing worse than seeing a lady cry. It's torture."

I looked at him in surprise. Sexy Trainer Dude gave off a strict, militant vibe, but getting part of my ear ripped off had shown me he wasn't all discipline and precision. He had a gentle side as well.

Note to self: Sexy Trainer Dude might actually be a gentleman.

And he'd been right about Miss Josie. When she saw my poor, bandaged ear, she wept. "What happened?"

Cedric stood behind her, looking less than sympathetic. Sexy Trainer Dude removed the bandage to show her the damage. "It isn't as bad as we initially thought," he said. "Just a tiny wound. I think it'll probably heal on its own."

Miss Josie hugged me close. "But what happened?" she asked again.

"He got into a tussle with one of the other dogs," said Sexy Trainer Dude. "And judging by the level of guilt and remorse Hans currently exhibits, we can safely guess it's him."

We looked through the window to the big dog area. Hans sat facing the corner, head bowed. He did indeed look sorry about what had happened. I wondered if this might mean he'd be more agreeable with me from now on.

Miss Josie's lips twitched when she saw Hans. "Yes, I'd say he's the one." She examined my ear. "You don't think he needs stitches?"

Sexy Trainer Dude shook his head. "I cleaned it before I bandaged it but put a little antibacterial cream on it when you get home, to be on the safe side." He put his hands on his lean hips. "I'm sorry. I have no idea why Hans would do something like this. We'll keep Capone in the puppy room for the time being."

"Thanks," said Miss Josie.

"You should have done so in the first place," said Cedric. "We were having brunch when you called. You interrupted us."

Miss Josie gasped. "Cedric—"

"And we aren't paying for this session," Cedric continued. "If we incur any vet bills, you will be held responsible."

Miss Josie put a hand up to stop him. "Enough, Cedric. There is no 'we,' and this is none of your concern."

He folded his arms over his chest. "Fine. If that's how you want things to be—"

"Yes, and you need to back off." She kept her voice low, but Cedric got the message. As he stomped off to the car, Miss Josie turned back to Sexy Trainer Dude, who'd gotten a little red in the face. "Capone is fine. I don't blame you or

Misty Mountain for any of this. Dogs will be dogs, right? Thanks for taking care of him."

He smiled at her. "Thanks for not blaming me," he said as he pulled a treat out of the pocket of his khaki shorts and gave it to me. Sexy Trainer Dude might not be the right Mr. Darcy for Miss Josie, but I liked him anyway.

"I'm so sorry you were hurt, Capone," said Miss Josie as we walked outside. "Poor puppy."

When we got to the car, she made Cedric get out of the front seat so I could sit next to her. I turned and looked at him, and I couldn't help but smile at the furious expression on his face.

It looked like I'd won this battle. Yes, I'd nearly lost an ear doing it, but it brought me one step closer to winning what mattered most—the war for Miss Josie's heart.

THIRTY-EIGHT

Things I like about Cedric:

1. Nothing.
2. Nothing.
3. Nothing.
4. Definitely nothing.

"Let's go through the books in the vault one by one," said Miss Josie to Mrs. Steele when we returned to the shop. Cedric left as soon as we got home from Misty Mountain, hopefully, to find a place to stay. The sooner he got off Miss Josie's couch, and out of her life, the better.

"What am I looking for exactly?" asked Mrs. Steele, a pair of dainty spectacles perched on her nose.

"Books with missing pages," said Miss Josie. "I've already found two. Both are completely ruined."

"Besides *The North American Indian*?"

"Yes," said Miss Josie, rolling up the sleeves of her white blouse. "Let's get to work."

Mrs. Steele made a tsking sound and heaved herself up

onto one of the high stools by a tall table next to the vault. Together they worked in silence for the rest of the morning. When Cedric came back, he uttered a brief greeting and walked up to Miss Josie's apartment. She followed him, and so did I.

Cedric sat on the couch, taking off his damaged loafers. He had a shopping bag next to him. He pulled out a pair of cheaper, and much less elegant, shoes and put them on his feet.

"I had to buy a new pair," he said. "Thanks to Capone."

"I'll pay for your new shoes," said Miss Josie.

Cedric's lips narrowed. "You ought to pay to replace the old ones. They were a great deal more expensive."

Miss Josie folded her arms across her chest. "Certainly. Send me a bill."

Cedric tossed down the box in disgust. "I don't want your money. I'm just irritated. I saved a long time for those shoes."

She sat next to him on the couch. "I understand. Were you able to find a place to stay?"

He shook his head. "I have a lead on a place for rent on River Road, but I can't see it until tomorrow. I'll have to stay another night."

Miss Josie stiffened. "Enough is enough, Cedric. You need to be out by tomorrow."

Cedric frowned. "I don't mean to inconvenience you, but I had nowhere else to turn." He ran a distracted hand through this hair, making it stand up on end. "There's something else, too. Something I haven't told you. I got laid off. Smythe's is downsizing. I need you, Josie. I'm desperate." When he reached for her, she hopped off the couch and moved to the other side of the room.

"I'm sorry for you, Cedric, but it doesn't change anything. I can't have you hanging around any longer."

His expression darkened. "Because of all the other men in your life?" he asked, his voice hard. "The vet, the trainer, the coffee guy?"

She narrowed her eyes at him. "Because of you, Cedric. Because of how you hurt me. Because of how much I once cared for you." The expression on her sweet face nearly made me weep.

He scowled. "*Once* cared for me?" he asked. "You mean you no longer do?"

She sighed. "It's over, Cedric. It was over a long time ago. Please move on with your life. And don't blame me because I want to move on with mine."

She went straight to her bedroom, closed the door, and locked it behind her. Cedric left the apartment and stomped down the steps. After giving a curt nod to Mrs. Steele, he went out to the back garden. I followed him.

For a long time, he sat on one of Miss Josie's chairs, lost in thought, a folded piece of paper in his hands. The paper looked an awful lot like the map of the garden Ms. Josie had found in Mr. Bartleby's last ledger.

Miss Josie came outside to tell him she had to run out to the bank for a few minutes, and Cedric nodded in response, sticking the piece of paper into his pocket where Miss Josie couldn't see it. As soon as she left, he marched over to the shed.

Cedric the Betrayer was up to something.

He stepped inside, grabbing a flashlight from a shelf next to the door. He knew exactly where to find it, which meant he'd been in this shed before. What was going on here?

He picked up a shovel, and turned, bumping right into me. "Get out of my way, you stupid dog."

He shoved me with his foot, and I hopped out of his way. He looked around a few seconds, and then started to dig up the dirt floor of the shed. The ground seemed hard, and he had to slam the shovel with force to crack the surface.

Rocco joined me; his head cocked to one side. "What's he looking for?"

I frowned. "I have no idea, but maybe he likes digging. Digging is fun."

Rocco narrowed his eyes. "It doesn't look liked Cedric is having fun," he said as we watched Cedric huff and puff, intent on his task.

Realization dawned on my little puppy brain. "Do you think he's looking for the missing books?"

"I don't know, but this isn't good."

"We need to stop him."

"Be careful," said Rocco, but I didn't listen. Instead, I plunged into the shed, barking my head off.

Curse my propensity for running headlong into danger.

"Get out of here," said Cedric, wiping sweat from his brow. He had dirt on his hands, and on his face. "Leave me alone, you idiot dog."

I refused to leave him alone. I had to stop him. If he dug up the missing books and took them away from Miss Josie, it would be a catastrophe.

Seeing no other option, I grabbed his pant leg with my teeth and pulled as hard as I could. I didn't bite him, but I may have yanked out a few of the hairs on his leg and I ripped his pants. He did not respond well to this. He turned to me, his face a mask of pure fury, and chased me out of the shed, wielding the shovel like a weapon.

"I'm going to kill you, Capone."

Note to self: Cedric is insane.

As he swung the shovel, I knew he sincerely wanted to kill me. Rocco knew it, too. He sat on the roof of the shed, howling and hissing at the top of his kitty lungs. I barked and dodged and weaved and ran as fast as I could around the yard, intent on avoiding Cedric and his swinging weapon of mass destruction. He nearly got me once, but I ducked and dashed between his legs. When I came out the other side, Cedric turned, the shovel high in the air, and screamed as he lowered it to the ground. At that moment, the side door to the garden opened, and Miss Josie and Mr. Nate stepped inside. Both of them stared at Cedric in shock.

He looked pretty terrifying, with his crazy eyes, dirty face, torn pants, and filthy hands. He took a deep breath, leaned on the shovel, and made a visible effort to compose himself.

"Josie," he said, panting slightly. "Back so soon?"

I ran over to Miss Josie and hid behind her, trembling. I'd never come so close to death in my whole life. Not when the horses back on the farm tried to trample me. Not when I'd gotten so sick from the peony bushes. Not when I'd eaten the whole bag of chocolate. Not with the German shepherds. Cedric wanted to hurt me on purpose, and he probably would have succeeded if Miss Josie and Mr. Nate hadn't shown up in time.

Miss Josie knelt to check on me. "What's going on here?" she asked. "Why would you attack a defenseless puppy?"

"Defenseless?" asked Cedric, letting out a sharp laugh. "You're hilarious. He's the one who attacked me. He bit me."

"He bit you?" asked Miss Josie in surprise.

Cedric showed her his ripped pants. "Your dog is out of control. What if he goes after one of your customers next? You need to make a choice here, Josephine. It's either him or me. I will not put up with this any longer."

My heart pounded in my chest. Oh, calamity. What if she believed him? What if she chose him instead of me?

Miss Josie rose to her feet. "I thought it was obvious, but if I need to say it I will." She looked down at me with a smile. "I choose Capone. He's my dog, this is his home, and neither one of us will put up with you or your nonsense any longer, Cedric. I'll pack your things and put them by the front door. You can pick them up in an hour."

Cedric stared at her in shock. "You can't be serious," he said.

"Goodbye, Cedric. Don't come near me, or my dog, ever again."

He let out a bellow of pure fury, and threw down the shovel, nearly hitting Rocco. "I won't forget this, Josephine. You'll regret you ever chose that animal over me."

She shot Cedric a withering glare. "Are you making a threat?"

Cedric shook his head. "It's not a threat," he said, his voice low and his eyes cold. "It's a promise."

THIRTY-NINE

Why I love Mr. Nate:

1. He always shows up when we need him.
2. He's protective of us.
3. He's kind to me.
4. He doesn't judge me when I'm naughty.
5. He gives me treats.
6. He plays with me.
7. He adores Miss Josie almost as much as I do.

After Cedric left, Miss Josie locked the garden door behind him and pulled me into a hug. Wisps of her hair had fallen out of her bun and tickled my nose, but I didn't mind. I licked her cheeks, wagging my tail so hard my whole body wiggled.

"I will never let that awful man near you again," she said, squeezing me tightly. "And I'm glad you chewed up his shoes. He deserved it."

"Did you hear what she said, Rocco?" I asked. "She chose me. She picked me instead of Cedric."

Rocco, who'd been rubbing back and forth against Miss Josie's legs, paused. "Of course, she did. Compared to Cedric, even you are quite the prize."

We went back into the bookstore to find Mrs. Steele putting on her coat and gathering her things, oblivious to what had just happened outside. "Josie, I looked through this pile of books, and all were intact." She tapped her hand on a tall stack of books next to the cash register. "I'll be back on Wednesday unless you need me tomorrow."

"Thank you, Mrs. Steele."

After she left, Miss Josie turned to Mr. Nate. "I have to go upstairs and pack Cedric's things. Do you mind staying here? I'm sure it'll be fine, but after what happened in the back garden, I'd rather not be alone."

"Of course." Mr. Nate sat down on the stool near the cash register Mrs. Steele had vacated. "Do you want me to look through some of these books while you're upstairs?"

"Are you sure you wouldn't mind?"

He gave her a crooked smile. "It'll be fun."

Miss Josie snorted. "You have a strange idea of what 'fun' is, Mr. Murray."

"I like this sort of thing." His gaze met hers, and he stumbled over his words. "And anything I do with you is fun."

"Oh." She blinked, adjusting her glasses. "Okay."

She turned and bumped into a table piled high with books on Samhain and Halloween traditions. Rubbing her hip, she hobbled up the steps quickly, muttering, "Ow, ow, ow," under her breath. I followed her, because I follow Miss Josie everywhere. I don't even let her go to the bathroom alone.

She packed Cedric's things, shoving them into a suitcase without folding them. It looked like she bunched them up on purpose. I understood why. After what he'd done to me outside, he deserved to have wrinkly clothes.

About to go downstairs, she paused, checking her face in the mirror. I thought she looked amazing, but apparently, she thought she needed some lipstick. She stepped into the bathroom to put it on, making her lips a bright, cherry red. She brushed her hair, letting it hang down to her shoulders instead of pulling it into a bun. Then she readjusted her bust area, which I found very odd. I tilted my head to one side as I watched her. What on earth was Miss Josie doing? When she spritzed herself with her honeysuckle and gardenia perfume, it finally dawned on me.

This was a mating ritual.

Uh-oh.

As she grabbed Cedric's suitcase and headed down the stairs, I wondered what I should do. I faced a conundrum. Seeing Rocco perched on the bookshelf near the bottom of the steps, I decided to ask him for advice. "She's falling for Mr. Nate. What are we going to do?"

Rocco paused in the middle of licking his private area. I felt sorry to interrupt, but this was important. "Do?" he asked. "Why should we do anything?"

He got me so flummoxed I stuttered. "B..b..b..but he's moving away. He can't be her Mr. Darcy if he's moving away."

Rocco squinted at me. "Her Mr. Darcy? What are you talking about?"

"Miss Josie needs to find her Mr. Darcy. All she seems to encounter are Wickhams and Willoughbys and Bingleys and Collinses. It's so frustrating."

Rocco's jaw dropped. "You're serious, aren't you?"

"Of course, I am."

"And you think the coffee guy isn't her Mr. Darcy because he's leaving?"

"Yes. Mr. Nate has done all the other things. He wrote her a letter like Mr. Darcy did after Lizzie spurned his proposal."

"Nate proposed?"

I shook my head. "No, but he wrote a letter."

Rocco rolled his eyes. "And writing a letter makes him Mr. Darcy?"

"It's not only that." I got agitated. "Captain Wentworth wrote letters, too. All the great Austen heroes did, but it's also the way he always looks out for her, and brings her coffee, and helps her stop Cedric from killing me."

"The last one is a negative in my book," said Rocco, but I knew he was joking. Or at least I thought he was joking.

"And he listens to her opinions, and he looks at her like she's the most beautiful person in the world." I paused, thoughts bouncing around my little Labradorean brain like ping pong balls. "Oh, calamity. He loves her. How terrible. He's not the perfect man for her."

"No one is perfect, pup. But he is imperfectly perfect in the best ways possible."

I stared at him, stunned. "That's the most romantic thing I've ever heard. Imperfectly perfect? It's like you just described Mr. Darcy. But what if he moves away and poor Miss Josie never sees him again?"

Rocco licked his paw and used it to clean his face. "Fortunately, you aren't the one who needs to make this decision. Your conclusions are whacked."

"What do you mean?"

"Humans move around a lot, but it doesn't mean he'll be gone forever. Even if he does travel, if he loves Miss Josie, this could still be his home."

Curse my tendency to jump to conclusions.

My eyes widened. "Beaver is his Pemberley?"

Rocco nodded. "Sad, isn't it?"

I pranced around, performing a little dance of pure happiness. "No, this is the best thing ever."

Mr. Nate and Miss Josie might be the Darcy and Lizzie of Beaver, Pennsylvania. I'd never been so excited in my whole life.

Miss Josie set the suitcase rather unceremoniously on the sidewalk in front of Bartleby's, and came back into the shop, stopping when she saw Mr. Nate's face. He leafed through the books near the cash register with a worried frown.

"What's wrong?" she asked.

"Take a look at this." He handed her a book, and she climbed onto the stool next to him. She paled as she studied it.

"So many pages are missing." She paused, a frown on her face. "But this one came from the pile of books Mrs. Steele already checked."

"Are you sure?"

She rubbed her head. "I think so. Maybe I misunderstood."

He reached for her hand. "You'll figure this out. I'm sure of it"

"Thank you, Nate."

She didn't remove her hand. He moved closer. The air hummed with an odd sort of tension as Miss Josie stared deeply into his eyes. Could this be the moment we'd been waiting for?

Rocco huffed and gave his tail and annoyed swish. "I wish they'd get it over with. This is so boring."

But we were to be disappointed. Instead of declaring

their undying love for each other at last, they spent most of the night poring over the books in Miss Josie's inventory. By the time they stopped, Miss Josie's shoulders drooped with fatigue, and they'd put nearly fifty books in a large box labeled "damaged."

"The first book was the tip of the iceberg," she said, her voice hollow.

"I'm sorry, Josie." Mr. Nate arms circled her protectively, and her head rested on his broad shoulder as if it belonged there.

"They fit together," said Rocco. I jerked in surprise. I'd thought he'd fallen asleep.

"You're right. They do. I'm surprised you noticed."

"I notice everything. I'm a cat. It doesn't mean I care though, just to be clear."

Note to self: Rocco might have hidden depths.

"I'd better go," said Mr. Nate, kissing the top of her head. "Will you be able to get some sleep?"

"Yes," she said. "Why are you so nice to me, Nate?"

He swallowed hard, studying her face. *"I cannot fix on the hour, or the spot, or the look or the words, which laid the foundation. It is too long ago. I was in the middle before I knew that I had begun."*

I stood up, nearly tripped over my big puppy paws. Did Mr. Nate quote *Pride and Prejudice* to her in the middle of our bookstore? It might have been the most romantic thing ever—even more than Rocco's "perfectly imperfect" comment.

Miss Josie seemed to agree. She put a hand over her heart. "I'm impressed, and I still can't believe you read the whole thing."

"I read every word. I watched the movie, too."

Her eyes narrowed slightly. "Which one? I love the

feature-length movie, but the BBC's production is more accurate." She gazed at him with an entranced expression on her face.

"Both," he said, his eyes on her lips. "I watched both."

This time, Miss Josie pulled him in her arms, making a sound of pure joy as her lips met his. She kissed him thoroughly (Miss Josie knew what she was doing), then he held her close, his forehead touching hers.

"I'm glad you made me read it," he said, his voice soft. "It helped me understand you better."

She reached up and tangled her fingers in his curly hair. "And I'm glad you made me drink coffee."

He let out a soft chuckle. "Really?"

She nodded. "Otherwise, I would have already fallen asleep, and I wouldn't have been able to kiss you goodnight."

She went up on her tiptoes to give him one soft, lingering kiss after another. And when Mr. Nate had to leave, they kissed in the doorway, like parting for even a few hours felt nearly impossible.

Cedric's suitcase was gone, which meant he'd come sometime during the night to retrieve it. Miss Josie waved a final goodbye to Mr. Nate. After he left, she leaned against the locked door, a sweet smile on her face, and I realized something important.

In spite of the missing books and the possible thievery of so many precious pages and the awful scene with Cedric the Betrayer, Miss Josie looked happy. And I wanted her to stay that way.

FORTY

Things Miss Josie likes to say to me as we walk:

1. Stop pulling.
2. Stop eating that.
3. Stop barking.
4. Stop being such a douche-canoe.

Miss Josie decided to take me to Brady's Run Park in the morning for a long stroll. She needed to clear her head, and I needed to get my wiggles out, but we stuck to the paved trail. Neither one of us wanted to encounter a bear again.

The leaves were changing in a brilliant display of gold, red, and orange, and the air felt crisp and fresh. I breathed it in. There was nothing as good for the soul as time spent in a forest. The peace. The calm. The serenity.

Well, it would have been serene. The only problem was I happened to be in an exceptionally barky mood. I barked at a jogger, at a leaf blowing across the path, at a maple syrup gathering vat, and even at my own shadow.

I do this often. Shadows are freaky.

As we rounded a corner on the path, I saw an older man walking toward us with an ancient basset hound. The man looked like Santa, with a white beard, portly shape, and wide smile. The basset hound was off-leash and hobbled toward me. At this point, I nearly vibrated with excitement, on the verge of losing it entirely.

The man didn't seem upset by my barking or my wiggling or the way I lunged toward his dog with a crazed gleam in my eyes. He may have been the most laid-back human I'd ever encountered.

"Why don't you let him say hi?" he asked, giving Miss Josie a smile. "He's being friendly, that's all."

Although she seemed nervous about the idea, Miss Josie carefully eased me closer. I sniffed the other dog and I stopped barking, a relief for all involved.

"Hello, puppers," said the basset hound. "My name is Priscilla. This gentleman with me provides treats. I'm sure he'll give you one if you're nice."

I greeted the man, tail wagging, and drooled all over his pants. He patted me on the head, and when I stuck my nose under his jacket, he laughed and a treat magically appeared in his hand.

"If you want this, you're going to have to sit," he said in a deep, hypnotic voice.

I planted my bum on the ground so fast Miss Josie gasped. There I stayed, still as a statue, until he gave me a treat. I took it from him gratefully and licked his hand afterward.

"They call me Biscuit Bob," he said to Miss Josie. "All the dogs know me. This little guy must be Capone."

"How do you know his name?"

He chuckled. "We heard you yelling at him as you approached. Noise carries in the forest, you know."

"He's right, it does," said Priscilla. "Did you honestly bark at your shadow?"

"Guilty."

"I bark at empty toilet paper rolls. It's a thing with me."

Biscuit Bob continued. "It sounds like Capone is on the rambunctious side, but don't be too hard on him. Labradors at this age are always energetic. You have a good puppy. I can tell. I'm never wrong."

I stared at him in surprise. "Is that true?" I asked Priscilla.

She nodded. "Biscuit Bob understands these things. He recognizes a good dog when he sees one."

Note to self: Biscuit Bob is my new best friend.

"Be a good dog, you'll get rewarded," said Priscilla. "It's canine karma."

"Canine karma?"

"The better you behave, the more treats and good things will come your way."

"Ohhh. Canine karma."

Biscuit Bob reached into his pocket and pulled out a handful of bacon-flavored treats.

"You're a dog whisperer, Biscuit Bob," said Miss Josie.

He smiled at her. "You learn as you go. And I carry a lot of treats with me. It makes me popular. If you don't mind my asking, why did you name him Capone?"

"It was the name the breeder gave him."

When Biscuit Bob bent over to pet me, I licked his entire bearded face. I'd never licked anyone with a beard before, and I liked it.

"I'm so sorry," said Miss Josie, pulling me away.

"Don't worry about it, and don't worry about the name

either. He is who he is, and you'll figure it out eventually. Sometimes the answer is right in front of you."

Biscuit Bob waved a cheery farewell as he walked down the path. Miss Josie repeated his words as she watched him go. "Sometimes, the answer is right in front of you." A smiled formed on her lips. "Oh, my gosh. We need to go back home, boy."

We got back to the shop as Mr. Nate arrived. He held two cups of coffee in his hands, and Jackson stood by his side. Miss Josie greeted him by pulling his head down for a swift kiss.

"Is this coffee for me?" she asked.

He nodded, looking adorably befuddled both by her question and her spontaneous show of affection. "Yes. It's Ethiopian. I got it from Equal Exchange. Ethiopia was where coffee initially came from, and they grow the best coffee beans in the world. I mean, Latin America has some fantastic coffee as well, and so do other countries in Africa, but Ethiopia's climate and the whole coffee-growing culture there creates the most consistently amazing flavors. Try it. You'll see."

Miss Josie took a sip. "Yum. Thank you."

Mr. Nate shook his head. "I can't believe the answer was so simple. Black coffee. I had you pegged for something completely different."

"Some surprises are good," she said, giving him a wink. Miss Josie was positively saucy this morning.

Even Jackson noticed. "What's up with all the flirting?"

"I have no idea."

Mr. Nate put the second coffee next to the cash register. "This is for Anne," he said. "Cream and sugar. Were you out walking this morning?"

She nodded. "Yes, and while I was out, I thought of

something. Well, thanks to Biscuit Bob, but I'll tell you about him later. First, would you like to help me solve a mystery?"

"Of course. But why do you remind me of Nancy Drew right now?"

"If this were a Nancy Drew book, the title would be *The Secret in the Old Shed.*"

Mr. Nate's eyes widened. "The shed. Cedric. The shovel."

"Exactly."

"Let's do this."

FORTY-ONE

A list of the roses found in Mr. Bartleby's back garden:

1. 'The Fairy'
2. 'Hertfordshire'
3. 'Bianco'
4. 'Our Beth'
5. 'Dracula' Rose
6. Rose 'Dorothy'
7. 'Yorkshire'

Although no longer blooming, the rose bushes stood in a neat row from the shed to the side door in the garden wall. Jackson and I sat near those bare bushes, waiting. It was so boring. Miss Josie and Mr. Nate had found the hole Cedric created in the floor of the shed, but they insisted on doing all the digging themselves. You'd think they'd appreciate the assistance of two world-class diggers, but they didn't want our help.

Well, I should clarify. Mr. Nate did the actual digging. Miss Josie, dressed in her pretty work clothes and heels, stood by and watched. By the time Gracie and Ms. Anne arrived, Mr. Nate was already sweating and covered in dirt. He'd taken off his jacket, and his white T-shirt clung to him, outlining the muscles in his arms and chest. Miss Josie stared at him, mesmerized. Ms. Anne fanned herself.

"I hate to miss the show," she said softly to Miss Josie, "but I have a hair appointment. Do you mind if I leave Gracie here with you?"

"Of course not," said Miss Josie, glancing at her watch. "The shop doesn't open for half an hour. I'll be fine, and Gracie seems to be having fun."

Gracie did seem to be having a good time. As Ms. Anne left, I realized all females appeared to find a sweaty Mr. Nate extremely attractive, even females of the canine persuasion.

"Hubba, hubba, ding, ding," said Gracie, practically drooling. "Now there's something I'd like to lick. Wow. I must be in heat."

"You can't be in heat," said Jackson. "You had your hoohaw removed."

Gracie gave him a dirty look. "My hoohaw is fine, thank you, and your lack of knowledge regarding the female anatomy is shocking. They removed my reproductive organs, not anything external, which is fine by me. I wasn't cut out to be a mother. I completely lack maternal instinct. I might be a bitch, but I'm not that kind of a bitch, if you know what I mean."

Jackson tilted his head to one side. "Wait. You still have a hoohaw?"

Note to self: Jackson is a pervert.

Gracie rolled her eyes. "Is that all you absorbed from what I said? You're such a dirty dog, Jackson. Grow up. Please."

Gracie turned her back on him, and when I caught Jackson staring at her fluffy bottom, I nudged him. "Stop it. You're being rude."

"Why? A dog can look, right?"

"Not if Gracie doesn't want you to look. It's called harassment. If you're not careful, canine karma is going to bite you in the—"

I was interrupted by the sound of Mr. Nate hitting something metal with the shovel. "What is it?" asked Miss Josie.

"I don't know." I peered around Miss Josie to see Mr. Nate lift a small metal box out of the hole he'd dug.

Miss Josie gasped, putting a hand over her mouth. "The safety deposit box. I can't believe it."

Mr. Nate lowered the box onto the table on Miss Josie's back patio. He was covered in dirt and sweat, but Miss Josie gave him a big hug. "Thank you, Nate."

"Don't thank me yet. We have to find out what's inside."

He lifted the lid. Jackson, Gracie, and I climbed up on chairs so we could see the contents. "What is it?" I asked.

"No idea," said Jackson. "I can't read. Can you read?" He looked at Gracie, his pug eyes huge and buggy in his face.

"I'm a dog, dummy," she said, giving her fur a shake. "Of course not."

I might not be able to read what was on the paper Miss Josie pulled out of the box, but I definitely read her disappointment at what she'd found. Her shoulders slumped, and she blew out a sigh. "I thought the missing books might be in here. Not this."

Mr. Nate looked over her shoulder. "A list of roses?"

"Yep. Seven different varieties. The ones he planted after Mrs. Bartleby died."

He frowned. "Mr. Bartleby planted the 'Dracula' Rose in memory of his wife?"

"I think it was one of her favorite books," she said with a smile. "They went to Whitby in England for their honeymoon because that was where Bram Stoker wrote it. Romantic isn't it?"

"I never thought about Dracula as being particularly romantic, but I guess you're right. Wait, there's a business card in here, too," said, Mr. Nate. "It's from an insurance agency. And what is this?" He asked, picking up a long pin with a pearl on one end.

"A hat pin. But why would it be in this box?"

"Maybe it reminded him of his wife."

Miss Josie sank into a chair. "This is so disappointing."

Mr. Nate knelt in front of her, taking her small hands in his large, dirty ones. "You're going to figure this out, Josie."

She gave him a watery smile. "I wish I had your confidence, but I'm being practical. One more thing is all it will take to put me out of business forever."

The words had no sooner left her mouth when we heard a noise from inside the shop. "What's that sound?" asked Nate.

Miss Josie's face paled. "Smoke detectors."

Mr. Nate opened the back door, and smoke billowed out. He covered his mouth with the bottom of his dirty T-shirt and rushed inside. "No," said Miss Josie. "Don't go in there."

It was too late. Mr. Nate disappeared into the smoky interior of the shop as Miss Josie dialed 911 with shaking fingers. "There's a fire at Bartleby's," she said. "Please come now."

Then she did something insane. She ran into the shop after Mr. Nate.

"Where's she going?" asked Gracie, pacing back and forth as the smoke detector beeped.

The high-pitched sound hurt my doggie ears, and the smell of smoke stung my nostrils. "What are we going to do?" I asked.

Jackson stood near the door, whimpering. "Nate? Please come back, Nate."

I shook from head to toe, every instinct in my body telling me to stay away from the smoke but I knew what I had to do. "I'm going in. If I don't make it, you can have my orange bunny, Jackson. Gracie, you get my bed. It's cozy. I know you like it."

They both screamed at me to stop, but I was a puppy on a mission. I had to save Miss Josie and Mr. Nate, even if it meant dying in the process.

I'm not exaggerating. That's how much I loved them both. It truly was impressive.

The smoke smelled terrible, burning my eyes and making it hard to see. I listened for the sound of Miss Josie's voice, and when I finally heard it, I barked excitedly. Sadly, it caused me to inhale a lung full of smoke and brought on a coughing fit.

I stumbled through the darkened shop, searching for her, coughing and wheezing. Miss Josie coughed, too, and shouted at Mr. Nate about the sprinklers. And I realized something.

It rained inside the bookstore.

This was not good. Water and books didn't mix. I'd learned about it my first day in the shop when Miss Josie instructed me never to pee on, drool on, or lick the books.

"A little water can go a long way in ruining a valuable piece of literature," she'd said, and this was not a little water. It rivaled a monsoon.

I found her and grabbed the bottom of her skirt with my teeth, trying to pull her out, still coughing my head off. "Capone. What are you doing in here?"

She looked soaked to the skin, and so did Nate. His white T-shirt now nearly translucent, reminded me of Colin Firth as Mr. Darcy in the BBC version of *Pride and Prejudice*. Not the stiff Mr. Darcy in a cravat, but the sexy Mr. Darcy after he swam in the pond at Pemberley. The Mr. Darcy who caused grown women like Miss Josie to get a little hot under the bodice.

Dear heavens. Mr. Nate was her Mr. Darcy. He had been all along, and it was so obvious now. Why hadn't I noticed it before?

I slumped to the floor, not from this startling realization but due to oxygen deprivation. Although Mr. Nate and Miss Josie coughed, too, my puppy lungs were much more susceptible to the dangers of smoke inhalation. I didn't see any signs of a fire in the shop, but my lungs felt utterly inflamed.

Miss Josie picked me up and carried me out to the front of the shop as the fire trucks arrived. Mr. Nate followed her. With both doors of the shop opened, the smoke cleared out quickly, but I still couldn't seem to catch my breath.

Curse my petite puppy lungs.

"Help," said Miss Josie, tears streaming down her smoke-stained cheeks. "My dog is having trouble breathing."

A burly fireman took me from her arms and put an oxygen mask over Miss Josie's face, then one over my face as well. Another fireman took care of Mr. Nate. I ended up vomiting all over the nice fireman. I couldn't help it. Once I did, however, I felt much better.

Miss Josie pulled me into a hug. "Why did you come into the shop?"

"He was trying to save you," said Mr. Nate, his voice raspy.

It made her cry even harder and hug me so tight it was almost hard to breathe. "You stupid, brave, wonderful dog. Don't ever scare me like that again."

After the firemen assessed the situation in the shop, the fire chief, Mr. Kevin Crawford, came out to speak with Miss Josie and Mr. Nate. "First of all, the three of you made a poor choice. Why would you rush into a smoke-filled building?"

"I thought maybe I could contain it and save Josie's books," said Mr. Nate. "We hadn't been outside long. I didn't expect so much smoke."

Miss Josie rested her head against his arm. "I went in because he went in. I couldn't let him be alone in there."

Mr. Crawford rolled his eyes. "And the puppy went in to rescue both of you ding dongs. Look, the first rule of fire safety is to get out and stay out. This situation could have ended badly. Thankfully, it looks like there was never a fire."

"What do you mean?" asked Miss Josie, lifting her head from Mr. Nate's arm.

He handed her something resembling a perfectly round charred bit of coal. "Someone daisy-chained together a bunch of smoke bombs and tossed them into your shop. It didn't do any harm itself, other than the smoke, but it triggered the sprinklers and caused a lot of damage. I'm sorry, Miss St. Clair, but can you think of anyone who might have a grudge against you? Someone who might want to cause problems?"

She and Mr. Nate looked at each other. "Cedric," they said at the same time.

As they gave Mr. Crawford Cedric's contact information, a small feather fluttered next to me. I pounced on it, stopping it with my paws. It stuck to the welcome mat by the front of the shop, and, as I sniffed it, a keen sense of foreboding grew in my heart.

Could this feather have come from the person who threw the smoke bomb into the mail slot? If so, Miss Josie and Mr. Nate suspected the wrong person.

As much as I despised Cedric, this feather didn't smell like him. It smelled like Mrs. Norris, the adorable, elderly owner of the haberdashery.

FORTY-TWO

The saddest moments in my young life:

1. Saying goodbye to Mistress Sue.
2. Finding out I'd been named after a scoundrel.
3. Seeing Miss Josie's face as she assessed the damage to her shop.

A few hours later, after showering and dressing at Mr. Nate's apartment, Miss Josie and Mr. Nate went into the shop to check out the damage. It was extensive. The only books not affected were the ones inside the sealed vault. Everything else ended up being nearly a total loss.

Ms. Anne came to get Gracie as soon as she'd heard about what happened. Gracie kissed me on the lips and told me I was the best and bravest puppy she'd ever met. Jackson attempted to do the same, his kiss so slobbery and disgusting I had to wipe my face off afterward. He made inappropriate noises as he did it and tried to slip me the tongue. It grossed me out, but Jackson was being Jackson, and I knew he felt proud of me, too.

"What am I going to do?" asked Miss Josie. She had on a pair of Mr. Nate's sweats and one of his First Impressions T-shirts. Both seemed miles too long for her, and she looked like a lost waif as she stared around the ruined remains of her shop.

Mr. Nate put an arm around her shoulders. "This is why you have insurance. It'll be fine." But the look in his eyes told me he worried, too.

We stayed the night at Mr. Nate's. He and Miss Josie slept in his bed, but there was no hanky panky (as Jackson put it) going on. They both fell into a deep sleep, locked in each other's arms. Romantic, and even better because they forgot to close the door to the bedroom, and we spied on them (aka watched over them) all night.

Mr. Nate's apartment, ultra-modern, sleek, and expensive looking, was the exact opposite of Miss Josie's. He did not own a single piece of antique furniture, and most of his books were either business related or sci-fi, except for the little leather-bound one with gold lettering Miss Josie had given him. Although it looked a bit out of place, it belonged there, the same way Miss Josie belonged with Mr. Nate.

How had I been so wrong? They could have been kissing and canoodling ages ago if I hadn't interfered. I never should have stuck my snout where it didn't belong. A mistake I hoped to soon rectify by doing what I could to make sure they ended up together forever.

Rocco came to Mr. Nate's apartment, too. He'd hidden under the bed at Miss Josie's after the incident, and it took us a while to get him out. He tried to act cool about it, but the poor cat seemed traumatized.

"There was so much smoke," he said with a shudder. "I thought we were all going to die."

"Did you see who threw the smoke bomb into the shop?" asked Jackson.

Rocco shook his head. "I was asleep. I never saw a thing."

"I think I might know who did it," I said, pausing for dramatic effect. "Mrs. Norris."

"The old broad with the hats?" asked Jackson, his eyes bugging out in surprise. Well, maybe not in surprise. Jackson's eyes tend to be buggy in general.

"Yes," I said and explained about the feather.

"Not exactly proof," said Rocco. "It could have come from her shop. It might be a coincidence."

My gut told me otherwise. "I think it's Mrs. Norris."

"What reason would Mrs. Norris have to vandalize the shop?"

We got our answer the next day when the insurance agent came. Mr. Nate sat next to the cash register, going through piles of books to see if anything escaped damage from the sprinklers. Mr. William Lucas, from the Big Beaver Insurance Agency, walked around the shop, ticking off boxes on a clipboard and murmuring to himself as he took notes. He turned to Miss Josie, who'd managed to procure an outfit of her own which didn't smell like smoke and gave her a tight smile.

"The good news is all damage to the building is covered, including both your shop and apartment."

"And the bad news?" asked Miss Josie, wringing her hands. She had on a somber grey dress and a black cardigan. It suited her mood.

Mr. Lucas eyed her with a sympathetic gaze. "Your inventory is, unfortunately, not covered by your current policy."

Miss Josie leaned against the counter. "What do you mean?"

He cleared his throat. "Insurance on something as valuable as books is a complicated process. Mr. Bartleby used a company called Regency for it. They're based out of New York."

"Why two companies?"

"Most experts agree you shouldn't insure rare and valuable books under a homeowner's or business insurance. A separate, fine arts policy is always a better idea. It's more cost efficient as well. Books like yours are like artwork, you know." He took a piece of paper out of his briefcase and adjusted the glasses on his nose. "According to our records, Mr. Bartleby's policy with Regency was up to date. The only problem is Mr. Bartleby did not list you as the beneficiary."

Miss Josie's eyes shot to Mr. Nate. "Who did he list?"

"Mrs. Henrietta Norris."

Miss Josie frowned, visibly confused. "How odd."

"Mr. Bartleby should have made you the beneficiary when he left the shop to you." Mr. Lucas took his glasses off his face and put them into the left breast pocket of his suit. "If Mrs. Norris is a friend of yours, perhaps you could explain the situation and ask for her help."

Miss Josie's face brightened. "You're right. I'm sure Mrs. Norris will understand."

After Mr. Lucas left, Miss Josie called Mrs. Norris. A few minutes later, the older lady arrived at the front door of the shop, accompanied by her boyfriend, Billy.

"Gracious, Josie." She stared around the shop in horror, hands on her cheeks. "Whatever happened?"

"Someone threw a bunch of smoke bombs into the shop." Miss Josie gazed at the damage, as if she still couldn't believe it herself. I stood next to her, protectively, wanting to shield her from any further pain. "It activated the sprinkler system and ruined most of the inventory."

"How horrible. Whoever would do such a thing?"

"I have no idea," said Miss Josie. "But I need a favor from you, Mrs. Norris. Mr. Bartleby forgot to change the name on the insurance policy, and you're listed as the beneficiary. Would you mind going to the notary with me to correct it?"

"Why, no." Mrs. Norris spoke in her sweet little old lady voice, but I saw something cold and calculating in her eyes. "I will not."

Miss Josie frowned in confusion. "Well, I can ask the notary to come here, if it's easier for you."

"No, dearie. You don't understand. I won't sign the policy over to you." Mrs. Norris had on a pale green dress with a matching hat. She adjusted her gloves, a smile playing on her lips. "The money is mine. Benjamin wanted me to have it, and, frankly speaking, I deserve it. He was my lover for a long time. Before I met Billy, of course."

Billy beamed at her, his expression positively gloating. As I stared at him, things clicked in my mind. His broad face. His big head. His barrel-shaped chest. The cold look in his eyes.

Billy was Charlie No Face. I mean, not the actual Charlie No Face, but the one who'd tried to break into the shop with pantyhose over his head.

How had I missed it? I inhaled deeply the way Uncle Clancy had taught me, and it confirmed my suspicions. I recognized his scent, and I recognized something else as well.

Note to self: Billy smelled like a criminal.

I should have picked up on it right away, but I'd been so

focused on trying to be a gentleman that I ignored what my Capone-ish instincts told me.

And Mrs. Norris smelled like more than mint and mothballs. She looked like a sweet, little old lady, but she smelled like a criminal, too.

"This will destroy me," said Miss Josie, coming out of her stupor. "It'll put me out of business."

"Tut, tut," said Mrs. Norris, squeezing her hand. "You're young. You'll be fine. I need money to finance my retirement. Young Nate here was extremely generous when he purchased my shop, but I could easily live another ten or even twenty years. I require liquid assets. Cash. It's fortunate Benjamin came through for me in the end."

"You can't do this," said Mr. Nate, his hand balled into fists by his side. "It's unethical."

"Unethical? A signed and notarized insurance policy?" She pulled an envelope out of her small, green handbag. "Here it is. Clear as day. If you have any questions, call my lawyer."

She and Billy turned to leave the shop just as Mrs. Steele arrived. She stiffened when she saw Mrs. Norris. "Henrietta," she said, giving her a curt nod.

"Lucy." Mrs. Norris inclined her head ever so slightly as she spoke. "Such a sad day. Poor Josephine lost nearly everything. You might be out of a job."

She emphasized the word "job" strangely, and Mrs. Steele's normally rosy cheeks paled. "I'm sure it's not so bad." Her eyes went to the soggy interior of the shop. The entire room smelled like stale smoke, and water still dripped from the ceiling in places. "Holy smokes."

"Exactly," said Mrs. Norris, with a sigh. "It's tragic. Well, we'd better be off. Billy and I are heading to Florida tomorrow. Good luck, Josephine. I wish you well."

They left and Miss Josie looked like someone had kicked her in the stomach. Mrs. Steele didn't appear to be much better. When the phone rang, Mr. Nate answered it. After he spoke quietly for a few minutes, he hung up, a strange expression on his face.

"Officer Stahl called," he said. "They questioned Cedric, who claimed to have been at a marriage counseling session with his wife at the time someone threw the smoke bombs into the shop. His alibi checked out. They have no other suspects."

"I can't believe this," she said. "It keeps getting worse and worse."

They watched Mrs. Norris and Billy cross the street arm in arm. The couple moved slowly, thanks to Mrs. Norris's advanced age. As Mr. Nate stared at them, his mouth drew into a hard line.

"Don't you think it's odd she carries the insurance policy around in her purse? Rather random, isn't it?"

"What do you mean?"

He stared down at her. "Perhaps the police are right. Maybe Cedric isn't the one who tossed the smoke bombs into the shop."

Miss Josie blinked in surprise. "Wait...you think it was Mrs. Norris?"

He shrugged. "Or Billy. And I might have a way to prove it."

FORTY-THREE

The surprising contents of Mrs. Lucinda Steele's handbag:

1. Homemade doggie treats.
2. A plastic, fold-up rain hat.
3. Cough drops.
4. A brown leather wallet.
5. Aspirin.
6. An old lipstick.
7. A jangly bunch of keys.
8. Something smelling an awful lot like thievery.

Mr. Nate left, and Mrs. Steele and Miss Josie stared around at the ruined interior of the shop. "It's going to be okay," said Mrs. Steele. "We'll get through this."

She placed her large purse on the floor, and removed her coat, taking it to the back room to hang it on a hook on the wall. I followed her, my tail wagging.

"I have a cleaning crew coming today, Mrs. Steele. The insurance company is sending them. They'll take care of the floors, which might get warped if they aren't dried quickly, and a few other things in the shop."

"What can I help you with?"

Miss Josie wrapped a lock of hair around one of her fingers, frowning. "Well, maybe you can help me go through the books. I need to separate them into three categories. Some are a total loss, others are damaged but could be repaired, and a few weren't affected at all. Those books should be packed up carefully and moved to my apartment."

"Did the sprinklers go off in your apartment, too?"

Miss Josie shook her head. "No, but it reeks of smoke. The cleaning crew will do what they can, but it will be a time-consuming process."

As they talked, I sniffed around Mrs. Steele's purse. Rocco eyed me curiously. "What are you doing, pup?"

I frowned at him. "Mrs. Steele makes the best dog biscuits and brings them to me in her purse. I smell them, but now I smell something else, too."

I stuck my head into her bag, trusting my instincts. Mrs. Steele's purse, more like a briefcase or a messenger bag, didn't suit a woman who wore floral print dresses and lacey cardigan sweaters. It was almost bigger than me.

Note to self: A woman's handbag is a mysterious thing.

At first, all I encountered was her wallet and some aspirin. Boring. As I stuck my head in further, however, things got more interesting.

I caught a whiff of an old book. The aroma caused a familiar tickle in my nose because it carried the distinctive scent of Miss Josie's shop. Not the way it currently smelled, which was an acrid mixture of smoke and sadness, but the way it did before, like vanilla and almonds and old leather.

I stuck my head in deeper, wondering what else I might

find, when I felt a tug on my collar. "Capone. What are you doing in Mrs. Steele's purse?" asked Miss Josie, nudging me away.

Mrs. Steele grabbed her purse off the floor. She zipped it closed, her movements quick and a little frantic. "He probably smells dog treats," Mrs. Steele said with a laugh. She patted me on the head, harder than necessary. "Silly puppy."

Putting her purse on the counter, she gave me a stern look, then she and Miss Josie went to the back room to search for boxes. Rocco jumped up onto the counter next to the purse and sniffed at it.

"What did you smell in here exactly?" he asked, staring down at me from his perch.

"She had one of Miss Josie's books in there, packed up in a mailing envelope."

"Well, I guess she could be mailing it for Miss Josie, couldn't she?"

"I guess, but there was something else, Rocco. Single pages inside clear sleeves. They smelled familiar. Do you remember the page tucked inside the ledger we found under the stairs?"

Rocco's eyes narrowed. "The one cut out from a book?"

I nodded. "Yes. The pages inside Mrs. Steele's purse smelled the same, like they came from one of Miss Josie's books."

"Hmmm. Let's see what Mrs. Steele is hiding in here. I can't open the zipper, but I do have one skill cats around the globe are famous for." He used the full weight of his furry grey body to knock Mrs. Steele's purse off the counter. It fell to the floor, and Rocco hopped down next to it. "We have to work fast. Grab onto the zipper with those fangs of yours and pull."

I didn't like the fangs comment, but I found the zipper and tugged on it. It was harder to open than I expected.

Curse my soft baby teeth.

Rocco sat on the purse and cheered me on. Well, let me rephrase. He called me rude names and told me to hurry up, but his weight provided an excellent counterbalance, and, at last, I felt the zipper move.

I worked and tugged and pulled, until I could stick my nose inside. I grabbed the envelope with the book, and was about to yank it out, when the door to the shop opened, and Jackson waddled over.

"What's up?" he said, letting out a loud belch. "Are you digging for treats?"

"Leave him alone," said Rocco. "He's working. We suspect Mrs. Steele has items belonging to Miss Josie stashed away in her purse."

"You think that nice old lady is a thief?"

"That's what we're trying to figure out. Are you going to help us or not, you dimwit?" asked Rocco, with a hiss.

Although Jackson did not take kindly to the name-calling, he joined me in trying to open the purse. I had the envelope in my teeth, and nearly got it out. Mr. Nate, unfortunately, noticed what we were up to and stopped us.

"What are you doing, Capone? Get away from there."

He put a cardboard tray full of coffee cups onto the counter and grabbed the purse. When I refused to let go, he gave me a serious look, lowered his voice, and said, "Drop it."

Sadly, it worked like a charm. Dang Misty Mountain and all those obedience classes. They made me too well behaved. I slumped to the floor, disappointed and discouraged. Why did I have to be so good?

Mr. Nate put Mrs. Steele's purse back on the counter, and I let out a whine. I'd been so close.

"What is wrong with you, boy?" he asked.

I licked his hand. I didn't blame Mr. Nate. He didn't know there could be stolen items in Mrs. Steele's handbag, and I had no way of telling him.

Gracie and Ms. Anne arrived, smelling of shampoo and the doggie groomer. Gracie had on a new pink collar. They both stopped and looked around in horror at the interior of the shop. They hadn't seen the full extent of the damage, and it was rather shocking.

Miss Josie and Mrs. Steele came out from the back, carrying several large, empty boxes. Ms. Anne hugged Miss Josie. "Josie. I'm so sorry."

"Me, too," said Miss Josie, taking a coffee from Mr. Nate and sipping on it. "Thanks for coming by."

"Of course," said Ms. Anne, taking off her coat and grabbing a coffee for herself. "We're here to help."

"Were you able to figure anything out, Nate?" asked Miss Josie, putting a hand on his sleeve.

He shook his head. "Not yet, but we have cameras trained on the sidewalk in front of First Impressions. When I heard about your break-ins, I added additional cameras on the side of the shop, and one to get a view of the sidewalk in front of Bartleby's. The footage is sent directly to my security company, but they promised to forward it to me as soon as possible. I took the liberty of sending it to the police as well. I hope you don't mind."

"Of course not," she said.

Mr. Nate looked at Mrs. Steele. "Speaking of thieves," he said. "I caught Capone in your purse. You might want to look through it to make sure nothing is missing."

She visibly flinched. "I will," she said, grabbing her

purse. My drool was all over it, but she didn't wipe it off. She clutched it close to her body.

Jackson, Gracie, Rocco, and I followed her when she went to the back room of the shop. After putting her purse high on a shelf, she grabbed me by the scruff of my neck.

"Don't touch my things again." Her eyes were cold and hard, and I saw a trace of spittle by her lips. Mrs. Steele was drooling. That could not be a good thing.

She put on her coat, shoving her arms into the sleeves with angry thrusts. Then she took a deep breath, visibly composing herself, and walked back to the main area of the shop.

"I'm sorry, Josie. I have to go. I have an errand to run. I'll try to come back later."

"Sure. No problem," she said, a confused look on her face as Mrs. Steele waved goodbye and hurried out the door. The sudden departure must have seemed odd, but Miss Josie didn't have time to focus on it. The cleaning crew had arrived, and men walked in and out of the shop, carrying buckets and ladders.

"What do we do?" asked Rocco. "She's getting away."

I sat up straighter. This was probably the worst decision I'd ever made, but we had no choice.

"We follow Mrs. Steele."

"Leave the shop?" asked Rocco, shrinking back.

I nodded. "We have to."

Jackson agreed with me. "He's right. I know a guilty face when I see one, and she looked guilty."

Gracie seemed less than enthusiastic. "I just had my hair done, and you want me to go outside? What if it rains?"

An ominous rumble of thunder sounded from the distance as if on cue. The sound made Rocco crouch low in fear.

"You'll have to decide for yourselves, but I know what I'm doing," I said. "I'm going out that door and tracking Mrs. Steele with my super sniffer. This is what I was born to do. No...this is what I was bred to do. And I won't let anyone steal from Miss Josie again."

"Fine," said Gracie. "If you're going to be all heroic again, I guess we can be heroic, too. But how are we going to get out?"

One of the men from the cleaning crew propped the door open. "Easy," I said, with a smile. "Follow me."

And, to my great surprise, they did.

FORTY-FOUR

What thieves have in common:

1. They're selfish.
2. They're greedy.
3. They don't tell the truth.
4. They sometimes make homemade dog biscuits.

Mrs. Steele did not go to the post office, the lying liar. She went in totally the opposite direction, and I followed her scent, keeping my nose to the ground as the blood of my ancestors pulsed through my veins.

"What's that sound he's making?" asked Rocco, decidedly uncomfortable with this adventure and flinching at each noise. Not an outdoor cat, by any means, this was a terrifying endeavor for him.

"You mean the chuffing sound coming from his nose?" asked Gracie. "He's following her scent trail."

"Why aren't you and Jackson doing the same?" asked Rocco.

Gracie looked at Jackson, and they both burst out laughing. "First of all, I'm a herding dog. Border collies, even the miniature ones, are meant to keep animals in line. We aren't trackers or hunters."

"You certainly keep us in line," said Jackson with a wiggle of his puggy eyebrows. I didn't understand how it might be considered suggestive, but somehow Jackson managed to make it sound lewd.

"What about you?" asked Rocco. "What were pugs meant to do?"

"Sit on the laps of kings," said Jackson, pulling himself up proudly.

"So, basically, you're useless?" asked Rocco.

"Look who's talking, fluff ball." Jackson let out a growl. Rocco responded in kind.

"Stop it, you two," said Gracie, keeping them in line as an excellent miniature border collie would. "Can't you see Capone is trying to work? And we have more important things to worry about right now than your egos. We're outside. Outside is dangerous. We have to be careful, and we have to stick together."

Rocco's eyes darted back and forth, and he jumped closer to me when a car sped past us. "She's right. I don't like it out here. We need to finish this and get back home as soon as possible."

"And we need to be discrete," said Gracie. "I'm shocked no one has noticed us yet, but it's only a matter of time before someone sees us and brings us back to the shop. We have to be quick and sneaky."

"My two favorite things," said Jackson, wiggling his eyebrows at her again.

"Why do you keep flirting with Gracie?" asked Rocco.

"She digs me. I can tell."

"Not going to happen, pug boy," said Gracie with a swish of her fluffy tail.

"We'll see, princess," said Jackson, waddling after her.

Note to self: Jackson is the most optimistic dog I've ever met.

We stayed on the edge of the sidewalk and ducked into bushes whenever someone approached. It took us some time, but, at last, we reached Mrs. Steele's house. Located on River Road, it was a neat and tidy Cape Cod painted white with blue shutters.

Staring at it, I imagined a kitchen with copper pots and beds of flowers blooming in the spring and summer. Now the beds were filled with nothing but brown leaves, which had fallen from the oak tree next to the house. Mrs. Steele's scent wafted strongly here, as did something else.

"It smells like Miss Josie's shop," I said, lifting my nose. "More than what could come from having one book in her purse."

We stood near a small window leading to Mrs. Steele's basement, and as I looked inside, I got a surprise. Rather than a basement filled with old lady things like porcelain vases and old coats, this resembled a warehouse. Shelves lined the walls, filled with identical cardboard bank boxes, each carefully labeled in black marker.

Not for the first time, I sincerely wished I could read. At the sound of someone approaching, we all jumped and hid behind the large rhododendron bush on the side of Mrs. Steele's house. From there, we could still see her porch, but no one could see us. A good thing, since I recognized the people on the sidewalk.

"Mrs. Norris and her lover boy," said Jackson. "What a surprise."

They knocked on Mrs. Steele's door, and she quickly

ushered them in. "We have a problem," she said, and she shut the door.

We ran up to the porch, and heard the murmurs of conversation from inside, but we weren't able to make out the exact words.

"What are we going to do?" asked Gracie, prancing in excitement. "We have to hear what's going on."

"Follow me," said Jackson. "Let's find another door."

He led us around to the back of the house and onto a small deck in Mrs. Steele's postcard-pretty back garden. Gracie, Jackson, and I stared up at the door knob, high above our heads. None of us were big enough to reach it.

"Why couldn't one of you have been a St. Bernard?" I asked, looking at the two small dogs next to me.

Jackson stood on his stubby back legs, reaching as high as he could, which wasn't high at all. "Wait. I'll get it."

Mrs. Steele must not have closed the back door firmly, because as soon as Jackson pushed on it, it opened, causing Jackson to land in an undignified heap on the floor.

"My hero," said Gracie with a snort, stepping over him.

"I meant to do that," said Jackson as he hefted himself up.

"If you two are done messing around," said Rocco, "I suggest we go this way."

We followed the sound of voices. Mrs. Steele, Mrs. Norris, and Billy sat in the front room, and we stood in the hallway, pressed against the wall like a criminal line up.

"Do you have the book?" asked Mrs. Norris. I stuck my head around the corner, and saw her sitting primly on Mrs. Steele's couch, with Billy next to her.

"Do you have the cash?" asked Mrs. Steele. She stood near the window, peeking through her lace curtains and looking furtively outside.

Mrs. Norris rolled her eyes. "For heaven's sake, they aren't after you, Lucy. We destroyed all evidence of what you stole from the shop with those smoke bombs. You ought to thank us."

"There was still so much more I could have taken." Mrs. Steele's voice came out as a plaintive whine, tinged with greed.

"Pish, posh. You took enough. Now give me the book, and I'll sell it through the usual channels. You'll get your payment once I do. Have I ever cheated you before?"

Mrs. Steele folded her arms across her chest. "The smoke bomb helped you more than it helped me, Henrietta. You now have the insurance money, thanks to the way you tricked Mr. Bartleby into making you the beneficiary."

"You're jealous you didn't think of it first." She let out a laugh. "You should have seen Josie's face when I told her Benjamin and I were lovers. It was most amusing. As if I would ever sleep with someone so old."

Mrs. Steele raised a quizzical brow at her. "But Henrietta, he was only a few years older than you."

Mrs. Norris waved a hand dismissively. "I prefer younger gentlemen. Like my Billy."

Billy lifted her hand and gave it a kiss, but he was no gentleman, and Mrs. Norris was no lady. They seemed more like monsters, and so did Mrs. Steele.

She folded her arms over her ample bosom and glared at Mrs. Norris. "Well, since your plan to take his money worked, I want my payment up front."

"I don't have the money yet." Mrs. Norris opened her purse. Green and covered in butterflies, it seemed like an odd choice for a criminal mastermind. "I'll give you a down payment. Let's say, ten thousand dollars."

Mrs. Steele's jaw dropped. "Newton's *Philosophiae*

Naturalis Principia Mathematica is valued at nine hundred thousand."

"We don't know we'll get that much for it. We aren't selling this at Christy's, you know." She reached into her purse, pulled out a wad of cash, and counted it. "I've meant to ask, how did you get your hands on this book, and why have you held onto it for so long?"

"I hid it," said Mrs. Steele. "When Mr. Bartleby was still alive. I shoved it in a box in the back room, mixed in with old tax records and such. When he realized a few of his more valuable items had gone missing, he grew suspicious. He locked up the back room and didn't give me a key. After he left Josie the shop, she kept it locked, too. I couldn't get into there until today. She opened it to let the cleaners in, and I jumped at the chance. I've waited years for this."

"It's too bad we couldn't get it sooner. Benjamin's mind was a mess toward the end, which was how I got him to put my name on the insurance policy. He kept forgetting things, losing things."

"Which makes me wonder..."

"Wonder what?" asked Mrs. Norris.

"About those missing books."

Mrs. Norris shook her head. "Do you know how many times my Billy has broken into that shop looking for them? They aren't there, Lucy. They're gone."

She let out a sigh. "Well, we had a good thing while it lasted. And now I'll have a nice little nest egg for retirement, too." She narrowed her eyes at Mrs. Norris. "Not as nice as yours, but I suppose we can't be greedy."

"No, we can't, especially if Josephine contacts the insurance company. In a rare lucid moment, Mr. Bartleby rewrote the policy, then hid the documents, the scamp. He told me all about it, but he couldn't remember where he'd put the information, so I think we're safe. Josie is the new beneficiary, but if she doesn't sign it in a week, it goes to me." She shook her head sadly. "Poor dear. I feel quite sorry for her."

"So do I," said Mrs. Steele. "But business is business."

"They are horrible humans," whispered Gracie.

"I agree," I said, and caught a glimpse of Mrs. Steele's purse sitting only a foot or so away from me. Rocco followed my gaze.

"Are you thinking what I'm thinking?" he asked.

I nodded. "This is our one shot."

"Maybe I can help." The voice came from a pure white cat perched on a table above us. He had one blue eye and one green. "I'm Casper. I'm staying with Mrs. Steele while my family is on vacation. She locks me in the bathroom and won't let me sit on her couch. I hate her."

"I feel you, dude," I said. "We used to have the same rule, too."

"Only for you, kibble breath," said Rocco. "Rules don't apply to cats."

Casper agreed. "I want to get even with her. I peed on her bed a few times, but I'd like to do more. How can I help?"

"Can you create a distraction, Casper?" I asked. This might work.

He grinned. "Definitely. Leave it to me."

I gave him a grateful nod. "Let's do this. Now."

We sprang into action. Rocco ran back into the kitchen. Casper took off full speed into the room, hissing like a maniac, and jumped on top of Mrs. Norris's hat. Mrs. Norris screamed, and as Billy and Mrs. Steele tried to yank him off, Gracie, Jackson, and I grabbed the strap of the purse and pulled it toward the back door.

We nearly made it out, but Mrs. Steele spotted us, letting out a high-pitched scream. We froze in mid-pull and that's when Casper, still perched on Mrs. Norris's hat, lifted his leg to pee.

"You'd better move," he said. "I can't hold them much longer."

"Bye, Casper. Thank you," shouted Gracie over her shoulder as we dragged the purse into the kitchen.

"My pleasure," he said. "We should hang sometime. I'll look you guys up."

Rocco held the screen door open for us. "Hurry up, butt sniffers. You can chat with Casper later. We need to go. Now."

He was right. We'd just made it out the door when we heard the heavy footfalls of Billy's massive feet.

"Run," screamed Gracie.

I couldn't go quickly pulling the heavy purse. Jackson grabbed the handle, too, and together we managed to get it out of the backyard.

"They're getting away," said Mrs. Norris. "Stop them, Billy."

Billy barreled around the corner. Although big, he wasn't fast or agile.

"Where are we going?" asked Gracie panting.

"The one place he can't follow us," said Jackson. He nodded to indicate a drainage pipe leading down to the river. Rocco ran into it, and so did Jackson. Gracie stared at me in horror.

"It's dirty in there."

I gave her a shove. Not the most gentlemanly thing I'd ever done, but necessary. The pipe, set at a steep angle, led down to the banks of the Ohio River below.

"I'll get you for this, Capone."

I heard Gracie's voice echoing through the pipe, but I had no time to dawdle. I hopped into the pipe and slid down bottom first, bringing the purse with me and landing with a plop in the mud near the river.

"Worst. Day. Ever," said Gracie, glaring at me. "Did we have to do that?"

"Yes, we did," I said. "I could never have outrun Billy carrying this purse. He would have caught me in no time."

Billy stood on top of the cliff, his eyes scanning the river bank, but he couldn't see us due to the dense foliage. "I lost them," he shouted. "But they couldn't have gone far. I'll head downriver to find them. I can't climb down from here."

"If he's heading downriver, we're heading up," said Jackson, starting to walk.

"But the shop and Miss Josie are in the opposite direction," I said.

"We've got no other option, pup." Jackson looked over his shoulder at me, his expression serious. "We need to get away from Billy, and it's nearly dark. It'll be harder to find our way back to our humans once the sun goes down."

"Well, this sucks." Rocco tiptoed through the muck, his expression one of pure disgust.

Grace's face mirrored his. "Ew. Ew. Ew. Was that raccoon poop? Gross. I smell something. It's like an animal crawled in a cave somewhere and died, and then their body slowly decomposed until there was only a pile of rotting flesh left and nothing else."

We all looked at her in shock, except for Jackson, who grinned and let out a soft chuckle. "He, he, he," he said. "Oops. I farted."

"Jackson, you are foul," she said.

"But charming and handsome, too." Jackson winked at her. "Come on, princess. I know you're out of your element, but we've got to move. You don't want to spend the night out here, do you?"

It was slow going with me dragging Mrs. Steele's handbag. It kept catching on roots and other things in the undergrowth. A distance which should have taken us ten minutes to cover took closer to forty. By the time we reached a trail near the bridge spanning the Ohio River and connecting Beaver to Monaca, I was exhausted, and it had started to rain.

"Let's rest a few minutes," said Jackson, shooting a sympathetic glance at me laboring under the weight of the purse, and at Rocco who seemed terrified of the precipitation. "We can take shelter under the bridge."

We scrambled to find a dry spot and cuddled up against the cold. As the sky darkened, our gloom increased with each passing moment. The rain pounded harder, and I doubted we'd make it much farther being so tired and cold and hungry.

"We should stay here until daybreak," said Jackson. "We'll get some rest and move on."

Gracie circled a few times before lying down. "Well, this is not what I'm used to," she said with a *hmph*.

"Same goes for all of us, peaches. We don't have an option, though." Jackson gave me a worried look. "Are you okay, Capone?"

I nodded, barely able to keep my eyes open. "I'm tired. This bag is so heavy."

"Sorry we couldn't help much," said Jackson. "Grace and I both have extremely stubby legs."

"Speak for yourself, puglet. My legs are perfect." Gracie sat next to Rocco, who snickered at the word "puglet."

Jackson didn't seem to notice. "Your legs are perfect,

Gracie. Perfect and stubby." Jackson turned to me. "Get some rest. I'll keep watch."

"Keep watch for what?"

A dark shape appeared next to us. For a moment, I thought it might be Billy. I yelped and backed up into the side of the bridge. Jackson, Gracie, and Rocco did the same, and we clung to each other, hiding as we slipped as far as we could into the shadows.

The tall man who stood before us smelled dirty and strange. He was thin, with a shock of red hair. He carried a flashlight, and when he noticed the purse on the ground, he stopped.

"Well, lookie here," he said softly, picking it up. "This is my lucky day."

As he trudged away with Mrs. Steele's purse in his hands, I slumped down to the ground, filled with utter despair. All our hard work had been for nothing. The purse was gone, and any hope I had of saving Miss Josie and her shop went with it. I let out a howl of pure misery.

Note to self: It's always darkest before it's pitch black.

FORTY-FIVE

Why friends are important:

1. They support your crazy ideas.
2. They pick you up when you're down.
3. They have your back.
4. They lick you in all the right places.
5. They never judge you.
6. They're willing to slap some sense into you when you're stupid.

"It's going to be okay, pup," said Jackson, licking my face in consolation.

"How is it going to be okay?" I asked, shoving him away. "When that man stole the only evidence we had to save Ms. Josie, we didn't do anything. We hid, like a bunch of wimps."

"What would you suggest we do, Capone?" asked Rocco. "Take on a human wandering around in the dark? We did the right thing. The sensible thing."

"The cowardly thing."

"You don't mean it," said Jackson, tilting his head to the side. "We were all so brave. We worked together to save the shop. We committed several misdemeanors, including breaking and entering and petty theft. We slid down a freaking pipe to land next to a raging river. We were total heroes, and we tried so hard."

"We failed." Too tired to argue any further, I stomped away from Jackson and flopped down next to the cement supports of the bridge with my back to my friends. Lightning flashed across the sky and thunder cracked as it rained even harder. I shivered, wet and cold, curling myself into a little ball of despair.

Slowly, one by one, my friends came to lie down next to me. They shared not only their body heat, but also their compassion. They understood why I'd gotten so upset and had already forgiven me for my outburst.

"Thanks, guys," I said, my voice thick with emotion. "I'm sorry about what I said. I'm the one who failed. I failed to make a better plan. I failed Miss Josie and Mr. Nate. I failed to be a good friend to all of you. I failed to control my anger. I failed to—"

"Shut up, numbnuts," said Jackson. "There is nothing to forgive. Go to sleep. You need rest."

I sighed and closed my eyes. I might not have much, but I had the best friends in the world.

The next morning, I woke to Jackson's butt in my face and the sound of his snoring. He had one paw on Gracie's tail, which may or may not have been inappropriate touching. Rocco slept on top of me, providing a warm feline blanket. He opened his eyes and stretched.

"The sun's coming up. Let's go." He sniffed, making a face. "Yuck. I smell like a dog."

Gracie woke up, too, moving as far away from Jackson as possible. He rolled over and farted.

"You need to change your diet," she said. "That is not normal."

I sat up, staring down at the river, as hopelessness consumed me. "What are we going to do?"

Jackson yawned and came to sit next to me. "We'll let the humans figure it out."

I shook my head. "They don't know about Mrs. Steele and Mrs. Norris. It's up to us."

"How can we help?" asked Gracie. "The purse is gone, and I'm covered in unspeakable matter. I think I rolled in sewage. Let's go home, Capone. We tried. It's enough."

About to get up and walk away, I noticed something black down by the river. It was Mrs. Steele's purse.

Without a word, I ran down the hillside, sliding in the mud. The purse had fallen down a steep embankment. I skidded to a stop. I might be able to get down, but how would I get back up?

Jackson, Gracie, and Rocco ran up behind me. "What's going on, Capone?" asked Jackson.

I pointed to the purse. "It's right there, but how do we get it?"

Rocco looked around. "I have an idea."

We moved a tree branch until it hung over the side of the embankment. He climbed down and tentatively stepped into the mud near Mrs. Steele's bag.

"Oh, this is horrible," he said, cringing in disgust. "I'm wet. I hate being wet."

"It's okay, Rocco." I kept my voice steady, trying to calm him down. It seemed to work. Rocco got the strap of the bag around the tree branch, and sat on it, holding it in place, as we slowly and painfully pulled the branch up the embankment.

It took a few tries, but, at last, we got it over the edge. Gracie, Jackson, and I flopped down in exhaustion. Rocco cleaned his paws.

"I've never been so dirty in my whole life. This is awful."

"Rocco," I said, catching my breath. "You're a hero and a genius."

"I know," he said, sniffing in irritation. "Can we go home now, please? I need time at a spa after this fiasco."

"Preach," said Gracie. "Me, too."

"First let's see if the book is still in here." I put my nose inside. Mrs. Steele's wallet was gone, but, to my great surprise, the book and papers were still inside.

"The thief probably took the wallet and tossed the purse," said Jackson. "They do it sometimes. I saw it on a cop show."

"Which means we have what we need." I wagged my tail in excitement.

"Yes," said Rocco. "But now we have to get it back to the shop."

It took a long time to pull the purse up the steep hillside, and even longer to drag it all the way through town. Block after block we trudged, until at last, exhausted, filthy, and starving, we finally reached the main street.

"We're nearly there," said Jackson. "I can smell the coffee from First Impressions."

"Thank goodness," said Gracie, and then she froze, her hackles rising. "Hide, everyone. Now."

Mrs. Norris and Billy stood on the corner, only a few feet away, with their backs to us. We hid behind a table in front of Don's Deli, but we were exposed. To make matters worse, as soon as I smelled the delicious aroma of meat coming from inside, my stomach reacted. It growled, because I hadn't eaten in forever, and I started to drool. The handle of the purse slipped out of my mouth, and I had to slurp my drool back in to keep my grip.

"We have to find them before anyone else does," said Mrs. Norris.

"The whole town is out looking for them," said Billy. "It's hopeless. We should cut our losses and get out of here."

She whacked him with her handbag, making Billy flinch. "I'm not leaving without the book, and you're going to help me find it."

Another waft of roast beef scented heaven came out of the shop. I tried to contain it, I really did, but my stomach rumbled so loudly, even Mrs. Norris heard it.

"What was that sound?" she asked, turning her head.

As soon as her eyes met mine, I knew we were in trouble. If she could beat up a giant like Billy, what would she do to us?

"Run," I yelled.

It came out muffled due to the purse strap in my mouth, but they understood. We took off down the main street of Beaver, running as fast as we could, but Billy quickly closed in on us.

"Run, Capone," said Jackson. "I've got this."

Jackson stopped suddenly, planting his portly pug body in the middle of the sidewalk. Billy couldn't stop in time. He tripped over Jackson and fell to the ground like a giant oak tree.

As Billy tried to get up, Gracie, Jackson, and Rocco pulled on his shirt and jumped on his back. Rocco hopped on his head, dislodging Billy's toupee. I hadn't even realized he wore one.

They had the situation in hand, so I ran past First Impressions and straight to Bartleby's. The door was propped open, so I flew in but skidded to a stop when I saw Mrs. Steele standing by the front window. She slammed the door closed behind me. I tried to backpedal, but it was too late.

"You've been a naughty puppy," she said. "And do you know where naughty puppies end up? In the river. Dead."

She reached for my collar, but I evaded her. I pulled the purse under a table and pressed my body against the wall. She knelt down, a nasty gleam in her dark eyes.

"You're a clever little thing, but it belongs to me. Give me the book. Now."

She crawled toward me, her expression murderous. I quivered in fear. This might be the end, and I was filled with regret. I was going to die, and I'd barely even lived. Even worse, I'd never see my darling Miss Josie ever again.

Then I heard the sweetest sound in the whole world. Miss Josie's voice.

"Mrs. Steele. What are you doing?"

Mrs. Steele jumped up, bumping her head hard on the underside of the table. I dashed around her, still pulling the purse, and went straight to Miss Josie. She gathered me into her arms. Mr. Nate stood behind her, holding Jackson and Gracie. Rocco had hopped onto a bookshelf.

"I'm never going outside again. Never, never, never," Rocco said.

Mrs. Steele gave Miss Josie a bright, brittle smile. "I wanted to help the poor doggie," she said. "He came inside and got all tangled up in my purse."

Note to self: Liars sometimes wear floral.

"Don't play games with me, Mrs. Steele," said Miss

Josie, her voice icy. "We heard every word you said. What have you stolen from me?"

"I've never been so insulted—"

Miss Josie cut her off. "Tell me the truth. Now."

I wiggled out of Miss Josie's grasp and stuck my nose in Mrs. Steele's beat up and muddied purse. Mrs. Steele tried to grab it from me, lunging toward me in a desperate attempt to retrieve it.

"Get out of there," she said. "That's mine."

Miss Josie stood in front of her, arms akimbo. "I don't think so, Mrs. Steele. Stay back. What did you find, Capone?"

I pulled out the book and all the pages in plastic sleeves, scattering them across the floor. Miss Josie's eyes widened in surprise. She picked up the book, carefully removing it from its puffy envelope. It was enclosed in a vacuum sealed bag.

"Newton's *Philosophiae Naturalis Principia Mathematica*. Mr. Bartleby told me he'd once tried to procure this. I thought he was imagining things. I should have known better." She gathered the pages tucked into plastic sleeves. "These were all taken from books in my shop, too. Mrs. Steele, why would you do this to him? To me?"

Mrs. Steele straightened her back. "I don't have to listen to any of this. I'm leaving."

"I don't think so." Officer Stahl entered the shop with Cedric. Mrs. Norris and Billy stood outside on the sidewalk, surrounded by policemen, and Billy seemed to be in handcuffs. He looked a lot older without his toupee. Mrs. Norris yelled at the police officers like an agitated little bird.

"Cedric?" asked Miss Josie. "What are you doing here?"

"I heard about the shop," he said, looking around. It had been cleaned and partially repaired, but most of the shelves were empty since the water damaged so many books. "I'm so sorry, Josie."

"Thanks, but what's going on?"

Officer Stahl put his hands on his hips. "When we went to speak to Mr. Churchill, his alibi checked out. A few hours later, we saw the video from the camera on the coffee shop. It proved without a doubt that Billy and Mrs. Norris were responsible for the smoke bombs. Although Mr. Churchill was no longer a suspect, he had an interesting theory."

Cedric stepped forward. "For a few years now, I've noticed odd things popping up on auction sites. I didn't realize until recently that they'd all come from this shop."

"And once we figured out who'd put those things up for auction," Officer Stahl nodded toward Mrs. Norris and Billy outside, "it wasn't hard to connect them to Mrs. Steele here. You have an interesting basement, ma'am. Quite the collection of valuable books and papers in there."

"You were in my basement?" Mrs. Steele sank into a chair. "I can't believe this is happening."

"Why did you steal from us?" asked Miss Josie, her face pale and tight. "And how could you have destroyed all those beautiful books?"

"Her name should have been the first clue," snorted Jackson as he waddled over to me. "Mrs. Steele. Get it. She steals things. He, he, he."

I shushed him. "I want to hear why she did it."

She spread out her hands in defeat. "I had three kids and no husband," she said. "They went to an expensive private school. I couldn't afford it on my own, and I had to pay for their college tuition, too. They'd grown accustomed to a certain lifestyle. There were things they needed, and things I needed as well. What else could I do?"

"You could have sent your kids to public school. They could have gotten loans for college. You had options." She shook her head, her soft blond curls brushing against her sad face. "Those books were rare and wonderful. You ruined them out of greed, and now no one can ever enjoy them again."

Officer Stahl took Mrs. Steele by the arm and led her to his police car. Mrs. Norris and Billy had already been taken away. Miss Josie gave Mr. Nate a hug, and then turned to Cedric. "Thank you," she said. "I can't believe you did this. After what happened with Capone—"

"Oh, I still hate your dog, Josephine, but I don't hate you. I owed you one, for how I behaved. You deserved better." He glanced over at Mr. Nate who picked thorns and brambles out of Gracie's fur and tried to act like he wasn't listening. Cedric gave her a wry smile. "And I think you found it."

Miss Josie's cheeks got pink. "I think you might be right."

Cedric raised a finger in the air. "Before I go, there is one thing. I'm convinced Mr. Bartleby hid something in your back garden. I tried to find it, hoping to surprise you and save the day, but I got interrupted by the hell hound here."

I wagged my tail at him. Hell hound? It sounded tough. Even Hans would be impressed.

"We did find something," said Miss Josie. "But it wasn't anything particularly valuable. It was a garden plan of Mr. Bartleby's rose bushes, a business card, and a hat pin..." Miss Josie's voice trailed off as her eyes met Mr. Nate's.

A hat pin? Had it been some kind of clue?

"That's too bad. I'd hoped something remarkable was out there, maybe even the Austen," he said. He glanced at his watch. "Sorry. I've got to go. I've got another marriage counseling session. Elinor is giving me a second chance. She's normally such a sensible woman, but for some reason she thinks I'm worth keeping. Goodbye, Josephine, and good luck."

Mr. Nate and Miss Josie watched him go, waiting a few seconds before dashing to the back room to get Mr. Bartleby's safety deposit box. Miss Josie pulled out the insurance card with shaking hands.

"Do you think this could have something to do with the policy on the inventory?"

Jackson, Gracie, and I all barked in unison, making Mr. Nate laugh. "It seems to be the popular opinion around here."

"Excuse me," she said. "I've got to make a phone call."

She went out into the garden to speak on her cell phone. While she was outside, Ms. Anne rushed into the shop. "Oh, my baby," she said, holding Gracie close. "What happened to you?"

"I was tired and cold and wet," said Gracie as she licked every inch of Ms. Anne's face. "And look at my nails. They're horrible."

Ms. Anne might not have understood Grace's words, but she got the gist of it. "My poor beautiful darling. I'll make sure nothing like this ever happens again." She glanced out the back window and saw Miss Josie pacing pack and forth in the yard. "What's going on?"

"She's talking to an insurance agent," said Mr. Nate. "About the inventory."

Mr. Nate and Ms. Anne went out to the garden, and we accompanied them. When Miss Josie hung up the phone, she lowered herself onto the bench, a befuddled expression on her face.

"What did they say?" asked Ms. Anne.

"There was a second policy. It listed me as the beneficiary. An agent is coming over right now to assess the loss." She seemed shell shocked. "I'm not going to lose the shop. It's going to be okay, more than okay, in fact. And I now have Newton's *Philosophiae Naturalis Principia Mathematica* sitting on my desk, thanks to my Labrador. Mrs. Steele stole it from Mr. Bartleby."

"You're kidding me. How much is it worth?" asked Ms. Anne.

"Close to a million dollars," said Miss Josie softly.

Ms. Anne let out a laugh. "Well, I guess you don't have to worry about the missing seven books anymore."

Miss Josie bit her lip. "I still want to find them," she said. "They're treasures..." Her voice trailed off as she looked around the garden. "Buried treasures."

"What are you talking about, Josie?" asked Mr. Nate.

She grinned at him. "I know where the books are hidden," she said. "Get the shovel, Nate. We have some digging to do."

FORTY-SIX

List of the world's cleverest and cutest bibliophiles:

1. Miss Josephine St. Clair
2. Mr. Benjamin Bartleby
3. Me.

Once again, we were out in the garden digging, and, once again, neither Mr. Nate nor Miss Josie wanted my assistance. I would have loved to help because I am an excellent digger. Some might even say I'm a natural.

Instead, I'd been instructed to sit on the patio and wait. It wasn't so bad. Ms. Anne brought us food, an excellent thing since we were all starving. She also gave us special treats. Jackson, Gracie, and I got bully sticks to chew. Rocco got catnip. In no time at all, he was high as a kite. He lay on his back, staring up at the sky, his mouth slightly slack.

"Look at those clouds. They're the most beautiful clouds I've ever seen. Are they singing? I think the clouds are singing."

Jackson nudged me, rolling his eyes, and I giggled.

There wasn't anything funnier than Rocco all doped up. I'd never seen him so chill.

Miss Josie was the opposite of chill. She nearly thrummed with excitement. Mr. Nate studied her with a twinkle in his eyes. "So where exactly are we digging, Josephine?"

She took out the map of the garden and put it on the table. Then she pulled out a list. "These are the books missing from our inventory," she said. "Now look at the names of the roses."

Mr. Nate leaned close, his hand resting casually on her back. "Are you saying..."

Miss Josie nodded, her curls bobbing as she smiled up at him. "I think Mr. Bartleby hid the books under his roses. If I'm right, *Dracula* will be buried under the 'Dracula' Rose."

"And Rose 'Dorothy' refers to *The Wizard of Oz*," said Mr. Nate. "But what does *The Velveteen Rabbit* have to do with 'Bianco'?"

Miss Josie grinned. "Margery Williams's married name was Bianco."

"Holy cow," said Mr. Nate.

"Exactly," said Miss Josie. "And all the other roses correspond with the missing books as well."

Ms. Anne, holding Gracie in her arms, looked over the list. "I'm guessing 'Our Beth' has to do with *Little Women,* and 'The Fairy' could be *The Hobbit*. But what about 'Yorkshire'?"

Miss Josie nearly bubbled with excitement. "*Jane Eyre*. The Brontë sisters were from Yorkshire."

After running his finger down the list, Mr. Nate paused. "Then is 'Hertfordshire' for *Pride and Prejudice*?"

"Yes," said Miss Josie. "And hopefully it's the rare signed first edition Mr. Bartleby talked about."

"That would be amazing." said Mr. Nate. "Do you think it's possible?"

She handed him a shovel and grabbed another for herself. "There's only one way to be sure."

After twenty minutes or so of digging, they hit something hard and heard a metallic clang. They pulled out a small container, approximately the size of a shoe box. It opened with an odd sounding *pop*.

"Mr. Bartleby sealed it," said Ms. Anne.

"He found a way to protect it from the elements," said Miss Josie, her hands shaking. A beautiful old copy of *Pride and Prejudice* had been stored in a thick, vacuum-sealed bag. It rested in the box next to documentation verifying its purchase. "And I'm sure all the other missing books must be here, too."

Mr. Nate let out a whoop and swung Miss Josie around in a circle. She laughed, lifting her face to the sky. Ms. Anne put Gracie down, and we pranced around the dancing humans.

"I guess we have some digging to do?" asked Mr. Nate, still grinning from ear to ear.

"I'll call for reinforcements," said Ms. Anne. "We could use some help."

"And call Officer Stahl, too," said Miss Josie. "The police will want to hear about this. We finally know what Billy was after when he broke into my shop."

As Ms. Anne ran to make the phone calls, Miss Josie stared up at Mr. Nate's face. "It's like my life is finally coming together." Her eyes clouded over. "Well, except for the fact that you'll be leaving soon," she said softly. "The thought of that makes me very sad."

"Does it?" he asked, his brown eyes warm and probing. "Why?"

She cleared her throat. "I met you during one of the worst times in my life. I'd lost so much and didn't think I could bear to lose anything else, so I concluded it was safer to distance myself from people. To shut myself up in this little bookstore and hide. But first Capone came into my life and forced me to get out into the world again." She smiled and scratched me behind the ear. "And then you started showing up with your coffee. Before I knew it, I slowly turned back into myself again, except I was braver, and stronger."

"And far more caffeinated," he said with a smile.

"Oh, yes." She placed a small hand over his heart. "Thank you, Nate. For the coffee, and for reading Jane Austen, and for always being there for me when I needed it most."

"Like when Capone ate the peony bushes?"

"Yes."

"And when he ate the chocolate?"

"Definitely yes."

Did they have to bring up every mistake I'd ever made? Geesh. Get onto the kissing part. Please.

Mr. Nate smiled. "I was happy to be there for you, through each one of Capone's bad choices and all of his intestinal distress."

Miss Josie put a hand on his cheek. "I'm so glad I met you, but I'll miss you, Nate," she said softly.

"No, you won't." He brushed a curl behind her ear. "Because I'm not leaving."

"What?" It seemed like Miss Josie couldn't quite breathe. I couldn't quite breathe either.

Note to self: Love is similar to oxygen deprivation.

"My home is with you, Josephine St. Clair, if you'll have me."

She wrapped her arms around his neck and pulled him close to give him a rapturous kiss. When they separated, Miss Josie practically glowed with happiness.

"I love you, Nate Murray. Haven't you figured that out by now?"

They kissed again, and Jackson sighed. I thought it was from deep emotion, but it actually could have been gas. One never knew with Jackson.

Jackson stared at Nate with affection. "He's a little slow," he said. "Lovable, but slow."

Gracie kicked him. "Shut up, doofus. They're getting to the good part."

Gracie was right. Mr. Nate gazed at Miss Josie, his eyes intense. "I love you. You've bewitched me, body and soul, and I never want to be parted from you."

I knew those words. I'd heard them before. I hopped to my feet, not wanting to miss a second of Miss Josie's reaction. "He's quoting Mr. Darcy again," I said.

"I think I might swoon," said Gracie, lying down and placing one paw over her face.

"Me, too," said Jackson, before letting out a long and nasty belch. I guess I'd been right about the gas.

Miss Josie and Mr. Nate ignored him. "If you keep quoting Darcy," she said. "I may have to ravish you."

He gave her a mischievous grin. "Let's save the ravishing for a time when we don't have an audience." He tilted his head to indicate Jackson, Gracie, and I all listening raptly to every word they said.

Rocco wasn't listening. He'd fallen fast asleep with his head in one of the empty planting pots. He may have been snoring. He'd gotten completely and utterly trashed.

Miss Josie nibbled on her lower lip. "But what about Seattle?"

"Why be the president of a company if I can't delegate a job or two to my managers? I have the best employees in the world. When I told them I wanted to make Beaver our headquarters, they went for it. They understood this is the only place I can be happy. And since I've now turned you into a coffee drinker, my life is complete. But there is still one thing I need to do."

"What?"

He nodded toward the book they'd dug up. "See if Jane Austen really wrote something inside that book."

After washing up and donning white gloves, Miss Josie carefully opened the sealed plastic package and took out the fragile, leather-bound volume. She looked inside, her eyes bright with excitement, and gasped when she saw the inscription.

"A novel of First Impressions written by Jane Austen. April 1813." Miss Josie's eyes shot to Mr. Nate.

"I don't understand," he said, his expression incredulous.

"I completely forgot it was the original title of the book," she said. "And Jane Austen thought it was a better one, apparently. Why did you choose that name for your café, Nate?"

He laughed, rubbing a hand against his jaw. "It had nothing to do with Jane Austen. My mom always said, 'You never get a second chance to a make a good first impression.' It became the motto of our company."

"Well, it was meant to be," said Miss Josie. "Obviously."

Mr. Nate pulled her into his arms. "And we were meant to be as well."

"Which is one thing we can definitely agree on." She went up on her tiptoes to kiss Mr. Nate and then put the book back into its protective sleeve. Ms. Anne rushed in as Miss Josie was placing it in the vault.

"Come on, you two," she said. "The cavalry has arrived."

The rest of the neighborhood joined in to help with the digging, and one by one, the seven missing books were revealed. The story made not only the local news, but the national news as well. The reporter interviewed Miss Josie about the books buried under the rose bushes, but they also discussed the heroics of three dogs and a cat and how a group of pets managed to find a book worth close to a million dollars and foil a group of thieves.

The next evening, Mr. Nate and Miss Josie lounged on the back patio hand in hand, sipping wine as the sun went down. Jackson and I sat at their feet, and Rocco rested on a folding chair a few feet away. He was a little hung over from all the catnip, and back to his old, grumpy self. Well, not quite as grumpy. I now knew his heart was as soft as his sweet, furry exterior. He just didn't like to show it.

Miss Josie stared at me, a small smile curving on her lips. "I've finally decided on a name."

I sat up, tail wagging. Was Miss Josie talking about me? Could this be the moment I'd been waiting for?

"For Capone?" asked Mr. Nate. "It might be hard to call him anything else at this point. I'm not sure another name will stick."

My shoulders slumped. Maybe Mr. Nate was right. I was far too Capone-ish for my own good.

Oh, calamity.

Curse my primitive nature.

"Al Capone's first name was actually Alphonse. It's a name shared by writers and painters and artists and kings. An extraordinary name for an extraordinary dog."

Mr. Nate smiled. "And that's his name?"

She nodded. "He's not simply Capone; he's Alphonse Capone. It's on his papers and everything. And, from now on, I think that's what I'll call him. Alphonse Capone. It suits him. But we'll keep it Capone for short. We'll only pull out the Alphonse on special occasions."

Mr. Nate agreed, and I thought I might burst with happiness. Not Darcy, but even better. Alphonse Capone. My name. The name I'd had all along and didn't even known it. The perfect name for me.

I'd found the perfect home as well. I had Miss Josie, whom I adored, and Mr. Nate, the best guy in the world. I had wonderful friends, including Jackson, who'd become like a big brother to me. Yes, I already outweighed him by twenty pounds, but he was older and somewhat wiser, so he'd earned big brother status. I had the sweet diva Gracie and the lovely Ms. Anne. I also had Rocco, who'd become my first, and best, feline friend. My life was complete.

And when Miss Josie gave Mr. Nate a sweetly ardent kiss, I knew I'd succeeded in that area as well. I'd found Miss Josie her Mr. Darcy, her one true love. Yes, I made a few mistakes along the way, but it had all worked out well in the end, as good stories often do.

Jane Austen couldn't have done any better herself.

EPILOGUE

The keys to finding a happily ever after:

1. Love
2. Friendship
3. Respect
4. Coffee
5. Lots and lots of books.

I believe Miss Josie did manage to ravish Mr. Nate that night. I couldn't say for sure. Jackson, Rocco, and I got locked out of her room, but, judging by all the lovey-dovey behavior we witnessed the next morning, I had to assume they'd done the deed.

Mistress Sue arrived a few days later, as promised, to check on me. Miss Josie and Mr. Nate greeted her nervously, but they needn't have worried.

"You're doing a fine job," she said, as I wiggled and wagged my tail and licked her. When she pulled a treat out of her pocket and told me to sit, I immediately complied. "And you've taught the pup manners, too. Well done."

"It took time," said Miss Josie. "We're not done training him yet. He'll start the next round of obedience classes in a few weeks."

"Excellent," she said. "You have to train a dog as much as possible while he's young, and socialize him, too. It's important. But he'll learn. He's the smartest puppy I've ever met."

Miss Josie folded her hands in her lap. "Can I ask you a question?" When Mistress Sue nodded, she continued. "Why was he the last of the litter to be adopted?"

Mistress Sue smiled and patted me on the head. "I couldn't let a dog like this go to just anyone. I had to find the right person, or I planned to keep him myself. When your friend, Anne, came to the farm, and told me you had a bookstore, I knew you were the right person for Capone, and this was the right place. He loved books and stories and watching PBS on the television. He was always a weird little guy, but what could be better for a dog that likes books than to live in a bookshop?"

If I could cry, I would have been weeping right now. I hadn't gotten adopted last because I lacked something. I'd gotten adopted last because Mistress Sue loved me and wanted the best for me. It was the most wonderful news I'd ever had.

"How did you come up with the name Capone?" asked Miss Josie.

"I named the puppies in his litter after gangsters as a joke and expected them to be given new ones as soon as they were adopted," said Mistress Sue. "But I'm curious. Why didn't you change Capone's name?"

"Because I love him for who he is, the good parts and the not so good parts. I don't want to change a thing about him. Not even his name. That's how it is when you truly love someone. You accept them, faults and all." Miss Josie's eyes met Mr. Nate's, and they both smiled. I smiled, too. I smiled so hard, in fact, I thought I might burst with happiness.

Not long afterward, on a cold November day, Mr. Nate showed up in the shop in a suit, carrying a leather briefcase. He looked like a gentleman, but, of course, Mr. Nate had been a gentleman all along—even while wearing torn up T-shirts and faded jeans. His actions made him a gentleman, not how he dressed. I understood it now.

Snow began to fall; fluffy, fat flakes whirled and danced as they covered the sidewalk and the street in a blanket of snow. Gracie sat inside with us, waiting for Ms. Anne to come back to the shop and pick her up. Jackson walked through the door after Mr. Nate, shaking the wet snow off his back.

"It's cold out there, puppy. I nearly froze my hairy butt off." He let out a chuckle when Gracie rolled her eyes. He loved to annoy her. It was a skill, but I wasn't paying attention to them. I stared outside, mesmerized.

I'd never seen snow before. It was exciting. I couldn't wait to go out in the back garden and play in it. Miss Josie had promised she'd let me out as soon as Ms. Anne came back. I nearly vibrated with anticipation.

She looked up with a smile as Mr. Nate came in. They'd made a date for dinner, and she'd put on a fancy dress, and had her hair up in a bun.

"Hello, handsome," she said.

"Hello, beautiful." Mr. Nate stopped, his face getting a little pink. He seemed oddly nervous.

"Are you okay?" asked Miss Josie as she walked over to him.

He took her hand in his. "Yes. No. I mean I have something I need to ask you." He went down on one knee, and Miss Josie gasped. I gasped, too. Could this be what I thought it was? Gracie, Rocco, and Jackson watched the scene unfold, just as entranced as me.

Mr. Nate cleared his throat. "Josephine St. Clair. I love you more than anything." He reached into the bag he carried and pulled out four rather old and battered-looking books.

I looked at Jackson, Gracie, and Rocco in confusion. "Books? I thought it was supposed to be a ring. Did I miss something here?"

"It *is* supposed to be a ring," said Gracie. "A big, sparkly, diamond ring. Ms. Anne has had quite a few in her day. She's been engaged half a dozen times at least."

"That's...a lot," said Jackson. "I don't think it's normal."

"If Mr. Nate is giving her books, there must be a reason for it," I said.

Miss Josie sank into a chair in front of Mr. Nate and took the books in her hands. "These were published right after Jane Austen's death. By her brother."

"Do you like them?"

"I love them. They are the first books to acknowledge her as the author of all her works. Oh, Nate. This gift is amazing."

Note to self: Books are the way to a lady's heart.

He lifted one of the volumes and placed a small box on top of it. "I thought *Persuasion* was appropriate, because I wanted to persuade you to accept this."

Miss Josie sat with the pile of Jane Austen books on her lap and stared at the tiny box. He opened it, his eyes on her face, and I saw the sparkle of a diamond in an elegant, antique setting. It matched the sparkle in Miss Josie's eyes.

"Will you do me the honor of being my wife?" Mr.

Nate's voice cracked with emotion. Miss Josie couldn't speak. She nodded her head, her lips trembling as tears filled her eyes.

Mr. Nate slipped the ring on her finger and pulled her into his arms. It filled my heart with happiness. Miss Josie had been alone for so long, and now she had Mr. Nate and me and Rocco and even Jackson. She had a whole family, like she always wanted. She had us.

When Ms. Anne returned and heard the news, she found a bottle of champagne stashed in the basement, a left-over from dear Mr. Bartleby, and popped the cork, toasting the happy couple.

"To the beginning of your story," she said, raising her glass. "May it be a happy one." They sipped the champagne, Miss Josie and Mr. Nate practically glowing with happiness. "By the way, I suspected this might happen."

"How did you know?" asked Miss Josie. She had one arm around Mr. Nate's waist and stared at him with absolute joy on her face.

Ms. Anne shrugged. "I've been engaged a few times myself," she said with a wink. "I know the signs. By the way, I have some news myself. I'll stop by tomorrow and share it with you."

I'd assumed Ms. Anne might be getting engaged again. Or perhaps she was going on a cruise. It was neither of those things. Ms. Anne walked into the store carrying something tiny and fawn colored in her arms.

"Um, what is that?" asked Mr. Nate.

"My news," she said brightly and set a miniature version of Jackson on the floor in front of us. "His name is Faraday, after the physicist, James Faraday. His owner abandoned him. Can you believe it? I found him at the shelter. He's only three months old, poor baby, and he needs some love, but he's a purebred pug, like Jackson. Gracie gets along so well with your dog, I knew she'd love him. I couldn't resist."

Ms. Josie knelt on the floor next to him. "Oh, my," she said. "He's so tiny. And adorable. What do you think, Gracie? Don't you love your new little brother?"

"Hmph," said Gracie. "The jury is still out."

Faraday stood in front of us, a little ball of trembling fur. As soon as the humans finished fussing over Faraday's over-whelming cuteness, we finally had a chance to introduce ourselves.

"Hi, little guy," I said, keeping my voice gentle. "Wel-come to Bartleby's. I'm Alphonse Capone, but you can call me Capone. The pretty girl over there is your sister, Gracie. Rocco, the cat, is on the shelf. He acts mean sometimes, but he's quite kind."

Rocco muttered a dirty word. Faraday looked up at him and narrowed his eyes, but I ignored Rocco to make the last introduction. "And this handsome dog is Jackson. He's a pug like you. Do you know what a pug is?"

I was about to start with an explanation about how pugs once sat on the laps of kings, but Faraday cut me short with one withering glance. "Of course I know what a pug is, you idiot." He rose on his four stubby little legs, meeting each of us eye for eye. "Prepare yourself to be dominated. You are my servants, and I plan to take over—first this bookstore, then the world. You cannot stop me. I'm Faraday the Fear-less, and I'm what laymen like to call an evil genius."

"Oh, hell," said Jackson. "When Anne said she had a surprise, I thought she was bringing snacks. This is a nightmare."

"Tell me about it," said Gracie. "At least you don't have to live with the little monster."

Faraday let out a decidedly evil laugh. It was strange to

find such a cute little package could contain such malevolence. "You're right, Mr. Fatso Jackson. I'm your own personal nightmare—" He got a far-away look in his eyes, then suddenly, and quite unexpectedly, peed on the floor. When he came out of his trance, he jumped, startled. "Oops. Excuse me. What was I saying?"

Ms. Anne interrupted him. She'd noticed the puddle, made a tsking sound and picked him up. "There, there, Faraday," she said. "Not in the store. I think we're going to have to call you Mr. Tinkles. It might suit you better than Faraday."

Jackson, Gracie, Rocco, and I looked at each other and burst into gales of laughter. Faraday climbed to the top of Ms. Anne's shoulder to glare at us as she carried him outside.

"I am not Mr. Tinkles. I am Faraday, the Evil Genius, and I'm going to make you pay. You'll be sorry you laughed at me. Consider it a promise."

Note to self: Faraday is going to be a problem.

ACKNOWLEDGMENTS

Thanks to my wonderful husband, for finally allowing us to get a dog. Thanks to Patricia Sutkowski for finding just the right puppy for our family, and Sue Varner for raising lovely Labradors. A big thank you to my editors, Ramona, Lara, and Marylu, and my brilliant cover artist Najla. Thank you also to my Mindful Writing group, and especially to Carolyn Menke for suggesting I make Capone a character in his own book. As always, sending out love to my Blankie Brigade (Kathie Shoop, Lori M. Jones, and Kim Pierson), because life is so much better with my tribe. And a special thank you to some furry friends, Jackson, Faraday, Townsend, Gracie, Wrigley, Uncle Clancy, Elliot, Casper, and Rocco.

ABOUT THE AUTHOR

National award winning author Abigail Drake has spent her life traveling the world and collecting stories wherever she visited. Abigail is a trekkie, a book hoarder, the master of the Nespresso machine, a red wine drinker, and a choco-holic. She lives in Beaver, Pennsylvania with her husband, three sons, and a mischievous Labrador named Capone.

ABOUT THE OTHER AUTHOR

Capone the Wonder Dog is a Labrador of impeccable grace and breeding. He enjoys walking in the meadow, chasing rabbits, and stealing butter wrappers from the garbage can. This is his debut novel, which he wrote with the help of his owner since he does not have thumbs and can't type. He dreams of one day becoming a bestselling author, and of catching the irritating robin that mocks him daily from the back patio.

ALSO BY ABIGAIL DRAKE

Women's Fiction

The Hocus Pocus Magic Shop

The Enchanted Garden Cafe

Delayed Departure

Sophie and Jake

Saying Goodbye, Special Combined Edition

Saying Goodbye, Part Two

Saying Goodbye, Part One

Traveller

Young Adult Fiction

Tiger Lily

Novellas

Can't Buy Me Love

Valentine Kisses

Short Stories

Into the Woods

ℏ can be obtained
ɩg.com
SA
ɔ300919
ɔLV00001B/111/P

9 780578 562667